Wild Passion

By Sheri Chapman

This book is a work of fiction. Names, characters, places and incidents are products of the author's imagination and are not to be construed as real. Any resemblance to actual events, locales, organizations, or persons living or dead, is entirely coincidental.

COPYRIGHT

Trient Press
3375 S Rainbow Blvd
#81710, SMB 13135
Las Vegas,NV 89180
www.trientpress.com
Ordering Information:
Quantity sales. Special discounts are available on quantity purchases by corporations, associations, and others. For details, contact the publisher at the address above.

Orders by U.S. trade bookstores and wholesalers.
Please contact Trient Press: Tel: (775) 996-3844; or
visit www.trientpress.com.
Printed in the United States of America
Publisher's Cataloging-in-Publication
data Chapman, Sheri
A title of a book :Wild Passion
ISBN Hard Cover:9781953975027
       Paperback: 9781953975034
       E-book: 9781953975041

CHAPTER ONE

Outside the Fortified Walls

The Sioux Nation had territories they claimed as their own, and unless an invasion occurred, they were fairly peaceful people. The Great Spirit blessed them with plants and animals to see to their needs. The Native Americans were appreciative and gave thanks to *Wakantanka* for every life they were blessed with to sustain them. They were careful not to waste anything.

Spirit Bear watched the white dogs from the first influx as they arrived in their horse-drawn white-covered boxes and settled onto his lands. The war chief studied them as they constructed the wall surrounding their wooden village. It angered the warrior to see how the *wasicu* annihilated the woods near their settlement, and they did not thank the life they destroyed. The white dogs acted as if they had a right to everything. Spirit Bear vowed to put an end to it. However, he was no fool. The chief wanted to learn the ways of these wasteful creatures before he made his move.

The early summer weather in the South Dakota Territory was hot and humid in 1803. Kaitlin Farley angrily brushed the rough dirt floors of their one room log home. It was quite tedious work with the sparse twigs she'd bound together and fashioned into a work tool.

Their home was the first one established outside of the robust settlement walls. Because there hadn't been any sightings of Indians for at least a month, her father and brother assumed it was 'safe' to build upon the rich plains. Many advised against the move and recommended they stay behind the firm security the town wall freely offered, but it was advice rejected passionately by her men folk. However, Kaitlin believed she knew the real reason behind their plight… or *flight*.

Light colored eyes wandered to the barren storage areas roughly hewn in the stout log walls. Kaitlin knew it was also too much to hope that her father or brother would bring home a rabbit or fowl for their evening meal; all they ever brought home were hangovers.

The young woman grabbed a basket she'd woven from long dry grasses gathered from the nearby stream's edge. For the time being, she gave up on cleaning the floors and headed for her only sanctuary. The cool water of the creek was the single place that seemed to soothe her frayed nerves.

After soaking her feet in the refreshing liquid, the honey-kissed blonde gathered poke, mouse ear, and water cress into her basket for a salad. She checked the wild peach trees and found several more had ripened since her last invasion. The deserted female had already been picking blackberries earlier that morning.

Kaitlin had no idea that she was not as unaccompanied as she thought. High on the hill above her, a lone Indian sat astride his mighty painted steed. His proud arrogance was not noticed as she gathered the plants she desperately needed for survival. The only movements on the stoic warrior was his raven hair as it ruffled with the caress of the breeze and his ebony eyes as he watched the white *winyan's* actions.

The war chief had been closely watching the activity of the white dogs for several moons. They believed it was safe for them to take more and more from the lands. They now were building their wooden boxes outside of the wall of wood, and they continued to deplete a greater circumference of plant and animal life around their settlements. They didn't even seem to notice the devastation of their ways! These strange fair-skinned men didn't care to preserve the natural balance of nature as did the red man. It angered Spirit Bear more than he cared to admit.

Spirit Bear would not tolerate much more invasion to the Great Mother's lands. The *wasicu* had no respect for anything held in high reserve by the Indian. He also had another purpose to his visit: a *wasicun* or two had been killing off a few members of his tribe. Those men would pay with their lives!

The white dogs did not even protect their *winyan!* The war chief's black eyes continued to follow the lone white female. She had honey-kissed skin and deeply golden hair that shone like a beacon in the sun. She'd been left alone for most days to gather plants with no one near to protect her. This golden-haired girl did not even have other *winyans* to accompany her!

Spirit Bear entertained the thought that maybe he should teach the *wasicu* a lesson. This was a definite future for the disrespectful white man, but maybe he would begin by getting a closer look at the woman who'd captured his attention. He didn't want to acknowledge it, but he *was* very curious about her…

Some sixth sense caused Kaitlin a moment of reprieve from her gathering. A chill sailed to her on the breeze, disrupting her work in the hot afternoon sun. She straightened up, tall and alert, and scanned the nearby land.

Kaitlin had an epiphany of her surroundings. She was always appreciative of the beauty of her backdrops, but suddenly she saw the thick, full woods as a place that could offer many spots to hide if one had a mind. With new understanding, she realized that even the tall grasses that relieved the trees could be good cover. Everywhere, danger could lurk: the rocks, the gentle hills, and the banks by the river. The young woman shook her head and scolded herself for her very active imagination; she assured herself that she was still alone on the frontier.

Kaitlin didn't notice the quiet movements of the brave who blended into the background as if it were as natural to him as breathing. Nevertheless, the single woman's hair continued to stand up on the back of her neck. Even though she chided herself for being afraid of *nothing*, the young female knew she was done gathering for the day. Once Kaitlin had thoroughly spooked herself, she knew she might as well head back to the safest place known.

With a rigid back, the solitary white female stooped to pick up her filled basket and quickly walked toward the cabin. When nearing her home, Kaitlin allowed herself one more wary look around. Her breath caught in her throat and her heart stopped momentarily when her eyes met those of the Indian's. The blonde froze: she could not have moved even if she'd wanted to.

A very handsome bronzed warrior was about thirty yards away from her, sitting astride a large painted stallion. The horse was free from any restraints that white man used to master the animals. However, the beast was completely under control. The dominant equine was just as quiet as its owner, standing with rigid muscles alert, ready to obey with any shift of balance.

The commanding man sat tall and erect as his onyx eyes raked her. He was physically honed to perfection. The sun accentuated his bare skin and danced along his prevailing muscles. A bear claw necklace hung over his sculpted chest: he was power personified.

The Indian had full lips that wore a hint of a sardonic grin, but other than that, his features were rock hard. Kaitlin instantly felt exposed. He was like a great cat; he could leap and take his prey in a single bound if he so desired.

Spirit Bear was very surprised when this beautiful white woman, all alone, did not shriek in fear and run away from him. Of course, he'd never seen a fair-skinned *winyan* this close before. His band had never been introduced to the ways of white man although he'd heard from neighboring tribes that the *wasicu* were weak and cowardly in their warfare. He expected their women to be even frailer than the men were reputed to be.

Why did this woman not try to escape? He could see her trembling. Her lips, inviting and pink, were parted in shock.

For now, Spirit Bear was content to observe. This golden female had surprised him in many ways. Her hair looked so sleek and soft, even when captured in the honey-colored bun that gleamed in the sun. A few tendrils that had managed to escape curled delicately around her face. Her eyes were amber, a shade darker than her hair, and contained hints of green. She wore a frayed gown; it was used but serviceable. He noticed she was slender in build but generous in areas that would please a man. And he was pleased.

Kaitlin finally came to her senses and took a slight step back. Her cabin was fairly close, but she could not escape from him if he didn't choose it. As she stepped back, the large horse took a stride closer.

It seemed as if the two war-like creatures had one soul, one mind, and one purpose. Somehow the warrior had communicated with his horse without movement. The bronzed man looked down his straight nose from his perch above. His piercing black eyes studied her thoughtfully.

"Please…" She choked out the nearly silent plea. "Let me go…" Her knees felt weak, and her body trembled with fear despite the heat of the day.

He was like a statue. The powerful man only sat and continued to gaze at her with his black eyes. She took another step back. Again, the stallion minimized their distance.

Kaitlin fearfully dropped her basked and turned to run. When she reached the door of the cabin, she wondered how she'd made it. The blonde dared to flash a look and discovered he was gone.

Kaitlin wasn't going to breathe a sigh of relief yet, however. She slammed the door and slid the 2 x 6 plank into place, effectively locking the door, before feeling a little safer. She sank to the floor in relief.

This was the first Indian she'd seen along the way. Like many others in her group, she'd heard the Indian stories. That was why the wall around the town was built. Although they hadn't had any trouble themselves, the frontiersmen had heard how others had met with terror, torture, and death.

Kaitlin couldn't figure out why the Indian had only looked at her. He didn't seem friendly at all, yet he hadn't harmed her. Still, she was very afraid. The young woman sensed that he'd definitely wanted her to feel fear.

Where there was one Indian, there was sure to be more. How could she collect food for her family if she couldn't leave the safety of her cabin? What protection was the log house if the Indian really wanted in?

Kaitlin didn't know how long she sat on the swept dirt floor and pondered these questions, but she realized that fear couldn't rule her life. The basket needed to be retrieved before the vegetables wilted and became inedible. Cautiously, she slid the board from the door and peeked out. Nothing seemed to be out of place. She dashed out, grabbed the carrier, and returned quickly. To calm herself, she began preparing the food.

A few hours later, both men of the household stumbled loudly into the structure. Both had red-rimmed eyes from hours of drinking. They were filthy and went straight to their pallets on the floor. Kaitlin sighed in disgust. She'd have to speak to them in the morning. Already their deep snores filled the small cabin.

Kaitlin absent-mindedly brushed at the golden tendril of hair that had escaped the rough bun she'd piled atop her head. A few tears squeezed past her control. *How could they leave her alone, isolated, day after day? How could they expect her to take this solitude?* She wished she'd never come!

After all her work that day, the stressful encounter with the Indian, her menfolk messing up her tidy house without a word, and then the fact that they didn't even to bother with the food she'd provided caused all of Kaitlin's tenseness and upset to surface. Kaitlin cried silent tears and mourned her old way of life. She mourned for her mother and for the death of her dreams.

Why had they come to this God forsaken place? What purpose did it serve? She must bear the burdens of life all alone! Even when her family was home, she was unaccompanied. A daughter shouldn't be forced to watch her father and brother's demise as surely as she'd watched her mother's. *And for what?*

The next morning, Kaitlin awoke early. The loud snoring of the men disturbed her, so she decided to gather more food. The young woman knew of a patch that promised many ripe berries for the picking. Her male relatives would still be in their chemical laden sleep upon her return.

Grabbing the basket, she carefully left the building. Kaitlin didn't bother to be quiet, but neither did she make noise to awaken the men. Although apprehensive about leaving, the white woman had no choice; one couldn't survive without food and water.

Kaitlin still shook when she thought of the virile man lurking in the wilderness. In fact, he'd visited in the few hours of slumber she'd been able to achieve. Her cheeks blushed when she recalled how her dream warrior had pressed his full lips to hers and how he'd pushed his manly body against her womanly curves.

The blonde shook her head and focused on reality. *How could she possibly be attracted to a barbarian?* Indians were known for torturing whites; yet, he hadn't harmed her. Still, she knew he was out there, and it left her quaking with alarm.

Kaitlin couldn't help but look around when she left the safe walls of the cabin. She silently slipped into the woods because the wildlife shouldn't be disturbed… or so she told herself.

The young woman quickly picked several varieties of fruit for their breakfast. She gathered plump blackberries, bright red cherries, and even ripe gooseberries. Her father didn't enjoy gooseberries much without the luxury of sugar they were too poor to buy, but beggars couldn't be choosers.

On the way home from the berry patches, Kaitlin stumbled across a large nest of turkey eggs. She sent up a prayer of thanks and carefully gathered the protein-laden shells.

As soon as she reached the house, Kaitlin worked at cleaning the berries and preparing the eggs for their morning meal. That afternoon, she planned on weaving a net to fish with. As much as she enjoyed berries, her body was beginning to crave meat.

Then men's snores continued to saw at Kaitlin's nerves, but the smell of scrambled eggs was better than the thunder of an approaching storm. The mouthwatering aroma filled the air and tickled the men awake.

Two sets of red, bleary eyes squinted into the dimly lit cabin. Kaitlin had the feeling her family was trying to remember where they were.

"Breakfast time," the young woman announced cheerfully.

The men groaned and rolled to their sides in an effort to assume footing on the rocking floor. The house contained no furniture. It had all been sold to pay for the ever-accumulating bills. Kaitlin was thankful for the four tin plates, cups, and forks she'd managed to salvage. Above all, she treasured her cast iron skillet.

Her father and brother shoveled food into their mouths, barely swallowing the first forkful before a new one was dumped in. After the eggs were demolished, the fruit received the same gusto.

"Father," Kaitlin began, "I don't know how safe it is here. I think we need to move back to town."

"Now, Kaitlin, ya know how I feel about that," Wayne managed between mouthfuls.

The young woman blurted out, "Papa, I saw an Indian yesterday!"

Silence greeted her revelation. After a slow minute ticked by, her brother's fork resumed scraping his plate in an effort to gather the last crumble of egg.

"I been meaning to talk to ya about that," her father stated.

"What? You know about the Indian?" She nearly stammered.

Ignoring the Indian sighting as if it were a figment of her imagination, her father said, "no, but I was jus' thinkin'. Yur right. Ya ain't should be out here all alone all day long. Jed has a pretty nice set up in the horse barn. He can shore do blacksmith work. He'd make a good husband for ya."

"Papa, I don't even like Jed! He's mean and rough. He drinks too much." The heavy accusation hung in the air between them.

"Like it or not, he has offered to take yur hand in marriage. He's a comin' for yur things today, so pack up."

"How much is he paying you, Papa? Is this little deal so you can pay off your gambling debt?"

Kaitlin cried scornfully. Tears welled up in her golden eyes.

Wayne's eyes widened in surprise at her accurate guess. He'd had to make a deal with Jed. He needed the money urgently, and Jed wanted Kaitlin. *It couldn't be that bad for his girl, could it?* Besides, it was time to marry her off.

"I knew it! You're despicable! Ever since Mama died…"

"You leave yur mother out of this!"

"You've sunk into a hole and took Bobby with you! You both drink your sorrows away, day after day! All of our money is gone!" she paused before beseeching him: "You can't do this to me, Papa! Please!"

"It's too late. He's a comin' fer ya." Kaitlin's mother and protector, Sybil, did not make it through the difficult and perilous journey. The angry river's tumultuous waters plucked her mother from the frail raft the men had constructed and sucked her into its murky depths. They'd never seen her again.

Kaitlin's eyes misted every time she thought of her mother. She missed her terribly! Sybil would never allow her father to do this to her! Her father and brother mourned her in much different ways. Each sought out the small shiny tin canteen that now seemed an extension of their arms. They gambled and drank their sorrows away.

The young woman felt all alone, bereft of friends and family. She blamed it all on the devil that lurked in the silvery canteens. Whiskey combined with

gambling were weapons used against her family; it
was artilleries they could not rise above.

With glistening eyes, Kaitlin turned to her brother.
Bobby carefully avoided her pleading gaze. She knew she
wouldn't find an ally in her sibling; he simply wasn't
strong enough to oppose her father.

"I hate you!" she yelled, whirling back to face the
man who controlled her fate. "I hate what you've become!
Look at yourself, Papa! I hope you can live with what
you've done!" Then Kaitlin tore from the house and ran
in the direction of the stream.

Bobby stood, ready to follow, but his father said,
"Let 'er go. She got nowhere ta run. She'll come back
when she's a ready."

Rather than wait for another confrontation, the two
men gathered their canteens and left. It was a long trek
back to town. Regretfully, they wished they still had their
horses.

Kaitlin stumbled towards the watercourse with
blinding tears streaming down her face. She let her legs
carry her to her dreaming spot, a little cove surrounding
the stream. A large white oak tree grew at an angle and
projected over the pool. It was a cherished place to sit and
dangle her legs over the water's edge.

Several large rocks lined the shore. The water
gurgled and whispered words of comfort to her. Fish
darted to and fro; they were curious yet cautious. This
was the very place she'd planned to spend the afternoon,
only she had planned to spend her time catching her first
aquatic meal, not crying.

"What will they do without me?" she moaned aloud.
Her father and brother were out drinking all

hours of the day. They had no idea what she did for them! They didn't and wouldn't gather food, firewood, and other needed items. *How would they survive?* Even worse, how would she?

Bradley, her solitary friend, had recently visited her. He'd gently tried to break the news that they had no credit and no money. They wouldn't be allowed to purchase anything further from the only general store in the area without some reimbursement first. Now her father wouldn't be able to buy provisions, and he was selling his soul provider!

Worse still, the young woman couldn't stand the thought of being at the mercy of Jed Coldwater. *What a perfect name for that awful man*, Kaitlin thought. He had icy water running through his veins, not blood, and he was meaner than an angry snake. How could her father marry her off to him? Yes, he was wealthy as far as the current town standing went, but there were certain limits that she didn't feel she could succumb to. *Not for anybody*. She remembered her last encounter with Jed as clearly as if it had just happened…

She'd just bought a bag of wheat to make into flour, as they couldn't afford the already-made version. Struggling under the weight of the bag, Kaitlin walked by the blacksmith shop. Jed sauntered toward her and leered impolitely.

"Ya need some hep, lil' missy? I shore cud hep ya out!" he said and wiggled his eyebrows suggestively.

"Thanks, but no," she said from under the strain of the heavy bag, "I can manage."

"Ya shore?" he asked as he approached her from behind. He grabbed her rear-end with grimy, sweaty hands.

"How dare you!" Kaitlin twisted around to face him. The grain bag crashed to the ground in her fury.

"I was only try'n to hep ya," he sneered. His mean eyes traveled down her reddened face and lighted on her heaving bosom. He licked his lips in a meaningful way. Then he rubbed his stubbly chin with his dirty hands as if contemplating his next move.

Jed took a step closer to her. Kaitlin was hit by his hot breath that stank of stale whiskey and tobacco. His filthy clothes reeked of horse sweat.

Kaitlin tried not to gag when he said, "I could hep ya out. Then ya could hep me out. I got a big itch fer ya."

"Get away from me," she hissed through clenched teeth.

"One day, I mean ter haf ya! I'll have yeh moanin' ma name after'n ya get used to it," he paused with a wink, "if'n ya catch ma meanin'!" Then his face split in a wide grin that showed brownish-black, uneven teeth. His rotted breath offended the very air.

Kaitlin didn't realize she had smacked him in her fury until she saw the red mark left by her fingers. She stood in the aftermath of her reaction, shocked at what she'd done.

Jed grabbed her arm and his enormous fist squeezed down with force. "Ya'll be sorry ya did tha', lil' missy!" he promised.

Kaitlin tried not to squeal in pain, but she could feel a bruise already forming under his abusive fingers. Thankfully, Bradley had just walked out of his general store and saw her standing in the road with her arm clenched by the hefty blacksmith with a large bag of grain at her feet. He came rushing over to her rescue.

"Miss Kaitlin, how are you?" he greeted her. "Do you need some help?"

Before the blacksmith could say otherwise, she smiled sweetly and said, "Yes, please, Bradley. I would appreciate your help very much!"

Jed hissed darkly, "We *will* finish this later," and stalked off.

Bradley, sweet Bradley, was her only friend. He'd saved her with his offer of help. She avoided town and Jed as much as possible.

A breeze lifted Kaitlin's golden tresses and snapped her back to reality. She climbed her special tree and sobbed her heart out. She had nowhere to run. There was nowhere to hide. The Boogeyman was coming for her.

A lone Indian warrior had watched the beautiful girl tear from her house. Unseen, he'd followed her to her special place. What could the *pron wasicun* have done to break her heart so? She appeared to be a good *winyan*; she performed necessary needs to care for the men in her life.

Without acknowledging it, Spirit Bear had much respect for the strong young woman. She took care of the men, not the other way around. This was much for any woman to do, especially a lazy white.

Spirit Bear turned his stallion toward the settlement. He was bound and determined to reveal who this threat was to his people. Since the white dogs had moved into the Sioux territory, three *Oglala winyan pi* had disappeared while they were out gathering food for their families.

Another incident occurred when a young brave, not yet in manhood, was found staked to the earth and left to die. One family in the tribe still mourned the *hoksila*, his body only placed on the scaffold one cycle of the moon before.

Spirit Bear's eyes narrowed. The filth that committed these crimes would pay. He already knew the gait, size, and weight of the horses in which the two culprits rode, thanks to his superior tracking skills.

As war chief of his tribe, he would initially assess the situation before gathering his troops to attack. Spirit Bear first needed to study these strange people. He needed to consider his enemy's strengths and weaknesses. By watching their living area with hawk eyes, he would also spot the murderers and take care of them himself should the opportunity present itself. And he would not be gentle.

Later that day, Kaitlin returned to the empty cabin. She had no belongings to pack aside from her cherished skillet. Her father had sold every other item she owned except for two frayed dresses and the tin wear. She was as packed as she could be. However, the young woman was determination not to go with Jed. That was a fate worse than death! She figured it was best not to be around when he arrived.

Kaitlin picked up her meager belongings contained in her weaved basket. Then the honey-haired beauty sat by the spring and finished her net. She spent the afternoon learning how to fish with it. Twenty attempts later, she finally caught the fat shiny bass. He was a beaut! The glossy fish had to weigh at least three pounds! Part of her wanted to share the good fortune with her family, but the other part still seethed at the injustice her father had committed. All Papa thought about was himself!

It was early afternoon when the solitary female heard a slight commotion coming from the cabin area. She was far enough away that she couldn't see anything, but a gruff voice was carried to her on the breeze. Kaitlin could have sworn that she heard Jed yell that he'd be back for her. Gritting her teeth, the young woman knew when she'd be ready to accept that her father had given her to the terrible man… Never!

The young woman gathered dry grasses for kindling, seasoned wood, and flint in which to start a fire. She placed three larger stones around the fire to support the skillet so that she could cook her catch.

With a sharpened knife fashioned from stone, the inexperienced female cleaned the fish. It was nearing evening when the water boiled in her skillet. The runaway had also gathered wild carrots and onions. Kaitlin added the fish and vegetables to the water to prepare a stew of sorts. Hopefully, she would have plenty for breakfast as well. The young woman

even found some sassafras for a morning tea! She smiled to herself because she'd successfully escaped evil one more day.

Sighing, Kaitlin climbed into her tree. She felt safer and more secure nestled in the branches. The natural screen helped to conceal her from prowling eyes. Of course, her scent was another story, but Kaitlin wasn't worried about animal prowlers. For the first time in quite some time, Kaitlin fell asleep with a full stomach.

The next morning, a strange grunting and snuffling-like noise awoke her. To her horror, the young woman saw a large black bear licking her skillet clean. *So much for breakfast.* That was okay with Kaitlin; at least *she* wasn't breakfast. It seemed like hours before the bear lost interest in the frying pan. Kaitlin no longer felt safe in her 'hideout'. The bear would be back; it was certain.

Spirit Bear could not believe his eyes when he saw the *ska winyan* leave the cover by the stream not long after his totem helper did. Had she stayed there all night to get away from the men in the wooden box? It was no matter. It was a sign from *Wakantanka*. A sign of what, Spirit Bear was unsure, but he pledged his protection to this lone *winyan*. He was drawn to her for some purpose. He vowed to find out why.

That afternoon, Kaitlin still was near the cabin, but she didn't dare go back. Thankfully, her clean belongings were with her, safely tucked into a small clearing surrounded by brush. The young woman knew the ticks would eat her alive, but that was much preferred to being at the mercy of Jed. Part of her wondered how her men folk fared their first night by themselves. Would they've had a change of heart?

Her hopes were dashed when she heard a heated discussion coming from the direction of the cabin…

"Where is she, ya filthy cheat?"

"I… I… I don't know!" Wayne stammered.

"Yuh gave yer word that she'd be mine. I'll kill yeh if'n I do'n get 'er. I mean it! I will *kill ye*! Yeh haf the money, now I want the gurl!"

"Give me time, Jed," Wayne pleaded. "I'll find her. I'll bring her to ya myself."

"I better have 'er by night fall, or I'm a comin' back. I got an itch in my pants I aim to appease tonight!"

Swallowing his fright, Wayne managed to croak out, "Jed, she's my only daughter. Be easy on her. Please!"

"Yeh shuda thought that one through afore ya made ar deal. We haf a score to settle, that gurl of yers and I. I'm a gonna teach her er place. Then she won' wanna cross me no more. I may make it to where she don' wanna sit fer awhile, but I ain't a gonna kill 'er. I got a plenty of luv for meh lil' missy!" he cackled gleefully. Then his arm surged like a frog's tongue and captured Wayne's throat. "See to it that I'ma satisfied. Tonight!"

Wayne's eyes nearly popped out of his head under the vice-like grip. When Jed released him, he mounted his horse and spurred it into a run without a backwards glance.

Kaitlin moaned softly. What was she going to do? A daughter couldn't be responsible for her father's death, but neither could she bring herself to become mincemeat of Jed's. The only person who might stand up for her was Bradley, but would he stand up to Jed?

Jed was an ogre of a man and had a nasty reputation. He didn't fight fair, and everyone knew it. It not only took a brave man, but also a strong and/or powerful man to stand up to him. Then, that man would have to watch his back for the rest of his life… or the rest of Jed's. *Why did her father ever get involved with the dealings of a man like him?*

Kaitlin found herself with a sudden headache. She knew the pounding in her temples was stress related. The only possible escape was to head for town. Maybe she could find a kind soul to board her out, or possibly, give her work of some kind.

There was no way a young woman alone could survive in the elements, not with a black bear lurking nearby… or an Indian. Kaitlin couldn't return to the cabin out of fear of her father taking her to Jed. She'd have to watch her step within the walls of the settlement as well. Jed was everywhere.

Her father, as sad as Kaitlin was to admit it, would have to own up to his own mistakes. She couldn't bring herself to sacrifice her life for him. The golden-haired girl knew it would only prolong the self-destructive path he was on, anyway.

Although she loved and worried about him, Wayne's only daughter couldn't release her hurt over what he was willing to sacrifice for whiskey and debt. Papa had no idea what she'd been through since her mother's death, what Kaitlin did for him, and how much she really cared. Now he'd sold her into the hands of a very cruel man who had nothing in mind but her torture. Kaitlin shuddered in revulsion at the thought.

With nothing else to do, the young woman stuck out for the settlement. Because she had to seek cover along the way, there was no way to make it before night fall. Still, Kaitlin had to put as much distance as possible between herself and the log home.

Sighing, Kaitlin stooped to pick up her meager belongings. She began the daunting task of trekking through the woods to the only civil gathering of whites in the area.

As the day swept into early evening, Kaitlin's feet began hurting. Women's shoes definitely weren't made for a lot of walking. The frying pan, also, didn't seem so heavy when the journey had first begun. She decided to make camp in a small clump of trees and finish the path to the community in the morning.

The honey-colored blonde took a long draw from the cool water in her canteen. She unwrapped a small swatch of material her mother had given her and pulled out a meager dinner of gooseberries. She preferred black berries, cherries, or peaches but didn't want to stain the last material memory of her mother.

Kaitlin gathered long grasses and wove a rough mat to curl up on. It would be silly to start a fire this close to town. She couldn't risk discovery from

Jed if he were out prowling nearby. Before dark, her exhausted body had drifted off to sleep.

Several hours before dawn, a shadow loomed dangerously over Kaitlin's sleeping form. Finally, Jed would settle this. The little tramp had evaded his grasp long enough. He lay down beside Kaitlin and laughed raucously. Oh, she'd be surprised with the way he had in mind to awaken her!

James, Jed's brother, waited in the patch of woods about one-hundred feet from where Jed was going to be having fun without him. James held the two horses quietly. He really wanted to be beside his brother, but Jed had wanted the Farley girl all to himself. He wondered if he was serious about the girl. James knew Jed wasn't the faithful type, but he'd mentioned he'd like to have some sons running around the blacksmith shop.

Jed had promised him that if he helped him find the blonde and get her back to his home, they would go out and catch more squaws. They could treat them as rough as they wanted and there was no one who would come to their rescue. No one was going to start a war over some red whores. *If they were dead, who were they going to tell anyway?* James smiled as memories took him away.

Something startled Kaitlin awake. It was pitch-black out, and the darkness was full of whispered omens. Everything else was silent. Waiting. She blinked several times into the tepid velvet, trying to adjust to the lack of light. She sensed a nearby presence. *Was it the bear?*

Then the overpowering stench assaulted her nostrils. She nearly retched in revulsion. Somehow, the smell reminded her of… Jed! With a cry of realization, she tried to spring to her feet. His hands must have been suspended over her, because he caught and crushed her body into his large frame.

"Ha! Ha! Ha! Got 'cha now, muh lil' vixen! This big bad wolf's gonna eat 'cha up! Yuh've been a very bad girl. Bad girls need ta be taught a lesson!" Jed taunted as he rolled her over to face him. He pressed her body even closer to his, leaving no doubt of his intentions.

Kaitlin screamed in horror. "Get away from me, you filthy beast!" she managed to screech.

"Go ahead and scream, honey. It turns me on!" Jed began to paw at her clothing. His huge jaws gaped open, and he tried to capture her lips.

"Oh, God, Jed! Please don't do this!" She struggled vainly and pressed with all her might against his chest. She scratched and clawed to escape. As she struggled, she noticed that Jed became more aggressive with his goal.

Jed rumbled in deep amusement, and his breathing rate increased. He was nearly panting on her chest. Finally, his sausage-sized fingers caught on the top of the weak fabric of her dress and ripped it.

The white creamy exposed skin gleamed in what little light there was. Kaitlin could see the whites of his eyes as they grew wider with his lust. Roughly, he grabbed and squeezed her chest. Again, Kaitlin screamed and flailed her fists on him.

"I cud make this firs' time a lil' easier if yuh'd cooperate," Jed's lust-filled voice croaked. "Yur so beautiful, missy. I gonna plant me a wee one in yer belly. Mabe ya won't be so keen ter get away then. But if'n ya like it ruff, I kin do that too. I will anyways, but I cud be persuaded to take it easy on yeh this fir's time. Hell, wu've got a might few hours ta kill!" He cackled with glee.

Kaitlin took a deep breath and consciously made an effort to control her wild panic. He'd just given her an opening for a different tactic.

"Sure, Jed. I just had to have you catch me first. It makes me really want you! If you'll just ease your weight off me a little, I could prepare myself?"

"Ya ain't goin' no wheres?"

"No. Where would I go?" A lump of sadness welled in her throat with these words.

Jed's voice held a touch of suspicion when he warned, "I will hurt 'cha on purpose if'n this is some kind of a trick. I aim ta have muh way with ya. I kin only wait a few more minutes, ya juicy number ya!" He pressed himself to her to prove his words.

Kaitlin forced a lump of bile down, "No, of course not," she whispered to hide the quiver of terror in her voice. "I just want to remove some of these layers so that this goes a little smoother."

The second Jed took his enormous hand off her, she jumped up and ran. Her heart pounded in her chest so fast she thought it might explode. The terrified woman heard him ripping the ground up behind her like an ox plowing the field. Luckily, Kaitlin was faster and more nimble.

Jed grunted in his exertion. His puffing was nearly on her heels! She felt the heel of his hand stab her in the back. She went tumbling to the ground. Her head hit something hard, and she saw stars. That's the last thing she remembered.

CHAPTER TWO

The Trail to Recovery

The next moment Kaitlin became aware, she felt someone dribble water into her mouth. Strong, gentle hands were on her. The blonde was cognizant of a presence, but she couldn't open her eyes. A cool cloth wiped her face, but still, her eyes refused to open. *Could this be Jed with the gentle hands?* Her mind screamed, *NO!*

Why couldn't she think clearly? What was this fog shrouding her mind? No stench assailed her senses, so it couldn't be Jed. What had happened? Where was he?

Strong hands lifted her and cradled her against a warm, rock-hard chest. *This was no Jed holding her so tenderly against such a fit body. The physical attributes didn't really fit Papa, but could it be him? Had he had a change of heart? Or was it Bradley? Who was caring for her when she couldn't care for herself?*

Spirit Bear was immediately aware of her change in breathing. *Would the winyan finally open her eyes?* Her spirit must be preparing her physical body to awaken. He protectively cradled her body closer to his chest. *Runs with the Wind* was so in tuned with his master's body that no instruction was necessary for guidance. The stallion instinctively did what the chief wanted; their minds were linked.

Behind the great color-splashed stallion, a line-back dun mare and a black gelding walked. Each was laden with a body draped just behind its withers. Spirit Bear was fortunate to be able to save the girl from the white snakes he'd captured although he'd had to mildly wound the men. Even though he'd taken pleasure in that, he hadn't killed the human dogs. He would take them back to the village for that. He was sure they would find a suitable end when he allowed the families of the missing maidens and the young boy to deliver justice.

It was a shame that the woman whom had touched the heart of his spirit helper had been injured. The filth tied to the saddles would pay for that as well. Spirit Bear's protective embrace tightened around the *ska winyan*. He couldn't help but to be attracted to this golden girl.

Although nudity was not uncommon in his village, he kept finding his eyes drawn to the ripped fabric of her dress that revealed a good portion of her creamy breast. When he'd gently picked up the girl, it'd nearly spilled out of her ripped dress. It had ignited a hunger for her that he could no longer ignore.

A buzzing and crackling noise in her ears finally stirred Kaitlin to her senses. She was on the brink of awakening. She felt her head cradled and lifted softly while something warm was dribbled into her mouth. She coughed and spluttered and finally managed to crack her eyes open.

Blinking in rapid succession in the dusk, she could make out a figure above her. Long, loose black hair fringed a very handsome but very warrior-like face. Those full lips she'd once dreamed of crushing hers were but a hand's reach away. Obsidian eyes shaded by black manly brows complimented his straight nose. High cheekbones and bronze skin left no doubt to whose arms she was nestled in.

Although she was aware he was helping her, it did not completely dispel the immediate alarm she experienced. Whites were taught to fear Indians. Whether whites deserved retaliation from the Native Americans or not, the red man was the one who'd earned the harsh reputation; he was seen as a savage with no morals or reverence for human life. Indians were incomprehensible and committed unspeakable murders and tortures against innocent civilians.

White man, however, was blameless in whatever pursuits he engaged in within the boundaries of the Indians' territories – or so the women folk were led to believe. With both cultures practicing vast differences in beliefs and philosophies, each culture unknowingly offended the other. Problems were bound to arise.

Spirit Bear felt the golden one tense when she saw who was holding her in an inclined position. *Did she fear him more than the growling ska sunka who had hurt her? Did she not understand what would've*

happened to her had he not intervened? Did her fear of him overrule her common sense?

He inwardly shook his head. It mattered not. The *wasicun* would pay with their lives. In a sense, she would, too. He'd saved her, but now she owed her life to him. She was his, by rights, and he planned on keeping her.

Kaitlin did not dare to move a muscle. When she came to, one of the first things she noticed was his reaction to her. His eyes, as black as midnight, had slightly narrowed. *What had she done to already insult this dangerous looking man?* She trembled at the thought. Sudden dizziness consumed her; she had no choice but to relax back into his stabilizing hands.

Spirit Bear brought the prairie chicken soup he'd prepared up to her lips. Her eyes were large chunks of amber in her face, but she didn't try to defy his help. Tentatively, the *winyan* drank the broth. Spirit Bear gave a slight nod of his head to indicate his approval.

From off to the side, Kaitlin heard a gravelly voice rumble her name, "Kaiiit-lliiiin… I think he liiiiikes yuh," James taunted.

Kaitlin saw her loathed attacker and his brother tied to separate trees.

"Shut up yeh fool!" Jed growled. "She is *mine*, not tha' dirty red skin's! As soon as I kin work these here ropes loose, I will kill tha' Injun and make 'er mine in *all* ways. Maybe I mite even switch tha' order up since he does seem ter haf an interest in 'er." He hacked out a laugh. "I think it might bother 'em to watch."

Jed then turned his attention to Kaitlin. "Say, if yuh can manage to git that Injun ta give me a drink a water, I mite not hold such a grudge agin' ya." Then he chuckled evilly.

Kaitlin shuttered in horror as she recalled what had nearly happened just before she'd lost consciousness. Her head still ached deeply. She tentatively reached up to feel her injury and found it newly dressed.

Jed could not contain himself and was unrelenting in his harassment of her. "I can't wait ta continue where we left off," he sneered. "I'll haf *both* of those pretty perks uncovered as soon I can!"

Flaming a deep red, Kaitlin looked down to see that her ripped dress did expose quite a bit of creamy flesh, but at least she wasn't falling out. She sucked in a breath and quickly tried to close the front of her dress when she realized she was still lying in the handsome brave's lap.

She hastily looked up into his gaze. She found that his eyes had traced the movement of her hands. He couldn't hide the quick amusement at her modesty; nor could he hide the flare of desire in his eyes. His pupils seem to dilate into pools of yearning that he rapidly masked by the hardening of his features.

Because James was angry at his brother and Kaitlin for his predicament, he continued to torture them, "Kaaaiiiit-liiiiin, see who else has noticed them purty knockers of yers? He'll be nibbling on 'em a'fore night fall!" Then he cackled.

Jed nearly roared, "Shut UP, James!! I'm a warnin' ya! I'll kill ya a'fore I kill that filthy lizard if'n yuh keep it up!"

"Aw, I'm just a scarin' 'er . Jus' like you was," he whined.

"Nah. I wuz serious; I weren't playin' with 'er. I aim to haf 'er and won't give 'er a rest until she bares me some young'ens."

Kaitlin shuttered at these words and moaned slightly as her head suddenly sent a burst of pain down her neck as a sledge hammer pounded rhythmic blows in her temples. The Sioux man silently got to his feet and rested Kaitlin's head gently on the ground. The next moment he was at Jed's throat with a huge knife. The very sharp tip was barely puncturing the area next to his voice box.

"*Pataka! Ho eyas wanna hecetu!*" the war chief tersely warned Jed.

"I think he wants yuh to shut up," James unnecessarily advised. "Yur scarin' his woman. He may wanna cut tha' voice box a yourn's out."

The warrior's fierce stare turned on James. It instantly silenced him. He didn't want any knife at his neck, even if it meant he had to stop wheedling his older brother.

A small bead of blood welled at the tip of the blade resting against the big blacksmith's throat. Wisely, Jed didn't move a muscle.

The native released the man suddenly and walked back towards Kaitlin. He lay down beside her and draped a shielding arm across her. Kaitlin was tense but didn't dare move. She heard Jed's angry intake of breath as *he* was forced to watch a hated foe lie beside the woman he'd chosen. When Kaitlin realized the warrior meant her no harm, she was finally able to relax her drained body enough to sleep.

At the first fingers of dawn, Kaitlin awoke and noticed the Indian already had the two captive men loaded on their horses. They looked very uncomfortable draped across the horses' backs like bulky supply bags. Their hands were tied behind their bodies and looped to the saddle horns.

Kaitlin brought her achy body to an upright position. Her world spun slightly, but it seemed to whirl less than the day before. Her movement captured the interest of the brave immediately.

"*Isica?*" he inquired.

"I – I'm sorry," she responded softly. "I don't understand." She pointed to her head and then her mouth. She gently shook her head 'no'.

"*Peslete*," he said in his strange tongue, pointing to her head. "*Isica?*" and he tenderly touched her injury.

She closed her eyes as the soft touch and the effort of sitting up caused the throbbing to resume.

"*Tos*," he said and nodded a confirmation. He whistled softly and his horse trotted to them. He retrieved a strange stretchy pouch and held it to her lips.

"*Yaskepa*," he commanded.

Because he placed the bag up to her lips, Kaitlin assumed he wanted her to drink. When she let the liquid flow into her mouth, a bitter tasted flooded her senses. She didn't mean to, but she turned her head and spit out the mouth full.

The muscular man placed his hand under her chin and turned her face so that she had to look into his. "*Yaskepa*," he repeated, firmly placing the bag at her lips once more.

Too tired and in pain to fight him, she swallowed three or four mouthfuls. He nodded once in approval and replaced the bag on his horse. Then he gave her more of the prairie chicken soup to eat. It had been warmed to a pleasant temperature. Kaitlin noticed he'd used her skillet; she nodded her head twice to show her appreciation.

After the food comforted her stomach, she tried to stand. She was very woozy and the spinning land made her dizzy, but with the Indian's help, she stood on her feet. When the world stopped rocking so heavily, she attempted to let go of the warrior's arm.

He immediately supported her weight by placing a steadying hand under her elbow. She'd successfully managed to stand without ripping open the quick but temporary repair to the bodice of her dress. Kaitlin considered it a small achievement.

The modest white was a little embarrassed of her next chore… She looked up into the handsome brave's face and tried to let him know she needed to relieve herself… without his assistance.

With a beet-red face, Kaitlin pointed to a patch of tall grass about twenty feet away. The warrior pointed to the reeds and raised his brows in question. Her face flamed more when he didn't appear to understand. She pointed again to the grass and herself and nodded. Then she pointed to the grass and him and shook her head.

The striking bronze man smiled slightly and began walking her that direction. She tried to stop him and shook her head no, but he continued to walk her to the spot she'd indicated.

"*Wistelkiya?*" he asked, his tone softer and gentler than she'd heard yet. He lowered his head to look at her, amusement evidenced on his lips.

"Um, sir? I don't know what to call you, but, um… I don't need your… assistance right now." Kaitlin tried to tenderly release his fingers from where he supported her.

Spirit Bear released her arm kindly but refused to leave. Because of her shyness, he presented his back to her so that she could take care of business. The warrior refused to leave her side when she was still quite obviously injured.

Kaitlin stood a few moments without moving. *What a stubborn man!* She felt she was quite capable of walking a short distance without assistance. She fumed. Even though it was necessary to relieve herself, it would be hard to accomplish this task with a man's feet and ears so close!

    Spirit Bear waited. He was amused at her defiance. Of course the *winyan* had no choice but to accept his assistance. She was weaker than she realized. The *sunka* had nearly killed her in his great lust to take her. Clenching his jaw, he felt the rage rack his body yet again. In Indian villages, *winyan* and *tiwahe wiconi*, family life, was cherished above all else.

    Kaitlin finished her business and waited for the copper-colored man to turn back around. She saw his hands clenched at his sides, and it frightened her. *Was he angry because she needed this time?* She didn't want to test his patience, so she studied him quietly from behind.

    The warrior's long black hair was braided in one lone plait today. It was adorned by two erect red eagle feathers tipped in black that were strategically placed on the back of his head. A few leather streamers festooned with bear teeth dangled subtly over his raven weave.

    He was about six feet in height and well-muscled. His broad shoulders tapered to narrow hips, and his back muscles rippled under the bronze skin even though he was merely standing. His defined shoulders bulged and his biceps and triceps coiled in unison with his clenching fists.

He wore soft leather leggings and a breechcloth. Decorated moccasins adorned his feet. He also had one leather arm band in which two more of the black-tipped red eagle feathers were attached. The bear claw necklace encircled his neck was tied at the back with a leather tong. He radiated unbridled maleness, wild and free.

"*Yucoya?*" he asked, disrupting her study of him.

"Um, I don't know what you just said, but I'm ready," Kaitlin answered gently.

When Spirit Bear turned to face her, the rage in his face melted. He didn't mean to frighten the *winyan*. It was her protection, or lack of, that brought about his anger for the white dogs!

"*Miye canzeka sni,*" he reassured her. He tried to let her know he was not angry. "*Uwa yo wanna.*" He lightly traced his finger down her shoulder to her elbow before supporting it once more.

Kaitlin was surprised that his touch could stir her so easily. It was if this virile man could read her thoughts, for he smiled. The unanimous human trait for joy and reassurance transformed his fearsome face into a striking one that all women would swoon before.

Noticing the shocked look on her face brought about by his smile, Spirit Bear grinned even broader. He realized the golden *winyan* found him attractive! He found that to be promising, for it would help her accept her place in his life easier.

Spirit Bear had never owned a slave before although in war with other tribes, it was common practice to take survivors as slaves. Usually only *winyan* and *wakanheja* were spared, for *wicasa* were too dangerous to let live. If they escaped, they were certain to return with reinforcements. Revenge and retaliation were sure things; they would take out their greatest *toka* before they entered the spirit world themselves. Women and children, on the other hand, were protected. Warriors did not kill them lightly.

There were two *wayaka* in his village now. One Pawnee *winyan* belonged to *Zuzeca Pazan*, which translated to Snake Strike. They were well-suited for one another. The villagers supported the name, *Nakpa Ihli*, for the *winyan*, for she made one's ear sore to listen to her complaints and vindictiveness. She'd been publicly punished many times for her disrespect. In fact, Spirit Bear suspected that *Zuzeca Pazan* took every opportunity to punish his *winyan*. He somehow derived pleasure from the deed, and that defied the Indian way.

The other *wayaka* was also Pawnee, a girl taken at the age of five. She was to be 'adopted' by the Oglala soon, for she was raised as one of their own. She'd been given as a gift to a couple who'd tried many times to have *hoksicala* but were unable. She was called *Unjinjintka Can Kosica* after the precious rose found in the desert. It was a miracle for a barren desert to nurture a rose, beautiful and bold, within the drab heated existence. Not only did it suit her life, but it also symbolized her personality. She now was seventeen winters and could take on a husband; she was not really considered a *wayaka*.

Focusing on his own *wayaka*, Spirit Bear patiently guided her back to where the *toka* were bound to their horses. His uninhibited stallion, *Runs with the Wind*, was ready. Kaitlin was amazed at the warrior's agility as he leaped onto the great horse without effort. He sat tall and proud as he reached a hand to her.

"*Uwa yo*," he said.

Because Kaitlin knew she had nowhere to go and no choice but to obey, she allowed the dark man to swoop her up with ease. She found herself cradled to his chest, much as a mother would a child. When she looked up to ask if he'd put her down on the horse's back, his face was a mere two inches from hers. It silenced the words before they ever formed on her lips. A hungry light flamed from within the swirling black depths of his eyes. Slowly, she watched him lower his full lips to capture hers.

The kiss was soft and gentle, yet demanding at the same time. He pressed his lips to hers for a few moments before catching her lower lip with his. His tongue traced a hot trail on the sensitive inner side of her lip. She drew in a sharp intake of breath, shocked by the intense fire he so easily lit.

Spirit Bear watched her eyes enlarge; the green in them began to swirl faster in the molten amber. He felt her heart beat strongly within her bosom that was pressed against his chest. She froze in alarm.

He was flooded with a strange, warm feeling for this lovely girl who had enticed his desire. He'd never felt so protective over a mere *winyan*, nor had he ever expected to. Slowly, he withdrew his lips from hers. He watched the windows to her soul as he did so.

Her startled eyes remained large and her lips were shining and parted with surprise from his kiss. She did not move but continued to gaze at him. He smiled slightly down at her.

Then Spirit Bear commanded his horse, "*Aglihunni.*" The coppery animal splashed with white tossed his black mane. His dark legs thundered in the direction of the Indian village. The large male's neighing cry ordered the other horses to follow.

Kaitlin was soon soothed back to sleep as a result of the pain-numbing drink that the Indian insisted she swallow. The horse's gentle rock as he galloped along the soft slopes helped facilitate her sleep by pounding a rhythmic lullaby. She now straddled the stallion in front of his owner, but the brave supported her sleeping form against his chest.

Behind the war chief, two men ground their teeth against the pain of riding their horses in this humiliating way. Oh, for freedom! Neither men had completely lost hope for regaining it; both were too consumed by the evil fire of revenge that burned brightly within them.

As the day passed, the horses slowed their gaits. The wild stallion still had not tired, but the same could not be said for the two white men's horses. Still, the animals seemed to go on and on.

The men were very thirsty, and their legs tingled with restricted blood flow. Their guts ached from where the saddles rubbed sores. They almost couldn't feel their arms anymore from the abnormal position in which they were forced to ride, and the sun beat mercilessly down.

Finally, when Jed and James felt they would surely die, the horses stopped. In a shady grove at the bottom of a rolling hill, the men were released from the animals' backs. They fell with a gust of breath, unable to stop their rapid decent. James groaned but Jed was too stubborn to give the Indian satisfaction.

Jed noticed Kaitlin was sitting prettily under a shady tree. She looked as beautiful as ever save for the ugly bandage wrapped around her head. Jed felt burning rage boil up inside him. He sure as hell didn't feel sorry that he'd caused her a headache! He didn't deserve to be treated like a damn Injun! She was going to pay just as much as the Injun would if he could ever get loose. The only difference is that the red man would die; she'd only wish she would.

The filthy savage came and stood over Jed. He roughly grabbed his arm and lifted him to his feet. Embarrassingly, Jed could not yet stand by himself. His legs and arms felt as if they had been shot full of led and drained of all blood; there was nothing left to supply energy to his muscles. Although he was a bigger man, the native handled him as if he were nothing.

"Yuh filthy snake! Wait until I'm free! I will cut tha' smile off'n yor face! I'll make ya a squaw 'afore I finish with yah!" However, Jed's threats had no power. The lack of water zapped any force behind his words.

James didn't bother to hold back his groans and moans as he was dumped unceremoniously by his brother's side. "Please," he gasped. "Water."

Kaitlin approached with the aid of a stick she used as a cane.

Spirit Bear turned to confront her. "*Iyotaka, wanna!*" he took a few strides to her and took her stick. He pointed to the tree where she'd been sitting.

"Please, Mr. Indian. Give them a drink." Kaitlin mimed drinking in the air and pointed to the men. "I know they are bad, but no one needs to suffer without water. Then I'll go back and sit down."

Spirit Bear was not in a negotiating mood. He scooped her up and took her directly to the spot under the trees. In a voice that could not be disobeyed, he commanded, "*Oyuhlagan sni.*"

Kaitlin was nervous but stood up for what she felt was right. "Mr. Indian, please. Just a little water for the men?" Again, she made a drinking motion in the air and pointed to the prisoners.

Spirit Bear's arms were crossed over his chest, but he nodded once. He'd planned on giving the *ska sunka* a drink anyway, but he didn't mind if she thought he did it because she'd requested it. They still had plenty of bark left in them, but he wanted them to continue to have endurance for the retribution they still had to pay.

Spirit Bear walked to the creek at the base of the hills to fill the *mniapahta*. For the first time, Kaitlin was left alone in the company of his captives.

"Kaitlin, get yur butt over here an' cut these ropes a' from me. Yu'd better hurry a'fore that red skin comes back." Jed used his softest, kindest voice in hopes of persuading her to do his bidding.

"Jed, Lord knows I hate this for you, but I can't help you."

"Shore ya kin. Yuh jus' come on over here and let these here ropes out so they kin be nice an' easy to move. Ya don' hafta turn me loose. I kin act like I jus' worked 'em loose on ma own."

"Jed, I'm more scared of you than I am of that Indian. He's tried to help me where you just hurt me. You would've raped me, and you nearly killed me!"

"Aw, shoot, Kaitlin! I was gonna sleep wit cha, but I got a rite to! I am ter be yur husband! Yur paw done turned ya over ta me. A'sides, that Injun's gonna do to ya the same as I waz! What wud ya rather haf, a filthy red skin a'tween yur legs or yur husband?" He waited half a beat before continuing, "Yu'd better hurry up an' decide! He'll be a comin' back a'fore long!"

"I don't know, Jed. You're mean and scary! I don't want to marry you." She wore a pouty frown of defiance before she stated with vehemence, "I won't!"

"If'n I swear ta leave ya be, will ya at least loosen these ropes up on me? James, too?"

Kaitlin looked worriedly toward the creek. "If he comes back and sees me by you…" she visibly trembled.

"He's gonna do that ta yeh anyways. I kin save ya. But only if'n ya turns me loose firs'." Jed did his best nice voice to help manipulate Kaitlin into doing his bidding. Scaring her about her destined future with the red skin only helped his situation.

Kaitlin stood in indecision, trembling with the knowledge that their uncertain future was in the palm of her hand. She was more frightened of Jed than she was of the magnetic warrior who'd only treated her with kind gentleness. Jed had shown her nothing but pain and humiliation. She knew she couldn't trust him; however, she knew that the men's situation with the

Indian couldn't be a good one. While he'd treated her with soft tolerance, the men were only shown power and domination.

"Damn it, Kaitlin! Get over here and git these ropes off'n me!"

Startled out of her ponderings, she froze. "It's too late," she whispered. "I'm sorry." Tears welled in her eyes but didn't fall. She was still weak from her injury she'd sustained by Jed's very hands, but her tender heart cried out for humane treatment of all people… even by those unworthy.

Spirit Bear wondered if the *winyan* would remain where he'd put her. He was pleased to see that she had, but he also discerned her trembling. Immediately, he knew the *ska sunka* had been biting at her again. He was very tempted to dump the water at their feet for upsetting her, but Indians were a proud people. Warriors, especially, could maintain control in many situations others could not.

He allowed the white dogs time to circulate their restricted arms. However, he'd show no more mercy. He roughly grabbed the men and leaned them up against a tree. After securing them, he lifted the *mniapahta* to first James's lips then to Jed's. Both greedily guzzled all the water they were allowed. A small trickle of liquid dribbled down from the edge of their mouths to their grimy chins, cleaning an unnoticed path on their unshaven faces.

Jed glared at his red enemy, trying to intimidate. The ebony eyes calmly stared him down until finally, the blacksmith looked away. Jed realized it was futile to try to be dominating when he was tied to a tree.

Spirit Bear returned to Kaitlin. He sat on the leather skin he'd unrolled and patted the spot beside him. "*Uwa yo, mitawa ogligle wakan mazaska zi, iyotaka.*"

Kaitlin had no clue of what he said other than he wanted her to sit by him. She obediently came and sat by the masculine form, secretly glad to be away from Jed and the pressure he put on her.

Spirit Bear motioned to her bandage and asked, "*Isica?*"

Kaitlin nodded. Anticipating her response, Spirit Bear retrieved the skin of bitter liquid that took away her pain. This time, she didn't hesitate to drink the sour medicine. In a short while, the potion had taken effect, and her eyes grew heavy.

Spirit Bear knew his *winyan* needed this break. He'd stopped for her benefit, not the *wasicun*. It was a normal for any tribe to rest during the heat of the day, but this was not usually utilized by the warrior society away from home. However, rest did benefit animals traveling during the hottest part of the afternoon.

After *wiiyayuh* began the decent from the highest part of the sky, Spirit Bear gently nudged Kaitlin. "*Uwa yo, Mazaska Zi Ista.*"

Immediately, her eyes opened. He gave her a few moments to awaken while he readied the animals and men. She couldn't help but to admire the way he easily lifted the bulky men onto the saddles of their horses. Still yet, she continued to be most amazed at his grace and power evidenced by his agile leap onto his war horse's back.

Kaitlin still wasn't used to the closeness of a man and the way the Indian swung her up onto the horse. Just as the warrior pressed her body back into his to give her support, Kaitlin caught Jed glaring openly at them. He mumbled something vile before they took off for the afternoon.

Traveling went similarly to the morning's trek, only hotter. By the time they rested that evening, Kaitlin was hot, tired, and her head pounded. When Spirit Bear jumped down and turned to help her off the big horse, she was already sliding into his arms without realizing she'd done so. Concern was etched in Spirit Bear's face.

Immediately, he set her down tenderly under a large tree. He unrolled the mat and began a fire. She didn't comprehend why they'd need a fire when it was so hot out. He took her beloved cast iron skillet and dumped water into it from one of his strange looking bags.

Kaitlin was content to watch his movements. She was fascinated by the way his muscles rippled under his flesh; they seem to dance seductively in currents. While he worked, his bear claw necklace made tinkling noises as they bounced against his chest.

Spirit Bear had a bag of medicines he wore attached to his waist by a thong. He dug through it and found fairly fresh St. John's wort. Kaitlin watched as he smashed it and added it to the bubbling water. He also added powdered plantain. Last, he took crushed slippery elm bark and added it to the brew. He boiled it for a few minutes and then removed it from the fire. She noticed he would glance towards her from time to time with a trace of concern etched in his features.

While the concoction cooled, he took care of the animals. He unloaded the men from the horses' backs and removed their saddles. He ran his experienced hand over the animals' legs to check for injuries from the hours of traveling. Next, he took a cloth-type material and rubbed the horses down. Last, he picked up their hooves and checked them for rocks. He allowed them to roam free to pick at the abundant grasses and drink their fill at the nearby water source. He knew *Runs with the Wind* would watch over them.

Refilling the *mniapahta*, he made sure Kaitlin drank her fill. Then he drank. He gave the prisoners their drinks as well. Kaitlin had no problem drinking the bitter liquid because her pain in her head was almost intolerable from the heat and the constant movement.

Spirit Bear helped Kaitlin lay back on the unrolled leather. He removed the wrap from her head. A large bruise that was a sickly green and black was visible through her hair line about an inch and a half behind her temple. Blood had oozed and was caked to the side, tangling her hair into clumps. Using the water from the boiled herbs, Spirit Bear gently cleaned her wound. Kaitlin closed her eyes against the painful assault but didn't try to resist.

"*Kanhtal*," he said softly. His masculine voice reassured and calmed her. He used the cooked herbs as a poultice for her injury. With fresh bandages, he redressed her wound.

Assisting Kaitlin to a reclining position, Spirit Bear whispered, "*Asniya wanna.*" Kaitlin had no problem following his order to rest; soon sleep would claim her.

When she awoke a few hours later, she saw the Indian had caught, cleaned, and was cooking a rabbit. Although wild game was lean, drops of juice and fat dropped off the spitted meat and hissed in the fire below. A delicious aroma sailed into the air. He'd gathered wild spinach and onion, and she noticed there were several wild plums resting nearby.

When the meat was finished, he brought her a section of substance. He'd cut off a small hunk with his knife and held it to her lips. She gingerly retrieved it with her teeth. The slight tang from the meat mixed with the garlic he'd obviously rubbed on it prior to cooking had her almost groaning aloud. She really hadn't had solid food since the fish.

CHAPTER THREE

Spirit Bear Discovers Weakness

Spirit Bear was pleased to see his *ska winyan* eat with hunger. She hadn't much of an appetite since the large *wasicun* had hurt her. Her current appetite led him to believe that the medicine he'd applied to her was beginning to take hold. It was the will of *Wakantanka* that her health was being returned to her. Spirit Bear offered a small chant of thanks.

He walked towards the bound *ska sunka.* He untied James's hands and handed him some meat and vegetables. James shook with hunger, but before he was able to grab his food, he rubbed his red wrists. They were raw, chaffed, and bleeding; thankfully, he couldn't feel the pain due to the numb tingling. James didn't resist the red man; he ate with relish.

After securing James back, Spirit Bear offered the same treatment to the bigger man. Jed's eyes were narrowed with hatred, but he also didn't fight. He, like his brother, rubbed his hands together for several moments before wolfing down his food. Drinking the last of the water from the skin the Indian held out to him, he contemplated his choices.

Jed knew that physically, he was no match for the Native American in his current condition; he was feeble from the hours of traveling bound to the back of a horse, and of course, the lack of a decent meal made him feel weak. He was the larger, more solid man of the two, but he wasn't packed with sheer muscle. Jed would still be willing to try to pulverize the red man with his bare hands, except he realized hands were no match against the Injun's piercing knife, bow and arrows, and who knew what else in his supply stash.

To be retied was certain death, Jed knew, but the damn heathen watched him like a hawk. Still, he'd managed to stow away a sharp rock. He planned on sawing through the ropes during the night hours when the filthy savage would be laying with his future wife. At least the loathed man hadn't yet taken his woman! That proved he was no real man at all.

Jed knew it was imperative to make his move tonight. Kaitlin was still pure for him, but once they reached the village, her time to remain untouched was very limited. Once they weren't traveling and that red beast took her into his dwelling, it was all over for her purity. When the red scum finished taking from her, who knew if he'd keep her indefinitely, kill her, or give her to his friends.

If Kaitlin was defiled by Injuns, Jed would never want her for his wife; he wouldn't take red man's left overs. Kaitlin was innocent and trusted the warrior just because he'd treated her with sympathy. She had no idea how appealing to every male she truly was.

He loathed his position. He didn't think it was wrong of him to take what he wanted – whether it was the rape and killing of the Injun maidens or of Kaitlin herself. What Jed Coldwater wanted, he took.

With regret, the blacksmith allowed the Injun to retie his hands. He glared at Spirit Bear with narrowed eyes to let the Injun know he wasn't intimidated. Jed felt more courageous because the stowed rock had given him hope. Maybe after he worked himself free at nightfall, he could kill the brave while he slept and then finish what he'd started with Kaitlin.

Jed's eyes roamed to where the large overo stallion stood. He'd take him as well. The horse would make him a load of money. He could breed him and fetch a handsome price for any offspring. Jed smiled at the prospect of having the woman he wanted, a fetching stud, and the announcement that he'd killed a dangerous Injun! The town would have to elect him mayor!

Spirit Bear was at last finished with his chores. He could ensure himself that the *winyan* was improving. Her rapid deterioration this afternoon had alarmed him. He knew it was simply the heat of the day, lack of water, and the constant movement, but he had to be sure. Head injuries were not something to take lightly.

When Spirit Bear approached Kaitlin, he noticed that her color had much improved. She still had a few dark shadows under her eyes, but she looked almost as well as she had that morning. He breathed a secret sigh of relief. *Wayaka* were not supposed to come to mean anything to the owner who captured or bought them.

It was especially important to maintain this unfeeling exterior when *toka* were around. The warrior who exhibited weakness before the enemy lost power; the protector could not show fault!

Spirit Bear thought about how delicate the balance of power was in the life of an Indian. For a warrior, his weapons and personal belongings held much power. If a warrior were able to obtain a possession of a foe, especially without injury to himself, it was considered a great coup. The foe would lose a little personal power due to the slight against him, making it easier to kill him. However, power could be regained. Any recovered items were also seen as a great coup. Performing acts of bravery or other daring coups would restore the native's honor in power.

If a *winyan* touched a warrior's weapons, they lost power as well. It was a serious thing for the woman if she defied Indian law. It could be death for the *winyan* if she knowingly touched weapons. Spirit Bear would ensure that his *ska wayaka* knew, without a doubt, that this could not be permitted.

Kaitlin watched the gentle yet fearsome warrior move toward her. She no longer panicked at his approach, and his medicine did wonders for her head. He was so calm and patient with her.

Still, she wondered why he'd bothered to bring her along. *What did he have in mind for her?* All the stories she'd heard were about rape, torture, and death. He'd done none of the above. She couldn't help her growing respect of him, nor could she prevent a warm spot in her heart from developing. It didn't hurt that he was the most handsome man she'd ever seen.

Spirit Bear sat on the hide beside Kaitlin. He offered her the *mniapahta* again and the *pejuta mniapahta.* He noticed she took small sips of both, but she didn't act as if either was an overwhelming need. This was good.

Spirit Bear pointed to the sleeping skin and said, "*Istinma yo, Mazaska Zi Ista.*" He made a motion of closing his eyes to let her know he wished her to sleep now.

Kaitlin had no problem with sleeping; it was all her body wanted to do since Jed had knocked her to the ground. She was thankful the dizziness was beginning to pass! The young woman just couldn't believe how weak she felt! She *hated* the feeling of being at the mercy of others; the blonde was usually the one who was in charge… to a degree.

She also wished she had someone to talk to; she'd been alone for so long! Although Kaitlin couldn't speak with others much at the cabin, she'd always enjoyed companionship.

Neither Jed nor his brother was those whom she would choose to associate with. The Indian, on the other hand, she had many questions for. Even if the blonde knew how to break the language barrier, the young woman was too afraid to pummel him with questions.

While she sat thinking about communication, Kaitlin temporarily lost track of time. The white female didn't realize that she'd done so until, suddenly, the warrior's features swam back into focus. She was consumed by the dark depths of his eyes. His intense gaze seemed to swallow her up.

"*Istinma yo,*" he said softly, repeating his command to her. His stern look had her lying down within seconds. He'd only been kind to her, but he still was so domineering! She looked up at the sky, aware that he was still studying her. Kaitlin held her breath, hoping to become less of an interest to him.

Spirit Bear could almost perform an immediate prayer ritual to *Wakantanka* for the return to health of the *ska winyan*. It was good to see she felt well enough to subtly challenge him. Her strength amazed him, both mentally and physically. His fascination of her only seemed to grow.

The day's dying light captured the gold in Kaitlin's honey-colored hair. It shimmered like a mountain stream running along its length. Spirit Bear picked up a tendril of hair and watched in awe as it curled around his finger.

Kaitlin was motionless, observing him as he watched her hair twine around his finger. To see this mighty warrior holding her hair like it was precious gold surprised her. He held such power in check. It was almost as if two people lived in the same body!

Black eyes met almond-shaped ones. Spirit Bear let the hair fall, forgotten, back to join the rest. She looked so beautiful in the fading light. Her sun-kissed skin was a compliment to the pink lips. Her flushed cheeks highlighted shallow hallows in her slender face. Delicate bones shaped her nose and brows. She looked like what the spirit of the sun would look like if she decided to borrow a *winyan's* body.

Kaitlin watched in slow motion as his head descended towards hers. Her eyes widened, but she didn't try to resist. His full lips meshed with her feminine ones. Leisurely, his mouth moved over hers.

At first her lips were unresponsive, but under his patient ones, they began to yield. She didn't return his kiss, but neither did she fight it. The pounding in her chest beat a rhythm to match his. His tongue slipped in the slight opening in her defenses and began to dance passionately against hers. Still, she didn't return the kiss.

"Lila wiya waste," he muttered huskily. *"Nimitawa ktelo."*

Once more, he began to seduce her mouth. His hand moved upward to support her head. His fingers caressed her hair as his mouth worked magic on hers.

She finally melted in his arms. Unknowingly, she lost track of time and place. All that mattered was the new sensations he was birthing within her. She made a slight noise of need, encouraging him to continue.

With his other hand, he began to roam her body. Immediately, he felt her stiffen. He noticed her eyes. They were wide with fear; she'd snapped back to the present and realized her predicament. If he chose, he would take her when and where he decided, and there was nothing she could do about it. The realization scared her.

He whispered, "*Kanhtal*," next to her throat.

"No," she requested in a low, quiet voice.

His finger traced her brows and down her nose. He gingerly touched her lips with his forefinger. The powerful man brushed the hair back from her face gently. The bandage he'd placed on her head was the only mar to her beauty. The *ska sunka* had much to pay for. His life would not be taken easily nor lightly.

Kaitlin was relieved but strangely disappointed when the virile male presented his back to her to sleep. Although her body was tired and needed sleep, the man beside her had awakened many things within her. The young woman's mind raced, and she had trouble quieting it down.

It was a long time before Spirit Bear felt Golden Eyes relax. *Mazaska Zi Ista* had many things to discover about the surprises in life. And he was just the man to show them to her.

Spirit Bear allowed himself to unwind and drift off. Slumber did not come easily or quickly when he had to *ka* near. Warriors did not naturally sleep soundly, for if they did, it might be the last time. Trained fighters honed their every skill: It was necessary for survival.

Like other warriors, Chief Spirit Bear had sharpened his skills until he was the very best. None could stalk, track, or kill more efficiently than he. He rarely missed when he fired his weapons, and none could defeat him in hand-to-hand combat. His war strategies were legendary. He'd more than earned his right to the title, chief.

Spirit Bear had been selected to begin his path down the warrior trail when he was three winters. The tribal elders and members of the warrior society used observation and visions when deciding whom to select for the most important job of protection. As they had predetermined, he excelled.

Chief Takes Chances had been killed in a raid by the Crow while defending his new child. After the village had recovered from his death, Spirit Bear had been elected to take his place. He was the youngest chief in the collaborative memory of the tribe to have this honor bestowed upon him: he had been a mere seventeen winters.

Before he was selected to take on the role of war chief, he was recovering from the Sun Dance. While his body healed, he mourned Chief Takes

Chances. Then, the responsibility of the whole tribe's lives lay on his shoulders as well. He didn't take the show of faith lightly.

He'd earned the name *Woniya Mato,* Spirit Bear, from a naming vision quest. The elders had agreed the name suited him well. Tribal members and the elders in the tribal council all laughed and joked in
a good-natured way about how he represented the essence of the *Cante Tinza,* or Brave Hearts Society. They agreed that the name was perfect for him for he was stealthy as a spirit, suddenly there then gone without a trace, hitting his enemies with the bear's ferocity. The name, Spirit Bear, was known to strike fear into the hearts of his enemies.

Not knowing about the sixth sense of a war chief, Jed had just sawed free of his bonds. As quietly as his legs would move, he went to his brother and put his finger up to his lips to specify he wanted him to be silent. Then, using motions only, he indicated he wanted James to gather the horses and supplies. He'd go and take care of the other… problems.

Jed quietly approached the filthy savage. He saw red every time he recalled that blood-thirsty animal nearly rutting on his woman. And damn her, she didn't try to fight him, neither. He planned on cutting the heart out of his captor while making her watch. No one treated Jed Coldwater like white trash and got away with it! No one. Then he would take his woman and his brother and go.

He'd planned on ravishing Kaitlin immediately, for he burned hot and furiously for her, but they had to be getting close to the heart of Indian Territory. He didn't want to take unnecessary chances. He wasn't a stupid man! Besides, he had all night, years of nights, for that.

A twig snapped somewhere in his dreams, and immediately, Spirit Bear leaped to his feet. All senses on alert, he scanned the near vicinity. Kaitlin lay sleeping soundly at his feet. It was not the *winyan* that had his internal siren blasting. His eyes narrowed when he saw the *wasicun* were missing. He unsheathed the knife strapped to his thigh.

The war chief crept with the night, blade in front, ready for use. His ears detected a noise. Spirit Bear noticed one *ska sunka* trying to saddle the black gelding quietly, but the big *wasicun* was not with him. The warrior had a debt to settle with both, but the big white man was the leader. Therefore, he would die hardest. Narrowing in on the younger brother, Spirit Bear stalked his prey.

Jed stood just barely beyond the vision of the Indian. Spirit Bear couldn't see him, nor could Jed make out the warrior. Because of this, Jed was not aware that the other man had been alerted to their freedom. He carefully proceeded through the woods in the dark of the night. Damn, it was hard to be quiet, even in early summer when everything was still lush and green! But thoughts of revenge drove him on.

James had a hell of a time catching the black gelding. The big horse of the Indian's kept blocking him from capturing it. The splashy horse would actually bare his teeth and lay his ears back until they were flat against his head! It beat all James had ever seen! When the mare had spooked at something and ran, the stallion's attention had been diverted. He took off after the female to regroup her with the other horse.

James grinned when he thought about how very like humans horses could be. The boy was off chasing after the girl. If he caught her, she might have to pay… just a little bit. He nearly whistled as he saddled the horse.

When the hair went up on the back of James's neck, he froze, then turned slowly. "Jed?" he whispered. Nothing was there, but now James was worried. He took a few steps in the direction of the Injun's sleeping spot. It sure was dark! If only he could see better!

Like a mirage, suddenly the big red man was before him, crouched like a panther ready to strike at him with a big knife! James nearly screamed. He stood, panicked for a split second, and then took out his sword. That was the first thing he'd secured upon gaining his freedom. He made sure he had a way to protect himself. The past three days had been hell! He,

James Coldwater, would rather die than be taken
captive again!

Slowly, the red skin moved forward, still ready to
spring in a moment's notice. James swallowed noisily; he
was sure his opponent could hear his fear. He stood with
his feet shoulder-width apart, holding his sword in front of
him. The trembling man grasped the handle so hard that
his knuckles were very nearly white.

The Indian's stare was fierce and powerful.
James's knees knocked with terror. He felt like a three-
year old up against his father in a game of wrestling: he
knew he didn't have a chance… unless Jed showed up.
Two against that Injun just might work.

"Jed!" James called shakily. Suddenly the
Injun let out a loud cry,
"*Hokahe!*" and charged.

James swung his sword wildly, hoping to slice
something on his foe. Spirit Bear moved like the wind. He
sliced the *toka* fingers holding the sword. James screamed
as he nearly dropped his weapon. Switching hands, he
held the large weapon with his left as he tried to ward off
attacks.

Again, the warrior charged. James held the sword
out defensively in front of him. "Come *on*, Jed!" He
yelled loudly. Shortly, the plea was followed with a
piercing scream. The saddled horse shied away from the
commotion and ran.

Kaitlin heard the scream pierce the night. She sat up quickly, trying to see what was going on. She noticed the native man was not lying beside her. Noises within the trees were coming from about thirty feet in front of her… fighting noises. The black gelding was saddled and tangled in brush just off to her left. Slowly, Kaitlin stood.

Jed finally reached the place where he could see Kaitlin. His brother had just screamed. He heard his earlier call for help and the Injun's war cry. He knew it was too late to help his brother, so he went for Kaitlin and focused on saving his own skin.

The burly man saw that the delicate beauty was standing on the skin that Injun had slept on with her. Red haze fogged his way to her, but he managed to reach her side in a few long strides. He gripped her upper arm in a death vice. She cried out with fright. She obviously heard the commotion coming from directly in front of her, and she nearly fell down when he grabbed her from behind.

"Shut yer trap! What in tarnation are yeh tri'n' ta do? We got to git ornselves outta here!" Jed said tersely in her ear. He dragged her to the horse. He ripped the tangled bridle from the underbrush and hoisted his heavy body into the saddle. He jerked Kaitlin up behind him by her arm. Whipping the horse, he wheeled it in the opposite direction as fast as he could.

Although hair streamed in her face making it even more difficult to see, Kaitlin managed to hold on. Jed didn't make sure she was secure before forcing the horse into top speed. She clutched at him in fear of the fall. She was still a little off-balanced from her head wound, and everything had happened at the speed of light.

"*Who screamed?*" She asked herself. She didn't want anyone hurt, but somehow the prospect of the handsome warrior being killed was a horrible thought to her. She sent up a silent prayer for her knight in bronze armor.

What would it be like to never see him again? He who'd stirred up things inside of her that she'd never felt before. Now she was at the mercy of Jed. That, in her opinion, was much worse than in the hands of the Indian. Somehow, she must convince Jed to take her to town. Then, maybe she could enlist the help of Bradley. For that, she'd have to evade Jed's rough hands. No one wanted a harlot for a wife!

The hard pounding on the ground during the night went straight to Kaitlin's head. Her injury had actually felt much better after the red man had administrated medicines to her earlier in the evening, but it was quickly returning to her former state. Before, when they'd traveled for three days, she'd been held and doctored. Now she had to grasp with every ounce of her being to keep from crashing to the hard ground: the blonde woman didn't know how much longer she could stay on.

After killing the *toka,* Spirit Bear heard Kaitlin scream in terror. He ran a few yards toward her, just in time to see the large *wasicun* swing her cruelly through the air and slam her on the horse. When she was barely hanging on, the *ska sunka* whipped the horse into a hard run.

A strangled cry of *"Pataka!"* ripped from his throat. He slid to his knees, anger boiling up hard and fierce. He threw his arms behind him and arched his back in anguish at seeing the only *winyan* who had stirred his heart taken from him. He offered a prayer to *Wakantanka* for her safe return to him. Clenching his jaw in determination, he whistled for his horse.

Jed continued to punish man and beast alike at the break neck speed for several hours.
He couldn't allow the Injun to catch up with him. For the first time, Jed was a little afraid. James, his brother, was dead; he was sure of it. Jed was unaccustomed to the guilt that was trapped in his mind as he sped along. *That Injun would pay!* He'd be back, and he'd bring his buddies with him. He'd kill 'em all!

Jed felt a feeble tug on his shirt. He looked back into the pallid face of Kaitin.

"I – I can't hang on anymore, Jed," she whispered.

He grabbed her arm and saw her wince in pain. Better to hurt her arm than to let her fall, he reasoned, because he wasn't stopping! He dangled her in the air before he was able to swing her onto the saddle in front of him. He didn't realize he had plunged her body down on the saddle horn. She cried out in pain before she succumbed to unconsciousness.

Jed didn't have time to worry about Kaitlin. When he swung Kaitlin forward onto the saddle, he caught a flash of color out of the corner of his eye.

Dawn was sending ribbons of light into the sky. Because of this, he saw the big stallion break free from the woods. Fear as he'd never known racked him. Whipping his mount harder, he leaned forward, urging it to greater speed.

Against the stream of pinks, blues, and purples, Jed saw the gilded edge of an arrow point shine from atop the tri-colored stud. Swallowing past the lump in his throat, his frantic mind grasped at hope: getting rid of extra weight was the key to his escape. The only extra weight that was expendable was the girl. It was the only way to save himself!

Regretfully, he started to drag Kaitlin's limp form from the top of the saddle. To prevent more guilt in his heart, he reasoned that he *had* to lighten his load. His horse was already slowing: it couldn't continue with all the weight.

Suddenly, the arm that was dragging the attractive woman's form from the saddle was rendered useless. An arrow marked by black tipped red feathers was deeply embedded in Jed's right shoulder. The move by the Injun barely prevented Kaitlin's fall; she was teetering precariously on the brink of tumbling into thundering hooves.

An idea came into the dull recesses of Jed's mind. The key to escape continued to be the girl! With his left hand, he laboriously pulled her up against his body. He gritted his teeth in agony of his shoulder, for it seared with heat and pulsed with pain with every beat of the horse's hooves. He held her so that if he was killed or his other arm was shot, she would die.

Jed heard a stream of what he believed to be Injun curses. Slowly, he reined in his horse and faced his ever advancing foe. With no prodding, the horse slowed, and then stopped. The gelding hung his head, his labored breathing filling the air.

The Injun approached, bow and arrow ready to fly in a second's notice. The great stallion came to a stop fifteen feet away. The mighty warrior's cold face was enough to strike terror into his heart if it hadn't already been brimming with it. The savage's bow was primed and ready for firing, and it was aimed directly at him!

Jed tried to show no weakness. He pointed to the savage's bow and arrow and made a motion for him to throw it aside. The Injun made no move to comply. Again, Jed repeated his sign language for the bow to be tossed aside. The warrior continued his frozen, hard stare. The only indication of his deep anger was the slight flare of his nostrils.

Jed was forced to an action he didn't want to take. He slowly placed his hand over Kaitlin's nose and mouth. Although she was unconscious, her body soon struggled for air under his hand.

"*Miye ahikte, ska sunka,*" the dark warrior's words were softly spoken but full of power. Jed needed no interpreter to understand that his opponent was promising him death. Scared beyond the point he dreamed possible, Jed did not lighten his grip on Kaitlin. If anything, he held her face harder. A slow, cruel smile slowly turned the ogre of a man's mouth upwards.

"*Hiya!*" Spirit Bear commanded loudly when Kaitlin's body began to vainly struggle to receive air in her burning lungs. The mighty warrior had finally discovered his only weakness: he could not bear to see this gentle woman die at the hands of his *toka*. With determination, he flung his bow and arrow aside.

"Oh, I see!" Jed stated. The grin momentarily wiped from his face with the force of his shock. "Yeh want this woman tha' bad?" he sneered. "I'd rather see 'er die that get yer filthy paws all over 'er! But since I kin do nut'in' about it rit now, yeh win. But lemme tell ya somethin' ya ugly savage! I'll be back fer yeh! And I'll take 'er in front a yeh. I won't never marry 'er after ya touched 'er, but I will still take me rightful share! Ain't nobody gonna get the last say with Jed Coldwater!"

With those words, he dropped the fragile blonde to the ground. Then he turned his fatigued horse and kicked his lathered sides. Before Jed was out of sight, Spirit Bear had reached Kaitlin's side. He held her still-shocked body and whispered words of encouragement to her. He wiped the hair back from her forehead. Chanting to *Wakantanka*, he performed the healing ritual that warriors execute when one of their own was injured. She was in the Great Spirit's hands now. Her body had endured so much!

Spirit Bear gently lifted Kaitlin's nearly lifeless body and carefully took her to a sheltered spot by water. He bathed her in *mni* to sooth her many bruises and forced more medicine down her throat. He stayed by her side to administer fluid, medicine, and prayer to her abused body. It appeared to be life or death for the first two days. Spirit Bear waited until her breathing stabilized before deciding to move locations.

Although Kaitlin needed many more days to recover before they traveled again, he knew it was imperative to move. If the *wasicun* reached the walls of the wood and alerted the others, they would both be in danger. His village was two days away, and he'd have to travel slowly, but if Spirit Bear could get Kaitlin to his tribe's medicine man, *Wawakankan*, she would have a better chance. Slowly, he began the arduous task of moving his *winyan* as easily as possible.

If he'd ridden hard, Spirit Bear could have made it home in a little over a day. Because he had to be so gentle and slow with many stops to care for the injured one, it took him nearly four suns. Her body was burning with fever when he arrived at his village despite his great care of her.

Most of the tribe came running to him upon his return. Many wore happy or worried faces, and all showed great curiosity over the *ska winyan* he cradled so tenderly in his arms. Satisfying none of the questions, he headed straight for his friend and medicine man's tipi, *Wawakankan.*

Once he reached the medicine hut, Chief Spirit Bear called out in a hoarse voice laden with concern, "*Anakiciksin!*"

Quickly, the youthful medicine man rushed from the wigwam and the two men gingerly carried their patient into the place of healing. Once Kaitlin was lying on a pallet, *Wawakankan* didn't pause to question the war chief. He began, instead, to carefully cut her weathered and filthy dress from her body. The medicine man made an exclamation and exhaled loudly when he saw the extent of the injuries of the *ska winyan*.

"What happened to her, my chief?" Wonder Worker asked in Lakota.

As they washed her body and administered healing balms and poultices to her many injuries, Spirit Bear told of his first encounter with the white woman and her life in the box of wood. He told of her flight and of the visit by his totem helper to her place of solitude. He spoke in awed reverence that she appeared thirty minutes later from the same spot as the great black bear, unscathed.

Spirit Bear then related his capture of the two enemies, *toka*, and how the big white dog had been attacking this beautiful girl in the dark of the night. He spoke shamefully of the escape of the big man, but how the younger *sunka* had not been as fortunate. In a voice laced with vehemence, Spirit Bear swore vengeance upon the *wasicun*, white man.

"You have achieved a great coup, *Woniya Mato!*" exclaimed the shaman. "You have taken the white girl from the enemy! Not only that, but you have taken his brother on his spirit journey. Some of our tribe will be avenged for their evil doing to our people!"

"Yes, but the one called Jed lives to tell of his escape, my *kola*," Spirit Bear let how he felt ring in his words to his friend.

"When you have rested, we can resolve this problem," *Wawakankan* confided.

"First we must wait until Golden Eyes awakens. She will have much fear in her heart to see that she is surrounded by many Oglala."

Hearing much more than what was said with just his words, *Wawakankan* looked deeply into the eyes of his *kola*.

"Let us hope it is the will of *Wakantanka* that she lives. She has a concussion, bruised and separated ribs, crushed muscle in her upper arm, and she had no air while her body was fighting heat demons. It is much to endure, but especially for a mere *winyan*."

Spirit Bear nodded his understanding.

"She means more to you than just a *wayaka*, slave, does she not, my *kola*?"

"*Tos*," he deeply affirmed. "Do what you can to save her. You will be well rewarded!"

Both Spirit Bear and *Wawakankan* worked long into the night. They changed bandages with fresh poultices every few hours. They spoke incantations over her bruised and battered body, and they forced liquids and nutritious broths into her nearly dehydrated throat. They also gave her willow bark tea to help keep the heat demons at bay within her body.

By morning, the men were taking shifts sleeping and watching over the *ska winyan*. Her color had improved some, but her bruises looked worse. Her body was a rainbow of blues, yellows, greens, purples, and shades of black.

"I will *kill* the *ska sunka* very slowly for what he did to her!" Spirit Bear cried. He paced with worry. His *wayaka* had not yet opened her eyes. It had been nearly three suns since they'd arrived in the village.

"Wait, my friend. Do not give up hope yet! See how she breathes not as deeply?" *Wawakankan* bought the pacing warrior before the still-fragile girl. "This means she will awaken soon. Still," he warned, "it may not be for several hours.

Finally, his words had taken the frantic edge of concern away from his chief. *Wawakankan* could now refill the dirt his friend had worn away from his floor. He smiled at his own humor.

As if reading his mind, Spirit Bear asked, "What brings a smile to your lips, Wonder Worker?"

"You, *Woniya Mato,* my chief." *Wawakankan* didn't elaborate, but the war chief was perceptive enough to know what his confidant was thinking.

"She is but a *winyan*, my friend. A *ska* one at that."

"*Tos*," *Wawakankan* nodded once in agreement. "But one with great beauty. Even under all the bruises on her body, one can see that the Great Spirit took much time in forming her."

"You look at her only as a healer, not as a man," Spirit Bear growled in a warning.

"*Tos, Wawakankan* agreed once more. With a hearty slap on his back, Wonder Worker said, "Let us eat."

An older lady, *Wawakankan's* mother, served the men smoked venison with many fruits and vegetables. She glanced under her lashes at the *ska winyan* who the whole village was speaking of. What a pity that the girl suffered so at the hands of her own people! Curiosity satisfied, she left quietly.

Stopping his mother, *Wawakankan* asked if she could find a dress for the girl, for he had to destroy the sad excuse for clothes she'd been wearing.

"*Tos*, my son. I will bring a *wahpaka* upon my return." Then she was gone.

CHAPTER FOUR

Kaitlin's Recovery

Kaitlin awoke to a mysterious rattling noise and a chanting voice. Blinking several times through a shroud of haze, she saw a man with a painted face waving things in the air. He was rattling a dried gourd and hollow bones over her. In his native tongue, his chanting was half singing and half rhythmic talking. His voice rose and fell in crescendos. As he worked, he did a mild dance she'd never witnessed before. He kept a drum-like beat with the timing of his feet.

Kaitlin's body felt very heavy and swollen, as if she'd had many bee or wasp stings. Her dry mouth felt like somebody had shoveled piles of dirt into it. A knife-like pain stabbed at her with every breath.

The scream she had building was trapped in her throat, threatening to choke her. The young woman wouldn't have been surprised had the man with the painted face reached out and sprinkled salt on her to prepare her for the evening's meal. It was then that she spotted Spirit Bear.

He hadn't yet realized that she'd opened her eyes. He was in a kneeling position, adding his voice to the chant the painted one was engaged in. Instantly, as though he could feel the caress of her gaze, ebony eyes met golden almonds. The heat was instantaneous. She felt the scream fade away. He was safety, and she knew no harm would come to her.

The shaman recognized of her state of awareness. When he finished his chant, he praised *Wakantanka* for hearing and answering their prayers. Spirit Bear's distinctive voice joined with his in offering thanks.

After the initial shock of figuring out where she was, the questions began pouring into her mind. *What had happened to Jed?* The last thing she remembered was almost falling off and Jed grabbing her arm and swinging her down on the saddle horn. She'd lost consciousness immediately.

She didn't think she'd ever see her handsome warrior again. She attempted a small smile and winced. Jed had managed to bruise her mouth and nose. *How in the heck had he done that?*

Kaitlin tried to lift her head toward Spirit Bear. "*Mni*, please," her scratchy voice croaked. Spirit Bear's brows shot up. Had he heard correctly? Had she asked for water in Lakota, the tongue of the Oglala? He retrieved the *mniapahta* and gently placed it to her lips. She drank greedily.

"*Oslohankel*," he cautioned her. He knew if she drank too much too quickly, she would become ill. With her level of bruising, that would cause her much pain. Before she was ready, he pulled the *mniapahta* from her trembling lips.

"Please, Mr. Indian!" She attempted to move her arm to reach for the water skin and then stabbing pain ribboned through her. Surprise at her body's level of agony, she gritted her teeth and did not try to move further. "*Mni…*" she rasped.

"*Hiya, Mazaska Zi Ista.*"

"You are wise to take the *mni* from her, my chief." The medicine man approached to look at the girl's face, color, and overall health upon awakening. "She can have more in thirty minutes." *Wawakankan* then added in awe, "You are right, *Woniya Mato*! Her eyes are golden! You have named her well!"

Spirit Bear watched as *Wawakankan* gently looked over his *winyan*. He lightly pinched the skin on her hand and watched it. He seemed to assess the amount of time it took for her skin to spring back smoothly.

Kaitlin lightly attempted to pull away but didn't struggle. She didn't like this painted Indian poking and looking over her, but pulling back meant using bruised body parts. She gave up the attempted resistance quickly. Lying back, she studied the hole in the top of his tipi as his prodding continued.

When *Wawakankan* lifted her supple leather covering, she felt a breeze stroke her body. Shocked at the prospect of being nude before two virile male strangers, she sucked in indignant air and struggled to lift the leather back into place.

Spirit Bear came to her side. He gently removed her hands from the covering. "*Hiya,*" he commanded kindly but firmly.

"No!" she strongly resisted him, then cried out in pain as she moved her bruised arm and ribs. "No, Mister Indian! Please don't let him touch me!" Her wild eyes entreated him, then looked frantically at *Wawakankan*.

Her pleading was futile; his role as medicine man was to attend to his patient. Tears leaked out of her eyes as he placed his hands upon her naked body. She turned her head away from the men and closed her eyes tightly. She might be forced to allow this inhumane treatment, but she wouldn't look as they touched her!

"She is full of fire, *Woniya Mato*," *Wawakankan* said with his voice filled with amusement. "It is good that she is weak," he laughed in good nature. "You might have trouble taming that one!"

Smiling at this friend's taunts, Spirit Bear nodded his agreement.

"I think we need to wrap her ribs and maybe her elbow with poultice and grape leaves. We can bind it with the leather strips. It will help keep her arm to her side as it heals."

"*Tos*, Healer. You are wise. Hopefully she will understand we are trying to help her."

Kaitlin continued to refuse to look at the men as they moved her body to wrap her ribs. It was so humiliating and degrading when they had to gingerly lift one breast then the other to secure the binding.

Spirit Bear could not help but to notice the little pink peaks harden in response to his touch. Without meaning to, his breath came faster.

"Not for some time, my friend," the shaman teased. "She will be too sore for what you have in mind." He did not dare to admit that the *ska winyan* had innocently worked her magic on him as well.

To return their minds from the path they walked, *Wawakankan* slowly pulled the cover back over *Mazaska Zi Ista*. Both men's eyes would sneak peeks on their own accord until her creamy skin on her chest was no longer visible.

When she was covered once more, Spirit Bear brought Kaitlin the *mniapahta*. She continued to refuse to look at him, even for the water her body cried for.

"Leave the water skin by her bed, Chief. She will drink when anger no longer holds her heart."

"I will allow this, for I know she hurts." Spirit Bear conceded. He decided to place a wooden platter of strawberries, sliced apples, and blackberries beside her. She would need to begin to eat real food as soon as possible. Fresh fruits were also packed with *mni* that she so craved.

When the two men exited the east-facing opening to the tipi, they didn't look back. They knew she'd be more likely to eat if they left her. They also knew she wouldn't try to escape. Not only was she sore from head to foot, but she had no clothes.

Kaitlin heard the men leave the tipi after they were finished humiliating her. She let out a soft exhale of pent-up breath. She turned to reach for the *mniapahta*. It was almost more than she could resist when the bronze warrior had brought it back to her, but her stubbornness had won! Now, however, she would drink.

The plate of fruit also looked delicious! Reaching for a strawberry, she gasped in pain. *Would every little move cause her to cry out?* She was determined it would not. Gritting her teeth, she reached out once more.

Lying back on the leather, she held the grasped prize loosely in her hand. With anticipation, she brought it to her lips. She nearly passed out when the unexpected throbbing knifed through her when she tried to open her mouth wide enough for the small item. No longer being careful, Kaitlin forced the strawberry past her lips. Chewing was agony, but she managed to successfully eat the red ripe fruit!

Exhausted, she let her heavy lids close once more. In moments, she slept.

Finally, *Woniya Mato* was able to address his people. He stood before his gathered community. They waited with anticipation to hear his words: there'd be a celebration in one passing of the sun! He would tell the story of his journey into the white man's domain, an enemy whom most of them had never seen. He'd relate how he came to be in the possession of the *ska winyan* and about how he's defeated one of the *toka*. Although he was still very angry about the other *wasicun's* escape, he needed to pump up his people about the situation. Later, he would rally a group to hunt the white dog down!

Instant milling of the people began when they heard the word, *celebration*. They all had much to do! There were varied and many foods to prepare!

Spirit Bear smiled to himself. He'd made his people very happy this day. They would soon have

their curiosity appeased. And of course, his people
would get to celebrate!

Wawat'ecaka, mother to the medicine man, sought
Wawakankan. She had in her rough grasp a fine, fawn-
colored leather dress made from a doe. Its fabric was very
supple and soft to the touch. A few beads and colorful
quill patterns decorated the garment. Light fringe clung to
the base of the dress. The neck was V-shaped, adorned
with more beads and quills. No sleeves were apparent on
the piece of clothing.

Wawat'ecaka also had a plain circular piece of
leather with a hole cut from the center and two side slits.
It was made with the same skill of the dress. Included
with the supple leather skin were two long braided leather
ropes.

"Here is the *wahpaka* you asked for, my son,"
Wawat'ecaka said.

"Thank you, mother. These are fine garments!
Much finer than I anticipated! Are you sure you wish to
part with these?"

"Yes, my son. Our chief, your friend, seems taken
with the girl. I feel sorry for what she has suffered by the
hands of her kind. It is my gift to her."

"You are very kind. *Woniya Mato* will be pleased.
But what is the cloth shaped like a tipi for?"

"I saw the injuries the girl suffers. She will not be
able to lift her arm to place the *wahpaka* on her body. The
other skin is so that she can cover herself

from curious eyes." As she stated this, her gray brows lifted in inquiry.

Wawakankan had the decency to look away from her knowing discriminations. "Your gift and skill will be celebrated soon, my mother."

"I will help the girl learn how to sew her own clothes when she has recovered. I am making her two day dresses. The fine *wahpaka* is one I made for myself long ago but never wore," she grinned. "I had sewn it before you were born." Patting her middle, she continued, "so I was never able to wear it. I don't want all my work to go to waste," she paused. "There are also two pair of undergarments for her."

"You are kind. I am fortunate to have one so generous for a mother. You make me proud!"

"It is I who is proud," the older woman stated. "You are a fine man who is gifted in many ways," she added, "There is one more thing for the *wayaka*." She brought forward a plain pair of moccasins made of the most durable leather but lined with the pliable skin she was so famous for. In addition, she also gave a fine pair of moccasins for more dressy occasions. On the border and across the top, colored quills and beads formed a matching pattern to those displayed in the dress. She handed them gruffly over, nodded her head, and with that, she left to help others prepare for the celebration.

When *Wawakankan* reentered his tipi, Spirit Bear was there. He was beside the *ska winyan*, watching her sleep. *Wawakankan* gave the clothing to the chief and explained the purpose of the circular garment with the slender rope braids.

"No wonder your mother has her renowned reputation as such a fine dressmaker! She can create anything from her one-of-a-kind leather! It is like rabbit fur to the touch but not so hot! *Mazaska Zi Ista* will be pleased!" W*oniya Mato* stared in amazement when he saw the dress *Wawat'ecaka* had chosen to give the white woman as a gift.

"Oh, my *kola*, is *Wawat'ecaka* sure she wants to part this this?" Spirit Bear exclaimed softly. "It is very fine. She could obtain much for this in trade!"

"She wishes to give it as a gift to your *wayaka*," the shaman stated.

"I shall tell her I am pleased." *Wawakankan* gave a nod of agreement. Spirit Bear said with worry, "*Mazaska Zi Ista* did not eat. I am boiling her prairie chicken stew with spinach and evening primrose roots. I also put in a few garlic, onion, and some carrots. I need a healthy concoction she can drink as well as eat. She is far too skinny! She has lost too much weight."

"Good choice, especially with the primrose roots. It will help her heal the injuries and bring her back to strength. That and the spinach will help build her blood for recovery and to hydrate her injured body. It is good to have a chief who also understands the power of plants for healing."

Spirit Bear nodded once and rose to check on his boiling food. Kaitlin should awaken soon. He wanted to have her eat almost immediately after she woke. Watching the food cook in the skin pot hanging over the fire pit, the powerful man also mixed gruel for *aguyapi*, Indian bread. Once the mixture was formed, he placed small pats on the heated stones next to the fire. In seconds, they began to slowly bubble and rise. A delicious aroma soon filled the tipi.

"*Woniya Mato*, you should not be cooking. That is woman's work."

Spirit Bear turned to look at him. "Think, *Wawakankan*, of the reception that *Mazaska Zi Ista* would get if I asked a *winyan* to stop preparing for the night's feast to come and cook a meal for my slave. I cannot imagine that a woman would feel kindly toward her for that. For *winyan*, preparing for the feast is a celebration in itself."

"You are wise, my *kola*." But *Wawakankan* did not add that it would not be wise for the chief to be seen serving his slave.

Spirit Bear had just finished cooking the last of the *aguyapi*, and still Kaitlin slept. In fact, she gave no sign of arising. He ate some of the meal himself and prepared for the rest of the morning.

Spirit Bear awoke early, a normal custom of Indian life. He knew the *wasicu* also awoke early, although not as early as the red man. Finally, Kaitlin began to arise. He went to her side and was the first thing she saw when her golden eyes opened.

"Mmmm, what is that smell? I'm hungry enough to eat a horse! I just can't seem to open my mouth wide enough," Kaitlin mumbled grumpily. For the first time, she'd gotten enough liquids in her that she needed to relieve herself.

"Um, Mr. Indian? I…" she paused. How in the world could she make him understand?

Spirit Bear smiled gently at her. He knew what needs one had upon awakening. He went to get her garments. He retrieved the circular cloth, the braided leather, and the under garment. He showed them to her, and at her nod, he motioned for her to sit.

A groan she tried to suppress ripped through her clenched teeth, but Kaitlin managed to sit with only minimal help from the Indian. He gently slipped the cut opening of the long circular leather over her head. He tied the leather braids around her so that her arms hung loosely outside of the soft folds but concealed her modesty. Enough of the fabric was left so that it hung three quarters of the way down her shapely thighs.

Soon, *Wawakankan* called from the entrance flap. The chief's voice boomed an invitation to enter. Both Spirit Bear and *Wawakankan* assisted Kaitlin to her feet. Her feet and legs weren't badly bruised at least. She was thankful for that. At least she could walk!

Only slight dizziness accompanied her upright position. The most frustrating thing was the weakness that she felt. She was unaccustomed to being handicapped!

Kaitlin was not a small woman. She was slightly taller than average and had a trim, muscular but feminine build. She was proud that she was strong enough to take care of herself and her family without the constant aide of a man.

If only the people at home could see the sad shape she was in now! Wouldn't her father be proud of the fine husband-to-be he'd sold her to? The woman still seethed over it when she allowed herself to think of it.

Kaitlin knew she required *Woniya Mato's* help to walk this time. With her uninjured arm, she leaned heavily on him. They walked a few feet to the tipi entrance. Clenching her jaw so she wouldn't cry out, Kaitlin maneuvered her body, with assistance, through the low opening. Both men had to help her to her feet once she'd gained freedom of the structure.

Kaitlin stood in wonder and blinked at her surroundings. The village was huge. Never had she imagined such a large gathering of Indians! The tipis seemed to stretch as far as she could see. She appeared to be at the heart of the society.

People milled around, doing chores. Men sat while they worked on weapons or skinned small game. Women brought wood and water back to their homes. Children frolicked and played.

The younger children stopped their activity to stare at her when her emergence became the focal point. Older children assumed the watchful yet appearing-not-to-watch stance as did the adults. Kaitlin could handle the stares of the young and innocent. Although she realized she had the attention of the entire village, none appeared to be blatantly staring.

Spirit Bear stood silently beside her, giving her senses time to register and absorb their surroundings. Without knowing she did so, *Mazaska Zi Ista* clutched his arm tightly. At last, she was ready to continue toward the privacy of the not-so-near woods.

Spirit Bear was pleased with the way she held her head highly and proudly. Her shoulders were taut and thrown as far back as she could hold them without intense pain. Honeyed curls rained in a cascade down her back, glinting with gold as it captured the light from *wi*.

The only visible bruising was that on her mouth and upper arm. Her lips and nose were swollen, and that area had a bluish tinge with green undertones. The bandage on her head still covered fading bruises from her initial injury.

Woniya Mato escorted Kaitlin toward the stream. He watched her eyes widen in wonder at the beauty of the village. It was so large, yet it seemed to be a natural part of the fauna surrounding it.

Near the happily chatting crystal waters, the horses of the village milled. Kaitlin saw the powerful steed belonging to the man next to her. Also present was the dun mare that James had been riding. Horses of many sizes and shapes formed a large band. They were trusted to roam at will. The Indian settlement was located half way up a majestic hill and nestled comfortably into the peaceful side. Thick trees of many varieties shadowed the border and offered excellent cover. One would not discern a fairly large town was tucked away in this area unless it was stumbled upon or it was a known location.

Massive rocks offered protection on one side. They could be used for sentinel duty as well as cover from enemies. About three hundred yards past the river bank, Kaitlin could see a lush green valley. The river winded through the prairie like a snake, trees speckling its path.

Woodland and plain animals alike mingled in the dell. There were pronghorn, bison, elk, and moose. Rabbits and fowl hid in the tall grasses. Carnivores that preyed on the herbivores camouflaged themselves within the shadow of the woods bordering the tall grasses.

Kaitlin could almost forget her physical pain and discomfort in the absolute beauty and serenity of this magical place. *Woniya Mato* couldn't help but to grin, for he enjoyed her sense of awe in this place he called home. It was refreshing for him to see it for the first time through her eyes. His smile broadened. Now, it was her home, too.

Kaitlin happened to look up into his tanned face while he smiled at her. The effect was dream-like. Here was the most gorgeous man standing beside her in this mythical place, smiling at her. For a moment or two, Kaitlin knew true happiness. However, her bladder's insistence brought her back to reality.

Spirit Bear knew she was ready to proceed. He helped guide her down a well-worn path flanked by the water way to the place where his tribe reserved just for this purpose. Near the end of the walkway, the trail veered from the river at a ninety-degree angle. The Indians had chosen this spot well; it was good for little else.

A stony spot with a sandy bottom was receded between two rock walls. The place had plenty of room for one to find an appropriate location to take care of personal business. There was plenty of sand to cover, and there was an area reserved that contained scraps of leather and other soft materials for toiletry uses. *Woniya Mato* turned back his back to let her have privacy. On the way back to the village, Kaitlin continued to gaze in wide-eyed wonder at the perfection of the land.

"It's so beautiful!" she breathed. She leaned more heavily on the man beside her for balance. She felt the power of his muscle ripple beneath the smooth skin of his arm. She gazed down and looked at her white hand on his bronze forearm. Then the young woman looked up again at his face. He continued as if he didn't notice her scrutiny as they traveled back toward the heart of the Indian town.

Instead of returning to the shaman's dwelling, Spirit Bear led her to an enormous and colorfully decorated tipi in the center of the village. Depicted on the side were scenes of buffalo hunts, war coups, and deeds of bravery and generosity. The central themes were a huge black bear rearing up on his hind legs with its mouth opened in a ferocious roar and a picture of warriors engaged in the Sun Dance. Once more, Kaitlin became so engrossed in the scenes painted on the leather structure; she almost lost herself in it.

Another smaller scene showed the sun beating down on the back of an eagle and a hawk. The hawk was the closer of the two birds of prey. Its feathers stood out drastically, a bright red with black tips. They flew above a black bird that strongly resembled a crow. Wind was coming from the east. Four sacred mountains dotted the landscape. Rain flew onto the crow while no water interfered with the attack of the birds of prey. The earth was visible below the flight of the wind warriors, and a river slithered beneath.

Kaitlin asked herself many questions. *Who'd painted this? Where did they get the paint? What did they use for painting utensils? Were these scenes of Indian life in general, or were they specific to the owner of the dwelling? Maybe her captor planned on introducing her to the chief. Could this be where the chief lived?* Kaitlin's mind traveled at the speed of light.

Gently, Spirit Bear led her to the side facing east. Close to the entrance, Kaitlin noticed a tripod of decorated poles. Upon it was a medicine sack covered by the pelt of a white wolf. The red man motioned for her to enter the open flap of the structure. He helped to lower her so that she did not hurt herself. After she entered, he quickly followed and helped her to her feet once more.

Kaitlin stood with Sprit Bear's help, expecting to see the fearsome chief of the village, but the lodge appeared empty. Kaitlin looked around.

The tipi was much larger than any in the village. In the center of the structure was the fire pit. Flat rocks lined the bottom. She assumed they were used to contain the fire as well as serving the purpose of cooking pans. A large skin pot was suspended over the spit, but thankfully, no fire roared below it. Strangely, Kaitlin noticed the chief also owned a cast iron skillet, just like her own.

A bow and quiver of arrows hung on a support pole near the entrance. Kaitlin noticed that all the arrows were made with red feathers tipped with black. Several spears leaned lightly near the bow. Higher on the pole two items were displayed: a tomahawk situated near a hardened leather and bone shield.

The picture painted on the shield's front was phenomenal! A large black bear, in the form of a ghost, was attacking and killing enemies with one swift swipe of its deadly paw. Attached at the top of the shield and the base of the tomahawk were a few black tipped red feathers. A flint rock and sandstone lay below the multitude of deadly weapons for honing sharp blades.

Kaitlin's eyes continued their exploration of the tipi. She noticed several sheathed knives hung here and there attached to the poles of the dwelling. On the far wall, woven mats of fibrous material lay on the floor. Bowls, plates, and cups were stacked neatly on one end. They looked to be made of bone and wood, not the tin she was so used to. Clay jars and water skins as well as bone and wooden containers that held herbs for medicinal and cooking purposes lined the mat near the point of where the wall and floor met of the moveable home. Dried fruits, nuts, and grains in more containers were suspended from woven shelves made from strong grasses and supple branches.

In another section, colorful mats of woven grasses formed a carpet. Upon the mats were several layers of supple furs. On top of that, leather skins were neatly smoothed. The skins were of leather similar to the soft fabric whispering on her body. Above what she assumed to be the bed, a fine fur of a black bear hung against the wall of the tipi.

Off to the side of the bedroom the intricate war bonnet of a chief was displayed. It was decorated with many rows of red eagle and hawk feathers. Leather streamers decorated with bear teeth and claws would frame the chief's face when worn. Beside it was the matching breast plate. It was decorated similarly, but also had painted scenes with bears attacking enemy tribes on the protective bone plates. There was also a feathered staff. The top was ornamented with the black tipped red hawk feathers. It was intricately carved with more scenes of bears, wolves, eagles and hawks, horses, fire, water, earth, and wind.

On the opposite wall of the bed, more furs and skins were rolled and stacked neatly into bundles. Other supplies added to the pile. In spite of the many things within the walls of the tipi, it was quite spacious. Really, it was surprising to find the home so roomy!

Kaitlin's eyes went to Spirit Bear. He was standing close to her, watching her reaction. She wondered what she was supposed to do now. Were they to remain standing while they awaited the return of the chief? She assumed the warrior knew the proper etiquette of how to treat the chief, so she'd try to follow his lead. In white culture, it was considered rude to enter one's house when they were not there. She was beginning to understand that Indian culture was vastly different from that of whites'.

Anticipating that *Mazaska Zi Ista* was weak and would need to sit, Spirit Bear lead her to the furs. He motioned for her to sit. The *ska winyan* shook her head; she seemed to be very uncomfortable. She wouldn't meet his gaze and continually wrung her hands.

Knowing that a tipi was a big change from the wooden box she was used to, Spirit Bear gently smiled. He again motioned for her to sit and sat himself. Tentatively, Kaitlin followed his lead. Stiffly, but as gracefully as possible, she lowered herself onto the supple leather. Her eyes would dart nervously to the open entrance flap.

Because Kaitlin was now able to move around a little more than she had been, Spirit Bear wanted to convey the importance of her comprehension of the taboo against women touching weapons, especially slave women! It was vital that she understood that this was forbidden now, for she would be left alone for a period of time when he went before his people during the celebration.

While waiting on the arrival of the chief, the warrior got up and approached the entrance flap. Kaitlin assumed he would look to see what was taking the Indian leader. Instead, the bronze man pointed to the large bow. "*Itazipe,*" he said. Then he pointed at Kaitlin and shook his head. "*Hiya, Mazaska Zi Ista.*"

She looked questioningly at him. Why was this man telling her not to touch the chief's bow? The thought hadn't even crossed her mind! Next she watched the big Indian point to the arrows. He repeated the process. He said, "*Wahinkpe*." He shook his head vigorously when he looked Kaitlin. "*Hiya, Mazaska Zi Ista*," he commanded.

The Indian warrior continued this process for all the weapons and also of the chief's ceremonial wear.

"I get it already," Kaitlin mumbled. "I can't touch any weapons or the chief's headdress. I wouldn't have anyway."

Spirit Bear looked at Kaitlin's sulky appearance. She seemed to understand. Good. He didn't want to have to become more assertive with her. Her body was too bruised for him to use force to get his point across.

A silent fifteen minutes passed when finally, *Mazaska Zi Ista* looked at Sprit Bear. She pointed to herself and said, "Kaitlin," and waited.

Spirit Bear pointed to her and said, "*Hiya, Mazaska Zi Ista.*"

She shook her head and said, "Kaitlin." More firmly, Spirit Bear reaffirmed. "*Hiya, Mazaska Zi Ista.*"

Ok, maybe her name translated to *Mazaska Zi Ista* in Indian. She still persisted. She didn't want to call her captor, "Mr. Indian" indefinitely, so she conceded. She pointed to herself and asked, "*Mazaska Zi Ista?*"

The red man nodded once and said, "*Tos.*" She motioned towards him and raised her brows.

His masculine voice reflected humor. "*Woniya Mato.*"

She copied him. "*Woniya Mato,*" she tested the foreign words on her tongue. "*Woniya Mato.*"

He nodded, repeating, "*Tos.*"

Nodding, she smiled. At least she had begun to break the language barrier, even if all she could say were 'no', 'yes', and the names of weapons!

CHAPTER FIVE

Kaitlin Adjusts to Life in the Village

It was nearing mid-day, so Spirit Bear planned on retrieving the nutritious meal he'd prepared for Kaitlin earlier. They would finish it off later this day. He'd also prepare fresh fruit for his slave. Then he'd insist on her resting.

When he started to exit the tipi to get the food items, Kaitlin startled him by grabbing him fiercely. Her eyes were wild when she saw he intended to leave her alone in the dwelling. She acted like they were trespassing on another's domain. He gingerly released her fingers and disappeared.

Kaitlin was attempting to pace with her frail body when he returned to his tipi. Why did she seem so nervous? She didn't seem to be so anxious in *Wawakankan*'s home! Now she could relax and eat. He'd be there with her.

Kaitlin was upset once he'd gone. Was this his way of telling her that she'd be staying with the chief? She was scared out of her mind. *Woniya Mato* had treated her so kindly, and he was so handsome. She didn't want to be with anyone else! Finally, she'd found a man she trusted!

She wondered what the new guy would be like if she were to stay in his home. Would he be power hungry and mean to her? Or… was the chief possibly the warrior's father and he still lived at home? However, the evidence in the tipi suggested only one person slept there.

Kaitlin breathed a sigh of relief at her captor's return. She walked as quickly to him as she was able and followed him like a puppy. The muscular man acted surprised that she was so relieved and happy to see him.

She ate slowly due to the soreness in her jaw. It was very swollen, but she managed to eat enough to take away the stabbing edge to her hunger. The young woman mostly stuck to the stew broth, for the fruit still hurt too much to go through the motions of chewing.

The soup had an interesting flavor; she'd never tasted anything like it. Really, it was quite good. With all the vegetables, it had to be good for her as well. She hoped she'd learn more about food gathering and basket weaving while here with these interesting people. She'd always had an interest in these areas, and who better to learn from but the natives of the land?

After she ate, *Woniya Mato* gently pushed her back into the soft leathers and hides and commanded her to rest. As long as he stayed by her, she felt she might be able to. She just feared being alone in the hut in case the chief decided to show up.

Several hours later, Kaitlin awoke to a happy drum beat. *Woniya Mato* sat close by, watching her. He smiled gently. Then he went to the flap of the tipi and called to *Wawakankan*. She noticed that he brought poultice supplies with him, and she groaned in dismay. Both men smiled secretly at her apprehension. She might hate it, but they both rather enjoyed it.

After her treatment, Kaitlin sat by the entrance to the wigwam. She was seething again, but soon her interest was raised. The village people seemed to be a flurry of movement. Fresh meats and vegetables were roasting. Firewood was gathered into a clearing close by the tipi she was occupying. There were people everywhere doing something. It was startling and amazing; Kaitlin couldn't take her eyes away.

Looking out the flap in an obscure way to avoid the people's detection, she noticed some Indians bringing instruments to the side of the same clearing that held the stacked wood. She noticed several sizes of drums being carefully placed on the woven mats constructed from reeds. Flute type woodwinds also joined the drums.

Kaitlin wondered what in the world was going on. It looked like they were going to have one big party! They'd cooked all day, had enough wood for a large bonfire, and now they were adding music to the events.

Kaitlin had finally relaxed about using the chief's tent. She felt he must be away on a hunting trip or something. Why, she didn't know, because they had all the fresh game they could ever want available at the base of the huge hill they lived on. She'd decided to stop worrying about it, but it struck her as odd that this village would want to celebrate without the presence of their chief!

As evening advanced, *Woniya Mato* approached her. He seemed to be attempting to ask her if she needed to go and visit the place by the river again.

She nodded gratefully. It was another slow trip partially because her sore body wouldn't allow her to travel quickly, but also because she could not seem to divert her attention away from the beehive of activity that the people were involved in. *Woniya Mato* was very patient with her and waited without irritation as she absorbed it all.

Upon her return, the warrior left her alone in the tipi. He moved quietly back toward the river. She wondered briefly how he'd like to be denied privacy when he wanted it.

When the handsome man reentered the tipi, he was clean. His hair was damp and hung freely down his back. He closed the entrance flap. He walked to the supply pile and took out a brush made from porcupine quills. He combed his long hair but did not rebraid it.

Next, he unfolded fringed buckskin pants and a beautifully fringed shirt to match. The soft leather was adorned with many colored quill patterns. It was an outfit worthy of any king. Kaitlin wondered if this man was barrowing items of the chieftain's. Maybe the chief *was* his father! With awe, she continued to watch.

Spirit Bear stripped to dress in his finery. Kaitlin flushed bright red all the way to the roots of her hair She'd seen her father naked once when he was very drunk and couldn't successfully pull up his trousers after relieving himself in the woods, but she'd never seen the fabulously fit body of a man in his prime! She couldn't but help to notice the difference!

Knowing why she flushed profusely, Spirit Bear kept his amusement to himself. He thought, "If she is embarrassed now, wait until she sees it when I make her mine!" He continued priming himself for the night.

Kaitlin watched as Spirit Bear took soot from the hearth and mixed it with fat. Then he made a stripe high on his cheekbones and across his nose. *Woniya Mato* mixed red ochre and the pulp of some type of red berries Kaitlin was not familiar with and drew a line on each side of his face under the darker one. He added three vertical lines sprouting beneath the horizontal ones. In a way, it kind of reminded Kaitlin of the feathers on the Chief's belongings.

This gentle man who'd administered her injuries now looked like a fearsome warrior who would not hesitate to kill. He represented all the horrible stories she'd heard about murder and torture. She couldn't stop the tremor from passing through her body.

Kaitlin nearly fainted when she saw *Woniya Mato* reach for the chief's bonnet. *Could he be…? No, surely not… but why would he be taking the Indian chief's headdress if he weren't the leader?* Kaitlin's heart beat erratically, and she suddenly felt weaker.

Woniya Mato placed the full-dress chieftain's bonnet on his head. Feathers and streamers plummeted down his back in a wild yet somehow organized array. At this moment, he didn't resemble anything Kaitlin thought him to be. He'd become a formidable leader of a very large tribe.

Kaitlin suddenly realized the drum beat had picked up in tempo. *Waniya Mato* walked to the entrance of the tipi and opened the flap. Although Kaitlin was not allowed to partake in the festivities because she was a mere *wayaka,* or slave, Spirit Bear didn't mind if she observed from the structure.

"*Opiye, Mazaska Zi Ista,*" he said, looking down from his height on her where she sat near the door. With his feathered staff in hand, he moved toward the opening. Then, like a mirage, he was gone.

Feeling more alone than she ever had in her entire life, Kaitlin began to tremble. She was the only white person in an Indian village! They were the enemy… *or she was.* The distinction was obvious. *What was she doing here?* Actually, she believed she knew the answer.

Woniya Mato had rescued her from the hands of an evil man, Jed, and then tended to her many severe injuries. She probably would've died without his administrations. She'd be sure to share his generosity with her people when she was well enough to travel back. She would also relay Jed and his treatment to her to the town council! They would surely stop his out-of-control behavior, no matter how much money he had!

Of course, James had been apparently killed by the chieftain, but Kaitlin was sure there was more to the story than she knew. Only Jed could tell her the full story, and she could be sure that he wouldn't be willing to share it with her!

Kaitlin looked out the flap. It appeared that the whole village had assembled in the clearing. On one side, *Woniya Mato* sat flanked by two other men with head dresses. Theirs wasn't nearly as elaborate as her chief's, but they were obviously prominent members of the Indian Society. Also present was the shaman, *Wawakankan*. He didn't wear a headdress, but he was painted up from head to toe and had some sort of a mask made of bone and hide which shaded the upper part of his face save his eyes.

The important men sat on woven mats made of willow reeds. Another reed mat was supported by a tripod of sticks to support the backs of each of the members of the tribal council.

A group of young women approached the center of the clearing. They were painted up. They wore woven skirts of intricate designs made from different colored grasses. They wore no other clothing other than jewelry adorning their hair, necks, upper arms, and ankles. They looked very young, as if they were facing womanhood for the first time.

The young maidens bowed to each of the council members, then bowed collectively to the crowd. Shyly, they began to dance, keeping time to the drum beat. Slowly, other instruments joined in. A rattle shimmered, and the lonely cry of the flute-type instrument accentuated the musical throbs. The deep voice from a male singer added to the ensemble.

After the women finished the dance for the crowd, they assembled and continued to sway as a group. *Wawakankan* took the center stage and began a dance of his own in front of the community. His body language painted a story even she could understand. At first, he assumed the fetal position. From his motions, he was born and flew through his childhood years. With his dance, he mimicked the growing portions of womanhood. Suddenly, he stopped. The timing of the drums was unbelievable. Total silence overtook the village.

Wawakankan then turned and bowed deeply to the young women. As he called each maiden's name, she would step forward and bow to the council and crowd. She would announce her new name for all to acknowledge. The multitude would repeat it back, and then she would walk off the stage. Her status was now one of woman, not girl. Each girl's name was called and the motions repeated. When none were left, cries of cheer filled the air.

Next, platters of food were brought forward by the women of the village. Steaming meats filled the vicinity with mouth-watering aromas. Cooked vegetables as well as raw ones were placed periodically. Serving dishes of fruits and other items that Kaitlin didn't recognize were also placed strategically for the taking. Council members were served by the new women of the population.

After all had eaten their fill and the trays were removed, the crowd quieted. There was more! Kaitlin watched with anticipation to see what would happen next. One of the young girls who'd just become a woman stepped into the clearing. She had changed into an old tattered dress that had seen better days. It had grayed with age and was laced with holes from use.

Wawakankan stepped forward and began a slow rhythmic dance to the slow beat of a drum around the young woman. He began to lightly chant and shake a gourd. Then he stopped with a drum beat. He called forth two people who looked old enough to be her parents and had them face the newly-announced-woman. Resuming his dance, the shaman made about five passes around the three of them.

Wawakankan placed his gourd rattle on the ground and picked up some horsetails. He began to waive them over the girl and then the parents. He waived them back and forth as the girl slowly stepped forward until she was very close to the pair. *Wawakankan* gave the horsetails to the three present. They began moving the plants over each other.

When the drum began to beat again, the three stood quietly while the other members of the tribal council stood and joined *Wawakankan*. They formed a happy and smiling circle around the maiden and her parents. The beautiful girl, just out of youth, trembled with… anticipation? Fear? Kaitlin was unsure.

Suddenly, the girl ran away from the group but returned a short while later wearing a beautifully decorated soft deerskin dress. It was very becoming on her. The leaders melted back away from the family to resume their seats while the community waited in quiet anticipation. The young woman held up the worn dress she'd been wearing.

Woniya Mato came forward. He held a long, deadly hunting knife. He took the dress from her and held it up for the crowd to see. Then he gave a mighty war cried and sliced the dress to ribbons. He turned to the girl who was now standing beside her parents. He waived the horsetails over all three and then presented the new family to the village.

The girl, *Unjinjintka Can Kosica*, as well as the settlement, would no longer recognize her Pawnee ancestry; the ceremony severed that part of her. The gathering went wild with cheering and clapping, welcoming the new *Oglala* woman into their midst. The three in the center of attention hugged and kissed each other with love and pride.

Next on the celebration agenda was for Spirit Bear to relay the events that led to his capture of the *ska wayaka.* None had questioned his bringing of her to the village, only of the circumstances for her deplorable state. He wanted them to understand the evil nature of the man called Jed. He was the one responsible, along with his dead brother, for the deaths and rapes of the three Oglala women and the tortured death of a young boy. Not only had he treated the Indians in this way, but he'd also been giving the same treatment to one of his own.

With his great speaking abilities and his reenactments of the events that had occurred, Spirit Bear relayed to his people the events of the past few moons. His people cheered for the capture of the *ska winyan* and the death of the enemy. Angry shouts went up over the escape of the other brother. Jed had committed horrible offenses against the Lakota; the white man's sins demanded his life in repayment!

Spirit Bear assured his people that once his slave, *Mazaska Zi Ista* as she was to be called, was better and more accustomed to their culture and customs, he'd take a war party and complete his mission of vengeance. Cheers and shouts of support split the air.

Woniya Mato had accomplished his goal. He wanted the band to understand that he was going to keep the *ska winyan*. She represented his great coup over the enemy, but also he took the young white for her protection. His people saw his generosity and bravery as an additional coup.

The rest of the night was spent eating, dancing, storytelling, and observing individual performances from the members of the tribe. Some sang songs. Others played musical instruments. Still others put on performances of one kind or another. Kaitlin found it all very educating. Before she knew it, she'd fallen asleep where she sat.

When Spirit Bear finally returned to his tipi, he smiled with fondness at his *ska wayaka*. She'd been so enthralled with the rituals of the Lakota that she'd fallen asleep watching his band. Gently, he scooped her up into his arms and carried her to his bed.

After lowering her onto the pallet, he removed the paint from his body. The chief took off his bonnet and hung it up on this special place, placing the ceremonial staff close by. Then he stripped. He folded and placed his ritual wear up.

Mazaska Zi Ista mumbled softly in her sleep and snuggled up against him when he lay beside her on the sleeping furs. His arms protectively circled her, and the relaxed warrior simply held her for a few moments. In her sleep, Kaitlin threw her arm over his chest and slid it down his body. Her hand came to rest on his lower belly, just below his navel.

The effect of her touch was immediate and intense. *Woniya Mato* lay, undecided. He really desired to take this girl who'd touched his heart and make her his in all ways, but he realized it was too soon for her to engage in such a physical exertion. He knew a woman's first time was not enjoyable for her. Not only would that be something she would have to endure, but her ribs would pain her, especially if she resisted.

Sighing aloud, Spirit Bear withdrew from her and rolled to his side. The bronze leader willed his mind to relax. It was some time before sleep was able to take him.

Spirit Bear was gone when Kaitlin awoke the next morning. There was a platter of leftover food from the celebration for her consumption. Kaitlin tentatively tasted foods that she'd never seen before. Although the food was foreign, she ate the new flavors with relish.

Shortly after she'd finished, an older lady was at the flap of the tipi. She came in and kindly gave Kaitlin a friendly smile. She motioned to the platter, asking in sign language if she'd finished. Kaitlin nodded with understanding.

The woman pointed to herself and said, "*Wawat'ecaka*." To ensure comprehension, she pointed to Kaitlin and said, "*Mazaska Zi Ista*."

Kaitlin accepted the name, believing she was given her own Indian name because they didn't know how to say 'Kaitlin'. She nodded again.

The woman motioned for Kaitlin to follow her. The injured white woman slowly got to her feet with minor support, her body protesting. She came through the opening flap and saw the woman intended to help her go to the Place of Privacy. Kaitlin smiled gratefully. She accepted the woman's arm for assistance.

Upon their return, the *Wawat'ecaka* brought her to a different tipi. In the yard sat the girl that had endured the intimidating ceremony of the night before. The shaman's mother motioned for Kaitlin to sit beside the other woman. She pointed to the girl and said, "*Unjinjintka Can Kosica.*" Then she pointed to Kaitlin and said her name for Desert Rose.

Desert Rose was separating grasses into different colored piles. She smiled shyly at the golden-eyed girl. Kaitlin reached for the grasses stiffly. She didn't just want to sit and do nothing; these people were helping her out, making her feel welcome, and treating her injuries. The least she could do was help them out until she was well enough to make the journey home.

Wawat'ecaka excused herself and went to the chief's tipi to do the *winyan*'s chores. It would be many days before the *wayaka* could fulfill her role in her new life. Gentle Rabbit would be certain to instruct the girl well, for she loved the chief as if he were her own son.

The motherly figure practically raised Spirit Bear, Wonder Worker, and their friend, Sky Warrior. Growing up, the three were nearly inseparable. Now Spirit Bear was head chief, leader of defense. Wonder Worker was shaman – medicine man, and Sky Warrior was lead peacemaker. He was in charge of the village affairs. He also was the protector of the village when the others were away on hunts or raids.

There was one other leader of the band. He was in charge of the hunting expeditions. He assembled the large hunts and conveyed the strategy that would be used for the taking down of large, dangerous prey. He was known as Lone Wolf. His name suited him well, as he was not one who liked to socialize a great deal. This stealthy hunter was more comfortable on his own, or in small groups. The only time he was at home with large groups was when he while leading a hunting party.

All of the leaders were single. *Wawat'ecaka* hoped that the newly blossomed women would catch the eye of some of them. It was time for the men in their prime to take a wife into their tipi.

Wawat'ecaka suspected that Lone Wolf had eyed *Unjinjintka Can Kosica,* but as was their custom, he couldn't indicate interest until she became a woman in the eyes of the Oglala. Then, possibly, *Unjinjintka Can Kosica* could help *Isnala Sungmanitu* overcome his shyness of crowds.

Her son was another matter. *Wawakankan* was friendly to all, but he didn't act seriously interested in just one maiden. He was content to play the field. He flirted with one and all. Sometimes medicine men didn't take a mate. She would see to it that he did.

Wawakte Towanjila, Sky Warrior, also didn't have an interest in a particular maiden. *Wawat'ecaka* knew that several young women would be happy settling down with him. All four young men on the tribal council were handsome. They captured the eyes of all single maidens in the tribe, even some from neighboring tribes. Gentle Rabbit would do her part to see them mated soon…

Desert Rose took an immediate liking to *Mazaska Zi Ista*. Without being told, she helped. She seemed genuinely interested in working with the weaving materials, and she was a quick learner.

The work that would've taken her three hours was finished in less than one. When *Unjinjintka Can Korsica* tied the bundles, she took down a basket she was weaving. Kaitlin watched enthralled. She tried to ask questions, but the language barrier was a deterrent.

Desert Rose decided to try to teach the Lakota language to Golden Eyes. She appeared adept at the tasks she was given, for she was already successfully beginning a basket of her own. Learning Lakota would benefit the girl; her life was now with the Oglala band and the white girl would need to learn to communicate beyond signing.

It was nearly noon, so *Unjinjintka Can Kosica* assisted the *ska winyan* back to the prominent lodge of the leader. She motioned 'rest' to Kaitlin. Then she smiled and left.

Kaitlin entered her tipi. She drank from the *mniapahta* and sat on the sleeping pile. It wasn't long before her lids were drooping. It'd been a busy morning for her recovering body. She lay back and slept.

When the golden-haired girl awoke, Spirit Bear was back in the lodge. He was sitting against his tripod willow mat, placing newly shaped arrow points on freshly created rods. He wrapped sinew with small amounts of rawhide binding to secure the arrow tip. He attached the feather guides at the end of the shaft in the same manner. Kaitlin was fascinated. She watched intensely.

Because he wanted this woman of his to ease into her duties so that she had the healing time needed, Spirit Bear allowed her to watch. *Wawat'ecaka* and *Unjinjintka Can Kosica* had given good reports of the white woman's willingness to learn. The slight exercise was good to loosen her stiff and swollen muscles.

Spirit Bear wanted to gather a war party to watch and possibly attack the *wasicu* around the next full moon. For this reason, he would make many new weapons. He only wanted to take the white dog that was known as his *toka*, or enemy, on this raid, but if he must, he would take more.

The ten warriors he would take with him also made similar preparations. They'd be ready! If they needed to, many more warriors had volunteered to come. Spirit Bear wouldn't be surprised if the whole community emanated.

After watching Spirit Bear's repeated actions for some time, Kaitlin became bored. She stiffly got to her feet. She wondered when her side would stop slicing at her when she moved her arm too much. In two weeks, there had been some improvement, but not substantial!

Without alerting her to his attention, Spirit Bear watched his *winyan*. He doubted if she even realized she sucked in breath from the sudden pain her movements caused. He was running low on the willow bark tea he kept brewed for her, so he stood, stretching his taut muscles. He went to one of the woven shelves and removed fairly fresh willow boughs. He started a small fire under the skin pot and poured water from one *mniapahta* into it. He added the willow boughs so they would seep their medicinal properties into the water for consumption.

He considered using other plants for their pain relief properties, but many of them required a ritual to prepare. Although he was practiced in the preparation of these medicines, he usually let *Wawakankan* do the honor.

It took much skill to prepare white hellebore's leaves and roots of the blue flag's. Both were excellent for pain relief, but if prepared the wrong way, both could be deadly. Willow bark tea, however, did not require a ritual nor was it poisonous.

Kaitlin couldn't figure out why the chief was cooking tree limbs. Surely he didn't expect her to eat that! The recovering woman could barely chew, so she doubted she could eat parts of a tree even if she'd wanted to! Of course, if he gave them to her to eat, how could she refuse? He'd saved her life at least twice that she knew of. Kaitlin would always be grateful to the warrior for what he'd done.

After the water had boiled for a while, Spirit Bear let the small fire die out. He would allow the willow bark to seep until the solution cooled. It was getting close to the time when *Wawakankan* would pay his daily visit to his patient.

Almost as if they were of one mind, *Wawakankan* appeared at the entrance flap. His deep voice requested permission to enter. Spirit Bear met him at the door. Kaitlin had backed up and was shaking her head, clutching at her poncho.

Spirit Bear and *Wawakankan* walked to the sleeping furs.

"*Uwa yo, Mazaska Zi Ista,*" he commanded.

While the chief battled wills with the white slave, *Wawakankan* prepared his supplies for use. He averted his eyes as if to not witness the clashing of wills and disobedience of the young woman unfamiliar to their ways.

Kaitlin had backed far away from the two men as she could. She knew the leader of the people was telling her to come over there, but she couldn't will her feet to obey. Although the innocent white girl had to admit that their medicine was miraculous, she'd rather do without than to flaunt herself. She was modest and would rather not come!

The large commanding figure of the Indians stood and prowled closer to her. Sternly, he repeated his words. "*Mazaska Zi Ista, Uwa yo!*"

Trying to show she was healed and didn't need administered to, she moved her arm. She didn't suck in the air as she wanted to, but the grimace gave her away. The Indian approached, still closer.

The chief's strong arm snaked out and captured her. He firmly grasped the back of her neck and escorted her to the furs. The dominant male was rather gentle with her, but she was still in too much pain to notice. Spirit Bear folded his arms across his chest as she obediently sat.

He gruffly said, "*Iyunka.*" Kaitlin lay back on the bed.

"She heals quickly, my chief!" *Wawakankan* said as he removed her old poultice wraps on her head and elbow and replaced them with new. He looked at the visible bruises on her head, face, wrist, and arm. They were more green and yellow than black, blue, and green. This was a good sign.

Spirit Bear was still slightly agitated with her, but he grunted his agreement.

"Do not be too harsh on the *wayaka*. She does not know our ways."

"*Tos*, this I know, my *kola*. In the world of the white man, do the women not obey the men? This behavior is strange to me."

Wawakankan began to lift the bottom of the poncho-dress she wore. Kaitlin started to move as if to escape.

"*Hiya*!" Spirit Bear sounded fierce. His black eyes were glittering, daring her to disobey further.

She immediately ceased movement when she caught the terseness of his command. His warm fingers found the leather strips and untied them. The virile male took the bottom of her garment and lifted it up in one smooth motion, revealing her upper torso. Immediately, her womanly parts responded to the kiss of air. Spirit Bear took a knife and cut the bindings holding the wrap over her wounded ribs. Splashes of blue were painted brightly over her skin, just below her shapely breasts.

Kaitlin's ribs labored erratically with stress. Spirit Bear saw that she wept. Tears of frustration leaked from her eyes as she screwed them shut. *Wawakankan* worked quickly and quietly so he could restore the *ska winyan*'s honor as rapidly as possible. The medicine man left silently when he finished.

Spirit Bear did not think *Mazaska Zi Ista* knew the healer had gone. A beautiful woman lay on his bed, exposed, with her breasts quivering with each ragged breath as she waited for the men to stop overseeing her health needs. The chieftain wanted to teach her a lesson about obeying. Gently, with feathery caresses, he touched her as he'd desired to for some time.

Golden eyes sprung open in shock. She was suddenly aware they were alone and of what the attractive man was doing to her. She shook her head against the strange sensations he aroused in her.

"*Hiya, Woniya Mato!*" it was whispered yet insistent. "Please… stop!"

His black eyes peered into hers. Almost as if to show her who was boss, he continued his playful exploration of her chest with light, gentle touches. Kaitlin began to squirm. A small gasp escaped her lips.

Spirit Bear had wanted to alarm her, to show her he was in control. However, it was he who discovered it was his captive who held the power. The chief had to stop. Slowly, the war chief lowered her garment. The vivid bruising on her ribs still did not allow for pain-free movement. He didn't wish to harm her; his only intent was to enforce obedience.

Spirit Bear rose from the tipi. With a muttered word, he grabbed a fibrous cloth, a fresh breech cloth, and his bow and arrow pouch. When he'd left, Kaitlin sighed with relief.

She was alone with her feelings. She felt so degraded and humiliated even though she realized they only had her best interest at heart. *But why did Woniya Mato do what he did to her? Why had her body responded so intensely?*

She paced. She could not seem to calm her warring emotions. She needed to get back home. Surely her father wouldn't insist she go to Jed now, not that he'd seen the cruel side of him. Bradley would be her last resort. However, she realized with regret that no man would ever affect her like *Woniya Mato* had…

Spirit Bear went to his favorite spot to bathe. A stony crevice flanked by deep green foliage housed a small spring that spilled and tumbled brilliantly down deep steel-variegated rocks. It chatted happily on its merry way to create a blue pool of deep water before overfilling and continuing its path to flow with the mother. It was a cool, refreshing place to visit during the hot summer months…. Or when the body was hot
with needs.

The leader of the band took the soapwort root he'd gathered and pounded it against a flat rock. Leaving the fibrous pulp on the stone, he stripped and dove into the crisp, invigorating waters. Spirit Bear returned to the stone, removed the pulp, and placed it on his head. Working the root fibers into his long hair, suds formed. The foam was also used to wash his body.

The warrior rinsed his cooled frame. With a cream constructed with cedar, he massaged it into his black length. He rinsed once more and returned to the bank of the sculpted pond. The dominant figure donned his clothes.

Woniya Mato whistled for *Runs like the Wind*. He leaped on to the stallion's back while looping weapons onto his own. It was time to bring home fresh game for supper. Thankfully, his mind was more chore-oriented.

Kaitlin was still pacing when *Wawat'ecaka* came to visit. She softly called to Kaitlin. When the motherly woman came inside the tipi, she motioned to Kaitlin's bare feet. The *ska winyan* didn't understand.

Wawat'ecaka pointed to her own moccasins, and then pointed to Kaitlin's feet again. *Did Woniya Mato forget to give Golden Eyes her shoes?* She would have need of them.

The elder went to the supply stash on the side of the tipi and retrieved the pair. The chief had hidden the decorated dress from *Mazaska Zi Ista*. Perhaps he wanted to wait until a special time to give them to her as a gift.

Wawat'ecaka gave Kaitlin the shoes for daily wear and motioned for her to place them on her feet. As soon as the golden eyed girl donned them, she felt their dream-like softness. She wiggled her toes in them, pleased.

Wawat'ecaka nodded, satisfied. Wonder Worker's mother then motioned for Kaitlin to follow her. They walked slowly, this time Kaitlin walked unassisted by a person, but used a sturdy stick the older woman had secured for her.

They went to a near-by meadow to collect tubers for the upcoming meal. *Wawat'ecaka* didn't expect the girl to really help, but she wanted to take her for a walk and begin showing her where and what to look for; each day, the girl should learn something. Kaitlin carried a basket of her own.

The woman would place the freshly dug tuber in a basket and then have Kaitlin find another plant to dig. The *ska winyan* learned quickly how to differentiate the plant they were looking for from the others. The slave felt badly that she wasn't yet able to dig. When Kaitlin had tried, she felt like she pulled a muscle across her ribs anew.

A short while later, the blonde tested the rib to see if it was freshly injured; luckily, it wasn't. She resolved her body was giving her a warning not to overdo it. However, her frame did respond favorably to the moving and walking. It took some of her stiffness away.

After filling the basket, they returned to the village. The Indian mentor used a hearth in the clearing and began a fire. Feeding the flame enough wood to get it going well, the motherly woman motioned to the *wayaka* to continue feeding it. Kaitlin stood in front of the blaze and soon had it crackling hungrily.

Wawat'ecaka cleaned the tuberous roots and then let the flames die down some. In the outside edge where hot ash had accumulated, the older woman placed the roots and pushed them into the ash with a stick.

Spirit Bear had just returned. He brought three rabbits over to where the women worked. Once he'd cleaned them, he gave them to *Wawat'ecaka*. The older woman skewered them and placed them on the spits above the flame. Feeding the fire a little more wood, she left momentarily.

The shaman's mother returned from her tipi carrying herbs which she sprinkled onto the meat. Slowly, as it grilled, *Wawat'ecaka* would turn it so that it didn't burn. Along with the tubers, she'd gathered wild carrots and green onions. She cleaned theses while the other things cooked.

Kaitlin watched and learned new ways to prepare food without her cast iron skillet. She'd cooked meat over an open flame, but the tuber cooking was new. The young woman wondered what they would taste like.

As she watched *Wawat'ecaka, Woniya Mato* watched her. Kaitlin was unaware that the great chief watched her every move with his ebony eyes. It was not long before *Wawakankan* joined their company.

The men visited, laughed, and joked while the women worked. Kaitlin tried to help, but she didn't know what to do. She watched as the medicine man's mother retrieved the tubers from the fire and removed the meat from the flames. While the things cooled, *Wawat'ecaka* made *aguyapi*. The skilled woman mixed the bread dough with the drippings she'd collected from the meat and kneaded it. Afterwards, raspberries were added.

While the bread baked on the stones near the fire, Gentle Rabbit retrieved plates and cups. With a knife, she sliced meat onto the plates, placed the tubers along with onion and carrot, and flipped the bread. Then she served the men.

Wawat'ecaka poured some kind of a drink into the cups made from horns and gave it to her son and their chief. The freshly made bread, hot and steaming, was also placed on the men's bone platters.

Next, Kaitlin watched as *Wawat'ecaka* fixed their plates. She included the same items, just in smaller portions. The elder also poured the drink into more horn cups and then served Kaitlin and herself.

The men placed their empty plates near the fire ring and stretched their tight bellies. *Woniya Mato* retrieved a pipe from the tipi and lit it up. The two continued to visit while they smoked.

Kaitlin watched *Wawat'ecaka* as she prepared her tuber. She waited until the vegetable cooled. Then she slit the skin and pulled on the ends. Fluffy white insides were revealed.

Kaitlin did the same to hers. The meal was delicious. The white woman was able to eat the meat and tuber slowly, but the raw carrots still made her jaw too sore to eat. The *aguyapi* was delicious. It was moist, steamy, and sweet. The berries gave it a tang that made it more dessert than bread. The drink in the cups was sweetened with berries as well. Kaitlin savored it as long as she could.

When the meal was finished, Kaitlin followed *Wawat'ecaka* to the river to clean the items. They also took care of personal needs while away.

The white girl studied the plates as she helped clean them. They were smooth and very white. They appeared to be made from the flat plates of a large animal's hip or shoulder bones.

When *Wawat'ecaka* and Kaitlin returned to the fire, the other important men from the celebration had joined *Woniya Mato* and *Wawakankan*. They also shared the pipe and visited. All eyes turned to the women as they returned.

Kaitlin shyly looked down. *Wawat'ecaka* smiled a greeting, rolled up the rabbit fur taken from the carcasses, and then headed to her home. Kaitlin started to go in the tipi but froze when she heard *Woniya Mato*'s voice calling her name. When she looked, he said the words that mean, 'come'.

Why did he feel the need to boss her around? In white culture, they never demanded that visitors 'come'! Kaitlin supposed it was because he was a chief and the leader of many people; *Woniya Mato* was used to having others jump to his every request.

Despite her thoughts, she came before the group of men. They simply stared at her. Then one of the men got up and approached. He grasped her chin and forced her to look up.

He stared intently at her face, examining her jaw where the bruising was still evident. The intimidating man focused on her eyes. It was nerve-wracking.

The bronzed male was handsome and fit, much like all the warriors in the camp, but none compared to their chief. The important figure then released her and walked a slow circle around her, making the young white quake with nerves.

"How much do you want for the *wayaka, Woniya Mato*? I have many fine things I will offer in trade for her," *Wawakte Towanjila*'s deep voice addressed the chief.

"She is not for trade, my *kola*."

"I could use a woman in my tipi to take care of the *winyan* chores," he continued. "Name your price."

"I could not part with her," *Woniya Mato* repeated. "I, too, need a *winyan* to clean around my tipi."

The other man resumed his seat silently. Kaitlin was then allowed to return to the chieftain's home. She did so quickly although she felt eyes following her until she disappeared.

Wawakankan also would like to trade for *Mazaska Zi Ista* but knew from his earlier teasing about the *winyan* that the chief felt more towards Golden Eyes than most would for a mere slave; however, *Mazaska Zi Ista* was not just any slave. She was a fine specimen of womanhood, one that made men of any skin crave to touch her.

Wawakankan also noticed Snake Strike watching her. *Wawakankan* didn't like *Zuzecan Pazan*. He had cruel eyes and a mean personality. He treated his slave horribly. *Zuzeca Pazan* had wanted to be a warrior, but thankfully, Spirit Bear also could see the man behind the façade. Snake Strike was a hunter by default.

Turning his thoughts back to the conversation, *Wawakankan* listened as plans were made. The men began to talk and strategize. The *wasicu* enemy would have no chance for escape.

    Kaitlin was restless in the tipi. *Why did Woniya Mato call her to the group of men? Why did the powerful male hold her face and circle her?* He said a few words she was familiar with but didn't know the meaning. He'd said '*wayaka*' when he addressed the chief. The white woman knew it was made as a reference to her. *Why were the men talking about her?*

    Kaitlin decided to try to work on stretching out her side. Walking and moving as long as she didn't overdo it seemed to relieve some of the soreness. Slowly, she stretched the arm up.

    The captive was asleep by the time *Woniya Mato* retired to his dwelling. He'd been trying to keep somewhat of a distance from the *ska winyan*. He kept reliving her face when he'd caressed her body. The possessive male longed to take her as he had no other.

    He avoided her by rising early and retiring late. Soon, she'd be well enough. He'd see how well she'd recovered in a week or two. He planned to make her his before he left to hunt the *toga*.

    The next morning, the white woman arose with the light. Spirit Bear was already gone. She kind of missed his domineering presence. *Wawat'ecaka* entered and was surprised to see Kaitlin had already risen.

'This is good', the old woman thought. *'She heals quickly. Already her body is recovering faster. I will teach her how to make her own morning tea. I will include herbs to continue promoting her recovery. Then she can help me make breakfast.'*

Wawat'ecaka lived alone. Her husband had been killed on a war raid five years back. She kept up her own tipi, her son's, and that of the chief's. Soon, though, it would just be her own and her son's. *Mazaska Zi Ista* would soon take over the care of the *Woniya Mato*'s lodge.

The war chief supplied meat to her and her son when Wonder Worker was immersed with work for the tribe. The three leaders of the council saw to it that the women who didn't have men to hunt for them were cared for. *Wawat'ecaka* loved the young leaders for their great hearts and kind spirits. She believed they were the best tribal council this branch of the Oglala had ever seen.

Wawat'ecaka began by boiling water. She wanted to show Kaitlin two of her favorite teas. One was sassafras, the other, mint. This morning, she'd begin with mint. After the water boiled, Gentle Rabbit added mint leaves. Then, for medicinal properties to help strengthen Kaitlin's immune system, she added purple coneflower blossoms. She didn't want Golden Eyes to use them every day, but for the next several days, it would benefit her.

When the tea was finished, she scooped out the herbs and then added a few drops of honey to sweeten it. After the combination cooled, she poured the brew into a horn cup for Kaitlin to consume.

Next, *Wawat'ecaka* placed goose eggs, wild mushrooms, and onions next to the still-going fire. Kaitlin motioned to her pan. Eggs were perfect for the pan!

Kaitlin motioned *Wawat'ecaka* aside. She'd make the breakfast for the kindly woman! The chief's captive wished to show appreciation for her new footwear. Wiggling her toes in her new, soft shoes, the blonde beamed. They were, by far, the best and most comfortable pair she'd ever owned!

With a flint knife, the white woman thinly sliced mushrooms and onions. She suspended the skillet the correct amount above the flame. Then combining her ingredients, she scrambled the mixture.

On two of the plates, Kaitlin divided the aromatic breakfast. *Wawat'ecaka* had never seen food cooked in a black pan before. She enjoyed the change. The elder woman even enjoyed being served by the *wayaka*. Her first impression of the girl was accurate. She was good, kind, and intelligent. She was a worthy slave for the great Spirit Bear!

After the breakfast was consumed and the mess cleaned up, *Wawat'ecaka* guided Kaitlin back to work with *Unjinjintka Can Koica*. Desert Rose was the skilled basket weaver of the community. Many baskets of all kinds and shapes were available. Colors and patterns varied on nearly every one. It was an honor to learn under one so accomplished.

Desert Rose gave Kaitlin's supplies back to her that she'd started the day before. She had a good foundation. Desert Rose could not find fault with it. With time, Golden Eyes could become as adept as herself if she chose.

When they sat and worked side by side, Desert Rose began to teach words to Kaitlin. Kaitlin learned words for fire, wood, cook, basket, grass, weave, patterns, and more. It wasn't long before they could hold a very simple conversation about basket weaving. Before noon rest time, Kaitlin repeated her new words back to *Unjinjintka Can Koica* to make sure she knew them correctly.

"Good," Desert Rose told her. She was proud of the new *winyan*. The girl had already warmed a place in her heart. With her intelligence and skill, she'd do well!

When Desert Rose began collecting things to put up, one of the men from the evening before approached the yard. He held cured furs in his hand: two nice rabbit and one of a red fox. He didn't look at Kaitlin; his eyes were only for *Unjinjintka Can Koica*. The soundless man stood, waiting for her to acknowledge him.

Desert Rose flushed when she saw she had a visitor. Men who hunted or fought to protect had very silent feet! She stood gracefully.

Lone Wolf said, "I would like a basket. I have these skins to trade." He seemed nervous. Kaitlin was not used to seeing a handsome brave, fit to perfection, act nervous around a mere woman!

Unjinjintka Can Koica took him to her supplies. She had many baskets arranged by use.

There were water proof ones, ones tightly woven for grain collection, and some loosely woven for whatever use. There were baskets for straining vegetables or teas and baskets for holding bathing items.

Kaitlin saw that Lone Wolf didn't know what kind of a basket he was shopping for. Desert Rose lent him a helping hand. Finally, a deal was struck. Desert Rose tried to tell Lone Wolf that three fine pelts for a basket were too much, but he insisted she take them.

Afterwards, Desert Rose had a dreamy smile on her face. Kaitlin smiled, too, for it was obvious her new friend was smitten. The white girl got to her feet and left her friend with a grin.

At the tipi, Kaitlin ate the food *Wawat'ecaka* left for her and lay down. Her morning had not been particularly strenuous, but she was still sleepy. Her lids drooped, and she fell immediately asleep.

Spirit Bear returned to the tipi and Kaitlin's sleeping form. She looked like an innocent angel sent from the sun, *wi*, and *Wakantanka*. He considered her a gift. As he had many times before, he offered a chant to the Great Spirit in thanks.

Dressed only in his breechcloth, he stretched beside her on the sleeping furs. He placed a possessive hand on her flat stomach. After she awoke and took care of her personal needs, it would be time for her treatment. He relished the thought of her rebellion.

Woniya Mato was already up when Kaitlin opened her eyes. She was pleasantly surprised to see her handsome warrior. She tentatively asked the simple phrase in Lakota, "Did you have lunch?"

Surprise lifted his brows. The chief nodded an affirmation. Then he motioned to ask how she'd learned to speak Lakota. Hoping she'd not get her friend into trouble, she shyly said, "*Unjinjintka Can Koica.*" She breathed a sigh of relief at his approving smile.

"*He's so handsome,*" Kaitlin caught herself thinking. "*His smile makes him even more striking. I shall miss him when he takes me back home.*"

CHAPTER SIX

Wayaka

Kaitlin drank from the *mniapahta* then tested the new language again. She told Spirit Bear she needed to use the Area of Privacy. The chief indicated that she could go on her own this time as long as she took the walking stick with her.

The white women showed her thanks with a smile and a slight nod. She left the tipi and headed toward the trail. When she began the path back, Kaitlin noticed a couple approaching. Nervously, Kaitlin watched.

The couple didn't appear to be getting along very well. The man was pulling the woman's hair until she arched her neck. He forced her to look up. Then he smacked her, knocking her down. Then the male would grab her hair again and haul her to her feet. The woman did not plead; she only glared with eyes full of hate.

Kaitlin couldn't help but to stare as the man dragged her closer. Suddenly, the Indian looked up and caught the blonde watching his every move. His eyes narrowed dangerously.

The white woman did her best to hurry and walk away, but the man was taking long strides toward her. His fists were clenched at his sides as the native stopped before her. His breath was ragged with adrenaline. The other woman sat where he'd left her.

Kaitlin didn't know what to do. She knew she'd offended the man by staring but was unable to stop. During her short stay in the village, the young white had never seen an Indian mistreat another. It'd shocked her. Surprise had covered the reasoning function of her brain… momentarily.

Now what? The trembling girl didn't know whether to step around this man and continue the path back to the village or stand her ground. The young woman knew meeting his eyes made him angrier, so she tried not to make eye contact. Kaitlin trembled when she saw the hate evidenced in his face and tight body. If the white woman knew the word for 'sorry', she'd have apologized. Instead the chief's slave merely stood there.

The man began streaming words in Lakota at her, but since they didn't deal with basket weaving, woman chores, or weapons, she didn't understand. Kaitlin just stood and listened to his incomprehensible rant.

The insolent little woman was too good to look at him when he talked to her? This lowly slave had been staring rudely at him moments before!? He didn't care who she belonged to, a slave would not disrespect a member of the tribe in this manner!

He longed to teach her in a way that would leave no doubt that he, a man, was in charge. He used that method often on his personal slave. It worked on her... for a while, anyway. Then she'd need to be taught another lesson about disobedience.

However, this slave didn't belong to him. Just how far he could push this possession of the chief's, Snake Strike didn't know, but he was willing to find out.

Suddenly, Kaitlin found her hair in the tight grasp of the man full of hate. He forced her to look into his face as he had the other woman. Kaitlin gritted her teeth in anticipation of the slap she thought was sure to come. He spoke a stream of rapid Lakota through jaws muscled shut. The blonde struggled to remain impassive. He shook her head and spoke in a more menacing manner.

Finally, the man jerked her head and pushed her down. Hard. Kaitlin fell back on her injured side. She felt the muscle cry out in protest, not knowing she did as well.

Instantly, it seemed, Spirit Bear was there. He whirled the man around to face him. Being a great warrior and chieftain, he didn't realize that he'd withdrawn his knife and held it ready in hand.

"You are always ready to strike a woman. Are you not man enough to face a warrior? I grow tired of watching you punish your slave like a dog!" Spirit Bear spat angrily.

Snake Strike's eyes grew large with shock in his thin face. He muttered something about Kaitlin staring at him while he reprimanded his slave. He appeared to be doing more stammering than defending himself in the face of the angry chief.

"Do not let me see you touch my property again!" Spirit Bear growled savagely. "As for your slave, I feel sorry for her. You need to reach in and find a heart, if indeed you possess one, and hope the tribal council does not grow as weary of this treatment as I. Now go before I really lose my cool!"

The man scurried like a mouse, snaking his hand out to grab his property on his way to cover. Spirit Bear was at Kaitlin's side in an instant. His warm tenor voice was heaven. She didn't know what he said, but he murmured to her in a soothing tone. He scooped her up as if she weighed nothing. Instead of walking to the village, he continued walking on the path that led up.

To her amazement, he led her to a crystal-clear pond with waters as blue as the sky. A willow tree along with other trees shaded most of the cool waters from the reflection of the sun. Spirit Bear sat her gently down and untied her leather cord to her dress. Before she could shake her head in denial, *Woniya Mato* said softly, *"Hiya, Mazaska Zi Ista."*

Kaitlin had been longing for a bath, but she couldn't raise her arms up to scrub her hair. After Spirit Bear removed her clothing and bandages, she moved quickly into the water to avoid his probing eyes. He stripped and followed her.

Kaitlin was mortified! *What if someone saw? What if she saw more than she intended?* She averted her eyes and missed his roguish grin. Mischievously, he approached her with soapwort root pulp.

The cool waters numbed the pounding in her side from where the horrible man had shoved her down. *Was that why Woniya Mato brought her here?*

Or was her stench too much to bear? She had to admit, she hadn't bathed in quite some time… since she was back at the cabin; she'd been too sick.

Oh, the water felt so invigorating! Kaitlin wanted to dive and play, but her body wouldn't cooperate! Suddenly, a shadow loomed beside her. The white girl covered her exposed chest as best as she could and looked up into the grinning face of the chief.

Spirit Bear placed something from his hands into her hair. Then, he worked it into lather. The chief couldn't wipe the smile from his face. Her feeble attempts to shield herself from his eyes amused him.

Once done with her hair, the war leader began on her body. Kaitlin shook her head with wide eyes, but the chief ignored her. He massaged the lather into her skin. He gingerly cleaned bruised areas and scrubbed healthy skin until it was pink. Although she tried to protest, he took extra time to make sure her chest was washed well.

Kaitlin felt like a little girl… yet little girls couldn't comprehend how he was making her feel. Just the intense way the handsome chief looked at her had her weak in the knees. His touch made her shiver with need. Standing in front of this god-like man, the woman in her was drawn to the raw magnetism emanating from him.

When finished scrubbing her body, the bronzed male gently indicated for her to dunk her head back. Still covering herself the best she could, his captive dipped backwards. Spirit Bear rinsed her hair. Then he took a pleasant strawberry-smelling cream and worked into her honeyed tresses.

Five minutes later, he rinsed her hair again. Cold, but refreshed and clean, Kaitlin wondered about leaving the pool. All she had to wear was her dirty garment. She couldn't go back into the village naked! She'd just wither up and die! It was humiliating enough the way it was, facing the man of her dreams in this fashion! Her teeth chattered as she soaked in the pool.

Her side was aching less than it ever had. The blonde assumed the cool waters worked their magic on the swelling and bruising. Spirit Bear donned his clothes and held up a finger to Kaitlin, indicating he would return shortly.

When the chief came back, he had a woven cover with an intricate pattern plaited into the material. He motioned for her to come forward. Blushing furiously, she stepped from the waters. She couldn't look at his powerful gaze. If the young woman had, she'd have seen raw hunger.

Spirit Bear wrapped his *wayaka* in the plaited blanket and scooped her up into his arms. He'd come back for her things later. Kaitlin was embarrassed! What would everyone think if they saw their chief carrying a naked white woman into his tipi? At least no one from the settlement would know about this! Her reputation would be ruined!

Snuggling into his arms more to avoid meeting Indian stares, she laid her cool cheek against his warm muscled chest. She could hear his heart beating. The young woman felt warmth for him rising in her. He was so kind! Who'd ever have believed that a chief could be so caring for someone who wasn't a member of his village?

Snake Strike watched the return of the chief and
the slave from the shade of his small tipi. Black anger
that always smoldered in his heart boiled fast and furious
on this day. The chief had humiliated him one too many
times. The first seed of resentment began when he wasn't
allowed to become a warrior as he'd always dreamed
because of Spirit Bear's power of persuasion.

Zuzecan Pazan also saw the way the chief looked
at him with disapproval reflected in his eyes. The leader
would realize what it was like to have a slave who didn't
want to mind! The insolent attitude of the *ska winyan*
was worse than that of his Pawnee's! When the white
whore healed and had real work to do, the true testing
would begin. The warrior would see! A firm hand was
the only way to deal with haughty women!

If Snake Strike caught the white woman alone
again, especially if she was away from publicly used paths,
he'd teach her a lesson about submitting to a man. She
was beautiful, and he longed to make her cower. He'd
wipe that smug stare right off her face! A cruel smile
twitched on his lips.

After depositing *Mazaska Zi Ista* on the sleeping
mat clutching her towel, Spirit Bear went to the hut of
Wawat'ecaka. Softly, he called her name.

"Yes, my chief?" she answered, coming to her door.

"I wanted to see if you had a dress made for Golden eyes. Her tipi-garment is so dirty. She just bathed, and I did not want to put it back on her until it has been cleaned," he answered. "I know she has the exquisite dress, but that is too fancy to ruin with daily use," he added.

The grandmotherly figure disappeared back inside her tipi and retrieved two soft garments. She gave them to Spirit Bear. He didn't take the proffered clothing.

"Give me ten minutes to treat her, and you bring them to my tipi. I want her to know who made these wonderful gifts."

Wawat'ecaka smiled and nodded. She loved the chief. He wanted her to have recognition for her skill. Not many would have been so thoughtful!

When Spirit Bear returned, he had the shaman with him. Kaitlin must have guesses what was in store, for she had put on her undergarment. She'd arranged the towel where it covered her modesty but would allow them to work on her ribs.

Spirit Bear could not suppress his humor. He laughed aloud.

Wonder Worker also smiled, "she has outsmarted you, my *kola*,"

"*Tos*, I will allow her this small victory. She has already had to submit to my bathing of her."

Wawakankan could not mask his surprise. "Don't get any ideas. I still plan on giving her five or so more travels of *wi* before I collect my debt." He patted *Wawakankan* on the back in good nature.

"You will still need to be gentle. These injuries can take two cycles of the moon or more to completely heal," the shaman advised.

"Give me credit, my friend. I know how to get what I want. She will enjoy it and give to me willingly."

Wonder Worker was not so sure. After the treatment of her injuries was complete, Gentle Rabbit brought forth the dresses. Kaitlin's eyes grew large in her wonder. Surely, the kind woman wasn't giving them to her! However, the blonde could see that she was! *Wawat'ecaka* shooed the men out of the tipi.

The older woman helped Kaitlin don the supple fabric. It was not easy as she still couldn't easily lift her arm much, but working together, they dressed that arm first, then the rest of her. Kaitlin stood and looked down at herself.

The dress was simply made. It was roomy, but clung to her lush curves in advertisement of her gender. The light brown material was so pliable; it almost felt as if she wore nothing at all! Kaitlin delicately threw her arms around *Wawat'ecaka*. She truly wished to thank her.

Wawat'ecaka looked down, touched by the girl's heart-warmed thanks. Then she motioned to Kaitlin to follow her out of the tipi. She wanted to show the men her creation on the model she'd made it for.

Both men stared. Kaitlin was embarrassed, but she did a shy twirl for them at *Wawat'ecaka*'s prompting.

"You have found a rare treasure, *Woniya Mato,*" Wonder Worker admired. He jested with his friend. "You must give me first choice if you ever decide to trade her off!"

Spirit Bear laughed with humor. His generosity was evident in his infectious laughter. "That will not happen, my *kola,* but if I ever decide to give her to another, it will be you."

The next three days were typically the same for Kaitlin. She learned the art of basket weaving each morning with Desert Rose. Her new friend would also review the Lakota language and teach her new vocabulary each day. It was a long, slow process acquiring a new and difficult language, but Kaitlin didn't give up.

The basket weaving, however, came naturally to Kaitlin. She'd already finished three. The first two baskets contained learning mistakes, but her third basket was perfect for holding grains. Now the white girl was ready to learn to weave waterproof baskets; they were the most difficult of the weaves. Lastly, Kaitlin would discover pattern-weaving. Patterns could make the most proficient weaver frustrated!

Before and after the visits at the family tipi of *Unjinjintka Can Koica, Wawat'ecaka* would teach Kaitlin the chores that belonged to the woman. She helped gather wood, cook food, clean the dishes, wash clothes, fill and return water skins, and straighten the tipi.

After rest time in the afternoon, Kaitlin helped *Wawat'ecaka* with her chores. It was a time of shared companionship. *Wawat'ecaka* was not of the same generation but was of a similar heart. The two women got along well and enjoyed helping the other with the chores.

At the end of the greatest heat each day, Spirit Bear would escort Kaitlin to the pool of blue water to soak her sore ribs. It was miraculous. The cold water removed the swelling, stiffness, and soreness, and the poultices helped to keep the pain away. Willow bark tea, as she discovered was made from the cooked sticks, helped, too. She was able to do more each day. Still, she tired more easily than she had before the experience with Jed.

Wawat'ecaka decided that Kaitlin was gaining strength. In several days, she'd begin to teach her the art of leather working. She asked *Woniya Mato* to kill a pronghorn. They were small but were ideal for beginning to learn the time-consuming art of making supple leather.

The curing of leather would keep *Mazaska Zi Ista* busy while their leader was away with the war party to hunt the white dog. Golden Eyes would, more than likely, miss Spirit Bear's presence. Gentle Rabbit noticed how the girl looked for him and followed him with her eyes when they were together. Being busy kept worry away. *If she realizes the danger of what the chief had planned to do... with a mere ten warriors...*

Woniya Mato lay down with Kaitlin during the hottest part of the day. Upon rising, he would take *Runs with the Wind* and hunt antelope. He wanted to obtain several carcasses because he would be leaving several days forth. He wanted to ensure that Kaitlin and Gentle Rabbit had plenty of meat while he was gone. Of course, Wonder Worker, Lone Wolf, and Sky Warrior would remain behind to keep an eye on his slave and to make sure they had plenty to eat, but it was still his ultimate responsibility.

About an hour and a half later, the wind whistled through Spirit Bear's hair. He rode his stallion down into the valley so that he could begin stalking the pronghorn. They were wonderful little animals for the Oglala. Their horns made excellent utensils, and their meat was heavenly. Obviously, *Wawat'ecaka* believed their skin made choice leather as well.

When Kaitlin rose, she went to *Wawat'ecaka* to learn about curing hides. She hoped to learn how to make the pliable leather that none other could compare to. If she could get the process down, she could maybe secure an income for herself and her family. She'd have to hide their income because otherwise, her father and brother would gamble and drink it all away.

If she could learn this process, she would be at the mercy of no man!

Jutting her jaw in determination, she arrived at Gentle Rabbit's dwelling.

"*Hau?*" she called, greeting the patient woman in her tongue.

Wawat'ecaka greeted her back. She guided Kaitlin out of the village to where the hides of three rabbits had been soaking in water in a place close to the river. Gentle Rabbit pulled one from the soaking spot. It dripped everywhere.

Kaitlin wanted to hold her nose. The smell of the hide and the water it had been submerged in was powerful. She watched as *Wawat'ecaka* took the hide to a wooden rack and spread it out. She tacked it down with small wooden pegs, stretching the skin as tightly as she could.

Kaitlin stood back and watched. She didn't know what to do, but she figured that was why Gentle Rabbit had her watch with the first skin. There were two more wooden racks waiting to secure a hide of its own.

After stretching the fur as tightly as possible, *Wawat'ecaka* retrieved a stone knife. The knife was not a meat-cutting knife. It was thick and rounded on the side from which it was held but narrowed down to a working blade of a thin, flat edge.

With this stone tool, *Wawat'ecaka* began scraping the underside of the pelt that she'd placed upwards on the wooden rack. She removed remaining meat, fat, and membrane with the procedure. Excess water was squeezed off the side with the junk she removed. In Kaitlin's opinion, the process was not a pleasant one.

When she'd finished with the one, *Wawat'ecaka* took the two remaining pelts from the soaking place. She stretched first one, then the other one on the second rack.

Kaitlin tried to remove the waste material as Gentle Rabbit had done. She still was not able to use her arm like normal, but she did the best she could. *Wawat'ecaka* had finished her second skin before Kaitlin was half-way done.

Gentle Rabbit usurped the third pelt from the *ska winyan. Wawat'ecaka* knew the girls' side still pained her, yet she had still made great effort to help. The respect Gentle Rabbit held for Golden Eyes only grew.

The girl's arm improved daily. Her ribs were allowing her a greater freedom of range, and the upper arm bruising had faded to mostly yellow. Her facial bruising, likewise, had mostly disappeared. Kaitlin was able to chew food normally at last!

Turning back to the chore at hand, Kaitlin was ready to see the next step. From a deep wooden bowl hardened by fire, *Wawat'ecaka* retrieved a brain of one of the rabbits. It was a ghoulish gray jelly-like substance. Gentle Rabbit sliced it with the stone tool and sliced it yet again. She took the smallest brain sections and began rubbing it into the matter-free side of the pelt.

Kaitlin wanted to retch when she observed this tactic. If this is what it took to secure hides worthy of a king, she would overcome her squeamishness. She'd also learn to deal with the smell.

She'd witnessed much worse things than brains smeared on a detached skin… *hadn't she?* Certainly, she'd witnessed more traumatic things, but none quite as appalling. Still, she forced herself to grab a section of brain and begin the same procedure on the skin she'd worked with.

When they'd finished the process with all three hides, Kaitlin felt sweaty, slimy, and smelly. She longed for a bath. *Wawat'ecaka* must have felt the same way, for she stood and led the way back to the village.

She motioned for Kaitlin to get a change of clothes, a rag, and a towel. This she did quickly. Then she followed *Wawat'ecaka* to the communal bathing place up the river from the Place of Privacy.

Kaitlin much preferred the privacy of the blue pool, but it was a special place to her. It was reserved for the chief and her. At least the communal place was gender-specific! The men bathed in a different location down the river from the Place of Privacy.

Kaitlin stripped and quickly entered the water. The white woman was not comfortable with nudity as her culture thrived on privacy. The blonde was not raised as the Indian. It was they who were comfortable with nudity.

Wawat'ecaka helped Kaitlin wash and condition her hair. She still could not raise her arms shoulder level without pain. The older woman had no qualms about playing mother; she rather enjoyed it. Gentle Rabbit couldn't wait until the day she became a grandmother. If only her son would take a mate!

After dressing in clean clothes, the women washed their smelly garments. Kaitlin had elected to wear the poncho garment. It was so easy to get on. She loved the dresses more, but until her arm healed, it was her clothing of choice.

Kaitlin was exhausted. Midday nap time was past, and they still needed to do the evening chores. Thankfully, most of the other chores had already been taken care of. She suspected *Wawat'ecaka* knew how taxing the tanning would be for her.

When they returned, Sprit Bear was also present. He had a female pronghorn and her baby skinned and waiting for them. The skins were rolled for easier carrying.

The shaman's mother instructed Kaitlin to begin a fire. While the white girl did her bidding, she took the hides to the soaking place. When Gentle Rabbit returned, she also had some water cress and poke leaves to complement their meal.

Wawat'ecaka began another fire. She suspended the larger carcass higher over the flame that did not blaze as hotly and began boiling water over the second fire. Kaitlin was surprised when the mother of *Wawakankan* wrapped the fawn in sage and poke leaves and nestled it into the ashes of a fire that had mostly died out.

The remaining poke was boiled in water. Next, *Wawat'ecaka* retrieved a bowl of crushed grains. She mixed pulverized acorns with grain powder. When the meal was close to being finished, she added water to the mixture. The gruel-like substance she then cooked on the flat rocks heated by the fire. When the *aguyapi* was finished, the Indian mentor drizzled honey over the top.

Kaitlin was starving and drained. She almost could not tolerate the Indian tradition of the men eating first. It seemed like forever before the men had finished their meal so they could consume theirs.

The meat fell off the bones in a steamy invitation. Kaitlin sighed in pleasure when the smoky flavor filled her mouth. It was so tender that one barely needed to chew.

The cooked poke reminded her quite a bit of spinach; she could tolerate it. The water cress, however, was very good. *Wawat'ecaka* had taken the drippings from the pronghorn and a solution made with salt brush and sprinkled it over the top of the cress. The result was a smoky meat dressing that hinted with the seasoning of salt. The water cress salad was nearly as delicious as the smoked antelope.

Nothing could compare to the Indian bread, however. The slightly nutty taste from the acorns along with the drizzled honey was better than the baked cakes one could buy in a store! Kaitlin savored every bite.

Wawat'ecaka shooed Kaitlin to her tipi when she saw the level of the girl's exhaustion. Gentle Rabbit would clean up and continue to watch the larger antelope cook. She appreciated how the girl was making her work load lighter and the day pass quicker. Besides, sleep facilitated healing.

Spirit Bear watched the swish of *Mazaska Zi Ista*'s dress until she disappeared from sight. He continued to visit while fashioning still more arrows. He'd just designed a new bow. He'd been testing it out and found with the slightly new technique used during its construction, he'd added about fifteen feet or more to his shot.

He told *Wawat'ecaka* to expect more meat in the morning. He wanted to kill at least two more pronghorn or one adult deer before his war party departed. She nodded in agreement. The meat would be welcomed.

Wawat'ecaka prepared the fire under the carcass. She wanted to continue to slow roast the meat. She stoked the fire so that it would smolder all night and continue to cure the adult antelope.

When she finally retired to her tipi for the night, the men also turned in. Spirit Bear stripped and lay down next to Kaitlin's sleeping form. She'd done well this day. She had dark shadows under her eyes, but a good night's rest would cure that.

The next morning, Spirit Bear awoke before Kaitlin as was his habit. She still didn't rise before *wi* began to lighten the sky. *Woniya Mato* began a fire to ward off the chill of the early morning. He also wanted to see his *winyan* in the golden light created by the flame. On this day, he'd make the girl his in every way.

Unhurriedly, he freed the leather cord that secured the garment to Kaitlin's body. Slowly, as not to awaken her, he lifted the fabric up. The beauty of her body, even with the maiming of the now-faint bruises, took his breath away.

His fingers began to explore. Slowly, he cupped a breast and ran a thumb over the peak. He smiled as her body responded to him even while it slept. The area around the hardened nub tightened under his touch. His administrations became more intense as he lowered his head to her skin.

What kind of a dream was this? Kaitlin felt a need roar to life that the woman didn't know she possessed. Her body cried out to *Woniya Mato* to be touched and explored.

Her dream warrior meshed his lips with hers in a hungry kiss full of promises. His lips and mouth worked wonders on hers until a mounting desire surged throughout her whole body.

She arched wildly under his roaming hands. In her dream, she could act as wonton as she desired! Her hands tentatively touched his muscled chest in awe. The warrior's taunt biceps bulged, and the captive couldn't help but to admire them.

She'd never had such a wonderful dream before! Never before had Kaitlin imagined such delightful sensations. No man had ever moved her in the way *Woniya Mato* did!

The innocent woman found pleasure in his administrations like she'd never known. She cried out with joy. The young beauty smiled with desire as her dream lover loomed over her. His ebony eyes looked intently into hers. Then the dream became a reality.

Once their bodies united as one, Kaitlin felt a stab of pain. However, he managed to mount her desires once again with his body, and she submitted to love.

When the warrior's caresses ceased, he propped up on his elbow and looked at her tenderly.

He smoothed golden tresses back from her exquisite face and whispered good morning to her. He smiled gently and spoke in a soothing tone. The handsome man revealed his sorrow that the first time was often painful, but that he never experienced a more meaningful coupling in his entire life.

Of course, Kaitlin didn't know his words, but she understood that he was treating her with reverence after they had… had… *after he had made love to her?* She watched as he got up and dressed. The warrior went to the river to bathe. Upon his return, he left to hunt and make final preparations before his leave in one *wi*.

Kaitlin was left to wonder about what'd just happened. *Was it really making love as her mind professed?* As she processed the events, she realized that she didn't know if he'd ever said that he loved her.

Did she love him? The blonde's heart beat faster when he was around, and her breath caught in her throat when golden eyes lit upon his bronze frame. There was a definite attraction, but *was that love?* They weren't even married! *Would he even marry her?* If not… *did that make her his… whore?* Kaitlin was suddenly appalled. He'd turned her body into a passionate weapon against her ability to reason.

Men! Jed professed to want to marry her, and yet he tried to take her against her will. *Woniya Mato* didn't take her against her will, but he'd turned her body into an unthinking machine. She really didn't have a choice after he had inflamed her so. She felt that he fully intended to heat her body with passion until it would not deny him, *but did he love her?*

These questions left Kaitlin in a saddened state. Her face flamed with embarrassed shame when she thought of her actions when she believed her passion to be a dream. *What must he think of her?* The young woman wondered how she'd face the day… or him.

Her mind wondered what man would want a tainted harlot for a wife. The blonde was sure the Indian chief would not marry a white woman. It would be similar to a white man marrying a squaw. There was no respect in the relationship. She'd never want that… yet it was too late now that she was no longer pure.

When *Wawat'ecaka* finally came to fetch Kaitlin, she saw the girl still was lying in her bed. Worried, Gentle Rabbit came to her side. Although the *ska winyan* was mentally distracted, the girl appeared well. The mentor wondered why she had this sudden behavior change.

Finally frustrated with Kaitlin's apathy, *Wawat'ecaka* shook her gently and motioned for her to follow. The blonde managed to raise herself up. The captive would rather not have to face Spirit Bear upon his return, so she followed Gentle Rabbit from the tipi.

Kaitlin was beginning to weave the waterproof baskets with Desert Rose. Her friend noticed a change in her normal cheery attitude. She tried to engage Kaitlin in the word game they played daily.

Kaitlin had been thinking about the terms used in reference to her in Lakota. She faced *Unjinjintka*

Can Koica and asked her in broken Lakota, "What mean woman?" and she gestured to each female present.

Desert Rose answered with a smile, "*Winyan.*"

Then Kaitlin asked, "What mean *'wayaka'*?"

Kaitlin watched the young woman's eyes widen in surprise. *How could she be the one to tell the ska winyan that she was a slave if she didn't already know?* Desert Rose decided to act as if she didn't understand Kaitlin's question. She would tell *Wawat'ecaka* about Golden Eye's strange behavior and question.

The morning went slowly for Kaitlin. She worked in a depressed, lethargic manner. She just didn't contain the unbridled enthusiasm as usual. The attractive white didn't ask unending questions about this method or that color or which grass. In fact, she didn't initiate further conversation past the slave question.

Kaitlin knew the word '*wayaka*' must mean something bad. She thought of possible meanings. *Did it mean whore? Conquest? Enemy?* It was evident that her young friend didn't want to reveal the meaning to her. It depressed Kaitlin further. Suddenly, she was homesick.

Finally, *Wawat'ecaka* came for Kaitlin. Desert Rose watched her friend go with concern in her features. She hoped her sadness would be worked out soon.

Kaitlin and *Wawat'ecaka* prepared a quick snack of smoked antelope for a light meal before the heat of the day. They'd already gathered wood, but the *mniapahta* still needed to be filled. Both women walked to where the spring spilled into the river. It was the best place to retrieve drinking water and fresh water cress.

Kaitlin looked up to see *Woniya Mato* guide his stallion toward the village from a distance. He had a large young buck lying across the horse's withers. Kaitlin drew in a quick breath and blushed furiously.

Wawat'ecaka was not so old and foolish that she didn't notice the breath and the blush from the *ska winyan*. She suspected what might be wrong with the young woman. The motherly figure wished to help Golden Eyes understand her position in Indian society, but she dared not interfere. She would, however, speak to *Woniya Mato* about the change in Kaitlin's demeanor. Maybe he could fix the problem…

Spirit Bear was waiting for *Wawat'ecaka* to return so that he could deliver the young buck. He was in high spirits, for finally he'd fulfilled what he'd longed to do since he first saw the *ska winyan*. She would never know how difficult it'd been for him to restrain. Next time, he promised himself, she would know more pleasure.

He saw *Wawat'ecaka* return and a listless Kaitlin trailing behind. Concern was etched in his eyes before he masked his emotions. It would not do well for any to see the tribe's chief concerned over a *wayaka.* He acted as though he hadn't noticed the women's approach.

Mazaska Zi Ista took the *mniapahta* into the tipi. Spirit Bear was reminded of a whipped dog with its tail between its legs. *Wawat'ecaka* came straight for Spirit Bear.

"My chief," she began.

"Yes, Gentle Rabbit? What ails Golden Eyes?"

Wawat'ecaka began, "I see you have provided us with more game. Maybe you should be hunting chief?" she jested.

"You are good for a man's ego," Spirit Bear responded with a twinkle in his eye. "But I think Lone Wolf would not give up his spot easily."

"You are right, Spirit Bear," she paused. Then she added, "The *winyan* has asked what '*wayaka*' means." She cast her eyes down.

"And what did you tell her, dear one?" he responded.

"We did not answer her question. She has come to her own conclusion. I fear it may be an unfavorable term."

"I will take care of the matter during rest time," he promised her.

"Yes, my chief. I thank you. I will begin to work on the new meat."

"It will save until after rest time if you wish," he replied. He'd already skinned the animal and rolled up the future leather for her transport.

"I believe I will work just a little before the heat hits fully," she responded. "Then I will rest."

"Yes, *Wawat'ecaka*," the mighty chief said as if he were addressing his mother. Practically, she was his mother. He'd been raised by the sweet lady since age nine.

His own parents had disappeared long ago. They'd been walking on a lover's stroll. When they didn't return, a search party had gone out looking for them. Many small parties found evidence of enemy horses, but no confirmation was found of what everyone suspected to be true.

Nearby enemy camps were raided and searched, scouts were sent to spy on enemy villages, but no trace of where they'd gone or what had happened to them was ever discovered. Spirit Bear had mourned for them for a long time, but eventually, all but his strongest memories had faded.

He walked toward his tipi and the woman trembling within. He'd try to break the language barrier and let her know that it was not just meaningless sex to him. He thought his actions immediately after their consummation would've made that evident to her, but women were fickle creatures.

If Golden Eyes could only realize how well she was treated. It was much better than her treatment by the wasicu! However, he knew that she'd have to come to that realization on her own.

The ultimate warrior sighed as he entered his domain. Kaitlin was lying on the furs with her back to him. He went to her and lay down facing her back. Spirit Bear saw her stiffen.

"*Mazaska Zi Ista,*" he gently called her name.

Just the way the chief said her name broke down her defenses. She began to cry quietly. She felt something for this man, and he'd made her body a traitor. She was crushed to realize that he would not marry her. Ever.

Kaitlin felt his arm gently under her and then he rolled her over. The blonde woman found herself cushioned up against his chest. He simply held her there and stroked her hair. The red man held the white female thus for a long time. He let her cry out her tears. Finally, she slept.

Upon waking, she was slightly more receptive. Although still sullen, she accepted the *mniapahta* he brought her. Kaitlin drank slightly with a shaking hand.

Spirit Bear got up and retrieved more meat. He also brought back an apple. He offered them to Kaitlin. He insisted, for he knew that her hands shook not only from nerves but also from not enough food.

The leader insisted she take a bite. Then he consumed a bite after her. Kaitlin's eyes widened. Men never ate with women in the Indian village! The chief, of all people, was eating at the same time as she, even sharing his food! *Mazaska Zi Ista* couldn't be more surprised.

Finally, Kaitlin muttered what she almost dreaded to ask. She asked *Woniya Mato*, "What mean '*wayaka*'?" She held her breath in fear that it meant 'whore' or something equally as vile.

Spirit Bear was silent for a moment. He'd known she'd ask. He tried to put it as gently as he could. He tried to point to Kaitlin and to himself. He voiced the words that mean they were together.

Was he trying to tell Kaitlin they were married?  No, she shook her head. That couldn't be true. After witnessing the big ceremony several weeks ago, Kaitlin knew that Indians would hold a ceremony to marry a couple… especially their chief! *So what could he mean? She was his whore?* 'Winyan' meant woman. So *wayaka* couldn't mean woman. *How could they be tied together otherwise?*

Spirit Bear knew he couldn't keep secrets or be deceptive in any way from Kaitlin, so he revealed what he knew would free the truth for her. He mentioned Snake Strike and Sore Ear. As he suspected, she didn't act favorably.

Kaitlin felt as if he had just slapped her. She drew in a ragged, sharp breath. "No! It cannot be true!! A slave? A slave? That is what I am to you?" Her breathing rate increased. She was nearing hysterics. "I'm your slave? You can do whatever you wish to me, and I have no rights? Damn you, *Woniya Mato*! Damn you!" she screamed.

She rapidly approached him and demanded, "Take me home!" and she pounded on his chest. "Take me home to where at least I have some dignity!"

Fire shot from the gold almond-shaped eyes. She glared, cried, and continued to pummel him. Spirit

Bear let her vent. She'd have to accept her place with him for he could never let her go.

"Why, *Woniya Mato*? Why?" she cried, spent. "I can't live life as your whore. I can't be a slave to your every desire! How can you expect me to be? You were so good and kind to me! Now I know it was all an act. You're cruel! I'm less than a human to you. I wish you'd just take me home!" And a plan was beginning to form in her mind.

After the heat of the day, *Woniya Mato* continued to shape and repair his many weapons. After the moon slept and *wi* began to light the sky, he and his warriors would embark on their trail to victory. He'd a score to settle with Jed, and it wasn't wholly what he'd done to the Indian maidens. It was also what he'd done… and *tried* to do to *Mazaska Zi Ista*.

Although he suspected she begged for her freedom or for a return to her *wasicu* life, Spirit Bear could never let her go. *Wakantanka* and his totem helper, the black bear, had both shown him the way to her. He'd no doubt he'd win her heart. Until then, she'd just have to accept her place in his life and on his mats.

CHAPTER SEVEN 

A Taste of Freedom

Kaitlin was more angry than heartbroken at the moment. She wanted to help *Wawat'ecaka* with the meat to expel some of her pent-up anger. Yes, she'd pummeled the mighty Indian chief until she had nothing left, but it was funny how fresh anger revived the energy levels in one's body.

She put every ounce of her energy into slicing and hanging the meat on the drying racks in the afternoon sun. She worked her arms until they felt swollen and raw. The beautiful blonde had knotted muscles that cramped. When the *wayaka* could work no more, she motioned to Spirit Bear that she'd like to go to the blue pool.

Taking in her exhausted state, her blood encrusted hands, dress, and body; he couldn't deny that a soak would do her good. He'd not pressed her to hold back in her angry actions. She needed to work out her frustrations. He knew, though, that her body would rebel. Yes, he decided, a cold soak would be just the right thing for her muscles.

He came with her. The *winyan* kept her back erect even when she wanted to sag with weariness.

She was proud; it was as though she'd been born Oglala and not a *wasicun*.

Kaitlin quickly hid herself from his eyes in the blue waters of the pool. He didn't swim with her, but came to watch over her. He wished to protect her from lurking dangers as well as from any temptations she might harbor in the face of her discovery of being his personal slave.

A person who'd mistakenly thought she was free might tempt to capture what she felt was taken away. The *sky wayaka* had been content just hours ago with her place in his life. Now he knew she'd need to be watched.

Kaitlin soaked her fatigued body until she could take the cold no longer. Her lips had a bluish tinge, and her teeth chattered uncontrollably. She hurriedly dressed and washed her dirty dress. Then the only white for miles returned with Spirit Bear, her master, she scornfully acknowledged.

Before he lay down, Spirit Bear prepared his things for the ride to battle. He wasn't sure what would happen with the outcome of the exhibition. If he wasn't victorious this time, he would see to it that he would be triumphant the next. He hoped to take the white dog by surprise. They easily had the warrior power to take the wood-walled settlement, but he wasn't necessarily ready to do that yet.

Woniya Mato knew the heart of the man called Jed. He was evil and would pay. He'd need to study the rest of the *wasicu* more before he could decide if they were all *toka*.

Spirit Bear reclined on the skins beside his *winyan*. He studied her features for a long time. Hopefully, his *wayaka* would be more accepting upon his return. As any enamored male, he hoped her heart would long for him during his absence.

The great chief finally settled his mind and was able to relax. He needed this night of rest because during the quest, he'd sleep very little. He wouldn't risk his life or that of his warriors to sleep deeply.

Spirit Bear awoke before *wi*. He'd spend the time before light kissed the earth with *Mazaska Zi Ista*. She may not be willing, but he could hardly refrain from taking her twice the day before. He'd have her once more before he departed.

Slowly, he began to stroke her body. He didn't know if her body would respond as it did the day before or if he'd have a fight on his hands the entire time. He hoped she'd grow to love his attentions as much as he loved to give it to her. He wanted Kaitlin to come to him freely without having to make her body betray her.

He removed her dress from his *ska winyan's* sleeping body. His hands roamed over her, slowly awakening her. He placed indulgent, butterfly kisses from her head to her toes. He blew hot breath onto her skin and tasted her body gingerly, softly. She sighed dreamily, a smile flirting with her lips. His captive grew closer to becoming fully awake.

The skilled Indian lover continued to touch and love Kaitlin's perfect body until he brought her to the brink of passion. Right when she cried out with pleasure, her eyes flew open. Her pupils were heavy with desire, and her body writhed with a deeper calling. He obliged her need with a need of his own…

Spirit Bear held her for a time in the aftermath of their lovemaking. He knew she still resisted her position in his life and the fact that he could make her body betray her. However, *Mazaska Zi Ista* didn't seem as distant after their bodies danced as she had the day before. The Indian male knew she'd discovered pleasure at his touch. He knew that very soon, her womanly recesses would crave his manhood, and he'd no longer have to take choice away from her by lighting her fires.

Woniya Mato whispered the words of his heart to her as he tenderly held her. The golden-haired beauty brought forth feelings in him that he never dreamed possible. He thanked her as well as *Wakantanka* for coming into his life. Spirit Bear swore he'd avenge her honor and, if it was possible, bring the enemy back for her to make peace with before Jed walked the spirit trail. When his manly heart felt satisfied that she wouldn't totally withdraw, he arose and gathered his prepared supplies for his departure.

Kaitlin watched him curiously. *Was he leaving? Perhaps her time for escape would come sooner than she anticipated…*

The honey-haired woman inwardly was upset that she couldn't seem to control her body when he touched her. The newly awakened female didn't want to have sex with him because neither had declared their love to the other, and they were not married.

A sudden thought wrecked her mind. *What if she got pregnant? What would happen to her? To her baby?* She was suddenly consumed with fear.

She was afraid of her future. *What kind of life would she have as a slave, even if she bore the chief a son? Would they send her away and keep her baby? Would he keep her as a slave and not allow her to be the rightful mother to her child?* She didn't know what rights a slave really had; none, she supposed.

What if she made it home and found out she were with child? Her reputation would be set for the remainder of her life. No one would understand the man she'd come to know. They would judge her and judge her baby if one had been created. A life of heartache would await her, for no man would take a woman who had an Indian baby.

Yes, she was very attracted to *Woniya Mato*; she even suspected she loved him. *What woman wouldn't?* He was handsome, protective, a good provider, and a fantastic lover. He was the leader of a huge community. No matter how she tried to justify loving the warrior, she couldn't be satisfied with the unstable life of a slave. She must escape before it was too late.

Spirit Bear prepared left over acorn stew, dried venison, and fruit for breakfast. After he ate, he disappeared into the darkness without a backward glance. A short time later, she heard horse hooves galloping away.

Kaitlin got up and made sassafras tea. She also ate the remnants of the nut-flavored stew and fruit. Then she did her womanly chores as she was expected to do daily. If she was to disappear, she'd have to do it when the village retired for the night. Otherwise, the alarm would be sounded, and she'd be discovered much sooner than if she left under the cover of night.

Wawat'ecaka was surprised to see such as change in *Mazaska Zi Ista* when compared to the day before. The girl had already made and drank her morning tea and did her chores! She must have gathered wood right when *wi* began to wake the earth.

On this day, the women began immediately to work the deer from the day before. They didn't want the meat to go bad, so it must be worked as quickly as possible. Much of the animal was dried. The ham was sliced and put into a pot with garlic, onion, carrot, tubers, and other plants Kaitlin did not recognize. A little of the salt brush solution was added as well to enhance the flavor.

This meal would last the two women and *Wawakankan* the day and part of the next. It made it easier to focus on drying the rest of the meat. After the meat was smoked and dried, they would work with the rabbit pelts again. The antelope and deer skin would also need working soon.

That was one thing Kaitlin noticed about Indian life; there was always something to do. Usually, there was someone to work with during the day as well. She enjoyed the company of the other women.

Kaitlin harbored a little guilt because she would not see the two women she thought as friends again. She wanted to learn so much more from them, but if she wanted to make her get away a reality, she would have to use the time in which her chief was gone.

After a morning of work, Kaitlin slept soundly. She wanted to be well-rested for her night journey. She would try not to work too hard in the afternoon so that she could conserve some energy.

Kaitlin feared traveling at night, but there was no alternative. She also desired to take a horse. Her escape would be much more of a reality if she could only secure a mount. Perhaps the dun mare would let her catch her.

Kaitlin quickly rejected this idea. Someone would notice her and become suspicious of her actions. She would simply have to leave on foot.

That afternoon, the women finished cutting up the meat to cure. They also managed to rub and stretch the rabbit pelts again. After they worked the brain matter into the hair-free side, they moved the hide as much as they could. They would do this daily for a week. When the brain solution was gone, fat would replace the rub.

Finally, it was evening time. Kaitlin washed her dirty body and clothes, filled several *mniapahta*, ate venison stew, and retired to her tipi. Inside, Kaitlin closed the entrance flap for privacy and began to gather food items. She placed the food and water skins in the basket she'd made.

After hiding her basket in case someone wanted to come in, she tried to lie down. She refused

to nap, for if she fell asleep, she might accidentally
sleep all night; she was so tired.

While waiting for night fall, Kaitlin also selected
a hunting knife to take with her on her journey. A good
knife was a person's friend in the wilderness. It helped to
secure food and ensure safety.

After selecting her knife, Kaitlin found an
appropriate sheath for it and a strap for securing it to her
thigh. There she would have easy access to it, and it
would be hidden from others' line of view. For now, she
placed it in with her goods in the basket and hid it once
more until she departed.

Just as the village was settling in for the night,
Kaitlin heard a man's voice calling from the entrance flap.
She answered. The manly shape of *Wawakankan* entered.

He studied her for a moment. She felt a little
nervous the way his eyes traveled over her body and
lingered on her for a moment too long. She remembered
the look on his face as he worked on her naked body.

Why was he here? He knew Spirit Bear was gone.
*Is that why he was in the chief's tipi now? Was he here
to take advantage of her?* She nervously watched him.

Wawakankan had a strange feeling about the *ska
winyan* of Spirit Bear's. When the spirits talked to
Wonder Worker, he listened. He felt restless on this night.
He wouldn't have been able to rest until he'd checked on
the woman with golden eyes.

It would've been hard for a blind man not to have noticed a change in behavior in both his chief and his slave. Spirit Bear had never been so happy and carefree before that *Wawakankan* could remember. The girl, on the other hand, had become more quiet and withdrawn. The only possibility would've been from the consummation of their mutual allure.

The girl may not realize her attraction for Spirit Bear, but it definitely was there. *Wawakankan* had seen how her eyes followed and appraised his chief on several occasions. He was sure *Woniya Mato* had been aware of it as well. What man would not notice an attractive woman's appraisal of him, especially one so in-tuned to others and the environment as a warrior would be? Still, a nagging worry harped from the back of Wonder Worker's mind.

Nothing appeared to be amiss in the tipi. Perhaps he was over reacting after all. *Woniya Mato* had not left any instructions for the girl in his absence besides to watch over her.

Wawakankan was tempted to bring her into his tipi for safekeeping at night, but he knew that it would be too big a temptation for him. If he admitted it to himself, the girl was special in every way. *Wakantanka* smiled on her, and she was beautiful. She had a gentle, care-free spirit that drew others to her. She worked hard and didn't complain. *What man wouldn't want her for himself?*

Instead of tempting himself and his honor, he went to retrieve his mother. *Wawat'ecaka* would be the perfect solution to his nagging fear. He couldn't allow for something to happen to Spirit Bear's property in his absence. That's what friends did; they looked out for each other.

Kaitlin breathed a sigh of relief upon *Wawakaŋkan*'s departure. She was fearful that he would want to make her sleep with him, or that he would stay in Spirit Bear's tipi. Either way, it would have foiled her plans. Thank God he wasn't into rape!

Kaitlin's relief was short-lived. A short time later, *Wawat'ecaka* came with her sleeping mats. They didn't trust her after all! At first, Kaitlin felt anger towards the older woman she considered a friend. Then she realized they were expecting her to attempt what she was planning on doing anyway. Her anger melted although her disappointment lingered.

It would just be a revamping of plans. She'd still make good on her escape. Vaguely, she wondered how long the chief would be gone. The young woman wondered what he was doing. Soon, she dreamed of him.

Kaitlin was barely conscious of *Wawat'ecaka*'s getting up periodically throughout the night. She'd go outside for a time and return to sleep. Once, Kaitlin's curiosity overcame her. She peered out into the darkness after *Wawat'ecaka*'s disappearance.

She saw the silhouette of Gentle Rabbit as she stoked the low fires around the drying meat. Kaitlin knew this action continued the drying process as well as kept predators at bay. It was quite ingenious!

The next morning, chores were completed as usual. Tea and breakfast were consumed. The fires were stoked. The meat would continue drying this day.

Before the noon nap, *Wawat'ecaka* took Kaitlin to the skins. They would let the young buck's hide continue soaking, but Gentle Rabbit took out the baby and adult pronghorn skins. She secured them to larger drying racks with the same process she'd used with the rabbits'.

Wawat'ecaka gave the smaller skin to Kaitlin to work with, and she took the larger one. Using the same de-mattering process with the hide knives, the women worked side by side. The smell was very strong, and the work was tiresome and gruesome, but Kaitlin tried hard to please. She truly liked Gentle Rabbit.

After one side was mostly matter free, the women removed the stakes from the hides and took them to the river to scour. Using gravel from the water bed, they rinsed and scrubbed the hair-free side.

Kaitlin followed *Wawat'ecaka*'s lead and staked the side with the hair up on the racks. They began the same process anew on the opposite side. This side took more time due to the hair removal. Kaitlin didn't enjoy the grisly task, but she honestly wanted to learn *Wawat'ecaka*'s technique at leather making!

During the hottest part of the day, the women rested. Kaitlin was glad to sink her worn body down to sleep! The heat made it difficult to sleep very hard, but with her body still recovering and the strenuous chores, she did manage to sleep for a brief while.

After awakening and visiting the Place of Privacy, the pair of women returned to work. They'd replaced the hides to soak during the period of rest because the heat would've dried out the furs, making it impossible to remove the hair. The work was slower, hotter, and more repugnant in the afternoon because of the remaining heat, but finally, the chore was completed.

The pair repeated the gravel-scouring process with the other side of the skins. Then *Wawat'ecaka* had Kaitlin follow her. She led her past the Place of Privacy and into a small cave in the rock wall. An overpowering stench assailed Kaitlin. She retched without meaning to. *Wawat'ecaka* smiled at her. She was amused at the white woman's weak stomach yet pleased with her determination.

The cave was really just a recess with a cover. After entering the one-person opening, only a small room was present. The reeking smell radiated from the fetid rock pool directly in front of them.

Kaitlin was abhorred with what she saw. A big flat rock as long as two men and as wide as one filled the room after one entered. The huge stone was hollowed out and filled with old urine and a small bit of defecation. The stench of old urine enhanced by feces permeated from the natural basin.

Gentle Rabbit went directly to this and tossed the pelts into the center of the mixture. Kaitlin nearly screamed. All that work! She just threw their hard work into excrement! Kaitlin was shocked and appalled!

Wawat'ecaka smiled in the face of *Mazaska Zi Ista*'s reaction. Not many liked to see hard work thrown into defecation! But it was a necessary evil to turn out the supple works-of-art and unique colors she was so well known for. Golden Eyes was fortunate that she was privy to the secret curing techniques that she'd perfected over her lifetime. Already, *Wawat'ecaka* loved *Mazaska Zi Ista* as her own.

After swirling the two pelts around in the fetid slop, the women returned to camp. They finished up chores and took soap and clean clothes to the bathing area. After washing themselves and their garments, they reclined for a while in Spirit Bear's tipi.

Directly after resting, the pair of women removed the dried meat from the racks and stored them in intestinal bags until they were needed. The stored meat was secured on the woven shelves in the tipis of Spirit Bear, Wonder Worker, and Gentle Rabbit.

Just after they'd finished eating the last of the venison stew in the early evening, a young child raced up to *Wawat'ecaka*. His eyes were large in his small face. Kaitlin guessed he must have been four years old.

"Come quick, Gentle Rabbit! My mother is giving birth!" he cried. "She called out for your help!"

Wawat'ecaka was also known as the village's midwife, so she went immediately to the hut of Quiet Deer. Yellow Feather, her husband, had joined Spirit Bear on warrior's duty, so he was not present to know he was soon to be a new father; the child was coming a little early.

Wawat'ecaka was not concerned. She knew the mother would've been, more than likely, worrying over her man's mission, and worry often brought on pacing. Pacing or other excess movement was likely to bring on labor if the woman was close; this was Quiet Deer's second child.

Wawat'ecaka was pleased for the couple. Most couples had children closer together than four years. There had been come concern that the first child, Red Squirrel, had been too much for the petite woman's system. She'd not easily conceived again.

Kaitlin returned to her tipi. She worried and fretted over the pain and labor of the woman in the throes of childbirth. Who couldn't feel for the woman whimpering in pain?

When dark fell upon the village, *Wawakankan* came into the hut of *Woniya Mato*. He would have to come to terms with his desire for the *ska wayaka*, after all. He sat on the sleeping mats of his mother.

Kaitlin sat on her sleeping furs and watched Wonder Worker on his. He'd situated his bed by the entrance of the tipi. She wondered what she'd done to deserve this mistrust. Yes, she planned on escaping, but she didn't think her actions had revealed this to anyone.

Was this shaman also psychic? Could he read her thoughts? She decided to try an experiment.

The young blonde imperceptibly studied his profile. He seemed to be in a sort of trance-like meditation. His lips worked subtly, and his eyes were closed.

She appraised him as a man. He had strong features. His red skin had a sun-stroked sheen that forecasted his health. He was muscular and lean as all the men in the village were prone to be.

His black hair was captured in two braids secured with thongs. He had strong brows over a slightly imperfect nose; it had the slight bump up high on the bridge typical to many Indians in the village. His jaw line was sturdy and powerful.

His cheeks were high, and his lips were full. He was graceful for a man, making normal movements seem dance-like. His eyes laughed frequently but could become tepid and murky when faced with healing illness.

His mind was quick and sharp. He took in a lot of information swiftly and reacted even more quickly. His knowledge of medicinal plants and spiritual rituals were astounding. It was because of him that so many could thank *Wakantanka* for their lives.

Kaitlin soon determined that her experiment was successful. She'd wanted to see if the Indian could tell that she studied him by concentrating on him. He'd gone from his trance-like state to full awareness of her. His ebony eyes opened and sought hers immediately.

Kaitlin had performed the trial but really hadn't expected him to sense her gaze. She hastily looked away and blushed deeply. The *wayaka* did not want to encourage him as a man seeking the company of a woman.

Kaitlin was deeply aware of his eyes still upon her. She felt awed by his power with the spirits. How else could she explain his sudden mistrust of her or his knowledge of unstated things? It was uncanny!

Her thoughts were broken by the four-year old boy. Red Squirrel cried out for the shaman, "*Wawakankan*!" he yelled loudly. "*Wawakankan*!"

Wonder Worker stepped out of Spirit Bear's tipi. Immediately, the young boy went to him.

"*Wawat'ecaka* told me to come for you," he explained with ragged breath. "She said for you to grab your medicine bag."

Wawakankan quickly went to his lodge to recoup the needed items. Then he disappeared towards the screams coming from the tipi half-way back in the village.

Immediately, Kaitlin thought of escape. *How could she think of leaving these wonderful people when a woman's life was on the line?* Kaitlin berated herself for being a horrible person.

However, she couldn't stop herself form sneaking to the supply pile and retrieving her escape basket. The only white in the village found herself strapping on her knife and stealing silently towards freedom. All who watched would think she was going to relieve herself. She tried to obscure the basket from her silhouette.

Once she was away from the immediate vicinity, Kaitlin broke into a slow trot. She didn't want to wear herself out immediately, but the young woman wanted to put as much distance between herself and the Indians in as short of a time as possible.

As she approached the river, the pretty blonde heard a sobbing noise. Her temptation was to steer clear, but curiosity got the best of her. Kaitlin stealthily approached the noise.

Her heart went out to the crumpled form lying by the place where they collected drinking water. It was the slave of Snake Strike. Ear Sore was weeping dejectedly. Normally, this was not a woman to show weakness.

Kaitlin hid her basket in the near bushes. Giving up her chance at freedom, she approached *Nakpa Ihli*. The caring white knelt beside the battered girl and softly swept her hair back from her face.

Kaitlin drew in a startled breath when she saw the state the other *wayaka* was in. Already, her eye was swelling and blacked with a bruise. Her lips were also swollen and dripping with blood. She'd vomited where she lay clutching her abdomen.

Kaitlin hugged her and crooned to her. She rocked the girl in her arms. *Nakpa Ihli* continued to weep softly. Kaitlin was not sure if she were aware that she was being held.

Kaitlin poured water from the *mniapahta* and wet the girl's bruised face. It seemed to work. The girl snapped out of her morose behavior and suddenly became defensive.

When the darker slave saw it was the mere white girl administrating her, Ear Sore relaxed. To Kaitlin, it was if she were suddenly aware of her surroundings. The battered woman straightened up from her crumpled position and looked at Kaitlin.

Slowly, the Pawnee girl figured out why the *ska wayaka* might be out so late. Ear Sore was not easily duped. She stood and went to the place where Kaitlin had hidden the basket.

"*Hiya, Nakpa Ihli,*" Kaitlin said firmly.

Nakpa Ihli stopped and turned with eyes narrowed with malice. The ill will was not directed towards Golden Eyes, however. Ear Sore motioned to the abuse she had suffered this night.

Somehow, through broken Lakota and sign language, *Nakpa Ihli* told Kaitlin of the horror she'd survived. The other slave also must leave this village. She'd kill herself before she'd submit to any more abuse at the hands of *Zuzeca Pazan.*

Nakpa Ihli refilled the *mniapahta* late in the night because the cold water helped keep her nausea at bay. She also had a greater thirst during this time. Snake Strike had followed her to collect water and confronted her about the frequent trips to the watering place. The Indian slave confessed she was with child, and she wasn't trying to escape him; it was the only way to keep the sickness at bay. Instead of understanding, her master had beaten, raped, and left his servant to deal with her injuries. He'd kicked her twice in the abdomen to punish Ear Sore for conceiving!

Did he think she wanted to have his baby? NO! Now his spirit would live on when all she wanted to do was kill him. *Nakpa Ihli* would be glad to lose the baby! Her eyes begged Kaitlin to understand and grant passage to tag along. Besides, she knew the land and how to cover a trail better than *Mazaska Zi Ista*. Together, they'd have more of a chance than if Kaitlin when ahead alone.

The blonde acquiesced. She retrieved her basket, and they were off. Kaitlin even let the other woman guide their escape. *Nakpa Ihli* had to be more familiar with Indian ways and would best know how to elude their captors.

The first mile was slow and rough as they waded in the edge of the river. The rocks were slippery in places, and it was difficult to remain upright, but both knew that water would erase their passage. When they saw a rocky bank with flat stones stretching on the ground for an extended expanse at lease a mile downstream, they took the opportunity to escape from the wet domain.

Nakpa Ihli led Kaitlin through a twisted path in the forest. They were careful to avoid limbs that would show signs of their route. Ear Sore did not want to follow the river much further as it snaked through the valley below the village. The young Indian woman was worried they could be sighted from above when *wi* lit the path.

The Pawnee girl knew the penalty of a slave who betrayed the trust of a tribe. Ultimately, the punishment was left up to the owner, but she'd seen slaves who were publicly beaten, or worse; some had had a hand or foot removed. Once in a while, slaves were even killed for offenses. Even that was better than returning to *Zuzeca Pazan*.

Nakpa Ihli did wonder why the *ska winyan* wanted to leave. She had the most handsome warrior in the whole village! He had a great heart, was generous and brave, and best of all, he was fearless in the face of his enemy. He had many coup and had earned the right to lead his people.

Spirit Bear was a notorious chief. Not many had the courage to face him in battle. Yes, he had a soft heart, but that wasn't a flaw! *Nakpa Ihli* heard he also had a slow hand from whispering maidens who sought his attention in hopes of becoming his radiant bride.

Spirit Bear did not take maidens for his own pleasure because he cared for their reputations and his as a leader. She knew that from his younger days, his reputation in all areas preceded him. *So why did the white girl run?*

Nakpa Ihli knew the true answer; it was freedom. When the freedom of choice and movement was removed, so was the will to live. Even in the best of circumstances, a slave could never be happy. The women trekked on.

By the time the sun was rising, Kaitlin was worn out. She looked over at *Nakpa Ihli* and saw that she was exhausted, too, but viewed the fierce determination to continue on the other girl's face. Kaitlin felt sorry for the woman she was beginning to know. She'd put up with so much at the hands of Snake Strike! *Nakpa Ihli* had to be hurting from head to foot, and on top of it all, she was pregnant!

Kaitlin heard how that a woman was often ill in the early stages of pregnancy. Most women in her

society back East rested frequently during the
nauseous time of the early months. Of course, there
were servants to wait on them hand and foot.

She sighed softly and continued to follow the
grueling pace set by *Nakpa Ihli*. The women stayed in
the wooded area as much as possible. They couldn't
chance being seen by Indians on missions. The pair also
tried not to leave a traceable path. This was very difficult,
for even grass would be crushed if one stepped on it, but
Kaitlin didn't truly believe that an Indian could track that
well, anyway.

"Unless *Wawakankan* led with spirit vision,"
Kaitlin thought. With that startling idea, Kaitlin stepped
up her pace. Her tired body revived for a time.

When the sun was high overhead, *Nakpa Ihli* led
them over to a small stream. They filled their water bags
and sat on the bank. Both women removed their
moccasins and dangled their hot, tired feet into the
soothing waters. Soon, they rinsed their faces, legs, and
arms. The water felt wonderful on Kaitlin's many
scratches.

Nakpa Ihli was pale. She looked ill again. She was
still sitting in a slouched way, and her hand was resting
lightly on her abdomen.

Kaitlin touched her arm softly. When *Nakpa Ihli*
looked at her, Kaitlin could see the girl's misery. Concern
immediately welled up in Kaitlin.

Nakpa Ihli tried to tell Kaitlin she just needed to
rest a short while before continuing. The battered girl
felt ill especially during the heat of the day; traveling
was too much for her until things cooled back off a little.
She led Kaitlin to a thicket and both crawled into the
thick brambles.

Immediately, the Indian girl was asleep. Kaitlin couldn't go to sleep, but she rested her body. She knew the grueling task ahead of them. Who knows how far they'd traveled? She couldn't remember how long it'd taken them to get to the Indian village from the white settlement.

Did Nakpa Ihli also plan on coming to the town with her? She didn't know how receptive the white people would be of an Indian, even if she'd been a slave of one. The Indian woman had been treated inhumanely! Kaitlin wished to help the girl.

During *Nakpa Ihli*'s sleep, she whimpered softly. At these times, she would suddenly clutch her stomach. Kaitlin soothed the best that she could. The blonde wiped the suffering woman's hair back away from her face and bathe her with water.

Finally, *Nakpa Ihli* awoke. She slowly returned to the stream and drank. She applied the cool waters repeatedly to her heated skin. Then she began to walk again.

Kaitlin was very worried for the girl guiding their expedition, but she could not get her to rest more. They would be in more danger if they stopped frequently. Besides, both were determined not to go back.

Kaitlin had never been so tired, not even when they made the long journey into this savage land. At least then she was able to ride an exhausted horse when her legs gave out on her. Now, travel was solely her responsibility.

The sweltering afternoon heat pummeled them. Early evening came, and the women passed a wild plum tree. Both made a beeline for the fruit. Grabbing handfuls, both women collapsed on the ground to eat the succulent fruit. Kaitlin also retrieved some dried venison she'd swiped from the newly stored meat in the tipi. *Nakpa Ihli* nodded her thanks. Ear Sore had to slice her food into small bits in order to get it into her swollen and cracked lips.

Kaitlin's stomach had been growling incessantly since noon. The women were more concerned with putting distance between the village and themselves. This was the first meal either had eaten since the night before; they were ravenous.

Kaitlin selected four more of the delicious plums and packed them into her basket for later consumption. The women dragged themselves to their weary feet and continued. By night fall, Kaitlin no longer cared if she left a path in their wake. *Nakpa Ihli* also did not seem to be as conscientious of this, either. In fact, at times, the girl seemed off balanced. Still, she led them on.

Night was worrisome. Not only was travel more difficult, but predators often hunted under the guise of darkness. Because she couldn't see, Kaitlin tripped many times, and her arms were scratched continuously. Sometimes, she even was slapped by tree limbs.

Her mind played tricks on her, and Kaitlin swore she could hear snakes slithering underfoot. Many times, she bit off a scream only to discover she'd stepped on a stick. Still, *Nakpa Ihli* trekked on.

She led them, step by weary step, until finally, near late afternoon the next day, exhaustion overtook them. They didn't even bother to eat. They just curled up under a low cedar and slept like the dead.

Back at the Indian camp, the child was finally born. It had been a long and difficult process. It took all of *Wawakankan*'s skill as well as that of his mother's to save the life of the woman and the child. Red Squirrel was finally big brother. His red wrinkled brother squalled at the stillness of the late morning.

Quiet Deer had much to be proud of. She had only screamed during the worst pain. Not many women experienced the kind of pain she had and lived to tell. She'd endured much the same of her first experience, and she'd been able to bring forth another child! However, it would be too risky for her to conceive again.

The neighboring tipi had been wonderful to provide both *Wawat'ecaka* and *Wakankan* with nourishment and *mni* throughout the long birthing process. Finally, Wonder Worker left his charges in the neighbors' capable hands. They would see to it that woman and babe were looked after.

Wawakankan went to the bathing place for men and washed the blood and grime from his body. He would seek his resting mats soon. He had not slept since the evening he was called to duty. Asking the spirits for help often drained him mentally as well as physically.

No sooner than he had dressed and returned to the village than *Wawat'ecaka* came for him. Her face was flushed, and she had a panicked look in her eye.

"What is it, mother? Has something happened to the new child?"

"No! My son! Oh, my son! It is *Mazaska Zi Ista*! She is gone!"

"Gone? Are you sure?"

"Yes. I checked the Area of Privacy, the bathing place, and where we collect water. I checked the tipi, where we work leather, and I even checked the cave of curing. She is gone," *Wawat'ecaka* said with finality.

"You are sure she is not collecting fruits or plants?"

His mother nodded.

Wawakankan took the responsibility upon his shoulders. Although he was not rested, he had more stamina than many. He went directly to the lodge of Lone Wolf. Then the two of them sought council with Sky Warrior and rapidly approached his hut.

Wawakte Towanjila was residing chief when *Woniya Mato* was not present. He brought the men into his tipi to discuss the turn of events. As he did so, Snake Strike came barging up. The small man followed the important leaders into the tipi without invitation.

"Where is she?" he cried. He ignored the narrowed eyes of the chieftain's. He looked wildly around the tipi.

"Whom are you speaking of?" the chief could not be rude unless truly provoked.

"*Nakpa Ihli*, of course! She is gone. Are you hiding her from me?"

"Do not dare to ask such a question in my presence! Of course I would not hide her from you unless there was a reason. However, we will discuss your treatment of her at the next council meeting." The three leaders nodded in agreement.

Zuzeca Pazan's narrow lips became a fine white line. His eyes squinted in a fury. "You cannot take my property from me!"

"The Council is the law-forming body in our village. If you remain part of this community, you will abide by the rules," Sky Warrior valiantly attempted to keep anger from his words.

"She is mine! She is pregnant with my child! It would be wrong to take her from me!" the small man cried hoarsely.

The three other men looked at each other in sad amazement. That did throw a damper on things. Nevertheless, his behavior would have to change towards her if they allowed him to keep her.

"We have important matters to discuss now. Leave us. We will consider your request when *Woniya Mato* returns."

The little man left the tipi in a cloud of black resentment. He already knew what that insolent chief would say. *Maybe he would leave this stinking village… after he found his girl!*

After the angry man left, the warriors continued their talk.

Sky Warrior began, "*Wawakankan,* I think the best thing to do would be to leave you in charge of things here. Lone Wolf and I will go after the girl."

Wawakankan shook his head. "It is I who should go. I gave my word to *Woniya Mato* that I would watch over the *wayaka.*"

"That may be so, my *kola,* but you are weary from duty. What if the woman or baby needs you again? I cannot perform the rituals or give the healing plants to them. It is you who must stay."

Both men looked to Lone Wolf. He was quiet but did lend his voice when he was needed.

"*Wawakankan, Wawakte Towanjila* speaks wisely. You are tired while we are fresh. We know you can assume chieftain duties in our absence. We can travel quietly and swiftly. Your greater need is here with the people," he paused to allow his words to sink in before continuing. "What if the war party returns, and they need treatment? If you were gone, important lives could be lost. Your place is better served here."

Wawakankan agreed with the logic presented by *Isnala Sungmanitu.* He would stay, but he'd help in the way he knew how. Before he rested, he'd prepare a ritual for *Wakantanka* to ask for the safety of all absent members of the tribe and for their safe and speedy return.

Lone Wolf and Sky Warrior quickly prepared light traveling supplies and weapons. Enemies were always abounding. Lone Wolf was needed on this quest, for his tracking skills were only comparable to that of the head chief's.

Wawakte Towanjila's tracking skills and abilities as a warrior were also highly honored. Lone Wolf had no doubt they'd have the *winyan* back in custody before the return of *Woniya Mato*. They'd leave her punishment in his capable hands.

It was early evening when Kaitlin was awakened by pesky flies. The annoying creatures aggravated her beyond belief! This time, she was kind of glad for their presence, nonetheless, because they'd roused her.

Surely their absence was missed in the village by now. It was more important than ever to press on. They also had to travel by foot where Kaitlin was sure; those tracking them would come swiftly by horse.

Kaitlin gently shook *Nakpa Ihli* awake. The girl's pallor didn't seem to be improving. Upon awakening, the young Indian woman retched up her earlier meal. The blonde did what she could to comfort. She held her hair and caressed her back.

Nakpa Ihli staggered to her feet. She noted the concern chiseled in the white girl's eyes, but she couldn't cave in and rest longer. They must press on! If only her stomach would stop cramping. Her lower back was beginning to ache and cramp now, too. She'd do her best not to show her pain to her new friend.

The women pressed on into the coolness of the night. They only stopped to rest their legs briefly and to drink from the *mniapahta*. Kaitlin noticed *Nakpa Ihli* was barely able to eat the plum that she gave her. Her lips had swollen even larger; the cracks had become crevices. Blood oozed from the side of her mouth, and her black eye had swollen shut.

If time permitted, she would make willow-bark tea for her friend. It would help lessen the pain of her injuries. She knew how from watching *Woniya Mato* prepare it for her.

Thinking of him brought his image to the forefront of her mind. He was so handsome! And he was kind… for the most part. Even though he knew how to make her body betray her, he'd been gentle when he took her.

If he weren't so attractive and magnetic, she could have hated him, but her mind and body were drawn to him in some inexplicable way. She shook her head with incomprehension.

Basically, if she thought about it, she was a slave to her father and brother, as well… in all the same ways save one. At home, however, she didn't even have respect! *Why was she leaving again?*

Of course, she remembered. *She was a free person with free will to do as she pleased.* Still, she did have a lagging doubt in the back of her mind. Jed. *What if her father hadn't reneged on his deal with the bully? Would her father really force her to marry Jed? She couldn't; she wouldn't!*

If she married Jed, she could see herself in the same situation as the woman weaving in front of her. She would end up pregnant without support, beaten, and treated worse than trash. She swore she'd kill Jed before she'd ever let him lay another hand on her. His hands only brought pain.

She really didn't want to resort to Bradley for help, but really, *what choice did she have?* If she returned to the cabin, *Woniya Mato* was sure to find her again. She couldn't imagine he'd be happy when he found out his prisoner had escaped the captivity of the mighty warrior and chief! He'd be forced to recapture her to save face. Honor and pride, it seemed, drove all Indians she'd met… except *Zuzeca Pazan*.

Within the walls of the township, she would be at the mercy of Jed if she didn't find another protector. Bradley was the only logical and ethical solution for her future. Still, she didn't love Bradley. She wasn't even attracted to him physically.

He was a handsome man, but in a slender, cultured way. He was tall and willowy even though he did possess muscular strength. He had soft ways necessary for selling to the public through his General Store.

Bradley was a good friend, so perhaps she could stand to live under his domain. However, he did not make her heart quicken or her step light as did the Indian warrior. Bradley just didn't possess the sheer male beauty of *Woniya Mato*.

She thought of Woniya Mato again, so quickly? She chided herself and once more, turned her thoughts deliberately back to Bradley. She knew Bradley held an interest in her, but she was one of the few attractive young women brought forth from the East. Not many women who weren't already married with children were available. None of them would have been allowed to come without proper escorts unless they were with their family. The smart ones had stayed behind.

It just wasn't fair! *Why were women treated like children?* Sure, the strength of men was needed for building houses and such, *but hadn't she proven she could survive without one?* Her father and her brother never brought anything home but themselves. She did it all, *so hadn't she earned the right to live independently without being harassed by unwanted attention?* She thought so!

If she could sell baskets and finish learning the art of leather making, she would open up a shop of her own someday! As she traipsed along after the Indian woman, Kaitlin allowed herself to dream of someday. She could remain a spinster for all of her live-long days if she so chose! *And maybe she would!*

It was nearing the time when the sun was beginning to rise when Kaitlin spied the familiar shape of a willow tree. She pointed to the willow and motioned to it. *Nakpa Ihli* listlessly plodded towards it.

Underneath the willow was a small pond. The women filled the *mniapahta* bags and sat for a short time. Kaitlin gathered willow boughs and broke them into smaller, easier-to-carry pieces. She secured them and selected pieces of bark from the trunk into her basket. Now she had something that might help ease her friend's discomforts!

The white beauty sat and removed her moccasins to relieve the soreness and weariness in the water. Never had her feet, legs, and back hurt like it did now. Her rib pain felt like a slap from a child when compared to the rest of her body. As they sat, Kaitlin handed the last plum to *Nakpa Ihli*. The Indian girl would have better luck eating it than the jerky with her abused mouth. As it was, even drinking caused the other woman to wince.

Soon, they dragged their weary bodies into motion again. Onwards they trudged. Kaitlin was no longer worried over every sound or the idea of being caught; things were not as scary when a body was exhausted, Kaitlin discovered. Nothing mattered except the endless plodding towards freedom.

They were finally five days away from the village, and Kaitlin began to think they had to be nearing the settlement, but she had no idea how far away they truly were. She had been unconscious much of the time on her trip to the village. In addition, they'd been on horses.

When the day was nearing the hottest point, Kaitlin became alarmed. They'd just stopped by the edge of a stream to fill their water bags yet again when *Nakpa Ihli* weaved and toppled over. Her friend was extremely pale and hot to the touch. She began whimpering and clutching her belly.

Kaitlin collected moss from a nearby tree and dipped it into the stream water. She bathed her friend's face.

"The *wakanheja* will not live," *Nakpa Ihli* told Kaitlin. "It will come now."

Kaitlin did not understand all of what *Nakpa Ihli* had said, but she recognized the word, *wakanheja*, from the night they stole from the village. That was the word that Red Squirrel used when referring to his mother's labor. *The child? Nakpa Ihli was going to miscarry? Is that what she was trying to say?*

Kaitlin tried to make a comfortable place on the ground for *Nakpa Ihli*. She removed her garment from her hot, sweaty body. She continued to wipe her face. *If only she'd thought to bring her skillet! Then she could prepare the willow bark tea!*

CHAPTER EIGHT

An Old Nightmare

Woniya Mato had finally tracked the big *wasicun*. He didn't have him in his sights yet, but he was close. The *ska sunka*, it appeared, had vengeance on his mind as well. This was good. Now he would make an easier, unsuspecting target for the chief and his warriors.

The powerful leader saw the signs of his enemies' journey about two to three days before his band would've reached the wall of wood. It was evident that Jed had a group of about fifteen men with him on the war path. They were headed toward the Bear Claw Clan of the Oglala.

It would take many more men than that to defeat *Woniya Mato*, Spirit Bear thought. They did not have the stealth or the skill of a warrior of *Wakantanka*! The white dogs would not see victory on this day!

The war chief could tell Jed was very close. The Lakota party found where the *wasicu* had made camp. The whites were sure enough of themselves that they dared to make a fire! If they only knew they were being stalked by the mighty Spirit Bear!

Woniya Mato noted that the enemies had split up for some reason. Had they become aware of the presence of those who planned to slay them? Spirit Bear motioned to his warriors to split up into groups of two and three to track down each of the white's parties. A hawk's cry would signal the other warriors that a white group had been sighted.

Spirit Bear and Yellow Feather teamed up to trace the leader of the *toka*, for *Woniya Mato* wanted to make sure he was the one to settle the score with the white dog and not a fellow warrior. The coward had five men with him; the other groups of whites had only had three to four. Spirit Bear smiled and looked forward to the confrontation.

His ears detected a noise near the bed of water ahead. The *wasicun* had even dared to start another fire! Not only were they cowards, but they were stupid as well! They would learn from their deadly mistakes. *Woniya Mato* would see to it that he was bothered by the great white dog no more.

Yellow Feather circled around, giving the chief time to strike first. Spirit Bear crept stealthily up to the undergrowth surrounding the small waterway. With his tomahawk in hand, the war chief leaped over the brush with a war cry and was prepared to a strike death blow. Instead, the sight that greeted him froze his hand.

The two *wayaka* from his village were close to the fire, not his *toga* he was primed to fight! He was fortunate, for he nearly killed the *winyan* of his soul! In a beat of his heart, he took in the scene and came to a conclusion of what was going on.

Nakpa Ihli writhed in the clearing in the process of miscarrying. The fire was warming a concoction of willow boughs and water in a stone bowl barely deep enough to contain the ingredients. Kaitlin was stooped low over the other girl, bathing her nude body and soothing her with words. Now, however, the attractive blonde looked at him with amber saucers in her face.

Fear as she'd never known racked her body. Kaitlin saw the man she loved as an enemy would see death swooping down upon him. His face was painted as it had been the night of the ceremony. The chief's honed body was taut with muscles straining with control. The tomahawk glittered high in the air as if preparing to slice down upon her, and the warrior's mouth was open wide as if calling the eagle of death to take her away. His war cry made her understand she had new things to learn about fear! Then the captive noted the chief's dark eyes; they were swirling with fury.

Woniya Mato wore thick buckskin leggings and a matching breechcloth. Both were fairly plain, but she could see his trademark black-tipped red feathers here and there. He wore no shirt and his bronze skin rippled with power. The leader's head was adorned with a single headband with several of his characteristic plumes waving above his terrifyingly painted face. His bear claw wanapin tinkled with pride from around his neck.

Kaitlin froze, trembling in terror. *Was he going to kill her? How had he found her so quickly? Did the shaman work such powerful magic that he was able to send a message via telepathy to his chief?* Surely, she deserved death in his eyes.

Why was he waiting? Did he want her to save the girl first? Still, she did not dare to move a muscle until he made the next move.

A cry from *Nakpa Ihli* brought them to their senses. Her body jerked with a spasm and then she curled into the fetal position. It was at this time that *Woniya Mato* saw her other injuries as well.

He grabbed Kaitlin's arm and hissed, "Who did this to her?"

Realizing the white woman still didn't understand him; he motioned to her eye and mouth and then pointed to the woman writhing on the ground. Spirit Bear believed he knew the answer. If he were correct, that problem would be dealt with upon return to the village, but he wanted to be sure the *toga* he hunted wasn't responsible.

Kaitlin, still shaken from her near death experience, looked down. Her voice was barely audible, "*Zuzeca Pazan*."

Kaitlin could see *Woniya Mato*'s fist clenched at his sides. He was a very angry man at the moment. The escaped slave knew she was the main cause.
She'd never feared the great chief before, but since she'd become a run-a-way who was now back in his hands, *would he have mercy?* She was frightened.

Why was he dressed this way? Was he hunting them? She dared not even look at him.

Woniya Mato untied a *mniapahta* at his waist. It contained willow bark tea. He never left without it when he was going on a trip for war reasons. The angry man held it to the bruised lips of *Nakpa Ihli* while supporting her head. The poor girl was so involved in the pain that wracked her body, she didn't respond. He forced her to drink as gingerly as he could.

Next, the chief took a packet of powder from his medicine bag and mixed it with water. When he had a paste, he forced it in Ear Sore's mouth. Then with a practiced eye, the gentle warrior examined her more closely.

He found the bruising on the woman's face appalling, but even more unspeakable was the black and purpling markings that crossed *Nakpa Ihli*'s abdomen. *Zuzeca Pazan* had beaten his slave way beyond belief! He'd caused her to lose the baby. Children were sacred.

Woniya Mato's jaw clenched as he gnashed his teeth. He was almost as angry at himself for allowing the exploitation to continue. The leader felt to blame that this level of abuse had been reached. The woman would live, but she couldn't take any more. Her body was tired of mending itself.

Had Mazaska Zi Ista ran away to help Nakpa Ihli escape Zuzeca Pazan's heavy hand, or were her reasons less noble? He'd wondered if she might try this while he was away. This is why he'd asked *Wawakankan* to keep an eye on her. It made him wonder why he had not.

His *ska winyan* would not look at him. It was good that she was scared. He'd let her feel fear of him for a while. The supreme fighter didn't trust himself to touch her at this moment; he *was* extremely angry.

Yellow Feather materialized beside him. They both looked down at the woman on the ground. Already the medicine *Woniya Mato* had given *Nakpa Ihli* was beginning to ease her pain. She breathed a little easier and was not curled up so tightly.

Within the hour, the worst had passed. *Woniya Mato* allowed Kaitlin to help the woman clean and dress. She would be too weak to travel for at least a day. Now the chief had to worry about having two women under his supervision while on a war raid.

While the females rested, *Woniya Mato* quietly took his teammate to the side.

"Yellow Feather, find the rest of our party and send them back to me. Our plans have changed due to the situation at hand. I will send a volunteer back with the *wayaka.* War is not a place for women. The danger is too great for us all while we must also protect them."

Yellow Feather nodded once and turned to do his bidding when a familiar voice slurred into the quiet stillness.

"Well, well, well! Looky what wuv here!" Jed came into the clearing holding a pistol in his hand. Five others followed his wake; the newcomers made a small horse shoe around the two women and men. Kaitlin was on one side while the warriors were on the other side of him.

"Looks like wuv stumbed inta a lover's lair!" he laughed raucously.

Jed was even more burly and rough than when Kaitlin had last seen him. The blacksmith's right arm was supported in a sling. In his left hand, he held the gun.

The attractive blonde had never seen two of the men with Jed. They were huge mammoths. Both were dressed in buckskin similar to Indian wear. The main difference in the clothing was the filth; it was stained with mud, debris, and something that could've been blood.

The first man was only a shade shorter than Jed. His hair was greasy and matted to his head. He had a black gnarled beard that hung half way down his distended stomach. His mustache flowed over huge lips and tangled into wads of food and grease as it merged with his beard. Kaitlin wondered if he had to cut the hair around his lips to open his mouth!

The second man had red hair. He was older and had no hair on the top of his head. He was a smidgeon taller than Jed. It was a race to see who was the filthiest between the two rugged mountain men. The second brother's mustache didn't tangle in with his beard, but it fell over his mouth in thin ragged wisps. Long, black teeth that were broken in places were easily viewed through the red straggles.

Both siblings were very stocky and heavy-set, and both had beady eyes. Each held a flintlock rifle in their club hands that were pointed at the Indian warriors! However, it was easy to see that Jed was their leader; they waited for his direction.

Kaitlin wanted to wrinkle her nose in disgust. She would almost wager they had many live vermin in their hair. Jed wasn't much better!

The other three men Kaitlin had seen around but didn't know very well. They weren't as filthy as the rest of the group, but they were well-known to her father. They loved to gamble and drink; this meant they were also under Jed's power.

The young white woman stood solid for a moment. Then the realization of what was happening sunk in. Now, the whole party she was with was at the mercy of Jed's group!

The braves didn't just freeze; they assumed a warrior's stance. Their tomahawks were in one of their hands and knives in their other. Slowly stalking forward, they assessed the six men who were their prey.

Jed laughed so hard he held his stomach. "Arn yeh gonna take meh? Jes the two o' yuhs? Agin orn six?" Jed mocked them again with his hearty laughter. "Yeh may not know it yet, but these here guns will stop yeh where yeh stand!" Of course, Jed had knives of his own to back up the guns in case they didn't stop the savages.

"Men," Jed continued. "This here is tha' Injun I was a tellin' yuh about. I want him taken alive. I don' care about this othen. Yuh can haf fun a torturin' him or yuh kin kill him fast. But I get the big un. He's a gonna pay fer what he did ter meh."

Jed turned to look at Kaitlin for the first time. "Gosh, I almost din't recognize yeh in yourn Injun wear. It suits yeh. How do yah feel about me takin' yer man here and torturin' him real slow like?"

"He's not my man, Jed."

"Well, he shore seems taken with yeah! Why, he even threw down his bow fer yeh."

"W - what?" her voice stammered.

"Oh, that's rit. Yeh were sort ter out o' it," he paused, eyeing the Indian men nervously for the first time. They were getting too close for comfort. "Herb, why don' yeh shoot the Injun with the yellow feather on his head? I don' care if'n yeh kill him orn not."

"No!" Kaitlin screamed.

A shot rang out from the black-haired man's flintlock. He must have been nervous, for he only grazed Yellow Feather's shoulder. He immediately began trying to reload his single-shot gun, for the flint lock was not convenient for multiple shootings.

The Indians stopped in shock. *What kind of evil magic was this?* These men could control fire with these sticks they held in their hands?

Again, Jed's harsh laughter rang out. "Nice shot there, Herb! Arn yeh a little nervous? Why, I bet we could haf them a puttin' on a song an dance routine down in the saloon after they really see what ourn guns kin do! Wu'll call thur act 'Dancin' with Bullets!'" He continued to laugh with vicious malice. Jed motioned to the men on the outside ring to move in on Kaitlin and Ear Sore.

"Kait, yeh kin come over ter me nice an easy like, and I'll haf some mercy on yeh. If'n I haf ta go come an git ya, yeh won' be too happy with ma treatment o' yeh."

"Jed, how about I come on over to you, and you let these others go? I promise to do what you say if you'll just let them go."

"Yeh'll come ter me anyhow. An' yeh'll do what I say, anyhow. Yer mine. A'sides, I got a score ter settle with yourn lover boy. More'n one. He took what was mine firs'. He's gonna pay fer that. He killed ma brother, an he took away the use of ma shoulder. I cain't forget that. Yeh, he's a gonna pay. I think aft'r I tortor 'em a'while, ya and me are gone a git all comfy like together and let 'em watch. I think tha'll tear him up mor'n anything else. Tha's what I think."

"You are a disgusting, vile excuse for a human, Jed! I *hate* you, and I always have! If you think I'll ever let you touch me, you're sadly mistaken! I'll see you rot in hell before you hurt any of these people, too!"

"Oh, honey cakes! Yer gett'n me all hot. I like to tame down spicy little hot dishes. I'll keep yeh fer a long, long time fer ma entertainment. Then, if'n yeh don' keep me good an satisfied, I may jus sell yeh ter the next man. I kin always replace yeh."

Jed no intention of ever selling Kaitlin. She was the prettiest thing next to sin that he'd ever seen, but the shapely vixen didn't have to know that. It would help keep her in line and doing what he wanted. He saw that she'd visibly paled under his goading.

"You're *despicable*! I *hate* you!" she spat.

Spirit Bear was electrified with this large challenge *Wakantanka* provided for him this day. He'd faced larger challenges than this before and lived to tell about it. He was cautious, more so than usual, for several reasons: the women and the strange fire sticks. Yellow Feather did not seem seriously injured, but his strange cut from the weapon bleed freely.

Woniya Mato had fought the great grizzly bear and the black bear both and lived to tell of it. He proudly wore their claws and teeth to advertise his bravery and daring. He'd mourned the necessity of taking the lives of those so powerful, but he'd done so under *Wakantanka's* direction.

The Great Spirit had shown him in a vision quest that if he could take the lives of both these animals in hand-combat, he would forever receive spiritual protection from them. It was not a task Spirit Bear relished, nor was it one he did lightly. Bears were highly revered for their power and strength. Mourning the animals after the fact was like mourning for a fallen warrior!

Spirit Bear only called upon the strength of these creatures when he truly needed their assistance. The woman he held dear to his heart was being threatened once again by the *ska sunka,* and he vowed to himself that this would never happen again. He also had the Pawnee *wayaka* and a fellow warrior to consider. The others in the war party could also be in danger from the fire sticks. *Woniya Mato* sent up a small chanted prayer to his kindred spirits.

Mazaska Zi Ista and the white dog seemed to be having a conversation. Spirit Bear did not know what was said, but Golden Eyes seemed to be pleading with the smelly coward hiding behind his fire stick. She seemed to becoming angry and upset.

Was she asking the white dog to rescue her, or was she pleading with him to release the Indian group? He'd love to know! When he took her back to camp and into his life, he would make her teach him the *wasicu* tongue. It would be a great weapon to have on his side!

Jed captured Kaitlin's attention again, "Honey, if'n yeh'll come over here, I won' shoot yer Injun feller." He paused before continuing, his impatience growing, "See here? I kin shoot 'em if'n yeh don' listen cuz I got ma gun trained on that pleasure center o' his. He won' be a givin' any more of what he got if'n yeh don' git over here now! NOW!" Jed's angry yell scared Kaitlin and made her jump.

"Jed, I'll come to you. Please, let *Woniya Mato* go. Let the others go. The girl is sick. She needs their medicine man."

The sudden revelation of the name, *Woniya Mato*, had a curious effect on the two burly men. Their jaws became slack and their eyes grew large with shock. Herb stopped trying to reload and Willy relaxed his hand on his gun. Their startled eyes met and communicated silently with each other. They were facing *the* Spirit Bear?

Jed continued his derisive taunting of his captivate audience. He was so absorbed that he didn't notice the reaction of the two mountain men.

"Boys, bring the purty woman ter me. Yeh all kin haf the Injun woman fer yer pleasure. She'll service yeh all. And I'll have ma turn wit this one. It is pure hell on them savages to haf to watch anothern take what they think is therns. O' course, this un took what wuz MINE!" Jed roared, startling the blonde and making her jump a second time.

"Kait, this is yourn las' time I'm a gonna tell ya. Git. Over. Here. NOW!"

The becoming white didn't want to go to Jed, but maybe she could help her Indian friends if she was beside the large man. If nothing else, she could bump Jed's arm when he aimed his gun at the people she so admired.

The captive still had the knife secured to her thigh. The white girl fully intended on killing Jed if he tried to rape her. She wasn't going to stand and take his scornful treatment meekly! She would also sacrifice her own self to protect these proud people she'd come to love.

Slowly, Kaitlin got to her feet. She began to move towards the white filth, but she couldn't help but to drag her feet. Spirit Bear became aware of her intentions.

His commanding voice halted her travel, *"Hiya, Mazaska Zi Ista. Oyuhlagan sni. Wanna."*

"Oh, looky! He's a tellin' his woman somethin'. I bet cha he's tellin' her to haf a good time. Don' worry. Yeh'll git ter see!" He cackled in merriment and rubbed himself suggestively.

Kaitlin faltered, teetering with indecision. Then she saw Jed make a dramatic motion of better aiming his gun on Spirit Bear's private area, so she trudged on.

"*Hiya, Mazaska Zi Ista!*" Spirit Bear did not yell, but his voice was full of power.

Even the *toga* before him trembled. The only one oblivious was the *ska sunka*, but he, too, would quake!

"Ye wan ter tell 'em, er should I?" Willy said, interrupting Jed's tirade and harassment of the pretty white woman.

"I will."

"Tell meh what?" Jed asked gruffly. "Tha',
um, this here Injun? He got a mean
reputation. He's a killin' machine! All the Injuns around these here parts knees knock together jes when yuh say 'is name!"

"So? They's just o' bunch o' heathens." "Jed,
we don' wan ter mess wi' em." "We already
got 'im whupped."

"No, we don'. Yeh jus don' understand. He's got the spirits on his side!"

"Yeh spooky ole hens! Who'd a thunk yuh'd be so chicken? I'll show yeh how powerful he is! Lemme git his woman secure, and he'll be a eatin' out a muh hand." He turned and motioned with four fingers for her to speed up her progress. He added for emphasis, "Now, Kait."

Kaitlin stepped forward. The two closest to her grabbed her arms. The becoming blonde didn't resist. They dragged her to Jed.

He roughly pulled her to his fetid chest. He slobbered his vile mouth over her face and tried to latch on to her lips. Kaitlin couldn't remain impassive under his wretched attempts to stoke *Woniya Mato* to anger. She twisted and turned, then coughed his putrid breath away in a vain attempt to escape his touch.

Jed looked at the mighty chief and saw his intimidating features harden into a mask of hate. It nearly made his heart leap in his chest. However, he couldn't resist making him even angrier. Slowly, he pulled Kaitlin's hands into his one large one; then he raised his arm up high, forcing her to nearly dangle before him. He bent his head over her neck and stuck his tongue out to taste her skin, all the while, he watched the warrior.

Kaitlin started to pull as hard as she could against him, but she was no match for his iron grasp. Soon, he was licking a trail down her neck to her collar bone. She hissed and turned her head away, squeezing her eyes shut. Unbeknownst to her, she let out a soft whimper of distress.

Woniya Mato watched the *ska sunka* bait his *winyan* into becoming his captive. He did not understand the conversation, only what he saw. The evil man laughed and mocked Golden Eyes.

Her body language told him clearly how much she did not want to go to the white dog. Spirit Bear suspected she argued for their sake. She planned on sacrificing herself to buy their freedom! *Wastelaka*, he silently called to her, *It is a trick. You cannot trust one such as him! Do not go!!!!* Then, he verbalized his order.

Spirit Bear saw that his command did affect the white girl. Then the white dog growled again and pointed his fire stick at his, *Woniya Mato's*, manhood! No *toga* threatened him or his *wayaka* and lived to tell of it. When Spirit Bear saw his hated foe paw and salivate on his *winyan*, it became too much.

Woniya Mato became the grizzly he was known for. The spirits hand answered his prayer; the bears' anger surged forward. Their supremacy flooded into his soul, creating pure, raw power. Spirit Bear's eyes were slits of wrath, and he breathed with predator precision. No evil magic would befall him or prevent him this victory!

He took out the two closest men almost simultaneously. One had a tomahawk lodged in his throat. The gruff man gurgled blood and finally drowned on his choked cry for life. The other had a knife protruding from his eye. He dropped his weapon and sunk to the ground, screaming in agony. Already, *Woniya Mato* secured his new bow and nearly had an arrow strung.

Almost as if cued, Yellow Feather took out another *ska sunka* with his tomahawk. Like magic, four arrows embedded themselves into the backs of the two mountain men still holding their flintlocks in terror. They dropped without a sound.

Appearing out of nowhere, Sky Warrior and Lone Wolf lent their expertise to the situation at hand. Earning a surprised smile from their leader, they returned the gesture. This day was good. *Wakantanka* was pleased.

Jed, terribly confused  on how the turn of events could occur so quickly, clutched his life line… Kaitlin. The Indians were closing in on him! *It's not fair*, he nearly whimpered. He'd worked so hard for this day of revenge! How could it be that he was going to be at the mercy of the filthy redskins… *again*? He would kill Kaitlin before he'd let them torture him again! Besides, if he was going to die, he would have the final revenge… and spare his pretty obsession as well.

"Kaitlin, yuh tell 'em to git back! Do yeh hear me? I got me one ball in this here chamber, and I'll use it on yer feller if'n they don' back off!"

Kaitlin would try to speak to her former captor. She only hoped he'd listen. She would not and could not risk the lives of so many from the Indian village – especially of the man she loved. These people had nursed her back to health! If *Woniya Mato* would listen, the chief and leader would continue his reign.

"*Hiya, Woniya Mato.*" Kaitlin held up her hand to indicate to the warrior they needed to stop their approach. She gestured wildly to the gun and then motioned to Spirit Bear. Again, she said, "*Hiya!*"

Yellow Feather seemed to understand. He rapidly told the others of the magic sticks that cut his arm without touching him. He pointed to his injury which was not critically deep but still oozed blood.

Kaitlin was almost being squeezed in two by Jed's sudden fear. However, she'd rather be clutched than licked. Besides, she didn't blame him for being afraid. Who wouldn't be in the face of death? Kaitlin briefly recalled her terror when *Woniya Mato* came at her with his tomahawk.

The young beauty couldn't say that Jed didn't bring it on himself. However, she was also petrified. The white girl had never seen violent death in person before; it was surreal. It almost felt as if everything were moving in slow motion!

Woniya Mato seemed to honor her request. He and the other warriors stopped where they were and were speaking to each other in rapid Lakota. With a nod, Yellow Feather, Sky Warrior, and Lone Wolf fell back. Only Spirit Bear faced Jed.

Woniya Mato motioned for Jed to throw down his weapon. Then Spirit Bear signed that he would do the same. He indicated he wanted Kaitlin released.
Whoever won the man-to-man contest would leave unscathed.

"I think he wants to fight you, one-on-one," Kaitlin revealed.

"No way! Thurs no way in hell I'll fall fer tha' one," Jed nearly whimpered.

"Jed, I'd say it might be your only chance. Indians are people of honor. They are only as good as their word. If they say you will not be attacked by all of them, you won't be."

Spirit Bear indicated once more for Jed to throw down his fire stick. He motioned throwing down his own tomahawk. Then he pointed to his knife and made a motion of Jed having his own knife. Spirit

Bear made it known that he challenged Jed in a hand-to-hand combat with knives. Again, to make it clearly communicated, *Woniya Mato* pointed to Kaitlin and made a sign of her walking away.

"Well, ta's not a fair fight neither. I only got one hand cuz o' him!" Without meaning to, he motioned to his shoulder and glared at Spirit Bear.

The chief understood. He even went as far as to offer to tie one of his hands to his waist during the challenge. Of course, there would only be one winner; it was a fight to the death.

"Jed, I'm sorry. You are clearly outnumbered. At least he's offering you a fighting chance."

"I got ma some moe help around chere somewheres. If'n they'd git over here, wuh'd still be victorious."

Instead of white men appearing, more of the mighty Indian warriors seemed to emerge, first in ones, then in twos and threes. Jed nearly cried like a baby.

All in all, twelve Indian men and one woman stood against Jed and the white woman he held in his hands. Jed knew escape was futile. If he killed Kaitlin, he realized they'd only make his death worse.

"How kin I be shore yuh'll follow through with yur words?" Jed screeched in Spirit Bear. "How kin I know yur tribe o' savages'll lemme go when I kill yur ugly face?"

Kaitlin tried to relate what Jed said with a few words of Lakota and sign.

How dare the white dog question his honor? Honesty was pride. If the chief said he would grant his *toka*'s freedom when and if he could slay his Indian foe, then the snake would live.

He knew that the *wasicu* did not live by the same code of ethics as did the Native man, so Spirit Bear made a show that his followers did agree and would abide by the word of their chief.

After swiftly relaying the belief of the *ska sunka* to his war party, a great shout of livid voices went up. They angrily made the motions that they would honor their chief's request. All knew, however, what the outcome of the confrontation would be. The white dog did not have a chance against the mighty spirit bear!

"Kait, yuh kin haf ma gun if'n yuh want it. Tha' way they cain't take yuh alive agin if'n yuh don' want. Yuh kin save that there bullet fer yerself," Jed tried to be somewhat gallant in the face of death.

Kaitlin slowly took the gun. She didn't have the courage to turn it on herself, but at least Jed would not have it to kill Spirit Bear. After grabbing the gun, she dashed away from his sweaty, dirty hands. She slowly pivoted to watch the interesting turn of events. She walked to her friend's side. *Nakpa Ihli* also was entranced. She'd never seen such savage yet dishonorable men before.

Woniya Mato gave his tomahawk, bow, and arrows to *Wawakte Towanjila*. Likewise, Sky Warrior bound Spirit Bear's hand to his side. He was only able to move his left hand. He did not want to give the white man any physical disadvantages. If the *wasicun* fought left handed, so would he.

The warriors formed a ring around the *ska sunka* and *Woniya Mato*. A knife similar to the chief's was thrown to Jed's feet. He picked it up.

Slowly, the two men began to circle each other. Brown eyes studied black and vice versa. Jed moved surprisingly well for his bulk, but Spirit Bear was an eagle in flight. This was his element; he wasn't war chief for nothing. He'd earned the right above many other worthy opponents.

Why didn't the filthy redskin attack? Jed was used to charges made by his foes. This man did nothing but nimbly move his body. *Was he trying to impress the others with his supple strength? Was he playing some kind of a game?* Jed was becoming angrier and agitated; it was his only defense against the fear plaguing him.

Spirit Bear watched the big *wasicun* go from fear to anger. This was not a good tactic. *Woniya Mato* had watched many men lose fights easily when they allowed the red demon to possess their control. Spirit Bear did not plan to ease the man's torture. He would not die quickly. He had much to pay for.

So the ska sunka waited for him to make the first move? So be it. With a harsh cry that stood the hair up on Jed's neck, the Indian surged forward. He nicked Jed's throat and danced back out of range when Jed slashed wildly toward the insult.

Again, *Woniya Mato* lunged. He nicked the other side of the white dog's throat and slashed his left shoulder. It wasn't deep, just enough to bring the fearful edge back into the blanket of rage. Spirit Bear wanted Jed to feel panic for a very long time; he wanted Jed to know he could have been dead twice so far had he chosen it.

"Why you!" roared the white man. "I will kill ya!!" and he charged, bellowing like a massive male bison.

Spirit Bear nimbly leaped aside. As the bull-like man passed, he kicked his side and punched his injured shoulder. Jed yelled in pain. Fear, anger, and pain fought for dominance in his body.

To goad his opponent, *Woniya Mato* laughed. His rich voice filled the air.

"*Mita ableza! Nita abuhingia kinyan!*" he said with humor.

His warriors' laughter joined his. They were enjoying the show. It was not often that their chief made a spectacle of another fighter. All present hated the swine that had abused and killed their women, and they loathed him for the abuse to the woman who now belonged to their prodigious chief! None would interfere, but they would watch and enjoy!

Time and time again, Jed attacked the big Indian. Every time he withdrew with more injuries. The chief, however, had none. The blacksmith, on the other hand, bled freely from many non-life threatening injuries. He'd been punched and kicked multiple times.

Normally, Jed had the upper hand. He didn't like being the mouse. If only he could turn the stakes! He was ready to do whatever it took!

The honor of the Indians would be null and void if he breeched the agreement made. Jed knew going in that it was a one-handed fight with a knife to the death. If any other tactic was used, the Indians would all attack him.

At this point, Jed didn't care. He just wanted to kill the hated foe in front of him. It was this man who caused him to tremble before him like he was a God. It was this man who had taken Kaitlin from him when he was going to make her his. It was this man who also stole his brother from his side.

This lone man was the only one to ever have the upper hand with Jed and live. Jed was not used to losing; he was desperate!

Woniya Mato noticed the change in the *wasicun*. Only the blind could not see that he looked wildly around for weapons with more range than the knife. His warriors had seen to it that the white dog did not have this option. Men without honor were not to be trusted.

The man called Jed did not lunge again, so Spirit Bear stalked forward. He inflicted more and more stab wounds on his opponent. Each became slightly deeper than the ones before it. He wanted Jed to feel his life flowing from his body and to experience the pain that accompanied it. He wanted retaliation for the women's and boy's life he had sacrificed.

This went on for hours. Jed's head dropped with fatigue, and blood covered him from head to toe, soaking into his clothes. His labored breathing filled the hour before dusk. The opposite was true for *Woniya Mato*; he didn't even look winded. He could've been walking in the prairie picking flowers for his mate from the looks of him.

Kaitlin could take it no longer. She didn't know why *Woniya Mato* tortured Jed so. Yes, he was evil and vile, but no man deserved this endless torture. Surely one such as Spirit Bear possessed such a thing as mercy! She came forward brazenly.

Nakpa Ihli must have sensed Kaitlin's intention. "*Hiya, Mazaska Zi Ista! Iyotaka!*" She grabbed a hold of her arm to prevent her interference.

Kaitlin was too distraught and pulled free. She marched forward and yelled, "*Hiya! Woniya Mato! Ayustankiya ye!*"

All eyes turned to Kaitlin. *Woniya Mato* said something rapidly to *Wawakte Towanjila*. The soft-hearted *winyan* could never understand what all the big *wasicun* had done and that he was only getting what he deserved. That is why women were not allowed to accompany war parties.

Spirit Bear understood her plea for him to stop. If the *ska sunka* had not committed such vile atrocities, he would've agreed that the *toka* had had enough, but he could not allow his *winyan,* a mere *wayaka* at that, to ever command the high chief!

Wawakte Towanjila immediately grasped Kaitlin in talons of steel. She struggled against him, but it was of no use. The warrior was made of iron. She could not pit her strength against his and hope to win.

Looking up into Sky Warrior's painted face, she saw admiration for her deed in his eyes. She also saw caution, for a *winyan* could not interfere. *Wawakte Towanjila* supported the leader fully, yet he could also understand the heart of the soft white girl. She did not understand their ways and was watching a man from her wooden village die a slow and agonizing death. She was forced to listen to his tortured screams of agony. It was too much to ask of any *winyan.*

Holding her body close to his stirred his senses. He longed for the white girl, and he also longed for the other slave. Both were very comely women. He would gladly offer protection to house them in his tipi; he could easily provide for both, and they seemed to get along well together. Maybe he could move *Woniya Mato* this time to hear and grant this request.

He knew *Woniya Mato* held *Mazaska Zi Ista* in high esteem, but it was possible that he might've lost interest after her attempt to escape his embraces. *How could any man tire of her, with her sweet smell and luscious shape? A man could hope, could he not?* He returned his attention to the uneven competition for life in front of him.

Kaitlin, however, couldn't bear to watch Jed's torture further. She studied the vibrant male who held her with a rock-hard grasp. He also radiated power. He was a powerful chief in the village of the Oglala, one step below *Woniya Mato*. In fact, Kaitlin recalled that he was the one who studied her face and walked around her soon after the arrival in the village.

He was like *Woniya Mato* in more ways than that. He also had the body born of a God. His skin was bronze but his was a darker shade than that of the chief's. He was very handsome as well, but Kaitlin still found Spirit Bear more becoming.

And the torture when on. Every time Jed's hoarse cry pierced the air, Kaitlin winced. She refused to look at the fight in front of her. She looked at the sky, the trees, anywhere but there. Once in a while, she would test the strength of the hands holding her, but the grip had not weakened. *Wawakte Towanjila*'s hands did not bite into her tender flesh, but neither did they allow for freedom of movement.

Kaitlin looked up just to see *Woniya Mato* inflict a deep wound on Jed's left arm. It gaped open and grisly bone slide gruesomely into sight. Jed screamed in horror and pain. Kaitlin's own miserable cry was lost in his. She sobbed and turned her face into the solid chest of *Wawakte Towanjila.*

"Please, make it stop," she sobbed. "Just make it stop!"

Wawakte Towanjila rather enjoyed watching the white dog die slowly at the fierce hands of Spirit Bear; it was not often one got to view such a supreme warrior fight in this way! Yet, he longed to comfort the fragile heart of the *winyan.* She should not be here. This was a man's domain. He saw that the other *wayaka* watched with an impassive face; she'd mastered the art of hiding her emotions.

Nakpa Ihli was able to watch. She never had seen anything of the sort! She breathed slowly and watched in awe. So this is how war was! She was glad to be a *winyan,* but she could relate to the treatment of the *wasicun. How many times had she been unable to protect herself against the heavy hand of Zuzeca Pazan?*

The difference between she and Golden Eyes was that *Nakpa Ihli* realized that *Woniya Mato* was a great-hearted man and a powerful leader who protected his people against evil. If he tortured the man, then it was for good reasons. Still, it was hard to watch for her; it brought back too many memories.

After eleven solid hours with no break for Jed, it finally ended. With an exhausted scream, it was over. *Woniya Mato* lifted Jed's head from his final resting place. With a war cry, he removed his scalp. He would present it to the families who still mourned for their lost daughters and son.

Kaitlin only caught a glimpse of the final ending to Jed's life. She shook and collapsed into *Wawakte Towanjila*'s waiting embrace. He could not stop himself from stroking her soft hair while she sobbed uncontrollably into his arms. He continued to hold her, wrapping her in arms of comfort as she lost herself in misery.

Why? She cried to herself. *Yes, Jed was evil, but did Woniya Mato have to desecrate his body? Did he have to torture him for grueling hours? Did he have to mock and play with his life so?* She knew that that was Jed's style, but she had not thought it to be Spirit Bear's!

Her picture of the chief's gentle nature and soft touch was shattered. She'd known he possessed a dominate side that wouldn't take no for an answer, but she wouldn't have thought the cruel side existed. *Until now.*

Gently, *Wawakte Towanjila* laid Kaitlin down and went to congratulate the mighty chief. He genuinely respected his leader and admired his prowess! He could only hope to be the fierce warrior that his *kola* was.

CHAPTER NINE

Return to Camp

After the many congratulations and pats on the back, *Woniya Mato* washed the blood of his foe from his body. He cleaned his weapons and immediately gathered all of his items of warfare. It was the first thing a warrior did every time a battle was fought. A man never knew when the next attack would come. It was necessary to be prepared.

Next, a fire was started. He and the others sat in front of the flames and chanted thanks to *Wakantanka*. Herbs were thrown into the flames, and fragrant smells radiated from the fire.

After the prayers of thanks were offered, *Woniya Mato* brought forth pemmican to eat. The two women sat on sleeping mats the men had generously shared for their comfort. They sat back from the fire and were separated from men, but they were close enough to prevent them from sulking off undetected.

Kaitlin had never eaten the popular traveling food. It was a roundish shape and contained pieces of meat, chokecherries, and was held together with paste-like glue. When Kaitlin bit into it, she discovered the white ingredient was fat.

Actually, the pemmican tasted delicious to her starving body. It was sweet with the cherries, had a hint of smoked meat, and was creamy in texture so that it melted in her mouth.

Kaitlin ate hers slowly, savoring the meal. She was so intimidated by *Woniya Mato* that she still couldn't look at him. Forever, she would see the glimpse of him holding up Jed's bloody head and issuing a cry of victory. Even worse, she could not repel the visualization of when the chief began sawing and detaching Jed's hair from his head. That image could never be forgotten, no matter how hard she tried or what she did!

In addition, *Woniya Mato* had not treated her as he had before she escaped from his village. He hadn't had a chance to really, but that idea didn't enter her head. She was now afraid of him. She wondered incessantly of what he planned for her punishment.

The look of dejection on *Nakpa Ihli*'s face said she was feeling similar worries. Her usual unreadable mask had slipped. Watching the demise of the white man had also affected her negatively. She was consumed with her return to *Zuzeca Pazan*. What he would do to her had to be similar of what *Woniya Mato* had done to the *wasicun*, she was sure!

The men, for the most part, ignored the presence of the women. They were not a part of men society, nor were they permitted to be. The women would be dealt with in good time. Now was the time for celebration.

Woniya Mato retrieved the ceremonial pipe for smoking. The men were in great spirits and boasted of how they'd so easily defeated the *wasicu*. They even had three fire sticks, two long ones and a short one to study. Lone Wolf would unravel the secret with Wonder Worker's help in the spirit domain.

Not only did they have a victory over the *wasicu*, but Lone Wolf and Sky Warrior had news to rejoice that involved Yellow Feather. He was a father again! He also received many hard slaps on the back.

Who could ask for victory better than that? The *ska sunka* had been defeated and had paid for his sins. A new baby boy was blessed into the village. *Wakantanka* had smiled upon them and was pleased.

Kaitlin and *Nakpa Ihli* were ready to retire for the night way before the men were. They could rest easier and for longer time periods, for they no longer had capture to fear. Kaitlin got up and went to the creek bed to drink and rinse her weary face.

She began to walk towards privacy so she could sleep the full night. If she didn't go before she slept, she awoke with the need. Then she did not feel as if she'd rested.

When she found a spot just far enough away to be out of the direct sight of the men, she relieved herself. She looked up after securing her undergarment into the black eyes of *Woniya Mato. Why was he here when she needed privacy? Didn't he have more important things to do like celebrate senseless slaughter?*

She shuddered under his gaze. She feared that he'd caught her to punish her away from the eyes of his men. She began to shake and looked down.

Had his victory over the ska sunka put this fear in her eyes? Spirit Bear grew angry every time he thought of her punishment under Jed's savage hands. *Did she not know that part of what he'd done was for her honor?*

Gently, he said, "*Uwa yo, Mazaska Zi Ista.*" Then he turned without touching her.

The bronze man could not bear to have her quiver with fear under his touch. Yet, he wanted her to be afraid. His reaction to her and of her response to him warred within him. The handsome warrior wanted her to have thoughts of passion and of desire when he was close to her, and yes, he admitted, he wanted her to fear. The leader did not want her to try to escape from him again.

Spirit Bear led her back to her sleeping mat and said, "*Iyunka. Istinma.*"

She knew she must lie down and sleep as he commanded. The captive watched his retreating back as he returned to the victory celebration. She sighed and rolled over.

Nakpa Ihli was already asleep. Kaitlin had seen *Wawakte Towanjila* giving her a drink from a *mniapahta*. Perhaps it was more willow bark tea or a sleeping aid. Lord knew she needed rest to help her body recover from the multitude of things it had suffered from!

Her body longed for sleep, but images of Jed's dead mutilated body kept creeping into her mind. It was a long night for Kaitlin. She knew that *Woniya Mato* came and stood over her before he lay down on the ground next to her. She feigned sleep.

The *wayaka* was surprised he didn't try to take his mat from her or to force her to share it with him. The distressed blonde knew he was still angry with her even though he didn't show it. Her desire to escape him was a slap to his arrogance, and pride was everything to a warrior!

Wawakte Towanjila came shortly after *Woniya Mato*. He crouched down and touched *Nakpa Ihli's* pale cheek. At least she had gained some color back, but she still had much to recover from. He placed a mild poultice on her lips and eye, but it was more like a mild wash to keep the swelling down; it would not irritate the sensitive tissues that sustained the injuries. Sky Warrior also lay on the ground beside her sleeping form.

Woniya Mato knew that *Mazaska Zi Ista* did not sleep. Her body was rigid although she attempted to relax it and feign sleep by forcing her breathing to slow and deepen; however, he knew better. A warrior's sixth sense was everything; without it, he didn't exist.

He longed to cradle her body to his and comfort her with soft words from his heart, but, as much as he hated to admit, she'd offended him. His love for her was strong yet he could not suppress his hurt. For that, he would treat her differently for a time. It would be just long enough so that she'd know what it was like to be treated more like a real slave.

He wouldn't be cruel, but all of her freedom would be taken. She would have a guard at all hours of the day, and he'd withdraw his tenderness from her. Still, he would not deny himself the pleasures of her body.

How could he? Even so, he realized that this was when the change in her occurred. She may not have run away if he'd waited to take her upon his return, but he could not. He had waited as long as he was physically able.

She was his and always would be. Having tasted her sweetness and knowing what she held in her heart, even the ways her eyes lit with discovery, he couldn't part with her now; not ever!

Finally, his *wayaka* slept. Frequently, she would whimper and cry out in terror. He even heard the words, "I'm sorry, Jed! So sorry…" before she'd roll over. He longed to comfort her, but unless she became extremely distraught, he would not.

The war party prepared for departure and let the women sleep while they gathered supplies. Gently, *Woniya Mato* and *Wawakte Towanjila* awoke the women. They drank, ate more pemmican, and were escorted to a more private location. Then the men rolled and secured the sleeping furs.

Once ready, *Wawakte Towanjila* lifted *Nakpa Ihli* onto his big grey stallion with a darkened mane, tail, and legs. *Woniya Mato* did likewise to Kaitlin. She trembled at his nearness.

The war party's cries pierced the air as they departed. Kaitlin was reminded of a pack of coyotes. As the horses began to gallop, she was thrown back against Spirit Bear's muscular form. He still didn't wear a shirt, and the gentle white could feel his muscles ripple under the supple doeskin dress, the only barrier between them. Immediately, she gasped and straightened her back.

Spirit Bear smiled at her shocked inhalation. His body had responded to her touch as hers obviously had to his. All was not bad in paradise. His *wayaka* longed to be in his arms as much as he longed for her to be there. *Mazaska Zi Ista* just wasn't ready to admit it.

As they rode, Kaitlin kept her back erect and straight. She leaned forward to avoid body contact as much as possible. She didn't want to make the chief angrier but couldn't handle his sheer male magnetism directly behind her.

The captive still quaked when she thought of what might await her upon the return to the village. The whole community had to be aware of what she attempted to do! If they weren't, they soon would be!

To save face, Kaitlin was sure she'd be punished. *What did they do to women?* She knew they attempted to give Jed a chance, but really, they just wanted to make it *look* like they gave the white man a chance; one he'd never had... the blonde was sure Spirit Bear knew it wasn't going to be a fair fight, but *Woniya Mato* didn't know that his life could have been taken by the flintlock; she did. That had scared the white woman more than she would ever admit.

As the day wore on, the enslaved girl couldn't help but lean back against her captor. His arm went possessively around her waist and rested on top of her thigh. A ripple of awareness mixed with fear overwhelmed her.

Kaitlin glanced down at his bronze arm. Even fairly relaxed, his muscles bulged. His embracing hand was strong and his fingers were lean. They tapered to rounded square tips. She'd watched them deliver ultimate pain, and the timid woman knew they could deliver supreme pleasure.

The *wayaka* shook her head. She would not think of that! It wasn't a union of consent! It was a joining of master and slave. She must never forget that! It was just hard to resist him because she found him so devastatingly handsome!

Woniya Mato smiled again as he saw Kaitlin shake her head in denial. She hadn't done so until he touched her. The eye-catching blonde wanted to refute their attraction for one another. Out of orneriness and wanting to teach her a lesson, he began to lightly caress the top of her thigh with his fingertips.

Mazaska Zi Ista froze and held her breath. He bent his head towards hers and whispered, "*Nimitawa ktelo.*" And she would be his: heart, mind, and body. It was a challenge. He'd never backed down from one before, and the warrior looked forward to victory once again.

The more her body rocked back against his, the more he wanted to take her. Pride was the only thing that saved them both. His *kolas* would never stop ribbing him. They'd say that a tiny yellow stone tamed the mighty spirit bear! No, he must remain cool and aloof.

He slowed his fingers on her shapely leg, for he was torturing himself more than he was her. *Woniya Mato* wondered if she'd felt the stirring of his manhood. Before he made himself more uncomfortable, the masculine male had to clear his mind of her.

How could he accomplish this with her so close? Her womanly curves were less than an arm's length away. And her scent… it wasn't as if she'd freshly bathed, but even the *winyan's* natural scent to him was stirring.

Interrupting his thoughts, *Wawakte Towanjila* called to Spirit Bear. "*Woniya Mato, Nakpa Ihli* needs to rest."

Glad for an excuse to ease his mind and body from the thoughts of taking pleasure with Kaitlin, Spirit Bear gestured with a light touch to *Runs with the Wind* to stop. He ran his hands up the sides of his captive's waist and under her arms to assist her from the heights of his stallion. The subdued *wayaka* gasped and flushed when his fingers lightly touched the sides of her breasts.

The white woman's legs nearly buckled when she reached the ground. The exercise she'd imposed on herself lately, the lack of sleep, and the riding for hours had zapped their strength momentarily. Still, the blonde managed to upright herself before *Woniya Mato* could assist her.

Kaitlin immediately went to *Nakpa Ihli'* s side. She'd been gently lowered to the ground from the back of *Wawakte Towanjila*'s grey stallion. The white girl was grateful for his tender treatment of her friend.

The women walked to a shady spot. The two chieftains unrolled the sleeping mats and allowed the women to recline upon them. Almost immediately, *Nakpa Ihli* fell asleep after drinking more of the willow bark tea.

Woniya Mato mixed up a paste and gingerly patted it onto the sleeping woman's injuries. He muttered under his breath something about *Zuzeca Pazan*. His friend, *Wawakte Towanjila*, hung by his side as he doctored the Indian woman.

The two men walked a short way from Kaitlin, speaking in quiet, low tones. The blonde probably couldn't understand what they were saying, but she strained her ears trying to hear anyway. *Were they speaking about the captives' attempt at escape and what punishments to enforce, or were they speaking of the injuries Nakpa Ihli had sustained at the hands of Zuzeca Pazan?*

The white was so full of anxiety that she almost could not will herself to relax. Without knowing it, her body began to weave with weariness while her eyes remained open. The last thing she remembered was *Woniya Mato* striding over to her and commanding her to lie down with a strict "*Iyunka*!"

When the golden beauty awoke, she was back on the horse in *Woniya Mato* supporting arms. She couldn't believe she'd slept that hard! Kaitlin had been moved off the sleeping mat, the mat had been rolled up, and then she'd been lifted on the great overo's back, all while she slept? That was crazy!

She was already uncomfortable. The captive needed to relieve herself. She was hungry, thirsty, and felt like she could sleep forever. Kaitlin tried to hold her discomfort to herself. That's what *Nakpa Ihli* would do!

Looking about, the white girl spied her friend. Ear Sore was still sleeping. The chiefs must be magic! Maybe the tender way *Wawakte Towanjila* held her was a good sign. *Nakpa Ihli* had enough worries in her life. A new home would be the best thing for her!

The Pawnee girl would have a handsome chieftain warrior to protect her from that nasty little man who lived to inflict misery on women! *Oh, please, God! Help my friend! Don't let her go back to his cruelty!* Kaitlin didn't realize it, but as she prayed, golden eyes stared at her friend and the man supporting her.

Wawakte Towanjila sensed her vision upon them and turned suddenly to look directly into Kaitlin's eyes. He smiled knowingly as he acknowledged her gaze and the possibilities it held. Flushing furiously, she quickly averted her assessment. *Woniya Mato*'s grip on her tightened possessively.

Was *Mazaska Zi Ista* looking for *Nakpa Ihli*, or was she admiring *Wawakte Towanjila*? *Woniya Mato* did not like the feelings of jealousy that rose up suddenly within him. If it was for her friend, the chief was fine with that, but if it was the man she sought, Spirit Bear would never let that happen. Taking a calming breath, he knew how to come up with a solution: First, he would watch more closely. He'd determine whether his *wayaka*'s interest was in her friend or his spirit brother.

Woniya Mato knew he could trust his fellow chieftain. A *winyan* could never tear them apart. They were brothers from as far back as he could remember. He'd just have to make it very clear to his *kola* that he wouldn't be the one to comfort her, even if she chose it! Kaitlin could have all the *winyan* friends she wanted, but men were another story!

Spirit Bear couldn't believe the change that had overcome him since he's first taken possession of the *ska wayaka*! Never would he have been jealous of his spirit brothers! Never would he have cared if a *winyan* preferred another over him! What came with the girl with golden eyes were feelings the leader had never experienced before.

What made the golden girl so different from the others? The handsome chieftain had many women throwing themselves at him! Many not-so-subtle suggestions were made for matrimonial arrangements to be prepared with selected daughters from home and neighboring villages. Parents did this with prompting from their offspring!

Several years back, when an experienced woman approach him with goodies, he'd tasted. He'd even taken, but the attractive warrior had been careful. He didn't want to be trapped into a marriage that he'd hate. None had tempted the chief in the slightest.

What was so mesmerizing about the white girl that made Spirit Bear determined to possess her fully? Was it because she didn't throw herself at him? He didn't think so. He knew the golden one was attracted to him. *Was it the language barrier?* Again, the bronzed man rejected that thought. He enjoyed a woman with a good brain and the conversations that came with them.

If it wasn't that Mazaska Zi Ista didn't throw herself at him and couldn't talk to him, why in the wild dogs did he have to own her heart and soul? He couldn't single out one thing; he'd found many.

The white woman's looks made him go wild. Her hair and eyes were unusual and beautiful, not to mention her incredible figure! The innocent girl's spirit was admirable, and her work ethic and enthusiasm for life were contagious. No, Spirit Bear couldn't single out just one mere reason why he was enamored with her. He could never let her go or his spirit would disappear.

Mazaska Zi Ista's tapping on his shoulder had him looking down into her wide-eyed face. She tentatively asked him if he would stop so she could have privacy. He shouted a word to the others and wheeled his horse toward nearby woods.

The golden-eyed girl was abhorred. Her captor dismounted and even walked with her! He knew she couldn't outrun him! Why did the war chief insist on accompanying her into the wooded area? Kaitlin was easily embarrassed as it was, but she saw the look of determination on his face: he wasn't leaving.

Blushing again, the shy girl gritted her teeth in anger. She needed to relieve herself, but it was so humiliating to have a man standing five feet away during the process!

Golden Eyes walked out without looking at him. She marched back towards his stallion and waited for him to help her onto the animal's back. Before the chief lifted her, he passed a *mniapahta* to her. If she hadn't been so thirsty, Kaitlin would have been tempted to reject his offer; however, she couldn't; she drank a lot.

After lifting her curvy frame back onto *Runs with the Wind*, Spirit Bear handed her more pemmican. She loved it! The white girl didn't think she could grow tired of the nutritious meal even if she consumed it daily. Kaitlin savored it as they traveled once more.

Finally, the sun went down on the first full day of nonstop travel, and the warriors stopped for the night. The same sleeping arrangements were made for Golden Eyes and Sore Ear. They got the sleeping skins and the men lay close by them on the ground.

The next two days of travel were much the same. The trek seemed to be nonstop with breaks at noon. *Nakpa Ihli*'s injuries were treated morning and night, and she was given plenty of water and willow bark tea to aid in her pain. If the Pawnee girl needed to rest more, a small extra break was provided.

The party continued to eat pemmican and sleep in the same arrangements. When the men conversed, they unceasingly spoke good-naturedly and patted each other's back in renewed victory. By noon the next day, they would reach the Oglala village.

The night before they were to reach their destination, Kaitlin couldn't rest. By the next day, she was sure she'd know pain and fear at the hand of *Woniya Mato*. Her anxiety levels were sky rocketing, and she was a tight ball of nerves. The recaptured slave was so fearful she quaked.

On top of that, the white girl noticed Spirit Bear watching her every move. If she looked to the left, he looked to see what and who she gazed at. If she walked to water to splash it on her face or dip her feet into it, he accompanied her. If Kaitlin needed to have privacy, she was denied that as well. Was he so determined to punish her that he couldn't allow her a little decency? It terrified her.

At least he slept somewhat apart from her. No sooner than the honey-skinned woman lived through her relief, she'd question why. *Was he trying to distance himself from her because he was about to kill her?* He hadn't been treating her same. After the first day of travel, he'd become even more cool and distant. It appeared to her that it was related to the approaching village: her death warrant.

"What is wrong with the *ska winyan,* my *kola*?" asked *Wawakte Towanjila*. "She weeps when she thinks no eyes are upon her."

"My guess is that *Mazaska Zi Ista* knows she is a slave and is now facing the knowledge she must come to me. She had no power to deny anything I wish," *Woniya Mato* replied.

"Have you grown tired of her? If you wish to send the *winyan* away after she tried to leave…" he paused then smiled, "my offer still stands. I will give you many fine things."

"No, my *kola*. I have not grown tired of her. Nor shall I." *Woniya Mato* struggled to remain impassive as the hand of jealously squeezed his heart.

"I want to ask you of the plans for *Nakpa Ihli*. You cannot send her back to *Zuzeca Pazan* before the council meets!"

Steeling his heart against his negative emotions, *Woniya Mato* pushed the possessiveness he was so unaccustomed to away. Then he answered, "No, I will not do that. What do you suggest?" he asked with a knowing smile.

"I would love to protect her and share my home with her. I would trade for the *wayaka*. She is a good *winyan*. She cannot be returned to the snake that strikes!"

"No, my friend, I will not do that. I think that it would be best that she stays with *Wawat'ecaka* until the council meeting. Then she will be yours. Let us meet to discuss the repercussions of what *Zuzeca Pazan* has done to her. I do not believe he deserves any trade for the *wayaka*. He lost the privilege by his own hand."

The men smiled in agreement and in camaraderie. Then they sat and smoked before retiring for the night.

Kaitlin knew he'd leave her alone as he had, thankfully, along the traveled path. Still, she silently wept with fear, for she'd understood snatches of conversation about the coming village celebration in one day. When the sun shone on the new day, was it to be her last? The captive was petrified about them publicly shaming her. *Would he whip her for all to see? Would he kill her with knife nicks as he had Jed?* Not knowing was almost worse than what she was sure to face!

When *Woniya Mato* lay down, Kaitlin still hadn't convinced her mind to rest. Tears continued to leak from her eyes. If only she had a friend to talk to. Yes, *Nakpa Ihli* was with her, and the blonde did consider her a friend, but she hadn't mastered enough of the language to really converse. Besides, *Nakpa Ihli* slept much as she healed.

Finally, Kaitlin cried herself to sleep. She had a horrid dream almost immediately:

Kaitlin was brought before the tribe during the celebration. All the Indians formed a circle around her. Woniya Mato was waiting for her, dressed as he had been on the day he'd slaughtered Jed.

The mighty chieftain stood before the waiting crowd with a huge bull whip in his hand. He ripped her clothes off for all to witness her nudity. Then the leader began to strike her. The whip bit her flesh deeply. Blood oozed and ran down her arm. He'd struck her in the same spot she'd seen the bone on

Jed's arm. She looked down, and her arm looked as grizzly as Jed's had.

Kaitlin screamed and tried to run as the whip bit her again. The laughing crowed pushed her back from their midst. Once more, the whip cracked. Again and again, deep wounds were inflicted on her body.

Finally, when the white girl was blood incrusted and exhausted, Woniya Mato lay on top of her as if to have sex with her in front of the crowd. He held a knife in his hand so that upon his completion, her final degradation would be complete: he'd remove her hair for all to see. The white girl screamed and screamed, locked in the nightmare.

Kaitlin felt his weight on top of her, and she fought madly. She would not be raped in front of the crowd if she could help it! At the very least, the golden-haired beauty wouldn't submit without a fight! The white girl twisted and turned wildly, pushing, pinching, scratching, and hitting. She continued to shriek in terror.

Woniya Mato didn't sleep. He was pumped to return to the village and concerned for *Mazaska Zi Ista*. His thoughts and worries jumbled together. He never slept during an outing anyway, but he usually was able to relax his rigid muscles.

Was his golden one so distraught over her recapture and what awaited her that she cried nonstop when his she thought none could see? What could he do to help her but not erase her fear of him? He wanted the *wayaka* to feel safe under his protection, but he also wanted her to fear him so his captive would not be so foolish as to run again.

Soon after she'd fallen asleep, the fair-skinned girl began writhing on her mat. Kaitlin twisted and turned and began to scream. Her legs jerked as if running.

Spirit Bear used his body to restrain her. In her sleep, the blonde fought him frantically. She even tried to bite him. The war chief lay on top of her to stop her flaying limbs, and he placed his hands on either side of her face to keep her from injuring herself or him. Quietly, the bronzed man spoke her name.

Tear streaked and eyes of misery opened to his ebony ones. Kaitlin knew what happened when he lay on top of her, and she began to shake her head.

"No… No… No… NO! *Hiya*! Not in front of the crowd, *Woniya Mato*! Take me to your tipi. I won't run away again! I swear it! If you must kill me, kill me before you rip my hair off!"

Woniya Mato did not understand her words, but he did comprehend her sheer terror. Her dream must be a flashback to what she'd witnessed. Sadly, he wished the *winyan* had not had to behold that. Women were not mentally strong in that area as men were. The striking warrior tried to comfort her.

"*Mazaska Zi Ista. Woniya Mato hiya wozan.*" He stroked her hair as he softly spoke. He kept saying words of comfort while he caressed her. It finally had a calming effect. His *wayaka* ceased her struggling and screaming. Golden orbs just stared into the hypnotic depths of his eyes.

Why was he being so kind to her? Why had he soothed the nightmare away? It had been so real! Doesn't he want me to fear what will happen to me? she pondered.

After the calm came the adrenaline rush. Kaitlin began to shake with fear of the dream and dread of her immediate future.

Woniya Mato rolled to his side and continued to stroke her hair in a reassuring manner. He held the blonde close in his comforting arms until she stopped trembling. Finally, she slept. This time, there were no dreams.

In the morning, Kaitlin awoke still locked in his warm embrace. The curvaceous woman shuddered as she recalled the dream. His scent and arms consoled her, and the captive was able to calm herself. Today was the day she'd find out her punishment. Maybe it wouldn't be as bad as imagined. *He'd comforted her, hadn't he?*

The *wayaka* didn't want to awaken the mighty warrior. She studied his handsome face. He was not so fearsome when he didn't have on the paint.

Kaitlin loved the perfection of him. His form was shaped directly from the hands of Gods. The blonde was mesmerized by his full lips; she remembered the magic they could work.

Traveling down, her eyes took in his masculine jaw line and the curve of his neck. Veins twisted under his skin in a very artistic way. They advertised good health and manly attraction on a physically fit athlete. It also spoke of strength and prowess. Continuing their scrutiny, her eyes admired his defined arms and muscled chest.

His eight-pack was visible on his abdomen as he breathed. The young woman's curious eyes traveled below his navel. He wore only a breech cloth; under it she could see that his hips were small and powerful, leading to the muscular legs that could move with the grace of a panther. His quads lined his skin clearly. He was a powerful masterpiece.

As she viewed his gorgeous body, Kaitlin's breath quickened. She recalled what he could do to her. *No, she must not think about that.*

She ripped her vision away from his body and into his knowing eyes. *How long had he watched her study him?* The innocent flushed immediately and tried to move away. Strong arms tightened the embrace and held her close in the brisk morning air.

It warmed *Woniya Mato's* heart to see he could stir desire in her without making the first move. His captive may feel mentally down about her recapture, but he knew she wanted him! It helped his ego that had doubted her feelings the day before.

Others in the camp began to rouse. The chief released her and began to prepare for the final leg of the trip. Had it just been warriors, they'd have finished the ride in the night, but they'd rested for the women. Yellow Feather had ridden ahead, anxious to see his new child and wife.

Weapons and supplies were packed quickly. The Indians mounted their steeds and galloped toward home. Again, the victory cry issued forth from each and every warrior. It was an eerie sound that had Kaitlin nestling closer to her handsome captor.

In late morning the band rode into the village. The great mob of people expected them, thanks to Yellow Feather. They swarmed around them and many greeted them and spoke at once. A few curious looks were directed toward the women.

The men dismounted and pubescent boys led their horses away to care for them immediately. The warriors spoke to family members and friends, all greeting the other in happy disarray. Already, many came up to *Woniya Mato* to congratulate him on his prowess over the *ska sunka*.

Woniya Mato made the announcement with the three other leaders that there would be a great celebration that night; it was expected. Roasting meats and vegetable smells already permeated the village. It made one and all hungry to smell such succulent aromas. They would be ready to feast with the celebration!

When the commotion died down, *Woniya Mato* led Kaitlin to their tipi. *Wawakankan* followed them. Upon entrance, he looked down dejectedly.

"My great chief, I have shamed you," he spoke with raw despair in his voice.

"No, my *kola*, you did not. *Mazaska Zi Ista* is the one who betrayed my trust."

"I am the man. She is but a mere *winyan wayaka*. She had just discovered she was a slave and had been left alone in the village for the first time. The spirits told me to watch her, along with your advice. I have failed you."

"Speak no more of this nonexistent insult. You saved the life of a woman and child. I believe that is more important than watching over the child-like behavior of a slave. No harm is done; she has been returned to me."

"Thank you, Spirit Bear."

"Speak no more of it. How is *Nakpa Ihli*? Have you had a chance to look over her yet?"

"*Tos. Wawakte Towanjila* brought her to me right away. She is resting now with the sleeping aid. The girl will still be able to bear children. She is lucky. I am told that *Zuzeca Pazan* is responsible for this?"

"I am afraid so."

"We will meet before the celebration to discuss this?"

"*Tos*. As soon as I secure my," he paused, "other problem." Both men's eyes went to the golden woman.

Kaitlin sat looking out the entrance flap at the beautiful scenery. She longed to be as free as the people who lived in the village, but she never would with slave status. The blonde watched the villager's flurry of movement.

She sighed, sending a flicker of sunlight dancing down her silky curls. Her shapely silhouette was perfectly outlined against the backdrop of brilliance. The *wayaka's* face no longer was marred by bruising. Her complexion was kissed by *wi*; the golden tint only accentuated her beauty. It brought forth the tawny sheen in her eyes.

Both men could only stare for a moment at her breathtaking beauty. She was a goddess given to their chief.

"What are your plans for her, *Woniya Mato*? She is too delicate of heart to bear much pain."

"I will not whip her or hurt her physically. She will have a guard placed on her at all times. She will not like this, but until she truly earns my trust, she will be watched." Spirit Bear sipped water then went on, "*Mazaska Zi Ista* will be brought before the council this night. We will decide if she deserved public shaming or if taking away all her dignity and pride will be enough. She will serve me in all ways."

"I am glad to hear your heart forgives her, my chief." Wonder Worker knew it was a light sentence for the crime the girl had committed.

"I forgive but do not forget. She has hurt me. I will hold my heart back from her for a while."

Concerned for the beauty's emotional state, *Wawakankan* asked, "Will she be allowed the company of others?"

"*Tos*. She may continue working and learning with the women, but she will be shadowed. If you will stay here to guard her, I will approach Young Elk to see if he will honor me. Some young men would look at it as a punishment, but he will not. He will take it how I mean it and do a good job. I will recommend to the council that in one cycle of the moon, he be admitted into the *Cante Tinza,* our own branch of the Oglala Brave Hearts Society for warriors. He has earned this right! Young Elk is an exceptional young warrior with outstanding promise!

Wawakankan was once again impressed with the honor and mind of the great chief before him. Not only was he kind, but he was fair. "This camp is fortunate to have you as chief, my *kola*."

With mutual slaps on the other's back, *Woniya Mato* left to find Young Elk.

CHAPTER TEN

Tribal Council

Kaitlin wondered about her fate. *When would he tell her? Would it be like her dream and the answer would come tonight at the celebration?*

She could tell with all the flurry of movement within the village that a great feast was going to happen. *Why wouldn't they celebrate?* They killed many white men and tortured Jed. They might have a lot of entertainment with what they planned for her!

Wawakankan was drawn to Golden Eyes. He knew she anticipated punishment and had no idea what to expect. He'd heard in great detail from *Wawakte Towanjila* about the great power and warrior's skills *Woniya Mato* held over the *toga*, but he'd also confided that he was concerned about the women viewing such a gruesome ordeal.

Golden Eyes seemed very shaken and remorseful. Her vibrations were ones of uncertainty and fear. *Who could blame her? Wawakankan* wanted to comfort her, but part of him was still upset for her taking advantage of that situation. She'd caused him to lose some of his power as a man. Now he'd have to earn it back.

Wawat'ecaka entered *Woniya Mato*'s tipi. She had smoked roast from a deer; *aguyapi* made with wild onions, garlic, and the salt solution; and *tinpsila*, sweet prairie turnips. This she'd prepared for the feast, but there was plenty to serve for the mid-day meal.

Wawat'ecaka smiled at Kaitlin. The older woman wanted the chief's slave to know she held no anger. *Who's to say what she would do if she were a slave? She'd have tried to escape as well.*

Woniya Mato arrived at the tipi. He was followed by a young man about fifteen winters old. The three males sat and were served the meal by *Wawat'ecaka*. Kaitlin continued to watch the hustle and bustle in the village. She didn't know what was expected of her at this time.

When the men finished, *Wawat'ecaka* softly called to Kaitlin and motioned to the food. Kaitlin didn't think she could eat due to the lump caused by the anxiety in her throat. She shook her head and motioned that she didn't feel well.

The blonde didn't think the men paid any attention to her until she heard *Woniya Mato's* command. He was suddenly behind her.

"*Uwa yo, Mazaska Zi Ista.*" He led her to the place by *Wawat'ecaka* and said, "*Iyotaka. Wate.*"

She'd heard the command to sit many times, but she was unsure of what else she was supposed to do. *Woniya Mato* continued to stand behind her, waiting. She looked up questioningly at him.

"*Wate,*" he said patiently. Out of the corner of her eye, she saw *Wawat'ecaka* come to her rescue; she subtly made eating motions.

To appease him, the slave picked up the succulent bread and nibbled at it. It seemed to satisfy the chief, for he resumed his seat with the other men. When she stopped nibbling, Kaitlin could see the chieftain make eye contact with her until she chewed some more.

"She seems obedient enough," Young Elk said as a compliment.

"Not well enough. That is why you are here. She does well when watched, but as you might have heard, she took advantage of my absence and left. For this, I cannot trust her. I need you to watch her and make sure she does not get into more trouble."

"Thank you for trusting me with your valuable property," he replied with a smile. Even the young man could see the value of the chief's slave. He would die for her if the need called for it.

"I do. That is why you were chosen. You have bravery and cunning beyond your years."

Ojilaka Hehaka smiled at the compliment. For the mighty bear to praise one not yet invited into warrior society was a supreme compliment. He nodded once.

"She has eaten enough to satisfy me. We need to hold council before the celebration this night. We have important matters to discuss."

Young Elk nodded once more to show he now considered himself on the clock.

"I want you to watch her everywhere she goes. If she must visit the Place of Privacy or needs to take a bath, you come to me if I'm available. I will escort her to those places. If I am not around, turn your back for a few moments while she takes care of her business, but that is all. If she is not done in that time, you will embarrass her to make a point. She can wait to bathe until I am able to accommodate her."

"Tos, my chief. I understand."

"Now I will introduce you to my *wayaka*."

"Mazaska Zi Ista, Uwa yo."

Kaitlin obediently got up and came to him. He stood her in front of Young Elk.

"Ojilaka Hehaka, Mazaska Zi Ista." He likewise introduced the names in reverse order. *Ojilaka Hehaka* met Kaitlin's eyes and nodded his head in acknowledgement. She was even more beautiful close up.

Kaitlin studied the young man with curiosity. *Who was he? Why did Woniya Mato introduce her to him?* The youth was fairly big, a head taller than she. He already displayed the masculine build that was typical of warriors of the village. His voice had previously deepened.

After the introduction, *Woniya Mato* prepared for the meeting at the ceremonial lodge. He did not paint his face yet; that would come later. He did, however, place the chieftain's bonnet on his head and grab the ceremonial staff. He ducked out of the tipi with a parting farewell to the both of them.

Oh, now she got it. She, who was eighteen, was to be babysat by a fifteen-year old! It was unbelievable! It wasn't that Kaitlin had anything against the youth; it was just the audacity of the insult that got under her skin.

Then the other implication of what she might need a babysitter for hit her. Maybe they didn't want her to escape her punishment. *Was that why she needed to be watched? Was the event to take place so dreadful that she needed a guard to ensure that she would be there to endure it?*

The four chieftains were present in the lodge. Incense burned over the open fire pit to encourage and invite spirits to attend. The four leaders represented the four directions. Four was a sacred number to the Oglala.

The leaders smoked the peace pipe. After visiting and retelling the events of the recent victories of the new baby, the return of the *wayaka*, and the defeat of the *wasicu*, they were ready to get down to more serious matters.

The men began discussing the slaves. *Mazaska Zi Ista* was the first on to be discussed. *Woniya Mato* was the one who had been wronged, yet oddly enough, he was also the one to defend her. The primary chieftain told of what she'd done and of how she'd been treated. The men listened with open ears and eyes to what their leader said, but they also listened to what their chief didn't say about the *winyan* who had so obviously won his heart.

When he'd finished with his version of events, *Woniya Mato* called *Wawakankan* forth to tell his side of the story. Wonder Worker revealed that he'd been told by the spirits that the golden-eyed slave would attempt escape. With a slight warning look for the high chief, he didn't mention his own shame in the matter.

After the medicine man relayed how the white slave had stolen away during the time both he and *Wawat'ecaka* had saved the new mother and son's lives, he added his own interpretation which bared much weight. *Wawakankan* spoke of how the *wasicu* and any slave, for that matter, view freedom. He spoke of how any might feel if that liberty was taken. The shaman brought up the point that it was difficult for men to relate to this. They were killed honorably where women were possessed and forced to do many things against their will.

Next, *Woniya Mato* resumed the floor and told of how Golden Eyes would be treated from this day forth until a future council meeting made other determinations. She'd basically be treated the same but with absolutely no privacy. He spoke of how the youth, *Ojilaka Hehaka*, had agreed to watch over the *wayaka*.

Spirit Bear justified why he felt like this was an appropriate punishment. He spoke of her courage and her determination and of her pride and willingness to learn new things. The fair-skinned captive always appeared to try her best. Love of life sparkled in her eyes. However, the punishment imposed would be adequate for privacy meant everything to *wasicu* culture. It truly would chastise her to have it removed.

The three other tribal members knew all of what had been stated was true because all were friends with the chieftain. They'd spoken many times of the *wasicu* and of *Mazaska Zi Ista*. They'd witnessed for themselves her sweet nature and innocence. They also agreed that this punishment was enough.

All present believed that she was a gift from *Wakantanka* because never before had their chief held interest in a woman over a night or two. They could all see for themselves what a precious flower had blossomed within their midst; they would not crush her.

Tribal custom often called for witnesses to be brought forth before a final decision was made. Therefore, *Woniya Mato* called another youth who often served as messenger to the council. Jack Rabbit was asked to have *Wawat'ecaka, Unjinjintka Can Koica,* and even *Nakpa Ihli* brought before them for this purpose.

Quick as a flash, Jack Rabbit was gone. The men spoke of other matters and smoked the peace pipe until one of the witnesses appeared. *Wawat'ecaka* was the first to arrive.

"*Wawat'ecaka*, thank you for blessing us with your attendance. Do you know why we've sought your presence at this council?"

"*Tos*, my chief. You wish to hear of the girl, *Mazaska Zi Ista*." The council men nodded confirmation.

Wawat'ecaka took a deep breath and began. She told of the way that the girl learned. After attempting something once or twice, she usually mastered the chore. From that point forward, she only honed her skill.

She told of her never ceasing chatter when she wanted to learn something new. *Wawat'ecaka* even bragged that the girl was so bright that she'd taken her under her wing to show her the famous tanning technique. At this announcement, the ceremonial lodge was quiet with the honor *Wawat'ecaka* had bestowed on the girl.

When Gentle Rabbit finished, they thanked her for her time. *Woniya Mato* escorted her to the entrance. Quietly, he asked *Wawat'ecaka* to prepare the girl for her hearing. He asked his motherly figure to dress the golden girl appropriately.

Next, *Unjinjintka Can Koica* entered. Her eyes held Lone Wolf's for a moment longer than necessary. She looked down to cover her colored cheeks.

"*Unjinjintka Can Koica*, thank you for blessing us with your attendance. Do you know why we have sought your presence at this council?"

"I believe you wish to hear about *Mazaska Zi Ista*."

Again, the men nodded.

Desert Rose told of Golden Eyes' mastery of basket weaving. She revealed that it took great skill to already be weaving waterproof baskets so quickly. *Unjinjintka Can Koica* also spoke of the *wayaka's* quick grasp of the difficult Lakota language.

"Of course, she can only talk to you about baskets, women chores, and that she can't touch men's weapons," Desert Rose joked. The men graced her with laughter.

"Thank you for your input." *Isnala Sungmanitu* got up to escort the basket-weaver out. When they escaped from the lodge, Lone Wolf appeared nervous. He acted as though he wanted to ask her something.

Unjinjintka Can Koica waited, for she hoped she might know what he sought. Finally, *Isnala Sungmanitu* asked her if she would honor his presence at the celebration. He received a blushing, "*Tos!*"

The final witness, *Nakpa Ihli,* was called into the lodge. They thanked her for coming. Her testimony was needed for two purposes: she would need to tell her side of the escape adventure, and she would also have to tell embarrassing personal information about *Zuzeca Pazan.*

Nakpa Ihli began by answering questions about Snake Strike's treatment of her. They asked about her beatings, vicious rapes, and other injuries. Shamefully, the Pawnee captive answered any and all questions.

The men were silent and tight-lipped throughout her revelations. It was much worse than they'd ever expected! They were ashamed that she'd had to endure so much!

Next, they gently asked *Nakpa Ihli* to recall the night of her escape. They asked for every detail. She began the sordid account.

Ear Sore told of being ill from the new life that had taken a hold in her body. She knew that any excuse to beat her would be utilized by *Zuzeca Pazan*, so she'd hidden the truth from him.

When he caught her secretly bathing her face and refilling the *mniapahta* late that night, she knew his mood. The *wayaka* knew she was going to get beaten no matter what, so she chanced the fact that he might have mercy on her if he knew she carried his child. Snake Strike had called her a whore and questioned who the father of the baby was.

He first brutally raped her, beat her, and kicked her twice extremely hard in her abdomen. He'd even held her head under water for over a minute. The abused woman believed he'd been trying to nearly kill her so that she would abort the baby; and she had.

Ear Sore spoke of Kaitlin reviving her shattered soul. She'd withdrawn into herself to avoid Snake Strake's viciousness. Kaitlin had brought her out of her shell. Then the pretty white and she made good on their escape.

The council thanked *Nakpa Ihli* for her honest account of the events and sent her back to *Wawat'ecaka*'s tipi. They closed the entrance flap and sat to discuss.

The men were impressed with the impact *Mazaska Zi Ista* had made on those she'd touched. They too had been moved by her special qualities.

Three of the four of the men wanted her for themselves.
A decision had been made; they would accept *Woniya Mato*'s suggested punishment as appropriate; she wouldn't be publically shamed.

Jack Rabbit was sent for Golden Eyes. Five minutes later, she stood trembling before the tribal council. The flap was sealed behind her. The challenge would be for the council to make her understand her consequences.

Kaitlin shook and quaked in front of the four men she found extremely intimidating together. As she awaited her death sentence, the men just stared at her for long moments. Her knees began knocking together.

If it were possible for *Mazaska Zi Ista* to be more radiant than she ever had, she'd accomplished it. The fawn color of the dress clung to her curves like a glove. Turquoise and amber beads were alternated along the hem, bodice, and collar of the garment. The V-shaped neckline dipped low enough to hint at Kaitlin's cleavage.

Blue and yellow dyed quills were woven in intricate patterns accented by more beads across the skirt and bodice of the dress. The light fringe on the hemline rustled softly when she walked. The border tickled her mid-thigh area. Beneath it, shapely golden legs were revealed. Her small feet were encased in matching moccasins. It was finery fit for a bride!

The *wayaka* flushed profusely and looked down, waiting for the judgment from the men before her. *Was what they had to say so terrible that they couldn't find the words?* She trembled as dreaded anxiety pulsed through her.

Finally, the masculine voice she knew so well spoke. "*Mazaska Zi Ista, wayaka ska winyan Winayo Mato.*"

So far she acknowledged her status of a white slave woman who belonged to Spirit Bear. Then his words began to run together. The blonde had no idea what he said. She looked down as tears welled in her eyes. *She would not cry, she told herself; she would not cry!* She would be brave as she faced death… courageous, unless her nightmare came to pass.

Spirit Bear did not begin with the formal council address. He knew Golden Eyes had not mastered the difficult Lakota language well enough to understand those words. He knew he'd lost her after announcing that the white slave named Golden Eyes remained his property. She shuddered before him in submissive acceptance. The white girl recognized whatever fate he dealt her.

Did she cry? Did she not know he was showing her mercy? He didn't think so. *Woniya Mato* rose and stood before her. Then he hooked his finger under her chin and gently forced her head up. Tenderly, the warrior wiped the moisture from her eyes. He cared not that the rest of the council, his spirit brothers, watched.

"*Mazaska Zi Ista*," he said and captured her attention so that it did not waiver. He signed to her that she would not die. Her punishment had already been given to her. The *wayaka* was to continue her life as she knew it with the escort of *Ojilaka Hehaka* or himself. She'd continue to have privileges as long as the *ska winyan* was escorted. She was not to go anywhere without one or the other of them. If she did, more severe consequences would be given. Then he asked Kaitlin in Oglala if she understood. She blindly nodded.

Could it be true? She wasn't going to die today? She was not going to be publicly humiliated? Oh, thank God! Kaitlin felt her knees weaken and give way.

Woniya Mato didn't realize she'd thought she'd die by his hand this day! How could he have let her believe that? His *Wastelaka* was so scared that she fainted into his arms with relief when she discovered she'd live!

He whispered apologies into her ear and held her beautiful body close to his. On this day, *Mazaska Zi Ista* was truly magnificent in her exquisite dress. He beamed with pride.

He turned to his council members and called over his shoulder, "I will return in a few moments." *Woniya Mato* planned on carrying his fragile flower back to his tipi.

"Remember it only takes five minutes to return to us," his tribal brothers responded and laughter followed him.

He grinned and shook his head at how his comrades tried to goad him.

Kaitlin quickly revived and was oblivious to the counsel's joking as she wept with relief. *The fair one couldn't believe they'd spared her! They'd really spared her!* She clutched at *Woniya Mato*'s strong shoulders and nestled her tear streaked face into the place his neck and collar bone met.

If Spirit Bear's heart hadn't been hers before that moment, it was now. She was so right, so good. Young Elk awaited their return. The war chief placed Kaitlin on the sleeping runs. He told her to rest while he returned to his council meeting. The most unpleasant part was about to begin.

When *Woniya Mato* returned to the ceremonial lodge, they became somber. No one enjoyed unpleasant situations. Jack Rabbit was called to fetch different members of the community who'd tell what they'd witnessed in relation to *Zuzeca Pazan* and *Nakpa Ihli.*

The council tried to be fair by calling some of those they believed might side with Snake Strike to speak, but all told the same story. They said the *wayaka* could do no right when in actuality, she'd done no wrong. *Nakpa Ihli* never complained or griped as she was reputed to do, even after beatings upon beatings. In the council's opinion, the only thing she'd done wrong was not to run from the abusive man sooner.

The last person they called to the lodge was *Zuzeca Pazan* himself. The four warriors were surprised to note that the one defending himself did not wear his preeminent dress when approaching the council. Most chose to wear their best when trying to impress the four or to entice them to take their side.

Snake Strike wore buckskin leggings that should've been made into glue moons ago. They were blacked with filth and crust. His breechcloth even had spilled food on it from days past. His shirt was in similar condition, and the perspiration that had stained under his arms must have done so for many passings of *wi.* To not dishonor him more, no one mentioned his sad state of wear.

"*Zuzeca Pazan,* thank you for blessing us with your attendance. Do you know why we have called your presence before the council?" *Woniya Mato* addressed him.

"Of course, I do. You brought me here to take my woman from me. Look what you've done to me! I am not made to do women's chores! I do not know how to wash clothes!"

Woniya Mato wondered if he didn't know how to bathe as well, but he didn't voice his thought aloud. Instead, he agreed, "You are correct. It has been brought to this council's attention many times over your cruel treatment of *Nakpa Ihli*. It will not be permitted to continue."

"But I captured her! Slaves are not honored guests among our camp! They must pay for being the enemy!" He wisely did not add, "Like YOU treat your slave as an honored guest!"

Woniya Mato continued as though he had not been interrupted, "Women are honored, even those of our enemy. They do not choose war. They own property and bear children. They do not attack us, nor should a man ever harm a woman with his strength!" Without meaning to, his fierceness was back, rippling through his body in a powerful omen. Spirit Bear, with a desperate struggle, replaced the lid on his anger towards the ill-willed man. The others felt the same way and began asking Snake Strike questions.

"Who was it that blackened *Nakpa Ihli*'s eye?" *Isnala Sungmanitu* asked.

"Who bruised her mouth and caused it to swell up so that she could not eat?" *Wawakte Towanjila* accused with a predatory gleam in his eye.

"And who," *Wawakankan* began but paused for dramatic effect, "caused her to lose the child she carried and bruised her internal organs?"

"It's a lie! I did not do that! She did it when she slipped and fell in the river. I tried to pull her out the only way I could. The rocks were slippery, and I dropped her. She hit rocks on her way down!" *Zuzeca Pazan* had not thought out his denial well. He was grasping at everything. Then he asked, "She lost the child?"

"You have defiled everything a woman stands for in Oglala society," *Woniya Mato* ignored his question. "Children complete our circle of life. That is how we, as men, live on. You have just killed a part of your spirit. For that, there is *no* excuse. You will have a punishment imposed," Spirit Bear spoke as if void of emotion. It took all of his expertise as a warrior and as a chief to do so.

"I denounce you as a hunter," Lone Wolf said. "No! You cannot strip me of my manhood! You," he began as he glared at the four men, "have already taken what was mine away!"

"You lose status as man in the village!" declared *Wawakte Towanjila*. He was not quite as practiced as *Woniya Mato* at masking his anger.

"You have proven you have a spirit of an angry boy rather than a responsible man. To this council, you are a boy, no longer a man!" *Wawakankan* announced.

"You will have to earn man status back. You must first prove yourself. When the council sees you are mature, you will go through the ceremony of being inducted into manhood with others," the head chieftain stated with finality.

"But they will be boys! You strip me of all honor! Give me my woman, and I will leave. I will take my things and go."

"She is mine now, *Zuzeca Pazan*! She will live with me after the ceremony tonight," Sky Warrior revealed.

"If I cannot have my property, I must be paid for her! What are you willing to give?"

"I give nothing. A boy cannot own property." "I. am *not*. A boy!" *Zuzeca Pazan* spat at *Wawakte Towanjila.* His veins were sticking out and his body was so tensed that he hunched over. His face and neck was a burning fiery red. Anger consumed him so that he cared not if he committed the worst mistake in his life by attacking the tribal council!

Wawakte Towanjila stepped forward to meet Snake Strike's unspoken challenge. The two angry mountain goats were about to ram heads. The men began to circle each other slowly. *Woniya Mato* stepped calmly between them.

"This stops now," was all he needed to say. Then he turned to *Zuzeca Pazan* and added, "We celebrate this night. If you chose to partake in the night's festivities, that is fine; you may. However, you will be brought before the community, and it will be announced what has been decided about your status."

"The four of you are too young for wisdom! Who decided you would make a good council? It is not right! You are awful: stripping a man of who he is. Completely! And then shame him in front of the crowd! You do not know what you are doing!"

"Be sure I know *exactly* what I am doing! If," Spirit Bear rebutted, "you do not wish to celebrate and desire to remain in your tipi, the council will not require your presence. We will still tell of our decision to the communal group. The choice is yours."

"This isn't the last of this!" claimed the little man as he stomped past the four men. His smell trailed behind him and left evidence that he'd been there long after he'd gone.

Lone Wolf joked, "I think the Fire Spirit wants to be blessed with more incense."

The men laughed to break the tension left in Snake Strike's passage. They returned to the ceremonial pipe and peace.

Finally, the council meeting was over. Each of the men returned to their tipis to rest. Later, they'd prepare for the celebration. Rest time was typically over, but many members of the society continued to rest longer than usual because they would be up long into the night.

Women were seen periodically checking on cooking foods. Children continued to play their games. Adolescent boys shot arrows through rolling hoops, wrestled, practiced hand-to-hand combat with sticks, and stalked each other as if they were stealthy hunters. Smaller children played stick and rock games or practiced throwing sticks at targets.

Children would be permitted to attend the early evening ceremony, but the late night festivities were for adults only. Mothers would take the children home and put them to sleep. They would either choose to sleep also or rejoin the revelry.

Kaitlin was still reliving her victory! She couldn't believe she'd been spared! The honeyed-blonde had dishonored the high king of the village and lived to tell of it! *But why? She could understand Nakpa Ihli, but her?*

Woniya Mato returned to the tipi in good spirits. The unpleasantness had been dealt with, and he had his golden eyed beauty back in his possession. There she would stay.

"Thank you, Young Elk, for watching over *Mazaska Zi Ista*. You will not be needed again until I come to get you in the morning."

"You honor me with this duty, *Woniya Mato*. Thank you for this pleasure. She is not what I expected in a *wasicun winyan*."

"*Hiya*, she is not typical in her race from my observations. I thank *Wakantanka* for her."

Once Young Elk left, *Woniya Mato* went to his sleeping furs. He hadn't rested well in many *wi* travels. He would rest now so he could be fresh before evening activities. To make sure Kaitlin didn't wander off, he called her.

"*Mazaska Zi Ista, uwa yo*."

Kaitlin was emotionally exhausted and could use relax time, but she was unsure of his intentions. He still scared her. She couldn't believe the man she found so gentle and caring when he attended her injuries could have been the man who killed Jed. She shuddered but slowly obeyed.

CHAPTER ELEVEN

Celebration

Mazaska Zi Ista looked like a scared fawn while she approached him with wide eyes. He knew she still saw the downfall of the enemy when she looked at him. That is not how he wished it. Spirit Bear wanted her to think of him with passion and longing, but with time, he would see to it that she did.

Kaitlin sat down the edge of the furs, her beautiful dress gracing her feminine moves. She perched as far away from him as she could and still have minded him. Softly, *Woniya Mato* called her name. Gold eyes met black. They held each other's gaze, each unable to let go.

"*Ahiyunka.*"

Kaitlin watched his full lips as he told her to lie down and sleep. She *was* tired. The attractive blonde didn't fight him and reclined her body. His masculine arms drew her against his body. Then he was still.

Confused by his treatment of her, Kaitlin lay there for a time before she was able to relax. *He didn't seem mad at her at all! Would she ever understand the man holding her?*

Several hours later, the *wayaka* awoke still embraced by the bronze arms. His breathing was slow and even, but she didn't know if that indicated sleep. The blonde woman reminded herself of the time she'd studied his supreme form. Kaitlin had believed him to be asleep, but he'd watched her peruse his body and arouse herself with his manly image! It'd been humiliating, but the white girl had been shamed many times in front of him.

With great care, the young woman tried to move out from under his arm. Instantly, it tensed, holding her in place. Did he tense in sleep, or did he know she wanted to move away from his intoxicating scent? His hard form against her back was disturbing.

She waited quietly for a time and then tried to move once again. This time she didn't try to leave but only rolled to her back. The chief's eyes were open, and he was watching her.

The white captive sucked in a breath and held it. He'd never treated her harshly with his dominant power, but she couldn't totally trust him not to. Kaitlin didn't expect him to beat her, really, but in the recesses of her mind, a suspicion lurked. The captive obeyed him out of fear at this time. He'd just granted her life; for that, she was thankful. *Would she always wonder when he had the power to take it from her?*

The bronze warrior propped up on his elbow so he could study her. Her bashfulness made her want to pull away, but Kaitlin knew he'd only make her submit. The white girl exhaled, and it calmed her. If the chief wanted to look, so be it, but the golden girl couldn't return his gaze, or he'd hypnotize her with his magnetic eyes and persona.

Woniya Mato smiled as he saw that see was determined not to look at him. What was she afraid of? The honey-haired beauty allowed him to look; she was smart enough to know if he wanted to gaze, he would. Her refusal to meet his eyes was a challenge Kaitlin subconsciously placed before him.

Unhurriedly, the warrior lowered his striking face to hers. He stopped a hair's breath before reaching her lips. Heavy lashes fluttered under his scrutiny.

Woniya Mato pressed a fleeting kiss on the tip of her nose and finally, gold eyes met black. They swirled with emotion. He could see the tiny lines of deeper gold in the tawny background. Slivers of brown and larger chunks of green also were sprinkled among amber rocks churning around her pupil. The almond-shaped eyes were thickly fringed with brown lashes.

The young woman's cheeks were slightly flushed. Perhaps it was from the heat, but he did not think so. He could tantalize Kaitlin no longer. Spirit Bear pressed his lips into the softness of her mouth. As his lips moved on hers, his woman tried not to respond; it only offered more of a challenge to a man who refused defeat.

Spirit Bear deepened the kiss. *Woniya Mato* tenderly drew in her lower lip, sucked on it, then released it. With the tip of his tongue, he traced her upper lip. The commanding man could tell it tickled her, but it also moved something inside of her. Her resistance was not as firm, for her breathing rate had quickened. The warrior drew back to study her.

With one of his hands, Spirit Bear cupped her cheek. His thumb stroked the softness. Then he lowered to reclaim and possess her mouth.

Her quiet exhalation was joined by a murmur made deep in her throat. It humored him that still yet, she resisted him. *Mazaska Zi Ista* tried to lie like a stiff board but was softening under his adept determination.

The commander released her mouth and nibbled and kissed her strong jaw. He worked his way back to her sensitive ear. Nibbling on her ear lobe, be breathed into it.

Kaitlin could not take it! Her ears were so sensitive! He made chills appear up and down her body. The beauty squealed and pushed at him. *Woniya Mato*'s deep laugh filled the tipi. With renewed determination, he bit the part of her neck in between her ear and her shoulder. *Mazaska Zi Ista* struggled desperately under him. Female squeals and squirming were of no avail. The blonde shivered and looked at the powerful man, knowing he was not going to hurt her. With her free arm, she rubbed her prickled skin to show how he'd made her cold.

Spirit Bear knew she had chill bumps. The tight nubs of her breasts were pressed into the fabric of the dress, advertising her condition. He groaned and moved away. With her mood now playful, he didn't want to move her reaction to him back into the fearful realm.

The commanding man would not take her unless she came to him willingly. *Woniya Mato* decided he'd to try to seduce her every night until she came to him freely. It was his intention, but Spirit Bear didn't know if he could follow through.

Sighing, the warrior stood up. He needed to relieve himself. Calling to Golden Eyes to follow, he escorted her to the Place of Privacy. Presenting his back, he relieved himself while his captive also took care of her needs.

When they returned, a young man had begun a drum beat announcing to the village that the festivities would begin soon. In the tipi, *Woniya Mato* began to prepare for the celebration by setting up his paints. The chiefs usually attended the festivities in full ceremonial dress. The warrior noticed that when he began to mark his face with his symbols, Kaitlin withdrew immediately. Gone was her playfulness from earlier. It was replaced by her submissiveness since her recapture.

"She relives the fight once more," Spirit Bear thought to himself. He wished he could help her deal with her fright, but the warrior knew she'd have to accept him for what he was. A mighty chief with an Indian village to protect could never denounce his fighter status. At least, he never would. Being a warrior was what he was; it was all he stood for.

Woniya Mato stepped outside the tipi. He called to *Wawat'ecaka* who came quickly.

"How can I help you, *Woniya Mato*?"

"Will you help *Mazaska Zi Ista*? I love her hair down, but in light of what we are celebrating, it is best if she wore more Native style."

"You would like her hair braided?" "*Tos*, that would be wonderful." "Do I need to change her garment?"

"*Hiya*, she is breathtaking. Your finery is above that of all others. It fits her to perfection."

Wawat'ecaka found that with age, she didn't flush easily. The older woman did so now under his praise. How could she enter the opening in his tipi to help the girl when her head was so swelled?

"Thank you," was all Gentle Rabbit could manage before finding that indeed, she still could squeeze into his hut.

Kaitlin looked up to see *Wawat'ecaka* enter followed by the fierce chief. Her mentor had a jar of something, leather tongs, and a porcupine brush. The captive was called back to the sleeping furs so that she wouldn't dirty her dress.

Wawat'ecaka began brushing her hair. The motherly figure rubbed a little bit of strawberry cream into the golden tresses so that it smoothed and combed more easily. Expertly, Gentle Rabbit weaved two identical braids into Kaitlin's hair and secured them with the leather strips.

Wawat'ecaka stepped back to admire her handiwork. *Woniya Mato* was right. This dress on the exceptionally pretty *wasicun* made her radiate beauty.

Her heart filled with pride that she was able to gift the sweet *ska winyan* with such a complementary wear. Gentle Rabbit believed that she'd made this dress specifically for Golden Eyes; she couldn't have matched her coloring better. It was the will of *Wakantanka*.

Kaitlin wondered what was expected of her during the celebration. She obviously was expected to go. *Would she sit with Ojilaka Hehaka or Woniya Mato? Why was she even invited?*

The white almost hoped she would sit by the babysitter. When *Woniya Mato* was painted, he frightened her. When he dressed as war chief, Spirit Bear was intimidating and powerful. He killed. She could not forget that.

When it was time, *Woniya Mato* told her to come and led her out into the clearing used for celebrations. A large bonfire was crackling merrily and would provide light for many hours. In the front of the fire, but far enough back to provide comfort from the heat, three sets of mats with support and one smaller mat without were waiting.

Kaitlin recognized *Woniya Mato*'s tripod willow back support. His ceremonial staff was also sticking in the ground by the mat. Draped over the back of his tripod was the skin of a white wolf. On top of the pelt was a breast plate made from many bones; it was painted and adorned with feathers and teeth.

On the opposite side of his seat was another tripod supporting an enormous head of a bear.

Streamers with black tipped red feathers and more bear teeth and claws dangled in layers amid small bones of some kind from the bear's head.

After adjusting to the shock of seeing such a massive bear head, she noticed a second bear's head placed slightly below the brown one. This one was black. It was very big for a black bear but could not compare to the grizzly's. It was decorated with streamers similar to the one above.

Then the white woman froze in her tracks; she could not go on. Slowly, Kaitlin began to shake her head back and forth. Trembling overtook her.

Beneath the bear heads, lying on the ground, were the three flintlock guns. And something else. The thing that made the blonde's hair go up on the back of her head was Jed's scalp.

Kaitlin could not sit by it. She just couldn't! Vaguely, she heard *Woniya Mato*'s command to come. When she didn't listen, he supported the back of her arm and dragged her to the designated spot.

He issued the work that mean 'sit' in Lakota. Twice. With gentle pressure, he forced her to sit. She could not rip her eyes off the shriveled remnants of Jed.

Kaitlin experienced flashbacks to that night. She saw for the millionth time how *Woniya Mato* had removed the blacksmith's hair. It was the most awful thing she'd ever experienced. The repulsive reminder lay feet from her!

Woniya Mato was concerned. He hadn't thought about Kaitlin's reaction to the *ska sunka*'s scalp. She removed her spirit from her body. It was like the *winyan* was a shell that mechanically did what was commanded... with help.

When *Woniya Mato* spied *Wawakankan*, he discretely motioned him over. Immediately, Wonder Worker assessed the situation. He left and returned with a horn cup.

"Have her drink this, *Woniya Mato*. It will prevent her spirit from hiding if it has not hidden well, but the *wayaka* may have emotion with what she will view this night."

Spirit Bear nodded and made Kaitlin drink the mixture.

"I think when the children go to bed, I will allow her to leave as well. In her fragile state, *Mazaska Zi Ista* could not handle reliving that night."

In thirty minutes, Kaitlin had recovered from her shock. She noticed that *Woniya Mato* had placed the offensive thing on the other side of him where his body blocked her view from it. Soon, the food was served. Because this celebration distinguished recovered life and victory, women were allowed to eat as soon as they served the men; they did not have to wait until the men finished enjoying the feast.

Under Spirit Bear's watchful eyes, she consumed tiny amounts of many mouthwatering foods. Berry juice was provided in multiple flavors. Kaitlin's was sweet cherry.

At the end of the meal, the white woman noticed the young male who'd begun the drumming had been replaced by a mature man. Maybe it was how he received training, the white woman validated. She noted the Indians trained in many ways.

Once everyone had eaten their fill, the ceremony was ready to begin. Dramatically, the drums stopped. *Woniya Mato* stood and moved into the cleared area directly in front of him so that he could address the crowd. All eyes were upon him; silent expectation filled the air.

"My people, we are here tonight to offer thanks to *Wakantanka*. He has blessed us many times. It is his will that two women were returned to us unharmed," he hesitated.

"Before we begin our victory ceremony over the *wasicu*, we have some things we need to address; things you need to know." He paused and scanned the crowd. He did not think Snake Strike would have the gumption to show his face, but he wanted to be sure.

"The first thing is that my *wayaka, Mazaska Zi Ista*, tried to escape our village on the night of Yellow Feather's second child." The group took in a breath. "But tribal council has reviewed this. *Wakantanka* has shown that it was His will that she was returned to me. Because of her spirit and heart, we feel the Great Spirit would want her punishment to be mild. It was determined by the council that she will be guarded at all times. Young Elk has accepted this challenge. Young Elk? Please come forward."

Kaitlin watched as Spirit Bear addressed the multitude. He said her Indian name within his speech addressed to the crowd. They collectively gasped and looked at her. She shrank from their eyes as much as she could.

Then the young man who followed her approached the chief and stood beside him. *Ojilaka Hehaka* was dressed similarly to a warrior. He'd painted his face in his own style and wore clothing of fringed and decorated buckskin with a matching breechcloth. She could easily mistake him for a man tonight!

The young male stood proudly as he was honored. His wise chief distinguished him with a deep responsibility rather than choosing not to announce his job to the audience. The people understood that he was being bestowed a high compliment rather than given a punishment to watch over a mere woman. *Ojilaka Hehaka*'s heart filled with love and respect for *Woniya Mato*.

Woniya Mato wanted to prepare the crowd. When *Mazaska Zi Ista* earned back his trust and he no longer needed *Ojilaka Hehaka* to watch over her, he planned on another ceremony. During this one, he would honor Young Elk and induct him into warrior society.

Next, he called forth *Nakpa Ihli*. Kaitlin thought she looked beautiful despite her evident bruising. The crowd, however, drew in a collective breath in show at the extent of her injuries.

Nakpa Ihli was dressed in deep brown. The rich mahogany fabric must've been made by Gentle Rabbit, for none could compare to it. The dress clung to her shape in all the right places.

Along the gentle scooped neckline and hem of the dress, bone beads were alternated with sparkly gold-colored pebbles and tiny onyx stones. A soft fray hung below the hemline and sleeveless shoulder area. It was a beautiful creation that looked very becoming on *Nakpa Ihli*. She wore matching moccasins.

Woniya Mato waited for the shocked murmurs to stop before he continued his address. "Many of you have witnessed *Zuzeca Pazan*'s treatment of *Nakpa Ihli*. Her bruising evidenced tonight was given to her by him days ago." Again the multitude drew in a breath.

"For this reason," Spirit Bear continued, "*Nakpa Ihli* no longer belongs to him. She will have a new owner from this point forward. She now belongs to our chief and leader, *Wawakte Towanjila*."

Sky Warrior walked forward and stood beside Spirit Bear. "In addition," the war chief continued, "*Zuzeca Pazan* will have punishment imposed on him for desecrating our traditional view of the treatment of women and life."

Lone Wolf approached the crowd and stood beside the other two chiefs. Wonder Worker also stepped up to stand with them. They wanted the community to know the decisions made were unanimous.

Isnala Sungmanitu announced, "*Zuzeca Pazan* had been denounced as a hunter. His rations will be provided for by hunting and warrior men of the tribe."

Wawakankan added, "He also has been removed from the status of man. Once he proves that he values life as *Wakantanka* desires, he may go through the rites of manhood once more to regain his rank."

Woniya Mato said, "The council has spoken, and so it shall be." The mass responded by cheers.

When it quieted down once more, Sky Warrior moved beside *Nakpa Ihli* and addressed the community. "*Nakpa Ihli* received her name from *Zuzeca Pazan* because he made up an excuse to punish her for her complaining nature. This has been found to be untrue. Therefore, she deserves a name worthy of her endurance and strength. She will now be called *Haspa Nableca*."

The community showed its support by voicing the name and saying it back. Apple Blossom, as she was not to be called, flushed profusely. She was only used to negative and punishing treatment. She was never recognized with honor.

Still shy, the young woman allowed herself to be led back to the chief's ceremonial spot in front of the bonfire. *Woniya Mato*, Kaitlin, and *Wawakankan* joined them as well, but Lone Wolf mingled into the crowd.

The drums began again and were accompanied by other instruments. Singers and dancers celebrated in *Haspa Nableca*'s rebirth into the camp, and they rejoiced in the punishment of *Zuzeca Pazan* for his dishonor of the ways of *Wakantanka*.

From a small dirty tipi on the outskirts of the village, a small man seethed. *How dare the chiefs of the council disgrace him so? They would pay! He would see that they paid if it was the last thing he did. He would get them all back! Then he'd leave.* Maybe he would even join the *wasicu* and lead fights against the Oglala. *What had the Sioux ever done for him? Nothing!* He would be glad to help with the downfall of the mighty *Woniya Mato*!

Zuzeca Pazan equally hated *Wawakte Towanjila*. Both Sky Warrior and Spirit Bear were too much alike. Just because *Wakantanka* had blessed them with height, muscular prowess, and a pleasing exterior which, Snake Strike hated to admit, women found enticing, they thought they had the right to play Supreme Being. *They already had it all; why did they have to take from him?*

He could hurt the two men most by taking their women. He would take both Sore Ear, as she would always be known to him, and Golden Eyes. If he couldn't take them alive, he would kill them as soon as the opportunity presented itself.

He'd have more luck by retaliating against the females. He knew with the sixth sense a warrior possesses, he'd never be able to sneak upon and kill either *Woniya Mato* or *Wawakte Towanjila*. If he challenged either one, he would never win the competition for he'd been denied access to warrior training. Hatred welled up within him so fast it almost took him by surprise.

He still couldn't believe they'd taken *Nakpa Ihli* from him. He knew it was because *Wawakte Towanjila* had decided he wanted her for his own. He'd seen the way Sky Warrior's eyes had looked at her womanly curves.

The child she'd lost had probably been his. That is why he was being so harshly punished for his treatment of a mere slave! He, a born Oglala, was treated with shame while his slave was honored with beautiful clothing and graced in front of the communal ceremonial place! He gritted his teeth.

Now, tonight, she would share sleeping mats with his hated *toga*. He jumped up and began pacing. If only he could prevent their union! *But how? What could he possibly do?* He grated his teeth harder in frustration.

Kaitlin watched the festivities from her honored position by the high chief. She'd observed the other celebration from the confines of the tipi, but somehow it was different this close. She saw the tribe's finery. They laughed and joked, and no one worked. It was as different as night and day. No wonder these people enjoyed sharing fun often and worshipping their gods.

Kaitlin's eyes widened in pleased acceptance as she saw Lone Wolf leading Desert Rose to his mat in the place reserved for the tribal council. She was on a date! She smiled with happiness for her basket-weaving companion. When her eyes met *Unjinjintka can Koica*'s, she nodded her head toward Kaitlin to indicate recognition of their ties.

Her friend blushed prettily when *Isnala Sungmanitu* brought her before the crowd. He didn't announce her presence, but all saw her take the place beside the hunting chief. It was a sign to all men that Lone Wolf had dibs on her.

Because the next large ceremony was to take place in one cycle of the moon, many competitions were included in the celebration. Young warriors would soon become men. In the upcoming gathering, they would become newcomers to the warrior and hunting societies. For this reason, they showed their acquired skills.

There were wrestling and arrow-shooting competitions. There were one-on-one combats. All involved, even those that lost, appeared to be good sports. Hearty slaps in appreciate were given upon completion of each opposition. Kaitlin watched it all with enthusiasm.

These people were so complex! She would have never known the depth of Indian culture had she not been brought to live with them. They seemed so alive! They made merriment of each part of life!

These Native peoples thanked everything. They even thanked tree spirits for willow bark! She was glad for the properties the willow provided as well, for she didn't know how she would have survived all her injuries without the pain reliever, but she would never have thought to thank the tree for what it had done for her!

When she compared the whites to the Indians, she found whites sadly lacking. They took everything for granted. Most were not thankful at all; they just took more and more, or like her father and brother, became obsessed and couldn't think beyond themselves and what they needed.

Spirit Bear watched Kaitlin's every move. His *wayaka* was so enchanting as she absorbed his people's happiness. The bright amber eyes took in every detail they could. The Oglala man watched awed, sudden understanding, and sometimes confused expressions play across her face. If the *ska winyan* only knew how he felt about her, but even he couldn't fathom the depths.

Woniya Mato had never met a woman like her before. He could not believe his good fortune. The leader thanked *Wakantanka* yet again for blessing him. Golden Eyes displayed a strong will combined with innocence that drew all of his protective instincts to the surface. She, more than anyone else ever had, made him feel like a man! The newcomer made him notice everything with fresh eyes. His heart warmed with her laughter at the young men's competitive moves.

Another hour of celebrating, feasting, and dancing flew by. *Woniya Mato* saw Kaitlin's head begin to droop with fatigue. He hated to end her companionship, but he knew his people waited for the real ceremony to begin.

Spirit Bear had a messenger announce by drum beat that the ceremony would begin in about twenty minutes. He took Kaitlin home and pointed to the resting place and told her to sleep. Then he returned to the villagers. The war chief didn't need Young Elk to watch over his slave for he could easily see his tipi from its prime location.

Upon his signal, the drum beat changed. To Kaitlin, it was an ominous sound; it was one that predicted death and destruction. Mechanically, the white captive removed her finery and folded it neatly. Then she brought forth her poncho garment. It was often used as a sleeping robe because of its level of comfort.

She tried to be a good slave and lie down, but the mesmerizing booming of the drum drew her like a magnet; she couldn't help herself. Kaitlin crept to the lodge's entrance. *Woniya Mato* had closed the flap, but she nudged it ever so slightly so that she could peek at the events as they unfurled.

The becoming blonde saw *Woniya Mato* dancing. Alongside him, Yellow Feather danced. Other people joined him. Two young men dressed to resemble women were also on the natural stage. The dancing chief and his warrior danced sneakily up to the two 'women'. One of the young men suddenly lay down and the other stood over him.

Spirit Bear acted like he jumped over something and raised his hand in the air as if to strike the standing-man-playing-a-woman. Yellow Feather danced into the scene from another direction. Then she saw six others dressed like white men melt into the scene forming a semi-circle. It was then that the realization hit the white girl: they were reenacting the scene!

Slowly, she relived the nightmare with them. Kaitlin saw a mountain man 'shoot' Yellow Feather and graze his arm with the flintlock. All the white men died save one who held one of the 'women'.

Woniya Mato motioned to the other Indian warriors to fall back, and the Indian playing Jed let go of the 'woman'. They began to circle.

It was too much! She couldn't watch anymore! Kaitlin ran back to her sleeping furs crying. She tried to cry quietly, but she sobbed aloud. *Oh, how could they celebrate such a horrid event? Wasn't it just today that she'd thought Indians were so much deeper than the whites?*

The drum beat when on and on. *Were they going to reenact the whole grueling eleven hours of torture that actually went on?* She didn't want to, but finally, she sneaked back to the entrance flap.

Haltingly, she looked out once more. This time, it was just *Woniya Mato* in the clearing. Only he was dancing his terrible ballet, but it was so much more. In his hands he held Jed's scalp! In morbid fascination, the slave was entranced to watch.

With the aberration in his hands, he twirled and changed directions rapidly. He'd hold the scalp high in the air and chant, then dip and whirl, moving his feet in rhythmic dance. This went on for a while. Then the tempo of the drums quickened.

Woniy a Mato moved faster and faster, his feet blurring with movement. Dipping, twirling, stomping, and arching his back as he held the hair up as an offering to *Wakantanka*, he became a melody. It was emotional and dramatic for all to see.

Magically, the chief and drums became motionless at the same second. Silence fell over the crowd. A desolate, sad melody and beat began.

A lonely figure came into the clearing covered in a cape made of white leather of buffalo hide. The person began to dance. This dance was not energetic, but mournful. Three men dressed as women and a young boy also walked onto the scene. They were dressed and painted totally in white.

The four figures slowly walked across the natural stage. Their heads were down in shame and the toes of their feet dragged the ground. Their walk also was slow and mechanical.

The dancer continued his white buffalo hide dance with the forlorn beat for a few minutes as the men-dressed-as-women and the youth crossed the stage a few times. He danced mournfully around them waving the white hide in their direction. He flapped the white leather as he weaved in front of it, around, and behind them. When the walkers were gone, the dancer did one more mournful spew across the clearing. Then he ran from the clearing and melted away.

Woniya Mato stepped forward and the drum silenced. Suddenly, a war cry split the air and the chief dropped to his knees. He held the scalp high over his head and continued the fierce sound until he ran out of breath. It sent chills up Kaitlin's back.

When he drew in another breath, the war chief arched his back and thrust his chest forward. He held his hunting knife up high. It cast an eerie glow in the bonfire light and flashed malicious intent in his hands. Instantly, *Woniya Mato* shredded the scalp into three strips. Then he relaxed. It almost reminded Kaitlin of a man being drained of energy.

When the great chief reclaimed use of his feet, three older couples were called to the clearing. He lined them up on the ceremonial ground, facing the community. All eyes were upon him.

"*Wakantanka* cannot replace what the *ska sunka* took from these good people," Spirit Bear began. "But their honor and that of their daughters: Laughing Brook, Blue Bird, and New Flower, have been avenged. Never again will the *wasicun* rape and kill our women!" Cheers and cries of victory rejoiced at his words.

"To remember them with honor, I give what is left of the *toka* to each of the families of these beautiful daughters. When you look at this, remember your daughters now walk with honor with the Great Spirit, *Wakantanka*." Spirit Bear stood before each of the couples, one at a time, with Jed's stripped scalp. Previous to handing it over, he knelt individually before the father figure, held the scalp up, and chanted with his eyes closed. When the chieftain stood, he delivered the hair piece to them.

Each woman hugged their husband with tears in her eyes. One openly wept. The three men comforted their wives with stoic dignity. They stood straight and strong, but the misery of mourned loss was reflected in their eyes.

When the sad but rejoicing couples rejoined the throng, *Woniya Mato* called a fourth couple to the stage. It was Rising Bull and Whispering Pine, the parents of Little Bison. They, too, suffered a great loss. Their child was a upcoming athlete sure to be inducted into warrior society. The council had watched him since he was five winters!

"I do not share the scalp with the parents of a future warrior. Instead, I give them the weapon used by the *ska sunka* who dishonorably stole their son's life. Eleven winters is not enough time to spend with a child!"

Whispering Pine's voice began a mournful song. The black-haired woman looked up with doe eyes as she sang the deeply emotional melody. Her husband began a background chant to accompany. When the song was completed, the distinctive chief knelt before them. He looked up into their faces and held forward a small, metal fire stick. Rising Bull accepted it.

Cheers again arose from the multitude. *Woniya Mato* waited patiently until the noise subsided before continuing his speech.

"Little Bison now walks honorably beside *Wakantanka* as a mighty warrior. Now, with his slayer avenged, he will enjoy this status for as long as the Great Spirit rules the skies." The answering prayers, victory cries, and songs were overpowering. When the voices receded at last, he added, "The tribal council has removed the fire from the stick, so it cannot cause any pain. Now, we rejoice!"

At last, the major ceremonial duties were completed. The rest of the night would be spent in reliving the victory, dancing, and feasting. Each person would retire when weariness overtook them. Spirit Bear walked among the celebrating peoples for at least another hour before retiring to his tipi.

Kaitlin was asleep, but he knew she'd watched the final ritual. He'd felt her eyes upon him as he'd danced. *Woniya Mato* wanted to spare her from reliving the terror, but he guessed that the suspenseful drums had her curiosity piqued.

The *ska wayaka* had trails of tears dried on her face. Her amber eyes were slightly swollen from emotional outpouring, but at least her drained body finally rested.

He stripped, refolded his ceremonial garb with care, and retired by her side. For a time, he watched her sleep. Then contented, he slept.

CHAPTER TWELVE

The Tipis of Isolation

Sometime before the waking hours in the morning, Kaitlin awoke with a swollen, cramping stomach. She knew that her time had started without having to see the evidence. Afraid to leave without permission, the white girl rolled over and tapped *Woniya Mato*'s arm.

Spirit Bear sat up, instantly on alert. *What was wrong? Did Golden Eyes have a night terror? Did she need to use the Area of Privacy?*

He could see her dim outline by the dying embers of the fire pit. She looked at him shamefully. She'd risen and gathered clothes neatly folded over her arm and pointed in the direction of the Area of Privacy.

The warrior stood with cat-like grace and held the flap open for her. He didn't question why she needed to take a change of clothes, but he'd noticed. On the way down, the *wayaka* tried to veer towards a tree. *What in the world was she trying to do?*

"*Hiya*," he spoke quietly but firmly.

"Please, *Woniya Mato*. I need to gather moss. It works to absorb my… well, I just need some." Kaitlin pointed to the moss and then to her clothes.

He shook his head. He didn't understand.
"*Uwa yo, Mazaska Zi Ista.*"

With great embarrassment, the gentle blonde stood before him, head downcast. Finally, she pulled forth her fresh undergarment. She pointed to the moss, then to her undergarment. Then she pointed to her stomach all without looking at him.

"*Tos*," he said, finally understanding what the *wayaka* was trying to let him know. Spirit Bear allowed her to gather quite a bit of moss. Then he escorted her to the place of privacy. Finally, he allowed her to clean her garments.

As bad as he hated to, the Oglala man led her to one of five tipis she hadn't noticed before. They set back from the village on the upper side of the women's bathing area. It was secluded but had easy access to areas that women needed to frequent.

Kaitlin looked at him questioningly. *Was she being punished for waking him in the night? He'd implied heavily that she needed to ask for an escort where ever she went, or punishment would be imposed. Isn't that what she was doing?*

Woniya Mato called at the flap of the nearest tipi. Finally, a woman in her early twenties answered. She gasped when she saw it was the chief. In rapid Lakota, he told her his *wayaka* had begun her monthly flow. He also stated that she needed to be watched at all times. The woman nodded understanding. She placed Kaitlin's wet garments over a nearby rock then drew her inside.

The young female pointed to an empty sleeping mat and turned to secure the opening flap. Tucking the moss under the edge of the mat, Kaitlin reclined.

Although the alienated captive was tired and still stressed from reliving the traumatic events recently endured, sleep was evasive. *Was the chief mad at her? Did she still belong to him, or was she now the property of the woman with her?*

The blonde believed her punishment was going to be that she was never allowed privacy. She wasn't alone now, but Kaitlin thought she'd have a male companion. *When would she ever figure out what was going on?*

It was a long time before the honeyed-blonde was able to sleep. She'd just managed a light doze when the first morning bird began to sing. Sighing, the light-skinned female sat up. There were two women in the hut: the girl in her early twenties from last night and a girl about her own age. Kaitlin could tell they wouldn't sleep much longer, for their breathing was not so deep.

There were three empty sleeping mats on the floor of the tipi that were unoccupied. A basket sat near the entrance flap filled with moss. Vaguely, she wondered why they needed such a large amount of moss. Several filled *mniapahtas* hung about the tipi.

Kaitlin lay quietly so that she wouldn't wake the others before they were ready. She wondered why these women were alienated from the rest of the village. Did they also commit some offense and were punished by isolation? It was all so overwhelming with the language barrier.

Finally, the older woman awoke. She nodded a greeting to Kaitlin. Then she tapped the other sleeping girl.

They motioned for Kaitlin to follow them. They went to a different discrete location for their relief. It was a rocky area above the place where the tipis sat. It was close to the lodges, but not so close that any smells would reach their temporary homes.

There was also a tiny spring that filled a small rock pond. The bottom of the minuscule pool was a large slate of what looked like flint. Its dark and lighter grey bands were clearly visible through the cold shallowness. It was only about four inches deep and three feet wide: not enough to bathe in, but the women used it to clean hands, arms, and body.

Kaitlin shook her head. Not only must she live separate from all the others, but she must even relieve herself and wash in areas apart. Then they covered used moss up with loose dirt. Kaitlin was surprised to see the other women also shared a time of menses.

Playful Otter told Morning Dove that this woman was the girl that was learning to weave baskets with Desert Rose. Playful Otter was friends with Desert Rose, and because of her curiosity, the basket weaver had already answered questions about the chief's slave.

Many women were inquisitive about Golden Eyes. She held some magic power over the chieftain. The white girl had won his heart where many others had failed before her. Some girls were not at all happy about her place in *Woniya Mato*'s life, but each would never confront the powerful man about it.

Both Playful Otter and Morning Dove, however, didn't have romantic interests in the leader of their community. Morning Dove was still considered newlywed. She was married to a hunter called No Noise. Playful Otter's heart, on the other hand, beat faster when the medicine man was around.

When Kaitlin's group was returning from the alternative place of relief, they met two other women. They were from the tipi that sat beyond theirs. Both stared openly at Kaitlin; it made her feel uncomfortable.

The two women leading Kaitlin didn't greet them, nor did the others attempt to say anything. They just glared at the white girl until they were past her. Kaitlin found her feet walking faster to keep up with the two in front of her.

The chief's slave noticed Young Elk making weapons from a hill on the opposite side of their location. He made sure she saw him watching over the tipis apart, but the young warrior-to-be didn't act as though he'd noticed them. His concentration appeared to be on the weaponry.

When the women reentered the hut, Morning Dove placed a skin pot over a fire and filled it with water. When the rocks by the fire were heated, she used a bone tong to put them into the water.

As the liquid boiled, the hard-working woman placed the roots of wild yams into the pot. She continued to add hot rocks and remove cooled ones for ten minutes. Finally, she took the pot off the fire.

Playful Otter held a thinly woven mat over a second pot. Morning Dove poured the concoction into the new container, straining it as she poured. Then she sat the root free tea in an area to cool.

Once it had gone from dangerously hot to the hot-but-drinkable stage, Morning Dove added enough honey to sweeten the entire drink. Playful Otter retrieved three horn cups and then filled the drinking vessels. They gave one to Kaitlin and settled down with a drink themselves.

The blonde captive didn't know what she was supposed to do, so she joined the others and sat to drink her tea. It was an interesting flavor. It was good to relax with new women and enjoy the beverage.

Each woman introduced herself. Then they said her name before Kaitlin could tell them, indicating they already knew who she was. They laughed in a friendly way at her surprise. The white girl didn't know how to react.

Both of the other women continued to smile at her to show they meant no harm. Then the younger of the two mentioned Desert Rose's name. Kaitlin assumed it was to show they were linked. Thus, this began a new bonding process.

The new acquaintances continued to sit. They conversed with each other and tried to include her. They continued Desert Rose's education of the Lakota language to Kaitlin so that she could expedite learning to speak with them.

The *ska winyan* was kind of glad that they were taking it easy and lazing around more than was usual for the Indian community. She really didn't feel very well, but the tea she'd consumed seemed to help her feel better. The other women poured some more for all in the tipi as they visited.

Kaitlin tried to question why they were in this tipi away from the rest of the village. Her new friends smiled and nodded as if in understanding. Both pointed to the moss, to their stomachs, and then indicated that for this reason, they were isolated.

Wasn't that strange? When a woman menstruated, she had to be isolated? Why? She wondered if it had to do with their religious beliefs. The others didn't seem to mind the forced time away from the normal daily rigors. Kaitlin knew she'd had menstrual periods before in the village, but at the time, she'd been unconscious. She wondered vaguely about how that was dealt with.

Soon, a voice called from the entrance. It was Desert Rose. She smiled at all present. She brought a basket full of vegetables, fruits, and dried meats. She told them she'd be back in the afternoon with another meal.

She called Kaitlin and brought forth her basket weaving materials so that she'd have something to do. Kaitlin was glad to be able to work with her hands. She couldn't freely communicate with anyone yet, and for that reason, felt a little alienated.

She was truly glad to share a tipi with these friendly women. The young white woman would've hated to share one with the females with cold stares! Pushing the others from her mind, the blonde girl began working on the basket.

Desert Rose made sure she stayed long enough to nod approval of her waterproof weave. She was glad to see Kaitlin in much better spirits than she'd been in of late. *Unjinjintka Can Koica* departed with a warm smile for all.

The other two girls brought out sewing. Morning Dove was working on a new pair of moccasins for her husband, and Playful Otter, or *Skeca Ecaca,* was making a dress for her little sister.

The day passed fairly quickly. Kaitlin learned a handful of new words and gestured a lot with her new friends. They seemed to accept and like her.

After the rest time, they returned to their personal place to relieve themselves. While they cleaned up, the other two girls joined them. One nudged the other when she saw Kaitlin. The darker female whispered something to the other and snickered.

Kaitlin turned to leave with Morning Dove and Playful Otter. At that time, one of new girls purposefully bumped into her. When Kaitlin glanced at her, the girl had a cruel smile on her face and a malicious look in her eye. She said something under her breath that didn't sound very complementary.

Kaitlin continued to follow her new friends. The whispering behind her back grew louder and was followed by mocking laughter. The chief's slave persisted to walk proudly with her back straight and refused to acknowledge them.

When they arrived back at the tipi, the women drank more tea and relaxed. Kaitlin pointed to the two figures coming back up the trail. From what she could understand between gestures and broken speech, one was a second wife to an older man in the community and the girl who'd bumped Kaitlin wanted *Wanyo Mato* for a mate. Opossum Eyes, as she was called, felt scorned by the chief when he didn't act interested in her attention. She became very negative toward any woman he displayed an interest in; Kaitlin resolved to stay as far away from them as possible.

Later, Desert Rose returned with *aguyapi, tinpsila*, the sweet radishes, and a ground roasted prairie chicken. The delicious aroma was tantalizing! Kaitlin was happy to be able to eat right when her stomach rumbled. No man got to dive in ahead while she had to wait!

As the women shared the tender, delicious meat, Kaitlin laughed and joined in the conversations as she could but soon found her mind wandering. She thought of *Woniya Mato* and wondered what his plans were for her. *Would he keep her indefinitely, or would he tire of her soon? If he did, would he return her to the settlement?* She was tired of worrying about her future, but she couldn't help herself.

For the millionth time, Kaitlin wondered why he wanted her. *Was it all for the sake of his honor?* He was so handsome and virile. *Woniya Mato could have any woman in the village for his wife, and he wanted her? Her status was below the lowest Indian!*

The striking chief made her feel so funny inside with the way he looked at her. His eyes seemed to consume her with fiery heat. The bronzed warrior made her shake with foreign emotion; he made her want him in a way she didn't understand. No other man had ever affected her in a similar fashion!

How could she stand to stay? If she did, Kaitlin's heart could never remain her own. The honey-skinned female still feared him and his fierceness, but there was something else there as well. Already, the warmth she felt for him threatened to break through her defenses. The white woman couldn't… *no, she wouldn't let that happen.*

If she tried to escape his soft touches and his disturbing embraces again, she knew the chief wouldn't be so forgiving. He'd made a point to tell her that her punishment would be more severe if she ran again. *Could she tempt fate?*

Then the young woman recalled Young Elk. With him watching over her and the women keeping an eye out as well, the captive would have to stay. It was almost a relief to know she couldn't try to escape again. Sighing, Kaitlin would just have to harden her heart and hope that her master didn't crush her. If she allowed herself to love him, it would destroy her for him to end up rejecting and sending her away.

When the blonde looked up from her ponderings, the other women were looking at her expectantly. *Had she missed something?* Kaitlin raised her shoulder questioningly and put a hand to her ear as if she didn't understand rather than didn't hear. They smiled and then said the very man's name she'd been thinking of.

They kind of giggled and pointed at the mats. *Were they asking her if she'd slept with him?* The private woman's face flamed at the suggestion. She looked down so they wouldn't see her embarrassment, but laughing met with her ears.

When Kaitlin looked back up, she saw they weren't making fun of her, but were kind of congratulating her. She'd captured the most eligible bachelor of the tribe! The slave wanted to tell them she hadn't captured him at all! He'd captured *her*, and *that* was the cause of his current infatuation.

If it wasn't for her being his war trophy, she'd never hold his interest. *How could he hold any true feelings for her when she couldn't even hold a conversation with him? How could he know she didn't have the same cruelty within her as did Jed?* The knowledge that their relationship would never last almost made the blonde's chin quiver with bottled emotion.

Suddenly the laughter died away. Her friends surrounded her with arms and pats. They knew it was an emotional time for women when each visited the Tipis Apart. Often women cried and didn't have a reason. Misunderstanding the motive for tears, they wished they could tell her she'd be back in the mighty chief's arms in no time!

After Desert Rose left, the women continued to drink the tea that helped with cramping and lounged around. It was so unlike village life that Kaitlin still couldn't believe it! She was glad to have this time to get to know these two nice women her age. Without it, she doubted she would have gotten to know them.

Just before dark, they all made one more trip to the alternative place of relief. With the tea they drank, it was necessary to visit often. Kaitlin was grateful for the plentiful moss and clean garment supply.

When she headed back in, the white girl glimpsed Young Elk's form. She felt sorry for him if all he had to do all day was spy on her. *He must resent it! She knew she would.*

Once they returned to the tipi, each retired to her mat. It reminded Kaitlin of sleepovers with her friends back east. The women, like young girls from her home, giggled and spoke past daylight hours.

Prior to when they reclined to sleep, Kaitlin heard Morning Dove's breathless murmurs of her husband, but she also caught wind of *Wawakankan*'s name. At that, she perked up. The golden-skinned girl looked at *Skeca Ecaca* in surprise. She shouldn't be surprised that such a handsome man would capture Playful Otter's interest, but she would almost bet if the handsome medicine man knew of it, he'd do something about it!

The shaman that knew it all did not suspect he had such a beautiful admirer? Kaitlin knew just the way to let him find out about it. She'd accidentally let it slip to *Wawat'ecaka*. The elder lady was a match maker if she ever saw one!

Before the white woman knew it, night had come and gone. The new day's morning was much the same. They relieved themselves, changed and buried moss, made more tea for the day, and laughed and spoke with gestures a lot. Kaitlin continued to learn more daily language from her treasured friends.

Unjinjintka Can Koica came with breakfast. She brought turtle eggs scrambled with onions and garlic. She accented the eggs with acorn cakes topped with maple syrup. To complete the meal, they also munched on fresh strawberries.

Desert Rose looked at Kaitlin's basket. It was nearly complete. She nodded in approval with a proud smile. For a surprise, she'd brought her own nearly completed basket. She wanted to show Kaitlin a particularly difficult finish weave that she saved for the outer rim. The basket top would be woven in color, making it an appealing item to fetch water or other things.

The intricate pattern was hard to do, but finally after five tries, Kaitlin caught on. The two women worked side by side; the mentor giving pointers for easier learning. Kaitlin stood, at last, holding up her basket for her friends to see. They all made appropriate noises of admiration for her accomplishment.

Happy to have taught her so well, Desert Rose was all smiles and nods. It'd be difficult to tell Kaitlin's baskets from her own. The next time *Unjinjintka Can Koica* worked with Kaitlin, she'd begin to teach her the more involved patterning. For now, however, Desert Rose needed to return to the village and her responsibilities. With a goodbye to all, she promised to be back early afternoon with another meal and provisions.

Satisfied with what she'd been able to do, Kaitlin poured more tea to celebrate. Then she sat by the women sewing to watch their technique. Each woman had a sliver of bone with a tiny hold drilled through the end. They used sinew and small pieces of rawhide to sew with. Morning Dove was nearly finished with the shape of the moccasin. This pair was for hunting; she would not decorate it.

Kaitlin studied the construction of the simple yet ingenious footwear. The bottom had a tough surface. It was almost as hard as rawhide but much more durable and pliable. The upper part of the shoe was made out of a very supple hide. A thick rawhide binding combined with sinew held the two pieces together.

When Kaitlin pointed to the upper part of the shoe, Morning Dove smiled and nodded yes. She knew Golden Eyes wanted to know if she had come from Gentle Rabbit. *Wawat'ecaka*'s leather was highly sought after, and she'd traded for it.

Hunting shoes had to be extremely durable yet flexible. The hunter had to stalk in them and thus, he must be able to feel the ground around him through the material. If he couldn't feel the earth, he was much more likely to step on something noisy and alert his prey to his presence. The shoes were half the success!

Kaitlin also watched *Skeca Ecaca*'s dress-making process. She'd cut the garment out already and was beginning to sew the sides together. For this, Playful Otter used soft rawhide. Sinew could be used for this as well, but sometimes it irritated youthful skin with its course texture. Her sister was only seven winters, so she chose the rawhide. Besides, she reasoned, the girl would outgrow the dress before the supple rawhide bindings wore out.

Before noon, the women made another trip to the refreshing spring area. Kaitlin took her newly completed basket. She wanted to fill it up with water to test its water-retaining abilities with her weave.

The honey-kissed blonde left it under the slight overhang of rock where the spring dripped into the stone bowl. There was just enough rock beneath it to keep it from the water's edge. Satisfied, she left it to take care of her other needs.

It would take a while for the basket to fill under the constant drizzle of water, so the women left it. They'd return later to retrieve it. The day was becoming hot and their aching bodies could use a little more tea and rest.

When the threesome returned for the basket, Kaitlin found an unpleasant surprise. Her basket was no longer under the rock where she'd left it. It was stomped and broken on the ground and contained used moss.

Kaitlin bent over the lost work dejectedly. *Who would do this? Why?* She'd never offended anyone other than the most important man in the village! *Was that why someone did this to her?*

The two women stood behind her, talking furiously. They were angry where Kaitlin felt upset and hurt. Unlike Golden Eyes, they knew exactly who'd committed this cruelty! With words of encouragement, they did their duties and escorted Kaitlin back to their tipi.

Kaitlin tried to ask if they knew who was responsible for her basket's destruction. They nodded: it had to have been Opossum Eyes.

This girl who had bumped into her had done this? But why? Kaitlin couldn't really understand. Opossum Eyes had a crush on *Woniya Mato*, but Kaitlin was powerless in his interest in her, *so why did she blame her?* If anything, the blame was Spirit Bear's. The war chief had chosen *her*. The Indian girl didn't even have dibs on the warrior, but jealousy did bizarre things to people.

The relaxed environment in the tipi was gone. Kaitlin's two new friends seethed in anger at Opossum

Eyes. She always interfered with others. She was a mean, selfish, vindictive person. She deserved a life as the mate of… *Zuzeca Pazan*! Of course, they didn't truly believe *anyone* deserved a fate that terrible.

A fresh attitude arrived with morning. They all laughed and conversed as the tea was made. Today they would gather pebbles at the spring for decorations.

Unjinjintka Can Koica brought a breakfast of flat cakes made of corn and wild raspberries. Playful Otter and Morning Dove told Desert Rose about the destruction of Kaitlin's hard work; Desert Rose was livid! Kaitlin tried to reassure her and had to deescalate her friend; she didn't want to be the cause of more strife in the village!

"If you'll bring me more basket supplies, I'll make another," Kaitlin said as she signed this to *Unjinjintka Can Koica.*

"You should not have to do this," her friend replied. "It is wrong what they have done!"

Kaitlin signed that she the practice was good for her.

Shaking her head, Desert Rose replied, "I will bring you more weaving supplies upon my return with your evening meal." Then she returned to the village.

"We will gather stone decorations after we drink more tea," Morning Dove stated. "This will be my last day here. My time draws to an end for one more cycle of the moon."

Kaitlin was surprised when she thought Morning Dove almost sounded regretful! Kaitlin would never regret her moon time ending! She did have to admit, however, it was a nice reprieve from the daily grind!

Within twenty minutes, the women were at the spring. The basket was gone. Kaitlin didn't have to ask who'd cleaned it for her. She felt warm thanks well in her heart. What sweet friends she had! She had more friends now than she'd ever had in her entire life!

Kaitlin learned the 'decorations' the women searched for were small pebbles. Unbeknownst to her, some rocks were softer than others. The Indians wanted the softer, more workable rocks, but they also would accept any stone with a ready-made hole in it. Drilling the holes was the hardest part of making jewelry or decorations for adorning garments.

Kaitlin found stones of light and deep blue chalcedony. She also collected obsidian, although hard, onyx, and the sparkly gold colored rocks that were frequently used. She gathered clear crystal and a few with a pinkish hue. They twinkled and sparkled as if winking at her.

The heat had increased by the time the women had gathered all the stones they wanted. There were more, but they'd depleted the major source for the time. Relaxed and back in good spirits, they returned to the tipi for their midday rest.

In the lodge, Playful Otter retrieved small leather bags and gave one to each of them. Kaitlin poured her collection into the bag. Smiling at her new pretty things, Kaitlin placed them on her sleeping furs.

The blonde reclined with the rest of the women. She certainly would miss Morning Dove tomorrow. At least she'd still share companionship with Playful Otter!

When Kaitlin awoke, the others were still sleeping. Quietly, she dumped the gems into her hands to admire. While she'd lived in the settlement and then her log cabin, she'd never taken the opportunity to do the things she'd enjoyed. It was simply survival.

The Indian's essence revolved around survival as well, but they also found time to enjoy and celebrate life; they gathered flowers and made beads. The women collected pretty stones. If only she weren't a slave, Kaitlin would love it here; but freedom was everything.

The women awoke and took their routine trip to the water place and back. They sat outside the tipi and just talked. It was too hot inside, and a gentle breeze kissed their damp skin.

Kaitlin chose to sit with her back to the tipis behind theirs. She could feel the cold glares collecting on her back. She wished it didn't have to be like this, but the choice didn't lie in her hands.

That afternoon, Desert Rose came with slain rabbits. She also had wild asparagus and carrots. From the ledge where Kaitlin had seen Young Elk, a mighty warrior astride a magnificent steed sat. His piercing gaze sought and held Kaitlin's.

Unjinjintka Can Koica said, "*Woniya Mato* wishes you a fine meal of fresh rabbit."

The women waved thanks to him. He nodded acknowledgement before turning his horse. He didn't look back.

Kaitlin discovered she'd held her breath once she'd been made aware of his prominent presence. He

commanded her attention, even if she was determined to
ignore it. When their eyes had met, it felt like she'd been
locked into a tunnel that radiated heat.

*What power did he have over her to affect her so
with only a look? Why did her emotions betray what she
fought so hard to hide from herself? Did this make her
bad?* She wasn't married to him!

She could not deny the domineering man made her
breathless with desire. *But desire for what?* Her body was
a traitor, for she didn't want him to lie on top of her. The
memories of the other things he did in intimacy made her
face flame. She could not lie, even to herself, about how
enjoyable that had been.

The women took the rabbits and began to skin
them. *Skeca Ecaca* lit a fire in the outside hearth and
prepared spits.

Kaitlin held the rabbits for Morning Dove as she
skinned them. Kaitlin had never skinned animals before;
the men had always done that. She supposed Spirit Bear
probably thought it wouldn't be a good idea for Desert
Rose to carry raw meat that far. She watched the process.

It was disgusting! It was almost as bad as
tanning hides. Her young friend split the delicate
underside of the rabbit Kaitlin was holding. Warmth
radiated out from the innards with a sickening smell.
The organs came out with a plop. They lay in a heap of
raw and quivering globs of grey and red.

Next, Morning Dove used a knife to separate the
skin and fur from the muscle. The skin didn't cooperate
easily with the Indian's administrations. Kaitlin noticed
the white tendons and connective

tissues just under the fur, but there didn't appear to be any blood. She found that strange.

    While the women worked, Desert Rose took out the basket-weaving materials from a bag and put it in Kaitlin's area inside the tipi. She was still angered at Opossum eyes for what she'd done. It was a great dishonor to destroy another's hard work.

    She knew one of the main reasons *Woniya Mato* had approached her was to see if Golden Eyes was okay. Young Elk may have witnessed the destruction of the basket, for the chief had known about it. He didn't come right out and ask her, but it was obvious to Desert Rose that very little escaped the knowing eyes of Spirit Bear.

    Woniya Mato secured meat daily for the women in the tipis of isolation. Most of the time, he gave Desert Rose time to prepare the meals, but today his timing was so that he delivered them to her just as she approached the outskirts of the area to take the basket supplies to Kaitlin. She personally believed he wanted to check on his *wayaka* himself.

    Spirit Bear was angry when Young Elk told him about Opossum Eyes destroying *Mazaska Zi Ista*'s basket. He was tired of the woman's interference in his life! Because he was chief, it was necessary to handle the situation with the insolent girl delicately. He didn't wish to destroy her, yet he was impatient for her desire for him to end.

Nonetheless, the chief couldn't allow her to disrespect others in the community. *Would his people see his wayaka as someone worthy of protecting from an established member of the tribe?* If anything, they would support his decision for mild punishment for Opossum Eyes if he went that route because Golden Eyes belonged to him, and for that reason, she was to be respected. Indians believed that all could earn respect, even a *wayaka.*

He longed for Golden Eyes to return. He missed her sweet smiles and quick looks. She gazed at everything with wonder. Most of all, Spirit Bear missed her softness secured in his strong embraces. He could not wait to taste her again. The masterful man hoped the first time he attempted to seduce her she would submit. He hoped he could abstain from taking her if she did not.

Woniya Mato's desire for *Mazaska Zi Ista* was renewed when he saw her standing with the others. When her heated gaze locked with his, it brought his repressed needs smoldering to the surface. He'd turned his horse away in order to maintain his air of command. He would never break the Indian laws for a *winyan,* not even *Mazaska Zi Ista.*

It was strictly forbidden for a man to have contact with a *winyan* while her spirit wrestled. Great power fought within her, and it would seek revenge on any man who neared the battleground. Often times, it took control of the *winyan's* body and caused her to behave and react in a foreign manner.

If a man happened upon a woman during menses without realizing it, it could cost him his power as a warrior or hunter. His weapons could fail him during war or in time of need when confronting a predator or dangerous prey. Even though the powerful chieftain knew this, he'd risked a moment of his time to deliver Golden Eyes personally on the night her spirit began to fight.

With only a snatch of time, his spirit wouldn't have been endangered. Still, men steered clear of the isolation area just to be sure. Never would one knowingly put his honor and manhood on the line for such a reason.

When *Mazaska Zi Ista* had been injured and her spirit wrestled, his life brother, the shaman, protected them from the spirits so that they could save the girl's life. *Wawat'ecaka* cleaned the girl up when it became necessary.

Woniya Mato freed *Runs with the Wind* so he could go back to the herd. Next, the leader found *Ojilaka Hehaka* to release him from duty. Spirit Bear would enjoy this time watching his *ska wayaka* without her knowledge. He melted into the woods to oversee her interactions.

Kaitlin and Morning Dove had just gotten the rabbits suspended over the spits when he returned. The rolled furs were placed neatly by the side of the tipi. Playful Otter prepared the vegetables.

He was surprised to see the closeness of *Mazaska Zi Ista* and the other two women. They treated her as a valued member of the tribe! They were honorable women!

He also saw how frequently the flap on the further tipi kept opening for Opossum Eyes to glare at Kaitlin. He was unsure how much of this behavior was encouraged by her tipi-mate, Stormy Night. He hoped that it wasn't much; the older girl should know better. At least the other women in the remaining three tipis appeared oblivious to what was going on.

Slowly, the roasting meat cooked and the mouth-watering aroma filled the air. The women sat in a group and laughed like old friends. It was satisfying for the chief to know his *winyan* was so welcome and safe with these trustworthy women.

When she was finished eating, Kaitlin put the remaining meat from the first rabbit on a bone platter. Then she added vegetables. To his surprise, she walked toward the tipi with the two women who spied on her with dagger eyes.

What was she trying to do, get attacked? She didn't know the heart of Opossum Eyes. The chief knew that she was a vicious person who loved to stir trouble. His heart wanted to call out to his *wayaka*, but he waited in silence.

Was she trying to make amends to this mean girl? She, who did nothing against others? Opossum Eyes had destroyed Kaitlin's hard work, and yet she was so thoughtful as to share a meal with them? His heart grew even warmer for the honey-haired beauty.

Both Stormy Night and Opossum Eyes scrambled out of their tipi to meet Kaitlin. They'd seen what she was doing, but were also surprised when she walked up to their tipi with a food offering. Normally, they had a long wait for Stormy Night's husband's first wife to bring food to them.

Opossum Eyes was not ready to make nice with the white woman. She stood with her legs apart and her arms folded across her chest. Her eyes were narrowed with hate as she looked upon the becoming girl who'd stolen the man of her heart.

The icy-hearted maiden didn't make it easy for Kaitlin. Golden Eyes tentatively approached her. She motioned to the platter that the food was for them. Deceitfully, Opossum Eyes didn't acknowledge that she understood.

Kaitlin came to stand directly in front of her and proffered the plate of food to her. Opossum Eyes quickly flipped the food onto Kaitlin's chest and smashed it against the fabric. She smiled when she noted the golden girl's eyes glisten with unshed tears.

"Why did you do that?" scolded Stormy Night. "I am hungry. It could be hours before Little Mouse comes with more food!"

"You would accept food from a whore?" asked the first woman from between gritted teeth. She expected support when belittling this foe, not ridicule. "I refuse. It could be poisoned."

Stormy Night said nothing. She was irritated over the loss of a good meal. She'd had to smell the tantalizing aromas for over an hour now.

When she could remain quiet no longer, she finally said, "You forget who brought the meat."

"I do not forget. He would not have poisoned it; *she* would have."

"You would do well to forget him, Opossum Eyes. He is mighty and can choose any. He chooses her."

"*Tos*, for now. But he will change his mind."

Kaitlin didn't know what else to do to show she wasn't mad and would like to get along. When the woman took her good will and threw it back in her face, the fair girl wanted to weep. *Hadn't she suffered enough?* She'd lost her mother, and in essence, also her father and brother. She doubted she'd ever see them again.

She'd lost her spirit and dignity; she didn't even own her own life now! What more did Opossum Eyes want? At least the other woman didn't appear to join in on ridiculing her. For that, she was thankful!

Kaitlin pulled the platter away from her chest and turned her on her heel. She wouldn't cry and give the spiteful girl satisfaction! Let them go hungry when there was plenty for all!

Kaitlin walked back to her tipi and ducked inside. Her friends around the dying fire followed her in.

Playful Otter came up to Kaitlin. "I am sorry, *Mazaska Zi Ista*. I did not think she would do this in the presence of Stormy Night."

The honeyed-blonde still had unshed tears glistening in her eyes, but she took a calming breath and replied with Lakota and mixed English, "The other did nothing. It was the entirely the girl with mean eyes. In fact, I believe the older woman reprimanded her with her mouth."

"That is good. Let us get you in clean clothes." The three left the tipi and went to the stone basin. Kaitlin had the root that made soap when pounded. She stripped and washed her body in the small pool. She was going to wash her garment, but Morning Dove quickly did so before she had a chance.

"Thank you, my friends! I will never forget your kindness and support."

Smiling back, they replied, "Nor will we forget yours. You, who dare to bring a meal to the vicious Opossum Eyes!" Giggling filled the air and the tension was broken.

Kaitlin donned her clean dress, grabbed the wet one, and they returned to the camp. They sat outside until dark fell, fed the fire more wood, and watched the crackling conflagration. Kaitlin had always loved to watch the red, orange, and blue flames lick at branches slowly before devouring them. When the moon lit the land, they retired for the night.

Spirit Bear seethed. How dare Opossum Eyes treat the tender gesture of *Mazaska Zi Ista* like that! That *winyan* was filled with bad spirits. Maybe she needed released from the demons, or maybe he needed to speak with her father about finding her a mate… in another camp!

He decided on the later… first thing in the morning. The mean maiden was of marrying age. Most marriages were arranged, and he had a friend in

the brotherhood just west of them. He was a Yankton
warrior with a powerful reputation. This man, Eagle
Talon, had spoken of his dissatisfaction with the women
in his band. He'd hinted at uniting their bands through
marriage, but he hadn't singled out any certain *winyan*.

Opossum Eyes wasn't the most beautiful or
desirable *winyan* in the group, but once a man got past her
derisive personality, she was pleasing to the eye. If she
were in a new environment without allies, she'd have to
be pleasant to make friends. Eagle Talon also had a
domineering enough personality; she'd present him a nice,
enjoyable challenge. *Tos*, this is what Spirit Bear needed
to do.

He returned his attention to the camp set apart
and enjoyed looking at *Mazaska Zi Ista* in the warm fire
light. The front of her glowed with gold and the back of
her was caressed with the silver of the moon. He could
catch snatches of conversation and tinkling laughter
from time to time.

Spirit Bear watched the women until they
entered the tipi for the night before he left them.

With morning, the chief paid a visit to Stands Tall.
The older man welcomed him into his home. After being
seated and waited upon by their wife, Stands Tall looked at
the chief with questioning eyes. It wasn't often that the
busy chief paid special visits.

"I have come to speak with you about
Opossum Eyes," *Woniya Mato* began.

The other man was silent. He knew the chief hadn't come to offer for her in union. His daughter was very strong willed, and she didn't always make decisions that made her father proud. He waited in near dread as to what the young chief would say.

"I wanted to see if you would be willing to join your daughter with a *kola* of mine in another village," he paused to allow his words to sink in. "He is an honorable man with a great reputation as a warrior. He has requested a union with a *winyan* from our community to unite our tribes."

Stands Tall breathed a sigh of relief. He knew it was time to tie his daughter with a man. Those here understood her moods and tongue. None as yet had made an offer for her. This would solve many problems though he hated to see her go so far. In addition, it was an honor for his daughter to marry a warrior with a reputation!

Knowing that typically, daughters remained near their mothers when united with a man in case of something happening to her husband, he said, "Does the chief agree to care for Opossum Eyes if this *kola* joins *Wakantanka*? I must be sure she will be cared for, as I grow older."

"*Tos*, you have my word. I will send a runner today to their village to see if Eagle Talon still wills this. I will have him make arrangements with his chief, Wise Owl, to ensure her continued care in case something befalls him. It will be two weeks before we hear anything. The camp is over five days' ride from here."

Both men stood and clasped each other's forearms in agreement. Then Spirit Bear left. The two men felt good about the decision concerning Opossum Eyes. She'd be honorably married and also could no longer cause problems in the village.

CHAPTER THIRTEEN

Expanding Skills

Kaitlin was sad to see Morning Dove depart with Desert Rose after they ate breakfast. She really liked her and her companionship. At least her other new friend, Playful Otter, remained. Morning Dove promised to return with the evening meal.

Once they were gone, Playful Otter got out drilling supplies and sat in the yard. She motioned for Kaitlin to get the stones she'd collected. The white girl wondered what they were going to do with them.

When she retrieved the gems, the honeyed-blonde handed them to Playful Otter who selected a smaller stone and placed it in a wedge-lever combination instrument made of bone. It held the stone fairly secure to prevent it from moving as she worked on boring a hole in one end.

The stone Kaitlin selected was semi-transparent. It was mostly a solid medium blue marbled with clear blue crystal. It had a natural indentation near the top half. It was this area that Playful Otter selected to begin to drill.

The bronzed woman took very fine sand and placed it in the groove. Then she took a rounded sliver of granite, stood it on end, and began to roll it back and forth between her palms while applying pressure to the sand in the indentation. Playful Otter continued this process for quite a while.

Finally, her brow sweaty from the movement, she stopped. She tapped the sand out of the hole and gently wiped it with her fingers. The beginning of a hole was evident. The width of the granite sliver on the stone was nearly transparent. A tiny speck had worn away so that a miniscule bright hole could be seen.

Playful Otter handed the equipment to Kaitlin to give it a try. The light-complected beauty took the granite, added sand to the hole, and began to do as she'd seen Playful Otter. The other woman had made it look so simple! She just applied pressure and rolled the granite over and over, back and forth, in her palm.

Kaitlin had trouble keeping the stone from slipping. The sand would spill and the rock would slip. *How in the world did she ever find the patients to learn this technique?*

For over an hour, Kaitlin worked and became frustrated with the drilling procedure. Finally, the hole was big enough for sinew to slide through. Kaitlin couldn't wipe the smile from her face.

Playful Otter handed her another stone. Kaitlin found, that indeed, her smile could disappear! However, she took it and began again. Already her neck and trap muscles burned with such intense use. Playful Otter began working with stones of her own.

When it was rest time, Kaitlin fell upon her mats and was asleep within minutes. Every time she closed her eyes, she saw blue stones. She dreamed of sand and granite rods turning back and forth.

After she awoke, the first thing Kaitlin thought about was all the work that was involved in preparing gems before they could become beautiful finery. It was dumbfounding! She'd never take decorative ornaments for granted again! Spirit Bear's *wayaka* lay quietly while waiting on Playful Otter to awaken; she dreamed of different jewelry she could to make with her collection.

In the afternoon, Kaitlin began construction on a new waterproof basket. She didn't have the endurance yet to continue drilling holes in the small stones as did her friend. They happily worked and talked the afternoon away.

Just before nightfall, Playful Otter told Kaitlin that her time in the tipis of isolation was coming to an end; she'd be leaving with the new sun. After they enjoyed breakfast together, she'd need to return to the camp.

That night, three new women arrived in their camp. They joined Kaitlin's tipi. One was a mature woman with two children who were being cared for by a second wife. Another was unmarried and just a year older than Kaitlin. The last girl was not yet inducted into womanhood, but her spirits had begun fighting; she was only ten winters.

The oldest woman was called Fresh Water. She seemed very friendly and motherly to Kaitlin. She smiled often and studied her from beneath her lashes. She was very good at calming the fears of the woman-child.

Kaitlin had noticed the girl who was close to her age before in the village. They'd gathered water at the same time before. Her name was New Moon.

The ten-year old was called Singing Cicada. Kaitlin poured some tea for her to help with belly bloating and cramping. For the youngster, thankfully, the spirit fighting was mild, and she really didn't require the tea, but it made her feel more grown up; she gratefully accepted it.

Kaitlin breathed a thankful prayer that she wasn't being left alone with Opossum Eyes. She didn't know if she could stand being isolated with her callousness! The *ska winyan* shuddered in horror at the thought.

When all was quiet, Kaitlin managed to sleep. It was the most restful night she'd spent in the tipis of isolation although more people were present to make night noises. Kaitlin didn't want Playful Otter to go, but she no longer feared her departure. Morning Dove brought Kaitlin and Playful Otter breakfast. The other women present would have someone bring food. They sat one last time together before Playful Otter had to return to the normal rigors of daily Indian life.

The day progressed much the same even though there were new people to get acquainted with. Kaitlin found that Fresh Water was very quiet, doing most of the chores unassisted. She appeared to prefer being the one in charge of the domestic tasks.

Singing Cicada, however, was a chatterbox. She incessantly asked questions and followed New Moon around. It was almost as if they were sisters.

Kaitlin sat quietly, watching, as she worked on her basket. New Moon approached her to look at her work. She nodded in appreciation then sat by Kaitlin.

Kaitlin could only haltingly understand her words. She heard her say, "You make good."

"Thank you," she said with a beaming smile.

Singing Cicada approached her after she saw New Moon sitting by Kaitlin. She felt comfortable in the tipi. She even blurted out a personal question.

"What's it like to be a *wayaka*?"

Fresh Water drew in a sharp breath. "Singing Cicada, you know very well the rules of society. We do not pry!"

"*Tos*, Fresh Water."

"You are nearly an adult. Already your spirit battles. Act like you will be going through the Rites of Womanhood soon."

"*Tos*, Fresh Water."

"I am sorry for Singing Cicada's rudeness. Please forgive her," said the oldest woman in the tipi. Fresh Water appeared to be taking responsibility for the young woman's words.

"It's okay," replied Kaitlin. She could see the naked curiosity in the three woman's eyes at the question. She didn't want to answer, so she returned to the basket weaving. She didn't like to think about being someone's slave.

"Desert Rose teach you?" New Moon asked, motioning towards her basket-in-progress.

"*Tos*."

"You are fortunate to have one so skilled to teach you," Fresh Water complimented.

"*Tos*, I agree."

For a while, all was quiet except for the chore noises that Fresh Water made. Both New Moon and Singing Cicada moved together and played a game in the dirt with sticks and rocks. It made Kaitlin smile as she watched them.

Through the open flap in the tipi, Kaitlin saw Opossum Eyes leaving right before the heat of the day. Again, she sent up an offering of thanks. At least she felt unthreatened now!

New Moon said, "I see you meet Opossum Eyes."

"*Tos*." She didn't offer more.

"She mean." New Moon received a look from Fresh Water. She continued, "Well, she is! Anyone who receives man looks, she gets mad at. Men will be men and look. She cannot stop it just because she wants to! She just wants all the attention for herself. She doesn't know how to get it, so she just gets bad attention by being mean."

"New Moon! Hush! You do not talk so!" Singing Cicada giggled behind her hand. All present knew the truth that only one dared to speak. As if it were a punishment for the turn the conversation had made, Fresh Water said, "It is rest time now. Lie down and sleep."

No one slept, but everyone rested and was quiet. Near the end of the time to rest, Kaitlin saw more new arrivals and one more departure. Kaitlin didn't know the first woman leaving. She was staying at a tipi further back, but she did see another run out to leave with her. It was Stormy Night. Kaitlin knew that her time to leave, as well, would most likely be in the morning.

After refreshing themselves and using the privacy area, Kaitlin attempted to drill more holes in her stones. She had two infatuated watchers. She tried to tell them that she didn't know what she was doing, but they were too enthralled to pay her any mind. It put more stress on Kaitlin to do a good job.

She managed to drill holes in two more stones before her arms screamed at her to stop. One was a light purple-pink hued crystal while the other was a black onyx. She'd spent hours drilling holes, and she only had four completed! It was frustrating and discouraging.

Kaitlin was relieved to see Desert Rose appear with her meal already cooked. She didn't really want to help skin an animal again! As they sat down to share a meal, Kaitlin saw may others bringing loved ones things to eat.

"Is this your last day?" Desert Rose asked her. "*Tos*.
I believe that in the morning I will be
free."

"This is good. I will bring breakfast to share and then we can walk back together."

Although Kaitlin only understood words here and there, she could fill in the blanks when they were speaking about daily rituals.

"Are you working on another basket?"

"*Tos*. I will show you." Kaitlin retrieved her incomplete work.

"This one is even better that the last!"

"I am glad to have the practice; it has helped me learn."

Desert Rose smiled with understanding. Then she gathered items to go.

"I will see you in the morning."

"*Tos,* will look forward to it."

When Desert Rose reached the outskirts of the boundaries, a lithe shadow of a man materialized. "I see she is not returning with you this night."

"*Hiya,* my chief." She masked her startled reaction. *Warriors moved with such stealth!* When his piercing stare caught her eye, she felt required to add, "But she will return with me in the morning."

"This is good. Thank you"

Desert Rose smiled and nodded. Then each went their separate ways.

Kaitlin had finished the bottom of the waterproof basket weave. It was very difficult to complete such a tight weave that even water could not escape from, but the challenge of the binding in which the bottom met the sides was even greater. Water found the weakest points. The white girl decided to work on that part in the morning when she was fresh.

Kaitlin sat with New Moon and Singing Cicada and worked on increasing her language. She pointed to her heart and made a beating motion.

"*Cante,*" New Moon replied. "If it is emotion you speak of, the word is *'Wastelaka'.* And," she paused and looked meaningfully at the sleeping mats with a sly smile, "*wikiskata*" would mean the attentions of *wica* to *winyan* at night."

Kaitlin's face flamed under her friend's inquisitive stare. Kaitlin turned to the tipi and pointed. Then she made motions to all the tipis in the apart location.

"Isnatipi."

Kaitlin made motions trying to ask her why. With the best way she knew how, Moon Eyes, with the help of Fresh Water, told her of how it's believed that when a spirit battles within a woman's body, she can become possessed as well as any who are near her. It could compromise a man's power. For this reason, she comes to the tipis apart.

The blonde only understood some of what the women tried to explain. She understood it had something to do with spirits. *These people were so very spiritual! No one in the white society would ever believe that the 'wild savages' were so religious and superstitious!*

Kaitlin lay down with the others but didn't rest easily. She knew that with the birth of the new day, she'd be returning into the village and the ever so watchful eyes. She'd also be near the powerful and dominating chief. The *wayaka* shivered at the thought.

During the night, Kaitlin awoke sweating in the heat. The extra bodies in the hut and the sweltering night had her almost feeling ill; the white girl walked into the yard.

A gentle breeze lifted her damp hair from her neck. She sat on a log made for that purpose by the fire pit. Stars twinkled merrily at her.

The honey-kissed blonde sighed. She piled her tresses in her hand and held her hair off her neck. She was tempted to go to the area of privacy alone to splash water on her neck to cool herself off but was worried that somehow her unaccompanied trip would be discovered.

Kaitlin didn't want to wake a woman in the tipi. They were all sleeping and this was hard to achieve on this humid of a night; still, she felt ill with heat. The white woman was undecided and was tempted to do the forbidden.

Then she saw him. *Woniya Mato* was standing in the place where Young Elk stood frequently to watch over the mini-village apart. His eyes glittered in the night.

Knowing she was watched, and realizing that he meant for her to know, Kaitlin walked to the area of privacy. She went straight to the stone pool and splashed water on her face. The young woman didn't stop there; she refreshed her arms, legs, and neck with the icy coldness. It was heaven.

The golden-eyed beauty realized her body no longer was menstruating, but she wouldn't admit that before morning. Kaitlin trembled when she thought of returning this night with the magnetic man. Yet, she was only prolonging the inevitable.

Slowly, the *wayaka* stood and prepared to return to the tipis apart. She didn't see the chief but knew he lurked nearby. Nevertheless, a strange prickling of her skin alerted her to a foreign presence.

Kaitlin heard a grunting noise. A rustling of the bushes and a digging in the foliage had her silent with fear. A pronounced sniffing noise slowly broadcasted a visitor. It was in the woods about fifteen feet in front of her.

Although the moon was fairly bright, the white-skinned woman still couldn't see clearly. A large shaggy-furred animal with a great sloping back was dimly outlined in the moonlight. It broke branches in the underbrush as it shuffled forward. Kaitlin stifled a scream. She'd never forget what a bear's silhouette looked like from her experience near the log cabin.

Suddenly, a hard wall of muscle supported her weak limbs. A strong arm circled her waist, and masculine voice whispered in her ear.

"*Ahan iwahwayela, Mazaska Zi Ista.*"

The captive would try to stand quietly; the war chief gave her courage. She knew a bear could easily defeat a man and woman team, but she instantly felt safer as his power radiated into her by his nearness. Kaitlin leaned back into his comforting security.

The bear continued to lumber closer. The couple stood meshed together, the man protecting the woman through his embrace. His hands were ready to retrieve weapons in a beat of his heart.

Within moments, the massive black bear stood on the path in front of them. She was less than ten feet away! Kaitlin was close enough to see the pale light from the moon reflected in her small black eyes. The bear stood still as her grand black nose twitched in the night air.

She made loud *hunka-hunka* noises as she studied the pair of humans. Finally, as if dismissing them because they were of no serious threat, she lumbered past. Two smaller shadows joined hers as they shuffled toward the chilled water to drink and cool themselves.

After the bears passed by, Kaitlin felt herself lifted and nestled into a warm solid chest. Spirit Bear retreated on silent feet. He carried her a safe distance away from the powerful mammals. On the fringe of the territory deemed as isolation, Sprit Bear allowed her to stand on the shaking ground. He supported his captive until she stabilized.

The white woman's eyes trailed up powerful bronzed arms until they reached his handsome face. A tender smile of relief was etched on his full lips, but the warrior's eyes sparkled with mischievousness.

More and more, *Wakantanka* gave signs to Spirit Bear that the white woman belonged to him, and her place was in the village! What more of a powerful sign could He have given to the chief whose totem was the image of a bear? Spirit Bear understood the signs of the Great Spirit!

"Until the morning, my sweet, golden bird," he thought. *"The Great Spirit has shown me you are mine and that no harm will befall you. The mighty bear is your kola."*

Woniya Mato looked down into her innocent face. Her amber eyes were wide with her recent fear and awareness of his commanding proximity. He tenderly stroked her cheek.

He walked her toward her tipi of one more night. Spirit Bear stopped before reaching the point where he'd begin to endanger his spirit. He reached down with his finger and applied pressure underneath her chin until Kaitlin's head angled up toward his. He electrified her lips with a tender caress. Then he was gone.

Slowly, Kaitlin's fingers touched where his lips had been seconds before. They felt as if burned by fire. It was crazy that his touch affected her so.

The white woman shook her head. A bear: a mother with cubs! She'd stood near enough to reach out and touch them and lived to tell of it. Never in her wildest dreams would Kaitlin believe that had happened.

Her warrior had been there to protect her. *How could she deny how he made her feel? He made her feel as if she could face anything! Anything except murder…*

The blonde returned to her bed and slowly allowed her body to relax. Morning would come before she was ready. It seemed seconds later, Fresh Water had the tea prepared.

Kaitlin arose and came to the fire. She smiled her thanks. Fresh Water smiled back. New Moon and Singing Cicada also joined the tea drinking.

The four women visited the place of privacy together. On the way, an object glimmered in Kaitlin's view. She stooped to see that it was. A large bear claw was wedged between two rocks. She dug at it for a few seconds before she was able to dislodge it.

"What you find?" New Moon asked.

Kaitlin did not know how to say 'bear claw', so she held it up for the women to see.

The others stared in wonder. A woman rarely discovered things of such great power.

Finally, New Moon said, "You find *mato ova.*"

The dawning of the word meaning for '*mato*' struck Kaitlin. *Mato* meant bear. She quietly studied the faces of the other for a few silent moments. Then, because she wanted to know what the chief's name, *Woniya Mato,* mean, she asked, "What does '*woniya*' mean?"

With a knowing smile, Fresh Water motioned to the air around them. Then she pointed to her heart, indicating her spirit, and motioned to the world around her again. Seeing Kaitlin's confused expression, she continued this by pointing to different things. Her new friend pointed to a tree, a flower, the water; the whole while she waved her arms around to indicate the spirit habitations around them.

At last, Kaitlin understood. *Woniya Mato* meant Spirit Bear! She grinned with pleasure. Then she pointed to herself. "*Mazaska Zi Ista*?" she asked.

Singing Cicada pointed to Kaitlin's eyes. "My name is 'Eyes'? How strange." Singing Cicada shook her head. "*Ista*," she said pointing to her eyes. Looking around, she finally spied a sparkling gold rock. Picking it up, she said, "*Mazaska zi inyan.*"

Still not comprehending, she said, "Oh, I'm Rock Eyes?"

Singing Cicada picked up another stone, this time a dull gray rock. She said, "*inyan.*" Then she held up a gold rock and repeated the same word. Holding up the gray rock again, she said, "*Hota inyan.*" Holding the gold one in the sun to capture the sparkling flakes, she said, "*Mazaska zi inyan.*"

"I'm Gold Eyes! I get it!" Excited with discovery, the girls spent the morning discussing the names of the people she'd met. Kaitlin didn't understand what the medicine man's name, *Wawakankan*, meant, and she knew that *Unjinjintka Can Koica* was some kind of a rose, but the blonde didn't understand what kind.

As though sensing Kaitlin's thoughts of her, Desert Rose came with a late morning breakfast. The five women sat and enjoyed the fruit and *aguyapi*. They laughed and spoke of Kaitlin's quick grasp of word meanings.

Fresh Water spoke of Kaitlin finding a bear claw and how that led to the understanding and discussions of names. Desert Rose looked in awed silence at Kaitlin. She, who shared the legendary Sprit Bear's tipi found a gift from a *mato*? This was a great honor! *Unjinjintka Can Koica* must tell the chief when they met him. She was sure they would meet him upon their return to the village.

After saying goodbye and giving quick hug to each person, the two friends left the area of isolation. Kaitlin proudly carried her basket-in-progress, her leather bag of gems with the drilling items given to her by Playful Otter, and her bear claw. They were joined by Young Elk as they neared the property line to the tipis of isolation.

Men normally walked in front followed by the women, but since Young Elk didn't always know the destination of the women, he followed at a leisurely pace. If one were to meet Young Elk, they would question if he was even with them if they hadn't been present at the ceremony where he was honored with the task.

Kaitlin hated to admit it to herself, but she was disappointed that Spirit Bear didn't appear to be around when she arrived back at the village. She'd looked forward to seeing him again with dreaded anticipation. She scolded herself for feeling disappointed.

The honey-haired beauty went into the tipi and placed her possessions against the wall with her other things. She couldn't help but to take a moment to fondle the exquisite finery of the dress that *Wawat'ecaka* had made for her.

CHAPTER FOURTEEN

Growing Closer

There was still at least an hour and a half of time left before the mid-day rest period, so Kaitlin wandered towards Gentle Rabbit's tipi. Young Elk grunted and motioned to the place where *Wawat'ecaka* worked with leather. The blonde turned toward it to help the older woman.

When she got to *Wawat'ecaka's* special spot, she saw that indeed, the friendly lady was hard at work on the task. The larger and smaller antelope hides were stretched taunt on two racks. They shone with a fresh coat of something.

Wawat'ecaka was bent over the deer hide in the soaking hole. She appeared to be scrubbing it. Kaitlin went to meet her.

Wawat'ecaka looked up and smiled her greeting. The thing *Wawat'ecaka* scrubbed had been soaking in the basin of waste! *How could she stand to touch the filth?* After the first powerful wave of stench assaulted her, Kaitlin nearly turned away. However, she knew to trust Gentle Rabbit. The elder was the expert on fine leather making, not she: there was a method to the madness.

Sucking in a deep breath, the white woman forced herself forward. She watched a moment as Gentle Rabbit scoured the hide with gravel to remove the embedded debris. Then she bent down to help.

Kaitlin found that she had to hold her breath in prevent the strong nausea from overtaking her before she could get close to the material. The overpowering stench permeated the leather. No amount of scrubbing could remove it. In the end, however, most of the fecal matter had been detached.

Wawat'ecaka then took the garment out of the soaking area. This area was a still pond separated from the main river. Gentle Rabbit used it to soak and scrub her leather.

After this process, *Wawat'ecaka* planned to wash her creation using the flowing water. She took a yucca plant and made soap. With the lather, she rubbed it into the texture of the leather. Again, she used gravel to clean it. As the elder worked the leather, soap, and gravel, she dipped the garment into the fresh river water. Kaitlin helped after she saw Gentle Rabbit's intentions.

When finished with both sides, Gentle Rabbit repeated the process. Then she stretched the hair-free pelt as tightly as it would go onto the new rack. They would allow the leather to dry during the heat of the day. When they returned, they'd work the brain solution into the hide.

Using more yucca soap, Kaitlin scrubbed her arms, hands, and face; she couldn't stand the thought of the filthy slop remaining on her when she went to her tipi to rest. The white girl wanted to be as clean as possible. She planned on taking a bath at the end of the day since it had been a week since she'd really been able to clean herself fully.

Wawat'ecaka patted Kaitlin's back in thanks. Then they went back to the village to rest. The blonde approached her tipi while Gentle Rabbit disappeared in hers.

When she got near her home, the captive could tell Spirit Bear was present. His powerful aura reached out to her before she could enter. He was sitting in his work space, designing another bow. He appeared to be attempting to make a longer base.

The warrior's ebony eyes captured hers, and he paused in his work to watch her enter. She felt his eyes follow her as she went to the sleeping mats and sat. Kaitlin removed her moccasins and lay back into the supple softness. She sighed with contentment.

The sleeping mats in the tipis apart could never compare to the graceful softness worthy of the chief's! The pretty blonde rubbed her cheek into the velvety feel of the leather and furs. She didn't realize obsidian eyes were still upon her.

Was this an invitation? Did the *ska winyan* know what she was doing to him? A man in need could only take so much! To see his female on his bed rubbing her face in the sleeping mat was almost more than he could take!

With purpose, he rose. Instantly, the blonde beauty froze. Her golden eyes watched him as he walked toward the sleeping mat. His heated gaze met hers and held it prisoner. Kaitlin stared as if entranced and watched as he removed his leggings. The warrior continued to hold her eyes captive as he reclined beside her.

"*Intinma, Woniya Mato*," she pleaded. She only wanted him to sleep. She was tired and didn't want to fight the battle of wills.

"*Hiya, Mazaska Zi Ista. Nimitawa ktelo*, you are mine, and I have waited for this." He propped up on his shoulder and looked into her wild eyes.

She could only stare as he traced her collar bone with his finger. Her heart beat madly under the fabric of her work dress. Slowly, he trailed his finger down the crevasse between her breasts.

The *wayaka* tried to roll away, as if to sleep. He chuckled at her feeble attempt to escape him. *Woniya Mato* took his arm and rolled her onto her back. Then he lowered his head.

Her large eyes watched him timidly as he lowered his lips to hers. He moved them sensually on hers. Kaitlin's breath came in shallow gasps, but she willed herself to remain still.

"Still determined to resist me, my *Wastelaka*?" he whispered into her lips. "We shall see…"

The chief deepened the kiss and explored the inner cavity of her mouth. His tongue danced against hers patiently. If the *wayaka* didn't have passion for him, he had plenty for the both of them.

The bear encounter had erased any doubt that she was for him. He hadn't forgotten his plan to seduce her into submission, but he didn't think he could refrain if she didn't submit. It had been too long, and he had great desire for this *ska winyan*.

Had not the spirit of the great bear shown him on more than one occasion that she was for him? It was the will of *Wakantanka*. No, Spirit Bear wouldn't feel any regret. She'd come to feel for him as he did her eventually.

He loosened the bindings on her dress. Her body was bathed in light coming from the *tipa*, or upper ventilation flaps in the tipi. Her breasts invited his lips to taste them, so he succumbed.

His captive lay under his hands as they explored every nook and cranny. They only thing that gave away her heightened state of passion was her rapid breathing and the hammering of her heart. Still, she just watched as his mouth and hands made love to her body.

At last, her body took control from her mind. The attractive white arched her hips and moaned. Spirit Bear smiled tenderly and began the mating ritual. Surprise entered her eyes as she looked into his striking face. This time there was no pain or discomfort!

Spirit Bear smiled down at her and nodded. Together they rode the horse of passion. After a time, he rolled off her and hugged her to him on the mat. "So it was good for you, *Wastelaka*. I am glad. It honors me to pleasure you."

Ashamed and embarrassed that her body had responded wantonly to him again, Kaitlin hid her face from him. To distract herself, she tried to remember what the word '*Wastelaka*' meant again. She knew it was one of the new words she'd learned back at the tipis apart, but the meaning kept eluding her…

Spirit Bear held her quite some time before he felt her body relax and sleep. He smiled down at her naked form, glad that *Wakantanka* had chosen him as her mate. He would guard her with his life.

The chief filled his sight with her until she awoke. When she opened her brilliant eyes and met his midnight ones, he smiled at her. Before Kaitlin could stop it, a tiny smile perked the corners of her luscious mouth. Then, as if to punish him for pleasuring her, she erased the suggestion of satisfaction.

He reached for her lips. She moaned and said, "Not again, *Woniya Mato*! Aren't you ever satisfied?"

But he only kissed her before he dressed. He could very easily have taken her again, but the warrior would give her time to adjust to the betrayal of her body. It would take a period for her mind to catch up and accept what her heart knew to be true.

Woniya Mato waited patiently for the woman of his heart to dress. He kept his back turned to give her privacy. He did it for himself as well. If he watched her graceful nude body for long, need would consume him once more.

"I'm dressed, mighty master," her mocking voice greeted him. He didn't understand her words, but he could grasp the tone. He didn't acknowledge that she'd said anything but simply went outside and waited for her to follow.

He took Kaitlin to the Area of Privacy and allowed her to fill their *mniapahta*. When they returned, he called to *Ojilaka Hehaka* and watched as they went back to the tanning area. Spirit Bear smiled at the haughty swing of her hips as she walked angrily away.

Spirit Bear knew that when her heart won over her mind, the beauty would beg him to love her, and he'd meet the challenge. He grinned mischievously at the thought.

The war chief turned back to work on the construction of the new bow. By experimentation, he'd discovered a way to add distance to his arrow flight. He was awed by the many blessings of *Wakantanka*. At the next celebration, *Woniya Mato* would demonstrate his new discovery if he'd perfected it.

Wawat'ecaka was already busy pressing the brain matter into the future leather when Kaitlin arrived. The young woman went to Gentle Rabbit's side and dipped her hand into the bone container holding a mixture of mashed brain and fat.

Kaitlin didn't think she'd ever get used to the slimy feeling of the slop they needed to rub into the hide. It felt like the bubbles of fat burst with goo when she pressed it. It made the blonde want to retch, but she scooped it up, pressed, and rubbed it into the hide regardless.

The stunning white girl worked the finishing materials in circles, back and forth, and up and down. She continued this until the section would absorb no more. Then she'd begin a new section bordering the old.

When the women finished one side, *Wawat'ecaka* turned it over and they began the opposite side anew. Kaitlin noticed that the second side seemed to go much quicker than the first. The last side was much closer to saturation after the completion of the first.

When it was done, the women shadowed by Young Elk returned to camp to begin the evening chores. Playful Otter and Morning Dove both waved to and greeted Kaitlin. She smiled in response.

Kaitlin was grateful to *Wawat'ecaka* for she'd already gathered wood for the day. The water was also collected after rest time. Mainly, it was just the meal that needed to be prepared and then the dishes would need to be washed. Last of all, Kaitlin desired a bath.

Woniya Mato returned shortly after she did and handed Kaitlin three already skinned squirrels. Still new at skewering, she studied the small frames for the best and easiest way to do this. She attempted it three times and nearly dropped the first small carcass into the dirt.

Spirit Bear smiled at her efforts. She saw him in her peripheral vision come to her aid. Gently, he took the frame from her hand and skewered it in one motion

"Show off," she grumbled. "You make it look so easy, but as you've shown me many times, your strength way surpasses mine!"

Kaitlin nearly bit her tongue as his smile widened at her grumbling. Fuming, she tried to do the next squirrel. It took her two tries, but on the third, she met with success. The third and final animal, she skewered on the second try.

As the small bodies roasted over the open flames, she peeled the *tinpsila* that seemed to be a major staple in the Indian's diet. The *wayaka* mixed the nearly powdered corn and wheat flour together and added water to make gruel. She sliced strawberries to sweeten the bread and mixed the dough together.

When the meat was nearly finished, the white woman placed the bread on flat rocks near the fire to cook. Soon, the meal was ready. She removed the first squirrel from the flames, placed two medium sized prairie turnips, and three pieces of flat bread onto the wooden platter she admired so many ties. Then she approached *Woniya Mato* with the provisions.

"My Lord, here is your food," she bowed low to show his royalty and supremacy over her. It was the only way she could face the power he held over every aspect of her life.

The warrior's eyes narrowed dangerously, for now they were in public. It was too hot to eat in the lodge, so they, like many others, ate out in their yards. He wouldn't allow her insolent behavior to continue. She would not mock him in public. He would tolerate some in private, but never in front of the eyes of the community. If he allowed it to go too far, he'd be forced to punish her, and he didn't want to do that.

He grasped her forearms holding the plate. His hands were glued to her, tempting her to fight him. Spirit Bear held her there for several long moments. When her golden eyes finally met his in tortured anguish, she cried, "What do you want from me? What can I give you that you have not already taken? Cannot I at least have my dignity?"

She bowed her head submissively, and he released her. He couldn't see the tears he knew streamed from her eyes.

"*Ho eyas wanna hecetu,*" he said gruffly. Kaitlin turned her back to her Lord and master to do his bidding. She continued to cook the *aguyapi* until the dough was gone. She removed the skewered meat from the flames and placed it on a bone platter.

Woniya Mato watched her as he consumed his delicious meal. He'd much pride for his *ska winyan.* Already she had mastered cooking meat over the open flame as well as the more difficult making of the *aguyapi.* For many, the correct amount of water and berries mixed into the dough was hard to determine. *Mazaska Zi Ista* had a natural talent for the correct consistency. On top of that, she'd yet to burn it or not cook it thoroughly; always, hers was perfect.

Spirit Bear was sorry he had to put her in her place. He knew she was still angry with herself for enjoying his attentions earlier that afternoon, but she didn't know what a serious fault it was for a slave to taunt her owner. It was especially dangerous to do it in public to the chief, no less!

He watched Golden Eye's stiff back as she finished the cooking chores. When he finished his plate, she offered him a second squirrel and more bread. He took seconds of both. It was a great honor to the cook to take more.

She grabbed the *mniapahta* and filled both of their cups with water. She sipped at hers while she waited for him to complete his meal. Still, she refused to meet his gaze.

When he finished, Kaitlin took his plate. She put the bones from his meal in a pile. The Indians, she discovered, wasted little. The tiny squirrel bones would be used for child spoons, jewelry, sewing needles, or something else. Never did they throw away anything.

Not wanting to eat, she put the remaining food on the platter and tried to take it in the tipi. Before she could make it three steps from the fire where Spirit Bear sat, his masculine voice called to her to stop.

She wondered what he wanted and silently griped to herself. Slowly, she turned into his heated look.

"*Uwa yo, Mazaska Zi Ista.*" He didn't leave room for her to disobey.

With unwilling feet, she approached him. Perhaps he wished to eat more. With hesitation, she proffered the platter to him. He shook his head and patted the ground next to him.

"*Iyotake. Wota,*" he commanded.

"You mean I can't even choose not to eat? I don't *want* to eat! I'm not hungry!" She didn't yell, but she wanted to! It wasn't fair that he commanded her every move! He told her when to eat, when to cook, when to lie down, when to sit, and when to allow him to make love to her! She did not want to live this life, *but what choice did she have?*

Dejectedly, the blonde sank to the ground. Listlessly, she picked up the Indian bread and nibbled on it. When she finished it, Kaitlin saw he watched her from the corner of his eyes. She picked up a small sweet turnip and ate that as well.

When the young woman attempted to push the plate from her, the chief nodded toward the squirrel. She didn't want to eat it, so she just picked at it. He finally withdrew a knife from the sheath attached to his leg.

Her eyes flashed a second of fear before he sliced the squirrel's hind leg from the rest of its body. He held the leg out to her and took the rest of the meat from her. He walked toward an elderly man living with his older wife and gave it to them to complement their meal. They thanked the chief and smiled their appreciation.

When *Woniya Mato* returned, he reclined and just watched her. He usually observed her with an emotionless mask. Normally one could not tell that he watched at all, so good was he at his technique. Now, however, the chief wanted her to feel the weight of his stare.

The warrior was willing to wait as long as he needed in order to ensure she did not pout her way to sickness. He'd force her to eat every meal in his presence rather than trusting her to keep her health up if need be. As always, he would be the victor.

When his *wayaka* finished, she gathered the dishes and put them in a pile. She disappeared into the hut. Upon Kaitlin's return, he noticed she had the porcupine brush, a towel, the strawberry conditioner, and soapwort. She also had a clean female breechcloth

and the cape-type garment *Wawat'ecaka* had made for her
while she suffered the greatest from her bruised and
separated ribs.

The attractive young woman approached him.
When she reached him, she stood silently in front of him
and looked down.

He asked her in Lakota, "Do you wish to
bathe?"

Kaitlin nodded without meeting his gaze. "*Tos.*
I will take you to our place after the
dishes are washed."

Kaitlin followed the approved distance behind the
intimidating leader of his people. She was so disheartened
that she had no power over *any* aspect of her life. She had
to be followed by a man even to use the restroom. It was
outlandish!

Even though she seethed with anger, she
couldn't help but to admire *Woniya Mato*'s manly
form in front of her. No man could compare to his
physique although some neared his build. Even the
way he walked advertised his great prowess and power.

His muscles rippled under the bronze skin. His
back radiated authority even as he swung his arms in a
relaxed mode. His wide shoulders narrowed to the small
but very male backside of him. Without meaning to, he
walked with silent feet and great stealth. She'd never hear
him if she didn't know he was there.

When she finished being a slave for him by cleaning his dishes, she had to go with him to their private bathing area. She wished he'd just trust her to bathe with the women. She didn't want to think about shared time together… alone… nude.

She flushed when she remembered the bath he'd given her. That seemed like eons ago. It was back in the time she'd innocently thought he was helping her to heal and get strong enough so that he could return her to her people. Now, however, she knew the true reasons he waited.

Surely her father or her brother looked for her! *Would Bradley try to rescue her?* If only the men in this village did not watch her like a hawk, perhaps she could escape again. *How could she ever hope to accomplish that while Ojilaka Hehaka or Woniya Mato flanked her everywhere?*

Kaitlin hurried and stripped when they reached the icy blue pond. She dove into the welcoming waters, cleaning away the stress of the past week from her body. When she washed her hair, she closed her eyes in the ecstasy of scrubbing and of the bubbles produced on her scalp. The *wayaka* felt revived and fresh when her hair squeaked with cleanliness. She dunked to rinse the suds from her hair.

When she opened her eyes, she didn't see Spirit Bear. She looked around for him. The masterful man was closer than she'd anticipated. He, too, had stripped and entered the cold calm waters.

He was close to her, closer than was comfortable. Kaitlin began to step tentatively backwards from him. He smirked and his eyes seem to glow with a predatory gleam.

Her commander closed the distance between them and captured her hands. He leaned over and looked down into her face. His black eyes sparkled with intention.

"Please, *Woniya Mato*. Just let me bathe!"

At first she thought he'd listen to her plea, for he took her hands and filled them with soap. With roguishness, he then placed her lather-filled palms upon his hard chest and washed his body with her hands.

She felt his nipple harden when her hands were forced to circle his chest. She groaned in frustration. Despite the fact she didn't want him controlling her life, she felt the monster within her awaken as she was forced to feel the smooth hard texture of his manly form.

His muscles were so clearly defined under her fingertips. Even though the water was nearly cold enough to cause hypothermia, his skin was hot to the touch. His muscles danced with sexual supremacy under her administrations.

It was exquisite torture. He was forcing her will to bend to his. She needed to hold on to the last thing that was truly hers: her mind.

Spirit Bear forced her to touch his body as she'd always longed to do. To feel the sheer power of his dominant form was all that any woman could dream of. *Why should she fight it?* But fight it, she would! She would prove to him that although he could force her to do many things, he couldn't force her to give him her soul.

The supreme male bent into the water so that their faces were almost touching. Then he crushed her to him in a passionate embrace. Evidence of his arousal couldn't be mistaken.

"*Canmihce*," Spirit Bear groaned deeply. "*Uwa yo miye, Wastelaka*" he requested huskily.

Spirit Bear knew she was as aroused as he. Only her mind kept her from yielding to him. He'd ask her to give willingly, but he would not beg. Before long he would do them both a favor and release their mutually pent up energy if she didn't submit soon.

Woniya Mato hadn't intended for his orneriness to reach this point. He'd only meant to tease her by showing her that she did, indeed, desire him, but he'd tortured himself as much or more than he had her. Now he was to the point of asking himself whether he should leave frustrated or have his will with her.

He knew each time he made her body turn against her mind, her resistance in thoughts grew. On the other hand, the more her body discovered pleasure with his touch, the more it craved him. Her body and mind warred with each other. He was curious to see how long one dominated the other.

He knew he'd have to have her again. Unless he appeased his organ's demand, he'd fight it all night. He'd end up having his will before *wi* awoke the earth. It was better to have it done with now. Then they both could sleep.

He should've known to be so close to her was to be weak with her. Her beauty and smell invaded every pour, every entry he had. The small white girl held such power over him; power she was unaware of. It was the Great War Chief who was at her mercy, not the other way around as she believed!

With a sound of great hunger, his lips claimed hers, and his mouth made her forget her determination to fight him. With one hand, he brazenly stroked her body.

Kaitlin clung to him. He supported her in their slippery environment that surrounded them. She felt his back muscles ripple under her hands. Cautiously, as if they had a mind of their own, Kaitlin's hands began to wander over his powerful frame.

Woniya Mato's lips seared hers in a crushing embrace. He worked them passionately until he felt the timid response of her tongue. His reaction was one that couldn't be ignored...

Although new to the art of love, this watery encounter was one Kaitlin could not have imagined. As they sailed back into the calm waters together, she became instantly ashamed of how easily she'd given in to him. Kaitlin quickly washed the feel of him from her body.

She froze as she felt him tenderly place the strawberry cream into her hair and work it through the length. The blonde stood quietly under his touch.

Spirit Bear made her feel many new things. His hands and body brought her many pleasures she'd never dreamed possible. All the emotions she felt were foreign to her. *How could he make her yearn to escape and have the will to stay all at the same time?*

When he touched her, her womanhood burned with fire! Then her body became a lustful entity. It acted wonton without her assistance or permission! It was the ultimate betrayal!

Never before had her body pulsed with desire. Just his nearness brought forth a deep awareness of him and their environment. *How was it that she'd never been so aware before?*

She rinsed her long hair by dunking under the chilly waters. When she resurfaced, the mighty chief grasped her hand and pulled her toward the bank. She followed his form from the watery domain with downcast eyes.

Woniya Mato held up a towel for his little golden bird. She kept her eyes diverted from his brawny frame. It brought an amused smile to his lips. His young flower was still too shy to meet his physique without shame? Maybe her desire was so strong for him that she feared stoking her flames by perusing his body.

I have loved you twice this day, Wastelaka. I will grant you freedom from my touch as you request, he thought. He stayed his hand and stepped back to retrieve a towel of his own.

Without meaning to, Kaitlin sighed with relief. His touch was too disturbing for her distraught emotions. She had a lot to think about!

She dried her body quickly and slipped on her clothes. She wrapped the towel around her dripping hair, twisted, and tucked the end next to her scalp. It seemed to help avoid soaking her clothes this way. She would comb out the mess upon their return to the tipi.

The timid girl picked up her soiled garments and then retrieved Spirit Bear's. She looked into the face of her bronze warrior with a questioning look. He answered with a nod.

Woniya Mato led her back down the river to where the women washed garments. He lounged his length against a tree as he watched her. Kaitlin found it difficult to concentrate with his dominant form lurking so close by. The chieftain didn't pretend to ignore her as he usually did. He watched her closely, and his *wayaka* found it unnerving.

Quickly, she finished the chore and stood. Kaitlin turned toward her owner so he could lead the way back to the village but paused when a familiar voice filled the air. Opossum Eyes approach from the path. The other girl hadn't seen Kaitlin yet, for her eyes were on the handsome chief.

"*Woniya Mato*! I have *missed* seeing you lately! You should come to visit our tipi. I can cook you a delicious meal you won't forget," she said suggestively. She made a beeline to where he stood. "I can make it as hot as you like!" she nearly purred.

Spirit Bear stood still, hoping his lack of response would be hint enough for her to stop her advance: it was not. Opossum Eyes walked up to him and rubbed her fingertips against his newly cleaned skin in a familiar fashion. She was so brazen; the Indian girl trailed her feathery touch onto his sculpted chest. At the same time, she made sure her breast "accidentally" brushed across his forearm.

Kaitlin's reaction was to draw in a shocked breath. It alerted Opossum Eyes to her presence. The other woman caught the look on Kaitlin's pale face and smiled with devilish humor. It was obvious to both Opossum Eyes and Spirit Bear that she was experiencing feelings of jealousy.

The bronze woman pressing against the virile man let her hand drop at an alarming rate to Spirit Bear's breechcloth. The reaction of the honed man was to side step her attempt at the speed of light.

"*Hiya!*" *Woniya Mato* caught the young woman's hands and held them tightly in one of his. He forced her eyes of hate for his *winyan* to turn to his.

With deep authority, he stated tersely, "Do not touch me so. You do not belong to me, nor will you. Act like you have dignity and honor. No man wants the leftovers of another's when he wishes to take a wife!"

When the chief released her, she sent a glare full of knives towards Kaitlin and ran away from the two at the edge of the river. The couple watched her go, each experiencing different emotions to her plight. Then the impressive athlete led the way back to his village.

Upon their return, Spirit Bear retrieved his new bow and arrows and went a short distance away to where the men and coming of age youth practiced their targeting skills.

Kaitlin collected her rock drilling supplies. She wanted intense action to keep her mind busy. Already she wondered at her reaction to Opossum Eyes rubbing against the man who'd made her love him.

The fetching blonde took her things to the front yard of the tipi and sat on one of the logs surrounding the fire pit. She retrieved an opaque rock with an iridescent glimmer. It was larger than the others she'd collected. It'd make a fine centerpiece in a necklace someday.

Kaitlin secured it in the bone wedge-lever and placed sand in the spot with the most natural indentation. Taking her granite rod, she began to pour her emotions into the rolling of the device in her palm. Eventually, through the monotony of the actions, the white girl began to think of Spirit Bear.

If he were divided into two people, she'd be head over heels in love with him. She'd never want to leave his side! He treated her with gentleness and respect. It was the man Kaitlin saw under the Indian.

The other side, however, was a powerful leader and protector of his people. The warrior would bend to no one. He'd never show mercy or weakness. *Woniya Mato's* command was to be obeyed at once, or the offender would pay the consequence. Sometimes the recompense was life.

This potent man owned her body. It'd turned traitorous and usurped her power on several occasions. If it'd already happened, it was safe to assume it was going to ensue again. It seemed now that she knew only pleasure beneath him and no longer pain, her response uncontrollable.

To give him her body was one thing. The striking warrior would caress her until she desired him; regardless, it was unthinkable for the power over her heart and her very soul to slip. When she'd felt the talon of jealousy over Opossum Eyes and the girl's familiarity with the gorgeous man, she'd condemned herself.

One day, as surely as he breathed, the arresting man would tire of her. He'd choose a woman of his own race, and she'd be left without his sweet kisses or overpowering embraces. She had to keep that knowledge alive in her mind so that she didn't give herself completely over.

What if Woniya Mato kept her when he took a wife? Again, Kaitlin knew she had to guard her heart. A mighty chief would someday want children. *Would he want half-breeds running around, or would he want a full-blooded child to follow in his path?* It was of no matter. She'd lost all control over her life. The white captive was at his beck and call, and he knew she could not resist him.

Looking up, Kaitlin watched as he stood still, pulled back his bow string, and hit his target accurately time and time again. Each time he nailed his target, the war chief would back up ten steps and string another arrow. Pretty soon, he was way beyond the other counterparts practicing.

Kaitlin watched as one by one, all on the field stepped back to watch the leader's performance. Sweat glistened on his powerful body. Muscles rippled as he continued to step back and aim.

When his pouch of arrows was exhausted, Kaitlin watched *Isnala Sungmanitu, Wawakankan,* and *Wawakte Towanjila* rapidly approach him with smiles and congratulations. Slowly, others joined the group. *Ojilaka Hehaka* retrieved Spirit Bear's arrows and brought them to him. He and the other youth Kaitlin didn't recognize used this excuse to approach the mighty warrior and congratulate him on his prowess. The athletic crowd flocked around their chief in awe.

Woniya Mato took his arrows from Young Elk with a smile of thanks. The youth bowed his head before his idol. At the encouragement of others, Spirit Bear continued to test the distance of the newly constructed bow. *Ojilaka Hehaka*'s worship reflected in his eyes as he watched the elder perform.

When the chief finished shooting targets, he was accompanied by the other leaders of the band. They all followed to his yard where Kaitlin sat. She felt like moving, but it was simply too hot to confine herself in the tipi, and she was not allowed to leave without *Woniya Mato; Ojilaka Hehaka* had been relieved of duty for the night.

"I must know this new technique," Lone Wolf said to Spirit Bear. They were sitting on the logs on the opposite side of the fire pit from Kaitlin.

"It is newly tested. I do not know if it will work on another bow. This one may be blessed by *Wakantanka.*" Although he believed his statement, he smiled because he knew his words would frustrate his *kola.*

"Do not be so cantankerous, *Woniya Mato*. Share your secret with the council members. If you cannot trust your spirit brothers, we have failed you," Sky Warrior helped in the pursuit of knowledge.

Lone Wolf added, "Think of our success for the hunt of bison! We would be blessed with more meat and hides in less time! You must give us time to construct new weapons with your technique!

Woniya Mato arched back his head and laughed heartily. "You honor me with this badgering. Come, my brothers. Gather around me so that I can share the secret of my success with you."

CHAPTER FIFTEEN

Much Honor

Kaitlin finally finished drilling the hole in the opalescent rock. She now selected a much smaller stone of onyx. The *ska winyan* already felt the intensity in the muscles in her neck and arms due to their isolated use. The young woman gritted her teeth with determination to drill at least one more hole and did her best to ignore the magnetic men enjoying themselves so near in proximity.

Night drew closer, and Kaitlin had just finished the hole in the small black rock. She took her supplies in their tipi and carefully put them up. All the flaps were open, but it was still hot.

Kaitlin had forgotten to brush her hair after the encounter with Opossum Eyes, so she took the porcupine quills and began to run it through her silken mane. She was surprised when there were very few tangles. The strawberry cream they made was magical! The lovely blonde needed to find out how they made that as well. She'd have many talents to support herself when she returned to her world.

The amber-eyed beauty brushed her hair until it shone. Then, due to the heat, she parted it in two pieces and braided each section and secured the bottoms with tongs. It was much improved, but she continued to be hot.

Kaitlin heard male laughter coming from the yard. She wished she were allowed to have friends visit. The lonely girl almost missed the days of the *isnatipi*. The women there had temporary lives similar to the men's.

It seemed to Kaitlin that the women did most of the work. The men appeared to hunt, to skin the meat most of the time, and to defend that village, but other than that, they didn't help with daily life. They build new weapons and shot them. They visited with each other.

The women, on the other hand, were expected to collect firewood, build fires, cook, and clean the dishes. Men got to eat first while then women waited on them. The females of the village collected all other food items and prepared them. Grains that were harvested had to be pulverized in order to make the *aguyapi* and other such dishes.

The women bared the children and raised them. They tanned the leather and made the clothes and shoes. They washed the garments and collected the water for daily use.

Females wove baskets and dried meat. The list went on and on. How could the men be so unfair? It just wasn't right! In essence, every woman was a slave of the man in the village. Men had physical strength but the women were the ones to work!

She noticed another vital difference in the Indian's way of life. All in the community shared a closeness that Kaitlin had never witnessed before. With a few exceptions, there was no animosity. It was like one large family. Each looked out for the other. The camaraderie was unbelievable.

Some specialized in certain areas. *Wawat'ecaka*'s leather. *Unjinjintka Can Koica*'s baskets. She was sure that Playful Otter also specialized in jewelry, but they didn't hoard their skills; they were shared… or traded for. It was amazing.

Woniya Mato entered the tipi undetected. *Mazaska Zi Ista* sat on the sleeping furs with her hair freshly braided, lost in deep thought. A hint of a smile teased her lips.

Spirit Bear hoped he was the cause of the smile. She was always so beautiful to him, but nothing compared to her when she smiled or reacted with enthusiasm to the life. He felt his heart warm with her love of life. It infected everyone.

The chief stood and watched her for some time. The beautiful blonde finally became aware of his presence and looked at him sheepishly. Her gold eyes flashed in the darkening tipi. He smiled to let her know it was acceptable to be lost in her thoughts, especially if they revolved around him!

His *wayaka* stood and retrieved a *mniapahta*. She let the refreshing water cool her parched throat. She'd not felt quite so thirsty until his presence dominated the structure. *Now how she was supposed to sleep?*

The blonde berated herself for not faking sleep. She wasn't sure if she fooled him or not, but most of the time, he left her be. Her face flamed as she recalled that he had roused her at least twice that day already, in a way that only he could.

She heard his command to come, *"Uwa yo."* He had reclined on the sleeping mat with only his breechcloth. Hypnotically, his eyes devoured her.

Kaitlin approached him as she knew she must. He patted the leather in front of him. A sexy smile spread across his firm lips.

Spirit Bear loved how her eyes became wide amber saucers when she was alarmed. He didn't intend to make her succumb to his will, but he loved to make her think he might. He had to be careful, though, or the games he played backfired on him. He mustn't let her know of the power she held over him.

He'd perceived the look on her face and the way it flamed when she thought of them together. It made him swell with pride that this beautiful woman thought of them that way. Already, he chipped at the ice she was determined he wouldn't melt.

Only today, his *wayaka* welcomed his passions! Her body no longer feared him, and he knew he brought her pleasure. Her physical self was already a willing captive, but her heart and mind still tried to resist. His smile broadened when he thought of the tempting challenge of winning her heart.

Mazaska Zi Ista lay beside him and held her breath. She placed her back to him and tried to relax. The robe she wore was very hot in the tipi, and he knew she wouldn't sleep with it on.

Woniya Mato began to untie the bindings to her cape-garment. The golden one sucked in her breath and grumbled something. She stiffly cooperated.

When he removed her outer wear, he allowed her lower region privacy by retaining her breechcloth. The amber-eyed girl trembled with expectation. He nearly fulfilled them, but twice already in one day would be hard on a body newly awakened. He could wait until the dawning of the new day.

Kaitlin shivered under his fiery gaze. He'd removed her clothes. *Was she allowed no decency? Why did he stare at her and smile his little smile? Was this some new form of seduction?* Well, he could lay there and smile all night. She would never make the first move!

The blonde was surprised when she was allowed to roll away from him and his swirling midnight eyes. He was still propped up on his elbows studying her, so the white girl made sure her arms covered her chest in the right places. If she was supposed to sleep, she could not.

Finally, she heard him recline onto the velvety leather. The dominate male gently touched her arm. She heard his masculine voice murmur, *"Istinma, Wastelaka."*

Early the next morning, there was a tap on the flap of the tipi. Lone Wolf and Sky Warrior waited for their chief impatiently. They were full of enthusiasm.

Spirit Bear arose and went out into the predawn morning.

"What is it, my *kolas*?"

"It is the white elk! He has been spotted! Come! Bring your new bow and arrows! Prove your stealth once again as hunter! It is a good omen. We are not blessed often with one such as he!"

Woniya Mato needed no other prompting. He donned his leggings, grabbed his weapon, and left. He quickly ran by *Ojilaka Hehaka*'s tipi on his way to secure his stallion. The chief needed to alert him to his departure.

While they rode, his spirit brothers could not help but to send a few sharp jabs his way.

"I am surprised we were able to rip you away from your *winyan, Woniya Mato*," came an unusual taunt from Lone Wolf.

The chief responded with a smile, "Had you waited until she was bathed in *wi*'s light, you would not have, my *kola*."

"She is beautiful." *Wawakte Towanjila* had seen just a glimpse of her nearly nude form upon Spirit Bear's sleeping furs. His body had reared a response.

"*Tos*, and she is mine."

To make sure his friend was not offended by his compliment, Sky Warrior added, "I am satisfied with *Haspa Nableca*. She is also beautiful. She heals quickly. After the ceremony of the next full moon, she will be mine in all ways."

They nodded, enjoying each other's jests. By mutual consent, they quieted and prepared for the hunt.

Kaitlin was fully awake now. With Spirit Bear's absence, she felt the chill in the morning air.

She quickly donned a dress. Then the white woman began her morning chores.

She made a mint tea sweetened with raspberries to help the adjustment from sleep to work. It was her favorite. When *Wawat'ecaka* came, Kaitlin had already gathered wood, water, and had breakfast cooking. Gentle Rabbit smiled in admiration. She loved this golden girl!

The women sat and shared the Indian bread and raspberries. Then *Wawat'ecaka* said, "Bring your basket. Today we will work on collecting *tinpsila*. We need to begin drying a supply for winter."

Kaitlin did not understand the fluency of the words said, but she did understand 'basket', *tinpsila*, 'drying', and 'winter'. She did as she was requested. *Wawat'ecaka* found a sharp stick for *Mazaska Zi Ista* to use to help her dig. It was too difficult to dig with one's hands all day.

Kaitlin noticed in surprise that the whole village of women seemed to have the same purpose in mind. "They all come?" she tried to ask Gentle Rabbit.

"*Hiya*, some are needed to stay to mind the children."

Kaitlin looked around for Young Elk. She hadn't noticed him since the village had begun to awaken. The youthful babysitter wasn't to be found, but she did notice *Wawakankan*. Her eyes rounded in surprise.

"Your son comes?" she asked.

"*Tos*. He comes for several reasons." She paused meaningfully. Golden Eyes had shame enough to look down. To help comfort her, *Wawat'ecaka* said,

"He comes for you, *tos*, but also to collect herbs and medicinal plants."

Kaitlin said, "*Wawat'ecaka*, I know one… who like him… but shy."

Immediately, the older woman's eyebrows shot up with interest. "*Tos*?" she nearly held her breath with anticipation.

"*Skeca Ecaca*, our very own Playful Otter."

Wawat'ecaka nearly cackled with glee. She could kiss *Mazaska Zi Ista* for this welcomed revelation! The girl was perfect for her son! This gentle and beautiful girl was whom she'd hoped her son would choose. Now he just needed a little gentle prodding.

Kaitlin smiled to herself as she saw Gentle Rabbit purposely find an excuse to go to talk with *Skeca Ecaca*. At least for her friends, dreams could come true! As they walked and dug, the women talked.

Kaitlin had longed for a day to visit with her friends. Even though it revolved around work, she got to speak with all those she'd met in the *isnatipi*. At least, all those she *chose* to speak with; Opossum Eyes kept far from her. Kaitlin was glad. If she hadn't been surrounded with her friends, the blonde was sure the mean-spirited girl would've found a way to needle her.

Playful Otter, New Moon, and Morning Dove ribbed her about her return to *Woniya Mato*'s tipi and his arms. They didn't understand her feelings about the man; she didn't herself. They teased her in good-natured fun and then giggled when she turned red.

They spoke of all the things Kaitlin had learned. Each asked about the skill they were teaching the pretty white girl. Kaitlin was doing her best to keep up all and do her best in all areas. She wanted each of her friends to smile with pride for their accomplishments as her teachers!

When baskets were filled of the sweet turnips, the women would return to the village only to retrace her footsteps and begin anew. This went on for the full day. The women rested during the heat of the day only to start fresh in the afternoon. The piles of *tinpsila* grew at a nearly alarming rate from Kaitlin's perspective.

Near evening, the women wearily dragged themselves back into the community. Spirit Bear hadn't yet returned from his great hunting expedition, so she didn't bother cooking. Kaitlin was so tired! She ate a dinner of berries, a left over piece of *aguyapi*, and one smaller *tinpsila*. Then she fell into the sleeping furs, exhausted.

Spirit Bear returned just after dark. He walked into the tipi to gather clean clothes. He smiled as he looked over *Mazaska Zi Ista*. She usually didn't make noise while she slept, but this night soft snores came from her.

He turned to leave. *Woniya Mato* wanted to bathe before he lay down beside her. He knew that if she saw fresh blood upon him, even a miniscule amount, the sensitive girl would go crazy.

The hunt had been an enormous success. Even now, the great elk lay slain and hung from a tree. After cleaning himself, he and the others would meet in the ceremonial lodge constructed around the sacred cottonwood tree. It was located close by, on the edge of the ritual grounds.

Because *Wakantanka* was so full of giving spirits, he also felt inclined to give. Prior to cleaning himself, he walked into the herd of horses. Choosing a yearling, he placed a woven leather braid around his neck. The foal looked much like his father, only he was a coppery sorrel overo.

Runs with the Wind had produced many outstanding horses in the herd, but Spirit Bear felt this was the most impressive yearling in some time. He led the colt back to the village. The chief stopped before the medicine man's tipi.

"*Wawakankan. Uwa yo.* I have something for you."

Wonder Worker came forward. His eyes grew large when shaman saw what the leader held before his tipi.

"My chief, what have I done to honor this?" he cried.

"Did I not tell you that I would reward you for saving *Mazaska Zi Ista*'s life when I brought her to this village?"

"*Tos*, but *Woniya Mato*, it is too much!"

"The life of Golden Eyes is worth much more!"
he responded deeply. "Honor me, and take the lead of
this fine young animal."

Wonder Worker had a horse of his own, but it was
a mare. He didn't need the mighty hunting and war horses
of most distinctive men in his tribe, but how could he turn
down the nobility of such a gift? He was a warrior at
times when it was needed, and he certainly hunted; the
medicine man decided he'd truly enjoy the challenge of
training a stallion.

Wawakankan smiled and took the leather braid
from his chief. He slapped the imposing man heartily on
the back. Then the shaman looked over the foal closely.

"He is his father all over again!" *Wawakankan*
exclaimed with pride.

"*Tos*, he only lacks his father's black points.
Otherwise, he is the same."

"It is you who greatly honor me, my chief! Thank
you!" He paused and looked down. "I do not earn this
gift." He thought of the time he was attending to Quiet
Deer when Golden Eyes stole from the village.

"I know not what you speak about. Of course
you earned it! I will clean myself now. Take care of
your fine yearling and then I will meet you in the
ceremonial lodge."

Wonder Worker nodded his mutual consent. The
men spoke long into the night. They
smoked the pipe of celebration and honored the Great
Spirit for his favor upon their people. They relived the
hunt for *Wawakankan*.

Both Lone Wolf and Sky Warrior had led the merry chase of the enormous bull in his prime. The animal had run for hours, advertising his strength and health. It'd taken forever to get close enough for a killing shot.

The two men teased their chief. They spoke to *Wawakankan* of how *Woniya Mato* had let them get ahead. Each had thought they would take down the majestic animal.

Before they could pull back the string of the bow, Spirit Bear had sent two arrows into the mighty beast's heart! On top of that, he was aiming from his motionless steed from about twenty-five feet behind them!

The result was twofold. The sacred animal had given his life, protection, and body to continue the preservation of Indian life. It had also proven the innovative technique for the new bow construction by their masterful chief! They would begin creating the special weapons soon.

After the artful hunt had been relived, *Wawakankan* proclaimed, "My chief, *Wakantanka* truly shines upon you. Never have our people been more blessed!"

Woniya Mato didn't know what to say to such a deep compliment. The chieftain merely bowed his head in thanks. After a few moments, they all smoked another round on the peace pipe.

Spirit Bear said, deeply moved, "This tribal council is truly representative of the sacred number four. You are right, *Wawakankan*. We have never been so powerful or so blessed before. It is a sign that the Great Spirit supports our rule."

When *Woniya Mato* returned to his tipi, he couldn't sleep. His body was so invigorated at his recent success hunting the great white elk. He sat on the mats by his *wayaka*, but his mind was still on the *hehaka* they'd killed.

White was a sacred color to the Oglala. *Wakantanka* did not bless many animals with this pelt color. The Indians did not take life lightly, especially with ones blessed white! Because of this, they'd also honored the spirit of the great elk and had thanked him for donating his life for their protection during their time spent in the ceremonial lodge.

Kaitlin sighed and murmured something in her sleep. "Bradley, please marry me. I can't live with papa after he tried to sell me to Jed…"

It turned *Woniya Mato*'s thoughts in an entirely different direction. Immediately, he bristled when he heart Kaitlin say Jed's name. *He still brings fear to her heart,* he thought. *She pleads with someone in her dreams.*

Spirit Bear felt helpless because he couldn't rid her nightmares of the *ska sunka*. He also felt pangs of jealousy that it wasn't his name she called to in her sleep. He knew the *winyan* couldn't help what she dreamed, but it should be he that filled her every need, even in her sleep!

The supreme leader paced the tipi for a time. He resumed a sitting position by the fireplace upon a woven mat. *Woniya Mato* chanted and closed his eyes for at least an hour.

When he lay down in the predawn hours, he'd released himself of negative emotion. It was vital for a chief to be able to do this skillfully in order to lead his people. Once more, he thanked the Great Spirit for allowing him this power.

Spirit Bear welcomed this early morning time. He loved to watch *wi* awaken this golden *winyan* of his… or he loved to awaken her himself! Choosing the later, he began to arouse her body…

Soon after a glorious time of shared passion, Spirit Bear opened the flap to his tipi. The position of the entrance flap advertised to others in the community the need for privacy. An open flap was an invitation for company while a closed one meant 'do not disturb'. *Woniya Mato*'s actions advertised they no longer needed privacy.

Within five minutes, *Wawat'ecaka* appeared with breakfast. Kaitlin had only just poured tea. Gentle Rabbit served the chief while Kaitlin sat subdued on her mat. The white girl couldn't bear to meet *Wawat'ecaka*'s eyes; she *had* to know why the entrance flap to their tipi had been closed for so long!

"Do you like the fresh elk meat, *Woniya Mato*?" *Wawat'ecaka* asked.

"*Tos*! It was prepared by an angel!"

The eyes of both foster mother and chieftain met. They smiled at each other in love and admiration. The elder lady could not miss a dig towards the man she claimed as son. "Hunting so late made you sleep the day away."

The dominant male bent back his head and laughed heartily. He wouldn't pretend to be offended.

"I was not sleeping, my mother. I was entertaining *Mazaska Zi Ista.*"

When both Indians looked at Kaitlin, the beauty flamed with embarrassment. If she had to service her chief, she'd prefer that tidbit kept private! The *wayaka* fumed in silence. Maybe the while village knew, but they didn't have to advertise the fact!

"She does not look pleased," *Wawat'ecaka* needled him in jest.

"She was moments ago!" he said while masculine laughter still rumbled in his chest. "She is bashful and doesn't like others to guess."

"I will leave her to eat in your presence, my chief. I will come for her after shame has melted away. I do not want her sullen this day. We have much work to do with drying the gift from *Wakantanka*. Elk make much meat!" She smiled at him.

"Then we begin to dry *tinpsila.*"

"*Tos.* That is a good plan." The mother figure turned to leave, and Spirit Bear called to her.

"*Tos*?"

"Have *Unjinjintka Can Koica* help you and *Mazaska Zi Ista. Haspa Nableca* would be good to help as well as *Skeca Ecaca.*"

Wawat'ecaka actually stepped back into the tipi. She looked at Spirit Bear in surprise. Did nothing escape the man's attention?

"How did you…?"

Again, *Woniya Mato* laughed heartily. Nothing could spoil his mood this fine morning! "I have eyes! Your son may not recognize the signs, but if all these named women help dry and prepare the fresh meat, in my mind, all have a claim. The council owns the meat because it is sacred. What better way, my mother, to have kindred spirits join than in a meal shared by those?"

"You are wise, my chief. *Wawakankan* will never realize the web he will become entangled in!" She cackled with glee. "Lone Wolf and Desert Rose, Sky Warrior and Apple Blossom, You and Golden Eyes… and Wonder Worker and Playful Otter. It is a dream come true!" Happy feet carried Gentle Rabbit to do his bidding.

Spirit Bear turned to Kaitlin. "*Uwa yo*," he called to her.

She shuffled to him. She still seethed at him inside. *He wouldn't break her will; he would not!*

"*Iyotaka*." She sat next to him in huffy silence. He placed the plate of smoked elk complimented with sliced apple and maple *aguyapi* in her lap. She looked up into his striking face. "Please, *Woniya Mato*. Take me home."

She knew he couldn't understand her, but she had to say it to appease her own conscience. She was falling hopelessly in love with him. The anger she held against him, or for herself for that matter, was not enough protection. She feared his touch because in his fiery embraces, she was beginning to welcome him into her heart.

Spirit Bear didn't know what she asked of him, but he heard her say the word 'please' many times. Most of the time it was when she was pleading with him and saying *hiya*. *Was she trying to tell him that she did not want to eat?* She had a very busy day of labor ahead of her, and she would need her strength. No, she must eat.

"*Wota*," he commanded. He pressed the plate into her lap and nodded his head towards it. Their eyes were still locked in a heated union. His dominant black eyes overpowered her pleading gold ones. He imposed his will upon her, and she was helpless but to do his bidding.

Sighing, she picked up the plate. She might as well eat and forget her ideas about returning to the white community. The meat *was* delicious…

Kaitlin was shocked to see such an enormous animal. They'd never get all the meat off before it spoiled! Even more surprising was the white appearance of the residual fur on the carcass. The head had been removed, so it was hard for her to determine if her eyes were deceiving her.

Wawat'ecaka had started drying strips of meat from the elk already. She had a rump roast stew cooking in two pots, and other selected pieces of meat were slowly roasting over a fire or were wrapped in leaves under hot ash. How one woman achieved so much was beyond Kaitlin.

Shortly after her arrival, Desert Rose and Playful Otter arrived. Kaitlin was overjoyed to see them. To top her spirits, Apple Blossom also appeared! Work wouldn't appear to be work today!

The men of the council sat nearby to watch over the women folk. Each had supplies for the making of new bows. They, too, would visit while they worked.

"How are you doing, Apple Blossom?" Kaitlin asked. She'd truly worried for her new friend. She felt confident that Sky Warrior was kind to her, but her injuries had been so severe!

"It is like I was born in the underworld and have emerged into the world of great spirits! I am treated like a princess when before I felt that my life was worthless. I am so *happy*!"

Of course, Kaitlin didn't catch all of what she said, but she did understand her body language. She smiled to show she was happy for her friend.

"How does Sky Warrior treat you?" Desert Rose asked. An undercurrent of curiosity was obvious among the women. So much was packed into the question.

Apple Blossom shyly smiled," He is very kind. He allows my body to heal before he makes demands on me. I am not used to this respect."

The women ribbed each other to tease her. "I think she likes him!" Desert Rose loudly whispered.

"Who wouldn't like a man like that?" Desert Rose teased. "He is hot!"

The four girls giggled. *Wawat'ecaka* made a show of putting more meat strips on the racks and checking the meat. She wanted the young ladies to have time to talk as girls were prone to do: about young men! She also began placing *tinpsila* on more drying racks. The community would be well prepared for winter with the security of bison meat!

Approximately half the village's women population had continued the chore from yesterday of bringing in the sweet prairie turnip for drying and storing purposes. The other half of the women dried the *tinpsila* and minded the youth. It was an awesome sight to see the whole population working in unison.

"I hear we are all dining together this evening," Desert Rose said when the teasing of Apple Blossom had died down.

"Yes, it is so," confirmed Playful Otter. She was nervous about being in the direct sight of the man she'd carried a crush on for so long.

"Ah, do I detect a state of nerves?" instigated Desert Rose.

Apple Blossom could not wait to test her newly acquired friendships by returning the man teasing. "Does *Wawakankan* stir your blood?"

The girls snickered when they were rewarded a blushing response. "I believe he does!" Desert Rose confirmed.

Kaitlin enjoyed the closeness with her friends, but she just couldn't get involved in the jesting of men. With her feelings all jumbled up concerning Spirit Bear, she didn't feel she could tease anyone. Yes, she was definitely attracted to the devastatingly handsome man. He stirred her senses beyond reason, but it was all against her will.

If one had a weakness, did one liked to be teased about it? She thought on that as the jesting continued between her friends. She decided that if a person had control over the situation, that yes, one would like to be teased. If the person had no control, the situation would not always result with favorable feelings…

"The women seem to really enjoy the slicing of raw meat," *Wawakankan* stated.

"When females get together, they can make any chore fun," Sky Warrior agreed.

"Are they always so noisy?" asked Lone Wolf. "They are like a pack of coyotes!" Male laughter greeted his observation.

"They speak of us," revealed Spirit Bear.

"Who else?" snorted Sky Warrior. His eyes twinkled with orneriness.

The men tried to concentrate on the new bow construction, but each man had a distraction close enough that his eyes would stray in that direction frequently. Still, they were able to make progress on the novel concept of bow construction.

Wawakankan had always enjoyed watching the women folk, but one woman in particular seemed to be catching his attention of late. He'd never noticed how attractive Playful Otter was before yesterday. She'd helped him gather coneflowers as she dug up the *tinpsila*, and she seemed a little nervous and breathless when he flirted with her. He knew it wasn't just his wishful thinking that her shiny lips parted in response to his words. She seemed to hang on everything he said to her. It was very good for a man's ego!

He'd also noticed her watching him from beneath her lashes. She was not one who was normally shy, but she seemed to be tongue-tied around him a lot lately. As an added bonus, the becoming girl got along with all the women his spirit brothers had interests in. Even now, he caught her sneaking glances at him from where she worked. Of course, Playful Otter caught him as well. He would have to think on this new woman of interest…

CHAPTER SIXTEEN

Love is Everywhere

Snake Strike stomped in rage within his tipi. Life was so unfair! He was stooping to do women's chores! He was cooking and cleaning for the first time in his life! He looked down at his filthy clothes. He admitted to himself that maybe he wasn't cleaning as much as he thought he was.

The denounced man was forced to take handouts from other families. He'd never been so shamed. Just to spite the council, Snake Strike was taking his bow out and killing his own prey. Of course, he couldn't be seen returning to the village with the meat, so he cooked and ate it out of sight.

Young boys were congratulated when they brought home something they'd killed! It was an honor to provide a meal before one was known to be a man. However, to shame him further, he wasn't allowed to provide for himself until he'd adequately 'learned his lesson'.

Zuzeca Zapan followed the two slave women around. He would find a time to strike them when they least expected it, but as for now, there had been little chance.

Wawakte Towanjila kept *Nakpa Ihli* confined to his tipi. He rarely even glimpsed sight of her. When he did, it was from within Sky Warrior's embrace. They would walk along like lovers with his arm draped over the whore's shoulders. *Zuzeca Pazan* roiled in a black rage when he thought of his *wayaka* taken from him and spending nights in another's arms, especially if that other was *Wawakte Towanjila*!

How it pained him for her to know she'd escaped his wrath! Ear Sore had gotten herself pregnant with another man's seed, ran from him, and then was honored! Snake Strike also couldn't admit that he couldn't stand the thought of her possible happiness. It was contemptible! He wanted her back beneath him! There was no greater pleasure for him than to hurt as he took. Once he achieved that, he'd move in for the kill.

If possible, *Mazaska Zi Ista* was even more closely guarded than *Nakpa Ihli*! When *Woniya Mato* wasn't around, she had the youth following her. He didn't have a personal vendetta against the boy as of yet, other than his association with the chief, but that was a black mark against him already. It was rumored that *Ojilaka Hehaka* would be selected for *Cante Tinza*, warrior status, at the next celebration. That, in itself, was reason enough to hate him.

When Young Elk was not following at the skirts of the golden-eyed girl, Spirit Bear was. Snake Strike had spied on them many times. He saw the two of them together in the pond of blue just days ago. He seethed to see how *Woniya Mato* treated this girl. It was like he felt she was above the Indian race! He treated her with warmth and respect! One could even assume that he loved her by the way he tried to please her! *Tos*, the down fall of the bear would be by the golden bird's death. He smiled in anticipation.

The best plan would be to attack the youth. Already the boy was a warrior in his stance and carriage. *Ojilaka Hehaka* could out shoot all of those his age and some already in warrior status. He'd the build of the chieftains. At that thought, *Zuzeca Pazan* gritted his teeth. *Tos*, he could widen his hate to include the boy. It would be easier on his conscious that way.

Zuzeca Pazan's best chance to strike down *Mazaska Zi Ista* was when she was watched by Young Elk. Neither he nor *Ojilaka Hehaka* had official warrior training as of yet, but more than likely, it wouldn't come down to combat between them. *Hiya*, ambush was more of a Snake Strike style!

The afternoon passed similarly to the morning. The women continued to cut strips of meat from the elk carcass to dry, and the men continued working on their new bows. The four women happily chatted while they worked. The four men did the same. Sneaked glances toward the other party persisted as well.

Wawat'ecaka placed the pieces of meat on the drying racks along with the *tinpsila*, and she watched the cooking of the choice cuts and stews. She wanted to give the young women time without her, and she wanted a meal fit for kings! A happy stomach made a man happy! A happy man would look to the women providers… and possibly find romance!

Near evening, the women stopped working on the elk. It was finally stripped of most meat. The next day they'd boil the bones and use the broth with their cooking. They'd also have the cleaned skeleton for utensils and other tools.

Each returned to their home tipi to gather a fresh dress and bathing supplies. The five women walked to the female's place. Soon they returned, cleaned and refreshed. Newly washed garments were placed on rocks and tree branches to dry.

While the women prepared the evening meal for consumption, the men also cleaned up. They brought their clothing back to camp for washing. The women usually did that for them in the morning when they retrieved *mni*.

Finally, the meal was ready. *Wawat'ecaka* had prepared a wonderful feast. There was ground-roasted elk tenderloin flavored with garlic, onion, and salt brush solution. She'd the cooked tubers in ash that burst forth creamy white fluff. There was roasted and raw *tinpsila* and wild strawberries. She'd also prepared *aguyapi* with meat cracklings and strawberries topped with a thickened maple syrup. Fresh peach juice was prepared to accompany the meal. Each modest woman served the man of her interest.

Woniya Mato captured Kaitlin's hands in his large warm ones when she gave him his platter. His mesmerizing eyes entranced hers, and a slight grin teased his lips.

Embarrassed that he'd boldly displayed affection in front of others, she flamed red and looked away. He was devilishly handsome and her breath caught in her chest. Her heart beat madly. The demure woman was ashamed she reacted so strongly with only a look from him.

When he released her hands, Kaitlin immediately found a food item to check on. If she'd taken time to look about her, she'd have discerned that none of her friends save Gentle Rabbit noticed their heated exchange. Each of her other friends were trapped with fluttering emotions themselves…

Lone Wolf nearly dropped his plate when Desert Rose brought it to him. He thought she was the most beautiful woman on the face of the earth! Just how her dark brows arched so finely over the thickly fringed eyes and the way her hair swirled around her tiny waist made it nearly impossible for him to concentrate on the delicious food placed before him. Desire for anything but her had fled his senses. When he took a bite of the first succulent item, he could've been eating saw dust.

Did other men feel as he did? Did the women they desire rob them of all wits and leave him weak in the knees? He was a hunter! All of his senses shouldn't be concentrated on just a woman. He tried to focus on the platter of food he held in his lap, but his eyes secretly watched *Unjinjintka Can Koica.*

Wawakankan was used to women flirting with him. He loved being the center of a beautiful woman's attention, but he was unaccustomed to the feelings he was beginning to experience around *Skeca Ecaca.* She seemed so shy of him! He'd never noticed Playful Otter's bashfulness before! *Is that why all of a sudden she was of interest to him?*

Most of the women he'd had dealings with were brazen. He'd been boldly pursued. Never before had shy maidens captured his attention.

When *Skeca Ecaca* brought his platter of food to him, her hands shook slightly. Her cheeks pinked when his hand brushed hers as he accepted the plate. Gently, he grasped her forearm and waited for her eyes to meet his.

Giving forth his most skilled seductive look, he thanked her softly. Playful Otter nearly stumbled under his scrutiny, but she managed to nod before making a speedy exit. An amused smile played with his sensual mouth as he watched her hasty retreat. *Tos*, he'd have to find more ways to wander in the areas she frequented…

Sky Warrior loved the graceful way Apple Blossom moved. Even though her bruising was still evident, she was gorgeous. Already she walked with dignity and pride. She didn't act as though she'd experienced significant trauma two weeks before.

In another two weeks, he would make her his in all ways. *Wawakankan* had told him of the seriousness of her injuries and had asked him to give her one moon to heal. He was impatient for the time to pass, but he granted the lovely woman this reprieve.

It was so hard not to take her in the nights when she was curled up next to his body. It was even more difficult when he comforted her after she cried out in fear of dreams when she was trapped with reliving the horrors of her past. He thanked *Wakantanka* that her spirit hadn't been broken under the heavy hand and cruelties of *Zuzeca Pazan.*

When she brought him his plate, she met his eyes directly. He saw no traces of fear for him, only trust and… *admiration?* Definitely, something along with the trust was there. He smiled at her, melting her with his haze. She was strong enough to not look away. She was entrapped in the confines of his stare.

Gently, he reached for his plate. He wouldn't embarrass her in front of the others. She returned his smile and lowered her lashes. Apple Blossom gracefully left him to eat with his *kolas.*

Haspa Nableca was on cloud nine. She was so happy! She'd endured hell and lived to tell of it. Now she was being rewarded with the most handsome of men! *Wawakte Towanjila* was more man than she'd ever hoped for. He was the answer to her prayers.

Not only did he possess the perfect body that rippled with muscular power before her, but he also was renowned for his prowess and courage. He had many coup although he didn't always leave with the others on war raids. His primary concern was protecting the village. He did go to war; however, if the movement was a strong one, for few could match him in the quest for continued life. However, the loss of both *Woniya Mato* and *Wawakte Towanjila* would be devastating on the life as they knew it in the Bear Claw branch of the Oglala.

The smoldering looks Sky Warrior sent her way made her tremble and want with a need she'd never experienced before. He made her long for him to take her. Never before had she wished for a coupling, for they were always associated with pain and humiliation. She knew that *Wawakte Towanjila* was different in all ways from *Zuzeca Pazan*. She waited with anxious anticipation for the ending of two more weeks…

After the men had eaten their fill, the women served themselves and enjoyed good food and even better company. The men joined the women and watched them as they ate. The *winyans* quickly finished and went to the river to wash the dishes.

The men formed a plan to intensify their ties to the women folk. Upon their return, the ladies sat and began to visit. In minutes, the men paired up with their interest and sat behind them.

"And then *Mazaska Zi Ista* took a platter of food to their tipi!" giggled Playful Otter.

"*Tos*, I thought she know I nice, she be nice," Kaitlin said in Lakota.

"Opossum Eyes? No way!" snorted Desert Rose. "I can't believe you were thoughtful of her after what she did to your basket!"

"I want no trouble."

"Well, you will get it with her. She wants the chief, and she's made no bones about it." Desert Rose advised.

"Yes, I saw," Kaitlin revealed.

All the women stopped to stare at her. Each wondered what she could've seen. Kaitlin realized that it sounded different that she had intended.

"I mean, she come on to him. He did nothing but make her go."

The three other women smiled and nodded at each other. The chief was truly wise!

"You are a lucky woman for one such as him to love," Apple Blossom said. "Now I'm lucky, too!"

Suddenly, masculine leggings were behind each of the girls. The line of conversation died on their lips. Each maiden was instantly self-conscious and uncomfortable with having been overheard.

Men dropped simultaneously behind each girl. Each male leaned forward as if on cue and looked over the shoulder of the woman they sat behind. Then they took each woman's free strands of hair and tucked it behind her ear. Every man in his prime smiled seductively into the eyes of the woman he lavished attention on.

In turn, the women flushed with pleasure and awareness. It was like a synchronized dance for each male did the same simultaneously with the other, and every female fluttered an excited response at the same time as others in the shared dinner.

Finally, Desert Rose, the most daring of the present females, placed her hand on the cheek of Lone Wolf. He was the most private of the males present, so he took her hand in his and stood. He said, "*Uwa yo, Unjiinjintka Can Koica*. Let us walk." He drew her to him, and they departed from the gathering.

Wawakankan followed Lone Wolf's lead and also enticed Playful Otter to walk with him. It was not considered improper to walk with a man alone as long as paths of frequent use were taken. Dark had not yet stole light from the lands, so no woman's dignity would be compromised.

Both *Woniya Mato* and *Wawakte Towanjila* were comfortable with the other's company. The women, likewise, also were comfortable. The shared experience on the trial of escape and recovery made a bond between the women and the men different than what the other couples experienced.

The leaders drew their women into their embrace, each leaned back against the powerful frame of muscles, bones, and flesh holding them. The men continued conversing while cuddling their female.

Kaitlin felt strange. Never before had the compelling chief displayed emotion in public. She didn't know how to react. *Was she supposed to sit still? Was she supposed to respond?* If so, she knew she couldn't. She chose to sit still in his arms.

His forearms rippled as he used his hands to speak with Sky Warrior. His biceps bulged, coiling and uncoiling, when he moved his arms. His coppery skin shone, and his veins were visible below the surface of his skin, winding on top of the clearly defined muscles. She was mesmerized watching him, infatuated with his brawn strength.

At last, night took the land. The walking couples returned. All four pairs sat around the communal fire of meat that still cooked and dried, speaking with each other. Finally, each person went to his or her tipi.

Wawat'ecaka couldn't be happier! She hoped to give her son lots of time to be enticed by Playful Otter. She'd have a talk with him about her reputation. He was known to taste what was offered. Wonder Worker couldn't play with the girl's heart. He'd ruin her chances of a good mating if he wasn't serious about her, but *Wawat'ecaka* planned to make his interest genuine…

The next morning Kaitlin awoke to love. Spirit Bear was especially tender with her and her feelings. He was always gentle to her, even when he turned her body against her, but this time the chief seemed especially patient and nurturing.

The blonde girl still could not seem to let go of her heart until he'd risen her passions to an uncontrollable level, but when he'd sated both of their overpowering needs, she clung to him as they sailed back into the calm harbor waters. He stirred such deep emotions within her. Kaitlin didn't understand how they'd grown to this level.

Spirit Bear propped up over her before removing his body from hers. He grinned seductively into her face. His eyes weren't masked of his emotions as usual. Something in them had elicited very powerful warmth within her.

The golden girl lost herself in his black depths of love and something broke free from her will. It was miniscule, but she felt the first pop. Kaitlin knew, without a doubt, she was helplessly in love with her domineering master. God help her, for she could not escape from his passionate embraces; nor did she want to.

Not willing to admit this to herself, she still vowed to always force him to make the first move. They weren't married, nor was it proper for them to share the sleeping arrangements such as they were. Kaitlin wondered if they'd ever be permitted to become husband and wife, or if it would always be a union of master and slave. She forced her thoughts from the depressing path they were taking. Deep down, she knew the answer.

Kaitlin realized Spirit Bear watched her as her mind had taken the detour. The unmasked love reflected in his eyes had been replaced with concern. His chiseled features were devoid of emotion, but a tiny worry line between his eyes gave him away.

Refocusing on his handsome face, she smiled. The tiny line disappeared, and his sensual lips teased a return smile. He was such a striking man. How could any woman not fall in love with him?

When he rolled to the side of her, he took her with him as he kept her locked in his embrace. Her bare breasts were nestled against his smooth chest. He looked down on her with tenderness. They stayed clasped together for a time. Each lover was staring into the other's face.

Finally, *Woniya Mato* rose and dressed. Kaitlin didn't remove her eyes from his form as he clothed. He turned, catching her in the middle of her perusal, and grinned at her. He lifted a mocking brow. Kaitlin swiftly looking away, refusing to admit she desired him as a man. He chuckled in humor.

"So the winyan finally admits to herself that she desires me. This is good! I am pleased. This is the first step she must take in giving her heart to me."

Spirit Bear waited until she sneaked a peek back to him. He stood quietly, deliberately, and answered her study of him. He let his eyes rake her golden body. His captive's breasts were large but not overly so and very firm on her body. Her tiny waist flared out to supple hips. She had long, shapely legs that made a man want to lick them up.

Mazaska Zi Ista's face flamed and she scrambled to dress. Male rumbling laughter escaped from him, deepening her color.

"Tos, this day marks a change in my little golden bird!" the chief thought, well satisfied.

"How humiliating!" Kaitlin seethed. How could she have let him see her yearning for him? He needed no encouragement to take her already! Did she want to be only a sex slave? The answer was *hiya*!

Kaitlin began the morning tea and went to the Area of Privacy. *Woniya Mato* followed behind her, but he did seem to be giving her increasingly tiny snatches of greater freedom. For example, she noticed that he let her go into the Area of Privacy without accompanying her inside as he had been. The *ska winyan* couldn't stand it when he'd stood four or five feet from her as she relieved herself!

When *Mazaska Zi Ista* came out, she bowed her head before the warrior and said the Lakota word for 'thank you'. He looked at her and slightly nodded, for his chief's mask was firmly back in place. Then she filled the *mniapahtas*. After gathering the wood, Kaitlin completed the tea and drank it.

Wawat'ecaka called the same people from the night before to eat a breakfast of elk, *aguyapi*, and fruit before beginning the arduous chores of the day. This day they would make meat broth, store the bones for tools, and stretch the intestines to dry for sinew. Then the other women would continue drying the many *tinpsila* as *Wawat'ecaka* and Kaitlin worked the hides they were curing.

In the afternoon, they were able to complete the deer hide. They began the soaking process on the great white hide of the elk. It would be a beautiful garment when it was completed.

At dinner time, the two companions headed back to the camp. *Wawat'ecaka* gave Kaitlin the rabbit furs, the two antelope skins, and told her the deer hide was also hers upon its completion. The young slave tried to let Gentle Rabbit know that this was too much, but the older woman wouldn't let her refuse to take the hard-worked-for items.

When Kaitlin entered the tipi with her arms full of stash, *Woniya Mato* looked up from his task in surprise. He paused then placed his chore aside.

"*Uwa yo, Mazaska Zi Ista.*"

The pretty blonde did as she was beckoned and came to stand before him.

"Let me see your work."

Kaitlin placed the furs and leathers on the ground in front of him. She watched as he examined each piece of work.

"You made these?" he asked, deeply impressed.

"I help *Wawat'ecaka*. I no do myself." "Very good job!" and he drew her to him. He pulled the pretty girl down into his lap. She watched his lips as he brought them down to her. They brushed across hers in a tantalizing manner. Just as her breath quickened, he released her with a mischievous smile. Then the dominant man resumed his work.

The next week passed much the same for Kaitlin. Each morning she woke to *Woniya Mato's* fiery wild passions. Each time she'd initially resist his intentions but yield as his expertise sent her sailing into no man's land. She'd succumb her will to his roving hands, mouth, and skills. Each day he chipped at her heart.

Then one afternoon, a band of Indians Kaitlin didn't recognize came charging on horses into the village. At first, she thought something was wrong. It looked as if another war party had shown, for the new men were painted up.

The color masks always worried Kaitlin, so she shirked back and melted into the leather siding of her tipi. Quickly, the quiet girl entered her safe domain. It was during the time where people arose after their rest time, so no one would question her presence in her tipi. She peeked out to see what was going on.

They were coming her way! Quickly, the golden one scampered back to the sleeping mats. Four Indian men followed *Woniya Mato* into his dwelling. They looked curiously upon her while the chief gathered various items.

She watched with large eyes as he then collected his peace pipe. Before exiting, Spirit Bear turned toward Kaitlin.

"We will have visitors this night. Make sure enough food is provided." Then he left and directed the band to the ceremonial lodge.

Kaitlin felt a flute of panic overwhelm her. Obviously these men were important. *So what if she messed up? Would he get mad at her? Did he punish slaves if they couldn't do what was asked in front of other people? Would she shame him?*

As the questions flooded her mind, Kaitlin wandered around the tipi. *What should she cook? What would be good?* She'd ask the advice of her savior, *Wawat'ecaka.*

Her feet flew on her quest to locate the mother of *Wawakankan*. Finally, she saw her by the drying racks.

"*Wawat'ecaka! Wawat'ecaka!*" "*Tos, Mazaska Zi Ista?*"

"*Woniya Mato* with four men. They painted strangers. He said cook enough. What I do?"

Gentle Rabbit calmed the panicked girl. "It's okay. I will help. I know just the thing." She went to her tipi and retrieved several large orange looking roots. She went back and got other strange looking items. These were longer and rounder, also a light orange color.

"These are sweet potatoes. It is a special treat! You will cook these along with the squash. You make excellent *aguyapi.* Mix your grain powder with acorn powder and the fruit of your choice. I have more maple syrup for it, and it will melt in their mouths! You will be the talk of the village! So do not worry," *Wawat'ecaka* soothed. "I will give you more of the ash-cooked elk and the stew with *tinpsila*, onions, garlic, carrots, and tubers. There will be plenty foods to tempt the men."

Kaitlin flung her arms around the motherly figure. "Oh, thank you!" she sobbed. She couldn't stand the thought of shaming *Woniya Mato*. Even more, she couldn't stand the stares from the scary men.

"Let us smoke before we begin," *Woniya Mato* told his company. The council was present with the

four guests. Eagle Talon came with Rain Dance,
Quick Feet, and Red Fox. All men present agreed.

"I take it you are interested in the marriage to tie our tribes together?"

"*Tos*, I am. I want to see this girl before I make a final judgment."

"You spoke to Wise Owl, your chief?" "*Tos*,
if I walk the warrior path with
Wakantanka, he will see she is cared for until she
finds a new mate."

"This is good." More peace pipe smoking ensued.

Sky Warrior's eyes met the chief's. He stood and called to Jack Rabbit, their normal messenger. He asked in a low voice for him to fetch Stands Tall, the father of Opossum Eyes.

"The girl's name is Opossum Eyes. She is headstrong and willful. She will be a challenge for you."

The other man smiled. "I like a challenge. I do not want a boring turtle for a wife."

"It is possible she will resist this union. She knows many in my village."

"She will adjust." Then the two men clasped forearms in mutual understanding and friendship.

Stands Tall entered the ceremonial lodge shortly after. All men stood as introductions were made.

"So you are the brave man who seeks my daughter for a wife."

"*Tos,* but before a final decision is made, I would like to meet her."

"Very good."

"Arrangements have been made with my chief, Wise Owl, for her care if I should walk with the Great Spirit."

The parent's eyes watered for a moment before he turned to retrieve his daughter. In fifteen minutes he was back. He brought the girl in with him.

Opossum Eyes did look becoming. She wore a newly constructed dress that still shone with oils of freshly made leather. Her hair had been neatly braided and hung to her hips. Her black eyes narrowed momentarily when they rested on *Woniya Mato*, but curiosity for her requested presence, the only female, overrode her other emotions.

The young woman looked around at the four strange men in the ceremonial lodge. She was nervous yet excited at being the only female with so many attractive males – all of whom stared at her.

Eagle Talon stood and approached the girl. "*Hau*, Opossum Eyes. I am Eagle Talon."

He captured her hand in his and studied them momentarily. His warmth encompassed hers. She couldn't help but to study the masculine form in front of her. *Who was this man? What did they want from her?* The way he looked at her made her warm even more than the day. She shifted her weight uneasily.

The man released her hand and walked around her. He picked up her hair to feel the texture. When Opossum Eyes looked up into his face, a gentle smile curved his lips. Nodding once to Stands Tall and *Woniya Mato*, he resumed his seat.

With the clue, Stands Tall walked his daughter back to their tipi. He turned and left her standing without a word. She was dying to find out what that was about. The Indian girl began to restlessly pace.

"*Tos*, she is just what I am looking for," Eagle Talon admitted. "She is an attractive female with soft, fine hair. She has strong hands and a good figure," he said once Stands Tall returned. "Come, let me show you gifts I have brought. See if this will suit you for the dowry price."

Stands Tall nodded. Eagle Talon led them to the shaded region beyond the village. The men's horses and supplies were stacked under the many trees. Picking up a large leather bag, Eagle Talon began to unload it.

There were many treasures inside: a bag of shiny multicolored stones for decorations that already had the many hours of labor involved evidenced by the drilled holes on their glossy surfaces; two woven rugs of wool-like fiber displaying colorful patterns in their weave; three hides of cured deer leather; three new *mniapahtas*; a cord of sinew; and a set of bone plates. A leather wrap was tied with braided leather cords. When Stands Tall unraveled it, it revealed a new hunting knife honed to a super sharp edge. One smaller bag held five newly formed sharp arrow points. Holding his treasures, Stands Tall stood and hit his chest once towards Eagle Talon.

"You honor me, Eagle Talon. I accept your generous gifts."

"I will stay tonight and leave in the morning. I will prepare my village for our joining."

"I will leave in three travels of *wi*. My wife and I will bring Opossum Eyes for the ceremony. She will have time to gather her things, prepare, and say her goodbyes."

Both men smiled in mutual respect. The deal was done. Stands Tall went to inform his wife and daughter while Eagle Talon returned to the council lodge.

By the time the men returned to the tipi of *Woniya Mato*, Kaitlin and *Wawat'ecaka* had the dinner prepared. Both women had worked hard and had already filled the decorated wooden plates and fire-hardened bowls with food. While Kaitlin handed the men the plates, *Wawat'ecaka* filled horn cups with strawberry-flavored sweet water.

The men ate in silence and the women stood ready to serve more food or drink in case any desired it. Finally, they rested as they watched for any who needed more service. When the men finished the superb meal and relaxed, the women cleared the dishes.

"Where did you find the *ska winyan*?" Eagle Talon asked.

"It is a long story, my *kola*, but we have all night."

"*Tos*, I have heard stories. Word flies far and wide of the many coup of *Woniya Mato*."

The chief smiled at the praise.

"What do the *wasicu* do now to strike anger into the heart of the mighty bear?" Eagle Talon asked, amusement sparkling in his eyes.

"What do you mean?" Spirit Bear inquired. "I know of the defeat of the trappers with the fire sticks. Then there was no further talk of conflict until the last new moon."

"What happened on the last new moon?" "Come, my *kola*. Surely you joke. No other holds the mark of *Woniya Mato* and his red feathers with black tips!"

Spirit Bear stood, serious and taut. "Please," he said with precision, "tell me of this event."

Somewhat unsure of the reaction of the powerful chief, Eagle Talon began a talk that enlightened Spirit Bear of unknown events.

"One of the warriors from my village found a small *wasicun* boy. He was sitting by the body of his father not far from the wall of wood. His father's body had many arrows of red feathers with black tips. This was not you?"

"*Hiya*! Someone impersonates me!" The war chief clenched his fists, making many veins pop out on his arms.

Eagle Talon had a thoughtful expression on his face. He said, "You may be right, my *kola*. The man and the two other *wasicu* found were riddled with arrows bearing your mark. Never before have I heard of the Oglala War Chief needing to aim so many times in order to kill his *toga*." He laughed to break the tension. "Normally men fall dead in fear at the name, '*Woniya Mato*'!"

Spirit Bear forced himself to stay calm. He would need to assess the situation. No one impersonated him and his deeds under the guise of his leadership without repercussions! Now, though, was not the time or the place. He had guests to entertain. His village was renowned for his generosity and kindness if deemed a *kola*.

While the men talked long into the night, Kaitlin cleaned and performed her womanly chores. Young Elk accompanied her on her trips to wash dishes and her other duties. Finally, when she could no longer avoid the tipi and the many men inside, she went directly to the sleeping mats and tried to ignore them.

Because she was the only attractive woman in a hut filled with vibrant men, she captured their attention immediately.

"Again, my friend, I ask where you found such a treasure? I have never seen one such as she!" Eagle Talon praised his *wayaka*. "Her meal was incomparable to many Indian-born women!"

Woniya Mato began the sordid tale of Jed and the capture of his *Mazaska Zi Ista*. Because of the gift of storytelling by the great chief, the four visitors sat entranced for many hours of the night. Each man would look with admiration upon the great chief, and they'd sneak peeks at the woman who'd piqued the curiosity of all.

CHAPTER SEVENTEEN

Zuzeca Pazan

When morning came, the visiting warriors of the Yankton band left. Spirit Bear called a meeting with the tribal council. The four men met in the ceremonial lodge directly after they'd eaten.

"I am told there is one who is masquerading as me near where the *wasicu* live." Spirit Bear revealed to his leading brothers. At the others' exclamations, he related Eagle Talon's words of the night before.

"I will take a small party with me to investigate these *wasicu* deaths. If I had committed this deed, I would take credit. I do not. I will discover who is doing this and why!"

The council supported *Woniya Mato*'s decision to take a small party of men to the wall of wood. Yellow Feather along with four other men would accompany the chief. He'd leave as soon as materials were gathered.

Spirit Bear planned on returning within a week so that he could give Young Elk time to learn of his adult name by seeking a vision from the Great Spirit for admittance into warrior society. He'd relieve him of his duties of watching *Mazaska Zi Ista* upon his return. She'd earned her trust by the way her resistance was dissolving toward him. He no longer feared her attempts to escape.

Although *Woniya Mato* gave the white beauty more and more freedom, he never left her totally alone. The next ceremony would be her official release from his lack of trust. He'd bestow full honor of trust upon her then… unless something changed his mind.

Spirit Bear returned to his tipi. Golden Eyes was not there. He walked to the leather tanning place. He found her working with *Wawat'ecaka* on the magnificent hide of the great white elk.

Even though the heat of the day had not yet hit, Kaitlin was hot and sweaty already. Her hair had been glued to her neck, so she'd braided it. It was the coolest and most tidy way she knew to deal with her wayward strands, but it didn't seem to stop them from escaping and continuing the attack on her neck.

The honeyed-blonde looked up in surprise from scouring the white hide with gravel when she saw the powerful frame of the chief outlined by the bank of the river. He approached the women as silently as he'd appeared. His polished stone eyes gleamed in admiration of their progress. Kaitlin stood up to give him her full attention.

Woniya Mato complimented them on the finery. He knew the leather would be above all other pieces of Gentle Rabbit's work. Nothing less would do to show appreciation to the essence of the white elk!

"The great elk's spirit is much honored," his mid-timber voice rang proudly to both women.

Kaitlin nodded once in gratitude of the compliment. She wiped a stubborn strand of hair from her face.

Spirit Bear softly called her to him. As the *winyan* approached, the warrior's magnetism reached out and trapped her in a sealed vacuum in which there was no escape. The white girl felt herself being drawn to him through no will of her own.

When Kaitlin was within arm's length of him, the chieftain reached out and grasped her shoulders. He looked down from his towering height and searched her face. His handsome features were mirrored with intention. With surprising need, Spirit Bear drew her to him and kissed her deeply.

"*Mazaska Zi Ista*, I must leave you for several passings of *wi*. You will be watched over by *Ojilaka Hehaka*. Do not try to deceive me." His dark eyes looked deeply into hers to see if she understood. Then he continued, "I will not tolerate disobedience. Upon my return, I will honor your behavior. See that I am not disappointed."

The beauty nodded her head; her eyes were golden saucers.

He turned to *Wawat'ecaka*. "You will see that she is looked after when the moon watches over the lands while I am gone?"

"*Tos*, my chief. She will be cared for and watched over. You have my word."

"This is good, my mother. I will go now." With that, he disappeared.

When the mighty chief and his warriors reached the outskirts of the area the *wasicu* claimed, the white men were in quite an uproar about Indians. Spirit Bear did not let himself be seen, but he saw the flurry of movements and the near panicked actions of the men inside the walls.

After scouting around, *Woniya Mato* discovered where the men had met their deaths. He'd even found several stray arrows embedded in nearby trees that had missed their marks. He thanked *Wakantanka* for this gift, for the construction of the arrows revealed subtle hints.

The arrows were poorly assembled. They were not of the status renowned by the *Cante Tinza*. They did not even appear to be of hunter's quality. Nonetheless, they were what was used to take the lives of three *wasicu*.

The feather guides used on the arrows were poorly dyed. They still contained chunks of red ochre with sooty ends. This, Spirit Bear determined, was another reason the arrows missed their marks. *How could the engineer expect the weapons to fly straight and true if they were of sloppy construction? Arrows did not follow the desired flight path with chunks of this or that weighing on their wings!*

The first several nights without *Woniya Mato* were welcomed, Kaitlin told herself. She didn't miss his hot kisses, his mesmerizing looks, or his tender embraces. She greeted the company of the woman who was very much like a mother with open arms.

Gentle Rabbit's kindness was all she needed… if only she could convince herself!

The chore of the new day was to begin gathering several kinds of berries for preservation. Winter was a difficult season, and the more the Indian village prepared, the more would survive the harsh months. The season for currants, buffalo berries, coral berries, and choke berries was beginning. The time for growth would continue for several months, but the Indians began gathering them as soon as they appeared.

Fresh berries were always used in their diets to provide many sources of vitamins. Those gathered but not used in a day would be dried. In this way, much would be preserved without undue stress and preparation.

Kaitlin, Gentle Rabbit, and Young Elk were joined by Desert Rose, Playful Otter, and Apple Blossom to pick the small fruits. The women went into scores of draws and ravines where the trees and bushes provided many locations of berries in fairly close proximity. Young Elk faded into the background.

Kaitlin looked around her in wonder. She'd never been this far from the village before. The beauty and serenity of the country never failed to leave her breathless with astonishment. She wandered away from the others, picking as she dreamed.

Before long, Kaitlin's basket was full. She discovered she was far from the others. In fact, no people could be seen at all! Not really alarmed because the white woman knew that Young Elk would be shadowing her steps, she began to walk back in the direction she thought she'd come.

In the distance, the blonde heard a rumble in the sky. Although not concerned because the atmosphere was clear, she picked up her pace. The white girl walked for a time but didn't see one person… *not even Young Elk!*

Kaitlin's heart began to beat faster. *What if she was lost? How would she explain to Spirit Bear that she'd become disoriented and was not trying to escape his wondrous arms? Would he believe her? He'd told her not to betray his trust…* The beginning of alarm swept over the captive. Kaitlin called out her friends' names.

The breeze picked up and blew blonde hair across her face. She wiped it away in frustration; the *winyan* was on the verge of panic! There was a hill directly in front of her. Kaitlin decided to climb it. Maybe the higher vantage point would show her the way to the others.

The wind was insistent now. It pulled at her hair, throwing it this way and that. The distant rumble was a roar and raced to meet the single white woman. Huge sporadic droplets of rain began to throw themselves at her. When she looked up, lightening split the sky in a threatening omen.

Kaitlin didn't see evidence of anyone around. In fact, the scenery was even more vague and unfamiliar. The crack of thunder bellowed just beyond her, causing a chill to race up her spine. A startled whimper escaped her lips as the lightning splintered a tree just to the left of her. Frightened, the lone woman began to run.

The rain launched an attack that slashed furiously at her. The torrent slapped her and temporarily blinded her. Stumbling, Kaitlin tripped and lay still in the mud and grass, a single sob escaped her lips and she waited for a small reprieve in the weather.

The lightening flickered in the face of the black, boiling clouds. The ominous wind was merciless, throwing abusive deluge at Kaitlin like daggers. The whistling squall made her hair nettles that stung and they abused her upper body. She simply couldn't stay in the open. If she did, the storm would tear her apart.

Just as Kaitlin rose to seek shelter, the water turned to ice. Harder and harder, the rubble struck at her, increasing in size and weight. Soon, it was no longer slivers of ice but hard balls of stone hurled form the atmosphere. The longer the frightened girl staggered in the open field, the more the hail bruised her flesh.

Crying with fright, Kaitlin finally managed to seek refuge under a large, thickly fringed pine. It was nestled in a grove of trees of several kinds. She hugged the base of the trunk in gratitude. The thankful girl still received a few slaps of ice, but only a fraction of what she'd face without the kind tree to shelter her.

Thunder and lightning continued its deadly dance in the skies. The trees bowed in submission, and the rain and hail punished. Kaitlin grasped the tree in fear and in relief. It now represented life to her.

The storm abated as quickly as it had struck. Its disappearance was accompanied by her strength. The blonde wept in relief that she'd made it through the fury of the gods, but her weak limbs wouldn't support her weight; after the force of adrenaline had abandoned her, she was left with nothing. She was trapped by her body under the pine in the grove of trees.

Kaitlin didn't know how long she lay under the conifer; only that night was usurping the light from the world. New fears griped her heart. She was all alone, weak and afraid, lost in the dark with no way of protecting herself.

The amber-eyed beauty was so wrapped up in her feelings that she didn't notice the sparkle of life glistening on the leaves and blades of grass. The night songs of frogs, birds, and insects fell upon deaf ears. The fresh smell of rain did not even revive her senses.

Kaitlin didn't know how long she shivered under the tree, but it seemed like forever. Finally, she tried to sleep. She knew it would be even more foolish to try to find her way home in the dark. She'd wait until daylight to try to get back to the others.

Bright and early, the mingled songs performed by a mockingbird awoke Kaitlin. The crisp world sparkled with new life and hope. The young woman stood on shaky feet. Feeling a twinge of hunger through her panic, she ate a handful of the berries she'd collected.

While the lonely girl ate the bittersweet fruit, a new sound floated to Kaitlin. It was not an unfamiliar noise, she realized, but a sound that squeezed her heart almost painfully tight with fear: it was the *hunka-hunka* noise of a bear!

Kaitlin looked around madly. She didn't see it, but certainly it was near. How else would the white girl be able to hear it? Surely her ears weren't playing tricks on her! Doing the most sensible things she could, the blonde woman scuttled up the life-giving pine directly in front of her.

Correctly assessing the origination of the noise, Kaitlin held her breath as she saw a large mother black bear and two cubs approaching her perch! The bears happily made an easy meal out of the tempting berries waiting for them under the tree.

When finished, the mother lifted her massive head, and Kaitlin could see the great nose twitching back and forth. The black receptacle sensed her nearness. Barely daring to breath, Kaitlin waited silently.

From her height, the white woman had a spectacular view. Still, it was difficult not to only focus on the activity below her swinging feet. Suddenly, a slight movement in the distance captured Kaitlin's attention momentarily from the bear: it was Young Elk. Only, he was acting oddly. He was hunched over when normally he had a tall, erect, and proud carriage. He walked as if he were in great pain. He seemed to be heading away from her.

Had the bear attacked him? What was wrong with him? If she could call to him, she would, but how could she alert him to her location if it would also alert a protective mother bear? Trembling, Kaitlin wisely held her tongue.

Was Ojilaka Hehaka looking for her? Surely he was! He would also be placed under the wrath of *Moniya Mato* if she was not discovered before his return! She watched helplessly as he haltingly faded from sight. The only thing she could do now was to remember where she'd seen him disappear and follow once the bear departed.

Abruptly, Kaitlin noticed another figure emerge from the spot she'd first seen Young Elk. She wasn't able to distinguish the figure, but he was coming toward her direction instead of following *Ojilaka Hehaka*'s steps. She sighed in relief. Rescue was close!

When the figure grew larger on the horizon, Kaitlin's eyes became wide with astonishment. This was not at all who she expected to recognize! It was the last person she ever wanted to see! *What was the vile little man, Zuzeca Pazan, doing out in this area?*

Kaitlin froze under the thick canopy of pine needles. She hoped his weasel-like eyes wouldn't detect her. She almost hoped he'd miss the presence of the bears and walk upon them. At least they would give her a fighting chance when they greeted him!

Snake Strike, unfortunately, recognized the unique shape of the bears rooting under the tree. Part of her prayers was met; his eyes didn't wander up the tree to discover her. Instead, they remained on the bear family.

Twenty minutes later, the great mammals grew tired of the spot, for the promise of berries had been depleted. They lumbered slowly away, rooting and foraging on route. At times, they would stop to dig a hole that would reveal some delicacy. Shortly after their disappearance, Kaitlin climbed down from the tree.

Immediately, she set off in the direction she'd last seen Young Elk. It was far from her savior tree, but she at last reached the place she thought she'd seen him travel. Perhaps if she hurried, she'd meet up with him. Walking swiftly, she let her feet carry her away from the bears and Snake Strike.

The sun was peeking over the top of the foliage when she heard a noise in the woods off to her left. A sense of danger swept over her. *Were the bears back? Had they traced her scent and followed her?* She tried to quiet her feet and the pounding in her heart as she traipsed onward.

Snake Strike could taste victory. He silently congratulated himself for his innovative plan. Now he'd forever rid himself of *Woniya Mato* and his delicious morsel of a slave. He couldn't wait to meet up with her and show her a thing or two!

He found where she'd climbed down the tree. She'd been in the conifer when he'd passed by! At least the bears hadn't finished her off; he wanted that pleasure. Due to the saturation level of the ground, he could see her trial easily. It was thankfully not covered well, for he didn't possess tracking skills. Basically, he could only follow if there was a blood trail, but since she'd recently passed, and he knew she was just up ahead. He circled through the woods.

Kaitlin knew the thing in the dense underbrush was trailing her. The footsteps would silence when she stopped to listen. Oh, how she longed for *Woniya*

Mato! She'd even be happy to see Young Elk! However, she feared it was Snake Strike stalking her.

Hurrying, she broke into a light jog. She did her best to avoid noisy areas. Things didn't crunch after the drenching rain, but the soft ground made sucking noises in places. Fear gripped her when she heard the pounding noise in the woods. *I was no bear preying on her!*

Kaitlin picked up her pace to a sprint. Risking a glance back, she saw her fear emerge. Snake Strike jumped from behind a tree with a vicious look on his face and was in hot pursuit!

No! No, it couldn't be happening! Where was her shadow, her guard against escape and injury? Why did it have to be the weasel-eyed man with an evil heart to find her?

Her breath knifed in her chest as she burst forward with sheer will to escape. Still, the small man gained on her. Spying a thick branch on the ground, the white woman scooped it up. If she couldn't outrun him, maybe she could injure him and then escape. Kaitlin turned to face her approaching nightmare.

When the repugnant foe noted that she'd stopped running, a malicious grin widened his face. Kaitlin had seen the predatory look before. She was a timid rabbit in the face of a hungry coyote.

Zuzeca Pazan laughed mockingly at her. *What attempt was this to elude him?* He'd be victorious. First, he'd play with her fear. He was the snake, and she was the mouse!

 *

Kaitlin warily held the branch-type weapon in front of her. She tested its weight in her hand. She'd never purposely hurt another before in her life, but the stunning blonde would to protect herself. She'd seen firsthand what he was capable of!

Snake Strike's wicked smile never left his lips. He began stringing words in Lakota at her, many of which she didn't recognize. *Zuzeca Pazan* made lewd gestures of his plans for her. His tongue flickered like a reptile's over his thin lips.

Adrenaline and fear pumped through the golden-eyed beauty's frozen veins. *"Oh, please, Woniya Mato,"* she silently prayed, *"find me!"* Kaitlin almost couldn't bear to look into the glittering narrow eyes of her opponent's. She knew she couldn't let her fear overcome her, or she'd be his prey in minutes!

Slowly, Snake Strike closed the gap between them. His evil eyes stared her down while his vile lips muttered insults at her in a constant stream. The small man made sure the white whore saw his muscles knot with anticipation of what they'd soon be doing to her. He could taste his victory.

Kaitlin continued to take a step back as he approached; she couldn't help herself. Never before had she been attacked in this manner! The *ska winyan* made sure her weapon was held loosely in front of her.

Zuzeca Pazan was in attack mode. He sprung forward. Kaitlin stumbled in a panicked attempt to avoid him. Suddenly, the blonde tripped and fell backward over a root and managed to drop her only form of protection.

In a flash, Snake Strike advanced on her with an assassin's pounce. He grabbed on to her foot. Kaitlin kicked crazily, smashing his face with her unrestricted foot. She clawed for her dropped club during the short reprieve. Feeling it, the determined woman swung wildly, making contact.

Snake Strike staggered back in surprise. Disbelief was etched on his bleeding features. With a snarl, he shook his head and surged forward with another onslaught.

"I am going to enjoy making you pay even more for that," he told her between gritted teeth. "You are going to make Ear Sore look like she bumped into a tree when I get finished with you! After you feel my wrath, I will find out what has infatuated the *chief* so much about you," he sneered, "but *I* will be the *only* one to find pleasure." Malicious laughter filled the air.

Kaitlin screamed in terror. Snake Strike grabbed both of her legs in a vice and dragged her back over the root. He made sure she bumped her head on it forcefully. The blonde knew it would do no good to plead with the devil, so the *wayaka* did her best to become a force to be reckoned with.

She heaved, twisted, and turned madly in his grip. The wiry man dropped her feet and kicked her viciously. Her hamstring cramped where he'd made contact, temporarily disabling her leg. Again, he kicked, this time he aimed higher and for much more tender spot. Luckily, his foot made contact with her derriere.

"I will take the fight out of you!" The Lakota man promised with another bruising kick landing in her hamstring. Kaitlin screamed wildly with agony and fear.

"When I'm finished with you, you will do anything I want to avoid further pain!" The wiry man gloated. "There. Will. Be. No. More. Defiance!" With each pause, he kicked.

A man materialized behind her. Snake Strike was in the process of kicking her again, reveling in her anguish, when the terse command came for him to stop. Both looked into the angry eyes of Young Elk.

Kaitlin had never been so happy to see him. She couldn't will her leg to function yet, but she tried to crawl away from Snake Strike. He didn't appear to notice, for he was angrily confronting the young warrior. The two men began to circle warily.

"You do not die easily! Leave now, or I will finish you off!"

"*Hiya*! It is you who will die this day!" "How are *you*, just a *boy*, going to fight me? You are injured. I thought I'd killed you, but now I see

I should have checked to make sure! Be ready, for
here I come!"

Kaitlin watched in revulsion as the two men met in combat. Neither had weapons, but the youth didn't move with the grace normally evidenced in his fluid motions. When he turned, presenting his back to her, her wild eyes detected two arrows piercing his body. Her eyes widened further as she noted that the *wahinkpe* bore a marked resemblance to those of *Woniya Mato's*. One was horribly close to where his organs used life's breath, and the other protruded from his outer back muscle.

Even though Ojilaka Hehaka had the more powerful build, how could he ever defeat the man who only suffered a bloody nose? Moving her injured leg, Kaitlin drug herself to the club nature had provided her.

When she looked up, Snake Strike had circled around enough that he'd backed Young Elk towards the root that had led to her downfall. Crying out to him, the white girl saw her warning was too late; the youth had already tripped and fallen on his side.

Snake Strike was on him in an instant. His hands pressed down with all his force on Young Elk's throat. The man-almost-warrior gasped and his eyes bulged. Kaitlin knew time was running out.

Using the stick to support her weight, the amber-eyed woman forced her leg to action. With a scream, she charged on one leg. Swinging crazily, the blonde hit where Snake Strike's back and neck joined, knocking him loose from his strangle hold on the boy. With narrowed eyes, the little man hissed and bulleted toward her. Kaitlin turned and raced, as best as she could, into the woods. She had just enough lead on the little man that she had a chance to hide.

Quietly, she dove into some brush and hid behind the large trunk of an oak. The white woman's ragged breath was sure to give her away. *Where was he?* He was close, she knew. *Did he see her dive behind the great tree, or did he search for her? Did she dare to find out?*

She *had* to look. Kaitlin had to be sure he wasn't finishing off the young man who'd interrupted her abuse and tried to save her. Golden eyes peaked from behind the fringe of leaves. Snake Strike stood just on the other side. He held the club she'd dropped! Thinking she'd hidden under a cluster of fallen branches, he struck down on them with excessive force.

A loud bawling noise broke the air. A black bear cub ripped from the underbrush in a frenzied panic. It favored its leg where the club had injured it. It tried to climb the nearest tree, but its leg was too sore. It continued to bawl incessantly.

Kaitlin took the opportunity to break out of the wooded area. Only temporarily distracted, Snake Strike refocused on the white girl. She ran toward the fallen boy. The vindictive man smiled. He'd take care of two problems at once.

When *Woniya Mato* thundered into the village, he was met by a somber *Wawat'ecaka*. Her head hung in shame. Immediately concerned, Spirit Bear dismounted and ran to her.

"What is it, my mother?" he asked.

"I have failed you, my chief. It is Golden Eyes. She has been lost."

"What? Explain what you mean, now!" Briefly, Gentle Rabbit told of gathering berries and then the powerful storm. She told of how Young Elk had temporarily lost her but looked for her even as they spoke.

"I am sure he will find her, *Woniya Mato*. He is a warrior in a boy's body!" she tried to sooth the man who was part of her extended family. The concern engraved on the chief's face did not fade. He turned to Yellow Feather.

"Find *Wawakankan*. Tell him I need him at once! You may tell him why... Tell him what we figured out at the wall of wood – who is responsible. I fear the worst!"

Confused but knowing it was best not to ask in the time of a crisis, *Wawat'ecaka* backed away from the intensity of the chief. However, her curiosity was brimming.

Wonder Worker and Spirit Bear bolted out of the village in the direction the women had taken to gather berries. It took a little while, but *Woniya Mato* found the evidence of where Kaitlin had spent the night. He tracked her and found where her path crossed two others.

Anxious as to what he might find, Spirit Bear swiftly followed the woman of his heart. Wonder Worker blazed the trail behind him. The two came quickly upon a grisly scene.

Kaitlin was stooped over an unconscious Young Elk. A loud bear cub's cry disturbed the morning air. Instantly on alert, Spirit Bear's eyes hunted for Snake Strike.

He saw the small man bullet from the woods like he was infected with the mad animal disease. His eyes were possesses with a furious glow. He had tunnel vision for the *ska winyan*.

Before he could think, Spirit Bear had two arrows ready for departure. One was in his bow, the other ready for instant restringing.

The command, "*Hiya!*" ripped from his throat without his knowledge.

The small man froze in his tracks. His trembling was immediately evidenced. He knew death was approaching. Turning, the diminutive male stumbled into the monstrous claws of an angry mother bear.

The two powerful Lakota leaders watched the demise of the snake weasel that had plagued their tribe for far too long. Cautiously, the men circled around to the woman stooped over the fallen warrior.

CHAPTER EIGHTEEN
Always and Forever

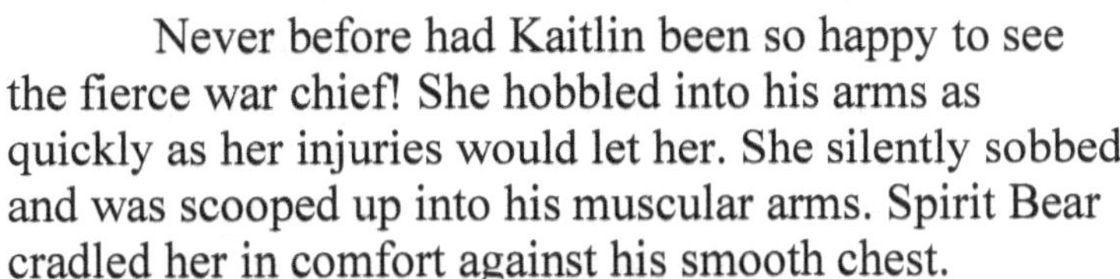

Never before had Kaitlin been so happy to see the fierce war chief! She hobbled into his arms as quickly as her injuries would let her. She silently sobbed and was scooped up into his muscular arms. Spirit Bear cradled her in comfort against his smooth chest.

Wonder Worker began chanting over the fallen form of Young Elk. Both kept a wary eye on the raging mother bear. When Snake Strike's screams finally ended, the protective bear seemed to sense the threat was gone. The great mother looked at the four humans before turning tail to comfort her young.

Finding her voice, Kaitlin said, "*Wawakankan, Ojilaka Hehaka* has two *wahinkpe* lodged in his back. I fear for him!"

He looked up from his work; black eyes silently thanked golden ones. Then he focused on the face of his chief.

"We need to move him into the medicine lodge as quickly as possible."

Gently placing Kaitlin on the ground beside her youthful protector, the two men immediately began constructing the travois. The arrows would need to be removed as soon as possible, but it was best to do this in the village. Upon the structure's quick completion, the men carefully placed the injured man upon it.

Woniya Mato positioned Kaitlin on the back of his stallion while he and *Wawakankan* carried the travois back to the village. Kaitlin couldn't help but watch the important males' muscles bulge with the strain of carrying the incapacitated youth.

When they reached the village, many members of the tribe swarmed to help upon the sighting of the group. Kaitlin felt loved and welcomed as she was surrounded by Gentle Rabbit, New Moon, Desert Rose, Singing Cicada, Apple Blossom, Playful Otter, and even Fresh Water. All hugged and patted her, and they talked in soothing, calm tones. The blonde girl felt reassured. *They only believed her to be lost.* Their eyes were filled with curiosity as they looked at the fallen youth being taken directly to the shaman's hut.

Many questions assailed her. All she had to say was, "*Zuzeca Pazan.*"

Both *Wawakankan* and *Woniya Mato* began a fire in the lodge. Incense was immediately thrown upon the flames. Within minutes of calming the crowds, Sky Warrior entered. Lone Wolf was on his heels.

After making sure everything was being handled with the care of Young Elk, the village chief left to help maintain control on the crowd. Lone Wolf tended the incense which brought the helping spirits into the lodge faster, allowing the other two men with the most medical knowledge the freedom to focus on their patient.

Wonder Worker rolled the young man gently to his stomach. He saw the two shafts protruding from his back. The one nearly centered in his back was deep, but it didn't strike vital organs. It did, however, separate the lateral muscle partially from where it attached. The injury would be slow to heal.

The other arrow was lodged in the outside lateral muscle, but it wasn't deep. It only took a slight tug to release the unwelcomed barb.

Realizing the youth's injuries were significant but not life-threatening, the chieftains relaxed. They began to smile as they discovered that once more, the spirits smiled upon them. The youth would revive shortly.

"I see you use the Seneca Snake Root on his injuries. Do you choose this plant for a particular reason?" Spirit Bear jested with Wonder Worker as he packed the wounds.

"A snake caused his injuries; it can also cure them."

Woniya Mato laughed, his eyes twinkling. He added, "Then I will make a rattlesnake weed tea to battle his internal injuries."

 *

That night the village waited with baited breath. The tribal council stood before them. A drum announced to the community an important message was about to be delivered.

"My people. I know you are curious about the recent events. Bear with me. I will tell all." He paused

as the crowd surged forward to hang on his every
word.

"Many of you know of the trouble we've had
with *Zuzeca Pazan*. He no longer walks this earth." The
crowd inhaled with anticipation.

"He has mocked me and our ways too long.
For this, *Wakantanka* takes him.
He abused Indian beliefs and defied them. He did not
honor life of those who create it."

Wawakankan stepped forward. "A great black
she-bear honored *Mazaska Zi Ista* and *Ojilaka Hehaka* by
saving their lives. She took *Zuzeca Pazan* as he attacked
them. His body will be recovered and put on the scaffolds
this day." He searched the crowd to see the effect of his
words. Then he continued, "It is a sign from *Wakantanka*
that more is destined from both Golden Eyes and Young
Elk. Otherwise, why would the Great Spirit have sent
such a powerful messenger?" he challenged.

"We celebrate upon the health and recovery of
Young Elk. I say he will recuperate enough in three
travels of *wi*," informed Sky Warrior.

The crowd conversed among itself as the chiefs
dispersed. Before Spirit Bear could go to his tipi and unite
with *Mazaska Zi Ista*, his duties as chief prevailed. It
seemed like hours before his people settled.

Kaitlin was so happy to be back in the safety of
the village. When the crowd address began, she retired to
her tipi. The golden girl was fatigued and hungry.

She hadn't eaten since the meal the day before unless one counted a handful of berries.

Wawakankan must have inherited some of his intuitive power from *Wawat'ecaka* for she seemed to know Kaitlin's every need and fear. Within minutes, Kaitlin had a large bowl of fresh fish stew. The bubbly brew had been thickened with the *tinpsila*. Carrots, onions, and fresh cabbage flavored the mixture. The salt solution, a favorite of Kaitlin's, added a zesty taste.

Freshly baked *aguyapi* accompanied the fish dish. It consisted of acorn powder mixed with fresh cherries. The juice Gentle Rabbit provided was also cherry flavored.

When Gentle Rabbit left her, she ordered the amber-eyed girl to rest. Gratefully, Kaitlin lay back in the supple furs and fell asleep immediately despite the drums and loud voices.

When *Mazaska Zi Ista* began to stir, she noticed a low fire crackled merrily in the pit. A profoundly handsome man beamed at her as she awoke. He wore only a breechcloth and a smile. He stood on muscular legs lined with sheer power and approached her in confidence.

The *ska wayaka* anticipated his approach. The chief softly stretched out beside her. Huskily, he whispered in her ear.

"*Wastelaka, nimitawa ktelo*, you are mine."

"*Tos*," Kaitlin finally admitted as she looked into his hypnotic gaze. His black eyes widened momentarily to hear her admit what her heart knew to be true. In fact, because she opened herself to him, the white girl feared she'd weep with gratitude to finally be back in his secure arms.

Kaitlin knew the war chief had noticed the welling in her eyes. He understood the meaning of her tears perfectly. He rolled on top of her, propping up on his arms on either side of her body so that his weight would not squash her. He held her face in his hands and told her with words and actions that everything would be alright.

The Lakota chief lowered his magical lips to hers in a gentle kiss. His *wayaka* met his passions. Again, she saw the subtle widening of his surprised eyes. She smiled softly in response.

Quickly, the kiss deepened and his hands began to rove. A throaty moan erupted from her, and he was happy that she also began a tentative exploration of her own. His body answered with an ancient need…

Finally I've broken her will to resist me, Spirit Bear thought. He lay beside her more fully sated than he'd ever been in his life. It was another sign from *Wakantanka* that she was meant to be his wife.

When he rolled to his side to speak with her, her golden eyes devoured him. He smiled and thought, *"You are ready so soon, my Wastelaka? This is good, for so am I."*

With the rise of *wi*, *Woniya Mato* took his love to their special location, the blue pool. Kaitlin wondered about his intentions, because for her, it was too cool in the morning for the icy waters of the spring fed pond.

"I brought you to the place that is special to me," his masculine voice informed her. "I want you to always remember our special times when you visit this place."

"*Tos*, I will, *Woniya Mato*." Kaitlin still felt very confused by his words and actions.

Before continuing his conversation, he spread a mat upon the ground. He added a supple leather skin to ward off the chilly morning air. He pulled her down onto it and covered them both with the leather.

"I brought you here for another reason," he said. His eyes looked into hers, serious, yet full of emotion.

"*Tos?*"

"I brought you here to ask you a big question." He saw her wonderment etched in her face. He allowed time for the impact of his words to affect her. The emotions flickered across her face as she thought.

What could he want to ask me? she wondered. *I am his slave in every way. What could he possibly ask of me that I haven't yet done? He even owns my reason to live,* she admitted.

"Do you have feelings in your heart for me?" Spirit Bear's warm timbre resonated.

Kaitlin could only stare at him. *Why could he want to know this? Was this his way of telling her he had alternative plans for her? Was he going to send her away? Or was he leaving?*

"Please do not send me away! I could not bear it!" She cried, her eyes swimming with tears.

"*Hiya, Nimitawa ktelo*. Always and forever, you will remain mine!" he said hoarsely, grasping her to him in a strong embrace. "Do not think I could do such a thing!"

"Then most certainly, *tos, Woniya Mato*. My heart beats madly with feeling when you are around."

"My biggest question," he said softly as he caressed her face with love, "Is will you become my wife? Will you let me own your heart and soul?"

"*Tos*! She cried with passion. "But do not tease me. This would be a cruel joke! How can a mighty chief marry a lowly slave?"

Wakantanka has shown *Wawakankan* and I, personally, that you are destined to be mine in all ways. In the eyes of the Great Spirit, we are already one!"

"I will marry you with honor!" she gasped. Shimmering tears dripped down her face. "It's a dream come true!"

"You must know, also *Wastelaka*, that you must denounce *wasicu* ways. You must fully embrace Oglala customs for us to be wed."

"*Tos*," she breathlessly agreed.

"We will announce our engagement at the celebration!" he said as he welcomed her into his arms. He lay her down gently in the sun-kissed light. Pulling the cover over them was all the privacy they needed.

When Young Elk was released from the medicine lodge, he went to the tipi of Spirit Bear. He asked the council to meet with him. Gladly, they amassed in the ceremonial lodge full of wise spirits.

"*Tos, Ojilaka Hehaka*? How can we help you?" *Woniya Mato* asked.

"I know that young men must seek a vision quest before they enter the ceremony of manhood." "*Tos*. This is so. Do you need time for this?" *Wawakankan* inquired.

"*Hiya*. Actually, I do not. This is what I wanted to talk with you about." He gathered his thoughts and took a breath. "During my recovery, I was visited by the Great Spirit. *Wakantanka* showed me he wants me to keep my totem spirit, the elk, as my main name. The vision I was shone was very similar to what I experienced. I saw a brave elk standing against an evil snake and a great bear. The elk knew when to stand strong and fight, and he knew when to retreat. I interpreted this as a sign by *Wakantanka* that my name is to be Brave Elk."

"Good, my *kola*. This, too, is a sign from *Wakantanka* that it is time for you to be inducted into manhood as well as the *Cante Tinza*. You will be a great leader some day!" As he stood with emotion, Chief Spirit Bear struck his chest with his fist once. The others stood and did the same.

When the meeting ended, a drum sounded letting the community know that the next day would begin the celebration. Only the council members and *Wawat'ecaka* knew of the chief's impending betrothal. Already, the couple had received many congratulations from their friends.

The next day was a flurry of movement for Kaitlin. Before she knew it, the food was prepared and the men were being served. The constant drumming numbed her. She felt like the time passed quickly. She was so high on Cloud Nine! She was actually going to marry the most powerful and sexy man in the world. His virility would be hers for all time!

The women ate with anticipation. The timing of the throbs was especially enticing this night. All knew it was an extra special celebration!

The first item on the festivity agenda was a recounting of the bravery of the teenaged warrior, Young Elk. Spirit Bear along with his council brothers chanted his coup and bravery for saving the life of the *wayaka, Mazaska Zi Ista.* They also told of his contest winnings.

Each boy to become a man was introduced independently. He stood before the community while his training and accomplishments were announced.

The rhythm was enthralling. Kettle and base drums beat a tempo for the wood and bone flutes they accompanied. Bone and gourd rattles added to the mixture and had Kaitlin swaying.

The upbeat music led to the masculine dance of the adolescents about to be inducted into the world of manly responsibilities. They circled the fire, dancing wildly. Their feet were a flurry of movement. They twisted and turned, flailing their arms with power. Their voices uplifted praise to *Wankantanka.* It was an awe-filled sight to behold.

After the dance, *Wawakankan* stood before the men standing in a line. Each stepped forward when Wonder Worker said their name. Lone Wolf placed a *wanapin* that related to each man's vision-quest around individual necks. Then Sky Warrior announced their new name to the congregation. The boy-now-man left the stage to roars from the crowd. This continued as each man was inducted.

Only two men were left before the collection of people: Young Elk and Wiley Dog. *Woniya Mato* took turns with the other three tribal council members going into depth of why these two men were being inducted into the warrior society in the Bear Claw Clan of the Oglala. The *Cante Tinze*, or Brave Hearts, did not normally accept men until years of displayed prowess and valor and many coups had been earned. These two men, however, due to the level of expertise displayed at such an early age, would be honored.

The detailed story of Snake Strike was told. The gathering loved the tale of bravery displayed by the youth. Sky Warrior called him forward to the tribal members.

"Lean forward to accept your *wanapin* in honor," *Woniya Mato* said loudly. Wonder Worker placed the totem around the youth's neck.

"The boy, Young Elk, is no more. Brave Elk now stands before you," Sky Warrior introduced.

Spirit Bear continued, "Brave Elk, protector of *Mazaska Zi Ista,* member of *Cante Tinza* Society, meet your people." Wild cheering and shouting went up from the multitude.

Woniya Mato took out his huge knife. It glittered powerfully in the light. The crowd watched silently with anticipation.

Spirit Bear held up his hand. Grasping the blade of the knife, he slid it down the honed tip, slicing the meat open. The three other members did the same with the war chief's knife. They sliced the hand of Brave Elk. The new member of warrior society grasped the bloody hands of his leaders.

Next, Wiley Dog was called forward. He received a fox teeth and claw *wanapin*. "The young boy, Wiley Dog is no more. Grey Fox now stands before you. Grey Fox, slayer of the mad wolf, member of the *Cante Tinza* Society, meet your people."

The bloody hand shake procedure was repeated with Grey Fox. Again, may voices shouted with admiration. When the mass calmed again, all tribal members sat except Sky Warrior.

"We have a special honor, one that has never before been presented to the Bear Claw Clan. This honor has not ever been bestowed upon an Oglala nation to my knowledge," the striking chief began.

Hurrahs went up and then a curtain of silence fell over the gathering.

"The council members were led to believe it was a sign from *Wakantanka*."

The multitude echoed praise, showing their belief also reflected this.

He continued, "The mighty bear showed herself." Again, the crowd roared then fell silent with suspense.

"She delivered *Mazaska Zi Ista* and Brave Elk from the hands of evil." Sky Warrior went on. "Both are destined for more than their station. One has become a mighty warrior of the *Cante Tinza* Society." He stopped dramatically. "The other," his eyes scanned many expectant faces, "will be joined to our chief."

The community went wild! They surged forward in congratulations. Before the crowd became too out of control, Spirit Bear stood.

"I want to address my fiancé," he began. "*Mazaska Zi Ista* has time and time again shown us that she has the heart of an Oglala maiden. She is brave and strong. She is skilled with her hands. She is wise," he paused. Winking at her, he chuckled, "although we all make mistakes." The villagers laughed with him.

Kaitlin was pink. She'd never liked being the center of attention. How could she resist the gorgeous man in front of her? The white woman lifted her chin and tried to meet the gaze of the Indian society.

"I give to my bride a bear claw *wanapin*. The she-bear herself donated a claw willingly to her." The crowd gasped. It was rarely heard of for a woman to receive such a gift, especially one who had been a slave!

"This was another clue from The Great Spirit that she was to be joined with me," once more, Spirit Bear laughed. "But I didn't understand the sign. The Great Spirit had to show me much more directly." His chuckles were echoed in the communal group.

The lithe man moved with masculine grace toward his betrothed. He whispered for her to lean forward. She bowed her silken head to accept the necklace.

Spirit Bear placed a lovely creation on her. The center piece was the single bear claw given to her on the night she first met the mother bear with *Woniya Mato*. On either side were opalescent rocks that gleamed pearly white, pink, and green in the light. The rest of the necklace was an intricate pattern of beautiful stones. There were golden Formica-flecked pebbles, glittering red-brown sand stone, and small onyx rocks that flanked reddish ones. It reminded Kaitlin somehow of Spirit Bear's symbolic colors.

"It's beautiful!" she cried. She jumped up and hugged him before she realized what she was doing. Then she jumped back as if he were hot to the touch.

"Oh, I'm so sorry! I hope I didn't dishonor you! The crowd…" she nearly collapsed when her nerves overcame her.

The community had watched her genuine reaction to the gift. How could any fault the love and respect for the chief so naked in her eyes? They clapped and cheered madly to show their support.

The chief drew her to him and held her tenderly in his arms. He cared not that the whole village witnessed his great love for his *ska winyan*.

"Soon, *Wastelaka*, but not soon enough, you will be mine, blessed by *Wakantanka* and joined for all time under Indian law."

<u>**Dictionary of Lakota words**</u> (as I understand them to be)**:**

Reference:
<u>**The Lakota Dictionary,**</u> *New Comprehensive Edition*
Compiled and edited by Eugene Buechel and Paul Manhart
University of Nebraska Press, 2002
and
On-line Translators

<u>**Single words:**</u>

1. *Ableza* - to notice, observe, be aware of, perceive
2. *Abuhingia* – to make a sudden charge/attack
3. *Ahiyunka* – lie down & sleep
4. *Aglihunni* – rest
5. *Aguyapi* – Indian bread
6. *Anakiciksin* – to come to one's aid
7. *Asniya* – rest (to heal)
8. *Ayucoya* – well done
9. *Canmihce* – I trust or believe; I want it very badly
10. *Cante* – heart
11. *Gopeca* – beautiful
12. *Hau* – Hello
13. *Hingnaku* – husband (on-line translator)
14. *Hiya* - No
15. *Hehaka* – Elk

16. *Hokahe* – Welcome! (greeting after "Hi")
17. *Hoksicala* – baby or child
18. *Hota* – rock
19. *Inyan* – gold
20. *Isnatipi* – Tipis in isolation
21. *Istinma* – Sleep
22. *Itazipe* – bow
23. *Iyotake / Iyotaka* – Sit down (or up)
24. *Iyunka* – Lay down
25. *Isica* – hurt
26. *KatA* – To kill or stun by striking/shooting, strike dead, knock unconscious, knock out (online translator)
27. *Kinyan* – to come or fly by
28. *Kola* – friend
29. *Mato ova* – bear claw
30. *Mitawa; mita* - my
31. *Miye* – I or me
32. *Mni* – water
33. *Mniapahta* – Water skin
34. *Ojilaka* – baby or young
35. *Oslohankel* – slowly
36. *Pataka* – come to a stop; stop!
37. *Pejuta* - medicine
38. *Peslete* – the top or crown of the head
39. *Pikila* – to be thankful, glad
40. *Ska* – white
41. *Sunka* – dog
42. *Tahca* – the common deer

43. *Tatonka* – bison

44. *Thawicu* – wife (on-line translator)

45. *Tinpsila* – sweet radishes

46. *Toka* – enemy

47. *Tos* – Yes

48. *Wahinkpe* – arrow

49. *Wakanheja* – baby

50. *Wanapin* – beaded necklace

51. *Wanna* – now

52. *Wahpaka* – dress

53. *Wasicun/wasicu* – white man / men

54. *Wastelaka* – love

55. *Wayaka* – slave

56. *Wi; wiiyayuh* – sun

57. *Wica / wicasa* – man

58. *Wicowe* – relationship as in brother or sister

59. *Wikiskata* – making love

60. *Winyan; Wiya* – woman

61. *Wiwasteka* – beautiful woman

62. *Wota; Wate* – eat

63. *Wozan* - to stun or cause pain by impact from a distance (arrow shot)

64. *Yaskepa* – drink

65. *Yazan* – Do you feel pain? (to feel pain)

66. *Yucoya* – Ready

<u>**Phrases:**</u>

1. *Ahan iwahwayela* – Stand quietly; Be still
2. *Ayustankiya ye* – Please stop!
3. *Hanhepi Waste* – good night (on-line translator)
4. *Lila wiya waste* – Very pretty woman
5. *Mitawa ogligle wakan* – My good angel
6. *Miye ahikte* – I will kill you!
7. *Miye canzeka sni* - I am not angry
8. *Nimitawa ktelo* – You are mine
9. *Oyuhlagan sni* – STAY!
10. *Tiwahe wiconi* – family life
11. *Wistelkiya* – Bashful (Are you bashful?)
12. *Uwa yo* – come here

<u>**Names of People:**</u>

1. *Woniya Mato* – Spirit Bear – War chief (main chief) – First kill at 12 winters (Night Hawk); (Sly Coyote was 8) then SB's induction into warrior society – parents "disappeared" at age 9. I have it in my mind he became chief at 18 and is now 23.
2. *Mazaska Zi Ista* – Golden Eyes (Kaitlin) - 18
3. *Wawakankan* – Wonder Worker – shaman also on tribal council
4. *Wawat'ecaka* – Gentle Rabbit – master curer – Wonder Worker's mother
5. *Isnala Sungmanitu* – Lone Wolf – hunting chief

6. *Wawakte Towanjila* – Sky Warrior – chief of village affairs
7. *Haspa Nableca* – Apple Blossom – Pawnee slave woman with Sky Warrior
    a. *Nakpa Ihli* – Sore Ear (Snake Strike) – Apple Blossom's first name
8. *Unjinjintka Can Koica* – Desert Rose (likes Lone Wolf) – basket weaver, Pawnee born but adopted by Oglala
9. *Skeca Ecaca* – Playful Otter (likes Wonder Worker) – drills holes in stones
10. *Ohitika Hehaka* – Young Elk – young man who watches over Kaitlin
11. *Watila Hehaka* – Brave Elk – Young Elk's warrior name
12. *Zuzeca Pazan* – Snake Strike
13. – Yellow Feather – member of the *Cante Tinza*
    a. Quiet Deer – Yellow Feather's wife
        i. Red Squirrel – Yellow Feather & Quiet Deer's first child
        ii.
14. – Moon Eyes (helped catch fish)
15. Fresh Water – shares teepee with Kaitlin in teepees apart – motherly to Singing Cicada
16. New Moon – shares teepee with Kaitlin in teepees apart
17. – Singing Cicada
18. – Morning Dove
19. Opossum Eyes – girl who is mean to Kaitlin and desires Spirit Bear

20. Stormy Night – girl who shares teepee with Opossum Eyes in the Teepees apart
21. Eagle Talon (Yankton Sioux – *future* husband to Opossum Eyes) shared mothers with Sly Coyote
22. Wise Owl – Yankton chief

<u>Names of Things:</u>

1. *Cante Tinza* – Brave Heart (warrior society)
2. *Wakantanka* – The Great Spirit (God)
3. Bear Claw Clan of the Lakota (Oglala Sioux) – Spirit Bear's branch of the mighty Sioux Nation

<u>TIME PASSAGES:</u>

1. Winter – year
2. Moon – month
3. Sun – day

<u>SPOILER ALERT TO FOLLOWING</u>

TIME LINE: Wild Passions

1. Began mid May
2. Ceremony approx. June (about a month later)
3. July when Kaitlin and Ear Sore escape
4. Early August isolation tepees
5. Early Sept when she is accepted as Lakota

<u>Author Bio</u>

Sheri Chapman loves to laugh frequently and enjoys life. She loves to write in multiple genres. From memoirs to paranormal, horror, and romance, she always has a computer nearby to write whatever inspires her. Being an author and Director of Human Resources for Trient Press is a dream-come-true for her.

Sheri has a few books on the Read-it-Before-You-See-It list. Wild Passion renamed "Captive Heart" will be filmed soon. "A Killer, Revisited" is also on the list.

Sheri recently retired from teaching in Missouri Public schools with thirty years of experience. She received her bachelor's degree and first master's in special education from Missouri State University. Later, she pursued administration and got a second master's and a specialist degree from Lindenwood University in educational leadership. Instead of working as a principal or in a district office, she decided to raise her favorite animal: Pomeranian dogs. Sheri raises exotic-colored fluffy babies and sells them to those who genuinely appreciate their little princess or prince. She is licensed and inspected by Missouri State, USDA, her vet, and AKC. Someday, when she has less on her plate, Sheri would love to show her dogs.

Sheri is the mother of four beautiful daughters. She and their father enjoy spending time with each other, family, and friends. Aside from reading and writing, Sheri loves animals and being outdoors. She likes going for walks, fishing, scuba diving, kayaking, playing games, and watching movies. She is a big Harry Potter fan.

More from Sheri

Chapman:

My website:
https://prayerpawpuppies.wixsite.com/authorsherichapman

Wild Passion *(Book 1 of the Passion series – historical romance)*

Wild Passion is COMING TO THE MOVIE SCREEN!!!

(It will be PG13 and renamed "Captive Heart")

*filming begins after 2020

Passions of the Heart *(Book 2 of the Passion series)*

Chief Spirit Bear: Rise to Power *(A Passion series story)*

<><><>

"Eyes with No Soul" *(YA paranormal suspense)*

COMING SOON:

A Killer, Revisited (Futuristic Detective, sci fi thriller)

To stay up to date with Sheri Chapman, you can follow her at
any, or all, of these sites:

Facebook Page (author):
https://www.facebook.com/AuthorSheriChapman/

Amazon: https://www.amazon.com/-/e/B07HMHB4BK

Goodreads: https://www.goodreads.com/author/show/8332075.Sheri_Chapman

Wattpad: http://wattpad.com/user/SheriChapman

Linked-In: https://www.linkedin.com/in/sheri-chapman-a256276a/

Twitter: https://twitter.com/Sheri7303